PRAISE FOR AUTHORS

Merline Lovelace

"**Merline Lovelace**'s *Mind Games* is an exciting
and skillfully told tale."
—*RT Book Reviews*

Lori Devoti

"**Lori Devoti** provides yet another
action-packed mythological tale."
—*RT Book Reviews* on *Wild Hunt*

Linda Winstead Jones

"*Raintree: Haunted*, by **Linda Winstead Jones**,
is nonstop action from start to finish."
—*RT Book Reviews*

Lisa Childs

"In **Childs**'s gripping tale...
there are some surprising twists."
—*RT Book Reviews*

Bonnie Vanak

"**Bonnie Vanak**'s *Enemy Lover* offers nonstop
excitement and great sexual tension."
—*RT Book Reviews*

CHRISTMAS WITH A
VAMPIRE

Merline
Lovelace

Lori
Devoti

Linda
Winstead
Jones

Lisa
Childs

Bonnie
Vanak

HQN™

ISBN-13: 978-0-373-77613-9

CHRISTMAS WITH A VAMPIRE

Copyright © 2010 by Harlequin Books S.A.

The publisher acknowledges the copyright holders of the individual works as follows:

A CHRISTMAS KISS
Copyright © 2008 by Merline Lovelace

THE VAMPIRE WHO STOLE CHRISTMAS
Copyright © 2008 by Lori Devoti

SUNDOWN
Copyright © 2009 by Linda Winstead Jones

NOTHING SAYS CHRISTMAS LIKE A VAMPIRE
Copyright © 2009 by Lisa Childs-Theeuwes

UNWRAPPED
Copyright © 2009 by Bonnie Vanak

Recycling programs for this product may not exist in your area.

CONTENTS

A CHRISTMAS KISS
Merline Lovelace

ABOUT THE AUTHOR

As an air force officer, Merline Lovelace served at bases all over the world, including tours in Taiwan, Vietnam and at the Pentagon. When she hung up her uniform for the last time, she decided to combine her love of adventure with a flair for storytelling, basing many of her tales on her experiences in the service.

Since then, she's produced more than seventy-five action-packed novels, many of which have made the *USA TODAY* bestseller list. Over ten million copies of her works are now in print in more than thirty-one countries.

When she's not glued to her keyboard, Merline and her husband enjoy traveling and chasing little white balls around the fairways of Oklahoma. Check her website, www.merlinelovelace.com, for information about other releases.

To Brad, my handsome nephew and Oklahoma's coolest state trooper. Thanks for the ride-along. And the stories of some of your wild stops. And all those "board meetings."
And most especially, for the joy your beautiful family has given me and Al over the years.

CHAPTER ONE

"WHAT THE—?"

That was all Sergeant Brett Cooper had time for when the headlights of his cruiser speared into the figure who seemed to have dropped out of the December night sky. She froze, caught like a deer in the swath of light, and Brett yanked the cruiser's wheel.

The black-and-white fishtailed wildly on the frost-rimmed dirt road. Brett had to employ every skill learned during his eleven years with the Oklahoma Highway Patrol to keep the squad car from skidding into one of the bur oaks crowding the narrow country road. Cursing, he pumped the brakes and brought the Crown Vic to a lurching halt.

His muscles had gone wire tight under the bullet-proof vest he hadn't had time to shed since coming off shift. Rolling his shoulders to unkink them, he aimed the cruiser's powerful side spot at the woman now lurching toward the patrol car. She threw up an arm to block the vicious beam, but not before Brett registered the essentials to call in a report if necessary.

Female, Caucasian or possibly Hispanic. No

blood or visible signs of injury. Hair, dark red, long and wavy. Weight, approximately one-twenty. Age, twenty-two to twenty-four. Height, five-seven or -eight, although some of those inches were due to her spike-heeled boots.

The knee-high boots were black, he noted with a cop's precision, as were her thigh-hugging leggings and the turtleneck sweater she wore under a silvery fox-fur vest. Perfect get-up for a cat burglar, except for the expensive vest. And the fact that there wasn't a house or a barn worth robbing within a thirty-mile radius.

"Hey!"

Her shout carried clearly on the frigid air. Weaving from side to side, she shielded her eyes with her bent elbow and stumbled toward the squad car.

"Thurn that thing awf."

The erratic movements and slurred speech made Brett roll his eyes. Not a wise move, given that his lids felt as though they'd been scraped with industrial-grade sandpaper.

"Great!" he muttered in disgust as he grabbed his flat-brimmed Smokey the Bear hat from the passenger seat and settled it with the chin strap at the back of his head. "Just friggin' great!"

Six days and nights on a statewide manhunt for the murdering bastard Brett had helped put behind bars five years ago. Another twenty-two hours pulling a double shift so his pal Dave could spend Christmas weekend with his family. To make matters worse, an Arctic blast had swept in early this afternoon, icing the roads and causing countless pileups. Now, less than two miles from his cabin and the sleep he craved, Brett had to run into a probable Drunk and Disorderly.

He kept an eye on the D&D as he exited his vehicle. He could have her on the ground in a heartbeat if necessary. She didn't look tough or belligerent, though. Only stoned.

"Stop right there, ma'am."

"Huh?"

"Put both hands up where I can see them, please."

Her right arm pushed into the air. Her bent left arm went up, as well, but quickly dropped again.

"I can't put my hanth up," she whined, swaying back and forth like one of those dashboard bobble toys. "The light…ith too bright."

Christ! The woman was so spaced-out she could hardly stand. Or sick. Her face was pale and white, almost translucent in the harsh glare of the spot.

"Turn away from the light," Brett instructed, "but keep your hands where I can see them."

The half turn almost proved too much for her. The needle-sharp heel of her boot caught in a rut and she rolled like a drunken sailor.

"Okay, ma'am," Brett said when she'd regained

her balance. "You want to tell me what you're doing out here on a deserted dirt road at 3:00 a.m.?"

She glanced from side to side. Her face took on an expression of astonishment, as if she was noticing the bare trees and dark, empty road for the first time.

"I, um, must be loth."

"Where's your car?"

"Car?"

When she glanced around again, baffled, Brett swallowed an impatient sigh. He'd better run her, see if she'd reported a stolen vehicle. He'd also check to see if she had any priors or outstanding warrants. Both were a distinct possibility if this was a chronic condition.

"Do you have ID on you?"

Lips pursed in concentration, she patted the front of her fur vest.

"I don't think so."

Her hands went south, and Brett tracked their movement closely. His interest was purely professional, of course. He had to make sure she didn't reach under the vest and pull out a concealed weapon. But he was only human. Watching her palms slither over slender hips and thighs did a number on his concentration.

"Nope," she announced. "No ID."

"What's your name?"

"Delilah." She thought hard for several seconds

before breaking into a brilliant smile. "Wentworth. Delilah Wentworth."

Whoa! Without the smile she was a class-A looker. With it, she damned near lit up the dark December sky.

"Where do you live, Ms. Wentworth?"

"I know that one!"

The force of her excitement made her sway so that Brett had to jump forward and catch her arm to keep her from toppling over.

"Denver." She beamed up at him. "I live in Denver."

He needed more than a name and a state to run her, but her face went blank when he asked for a social security number.

"Date of birth, then."

"May thixth. Eighteen eighty-eight."

"Right."

He made the mental correction. A DOB of May 1988 would put her age at twenty. Younger than he'd estimated, and under the age for legal consumption.

"How much have you had to drink tonight?"

"I haven't. Drunk, I mean." She dropped her gaze to a spot just below Brett's chin. "I need to, though," she murmured. "I'm thoooo thirsty."

"What did you take?"

"Huh?"

"Are you on drugs?" he asked patiently. "Or medication?"

"Yeth! The dentith shot me full of something."

"Dentist?"

"I chipped a fang. On Christmath weekend!" Her auburn brows snapped together in a scowl. "You ever try to find a dentith during the holidath?"

"No, ma'am."

"Ith not easy." She stabbed a forefinger in the direction of her left cheek and glared at Brett, as if her dental problems were his fault. "I don't know what he gave me, but the whole side of my face ith numb."

That explained the slurred speech and dilated pupils, but not what she was doing out here, alone and on foot, miles from the nearest town.

Brett swallowed a grunt. Sleep would have to wait another three or four hours while he drove the woman back to the county jail.

Or…

He could take her to the nearest motel and let her sleep it off. It *was* Christmas weekend, after all. And he was so tired his bones ached. He looked her over once again and decided to give both her and himself a break.

"I'm going to drive you into town and get you a motel room. But before I put you in the squad car, I have to do a cursory pat-down. You're not under arrest," he assured her when she blinked at him, wide-eyed. "I just need to make sure you don't have a weapon on you."

Not likely, given those hip- and thigh-hugging pants. But the furry vest might have an inner pocket and the knee-high boots could conceal a knife.

"Put your hands on the hood of the squad car, please."

She wobbled the last few steps to the Crown Vic. When she leaned forward to plant her palms on the hood, her vest rode up to display a nice, trim rear.

Brett eyed it appreciatively but was careful to follow procedures for patting down a female. He used only the back of his hand on her upper torso. He had to slide his palms down her thighs and calves, however, to check inside the boots. He was pretty sure the search didn't take longer than absolutely necessary.

"All right, Ms. Wentworth, let's get you in the car."

She pushed off the hood and tried to swing around, but her ridiculous boots tripped her up again.

Brett caught her. Again. This time, though, her knees gave out completely and he had to scoop her into his arms to keep her from collapsing in a disjointed heap.

Her head lolled back. He could see the thin, golden-brown rim of her irises surrounding huge pupils. Whatever the dentist had pumped into her was powerful stuff.

Brett couldn't pull his eyes from hers. The pupils

were so deep, almost mesmerizing in their intensity. He felt as though he was falling into their dark, compelling depths when her mouth curved in a slow smile.

"I'm thoo thirsty," she said again in a throaty murmur that kicked up his pulse. "I had just begun to feed when I chipped my fang."

She slicked her tongue to one corner of her lip. Brett's mouth went bone-dry as he followed its progress.

"May I drink from you?"

His heart hammered against his Kevlar vest. The urge to crush his mouth down on hers exploded inside his belly. He fought it, but the effort made him dizzy.

"Yeah, sure. I've, uh, got some bottled water in the squad car."

He hefted her higher in his arms and started around the hood. Before he'd taken two steps, she'd nuzzled her face against his neck. An instant later, something sharp sank into his throat.

Eleven years on the force had conditioned Brett to react to any situation with lightning reflexes. He knew he could take this woman to the ground, yank her arms behind her back and cuff her before she drew another breath. Yet he didn't move, didn't blink, didn't so much as tighten a muscle.

The sensations spreading through him were like nothing he'd ever experienced before. They came in waves, each one stronger and faster than the next. His weariness evaporated, and pleasure rolled over his body.

The woman in his arms shifted, pressing closer, and pleasure became desire. Hot, heavy, urgent. Within seconds he was rock hard and aching below his Sam Browne belt. Then, just when the erotic sensations grew so intense they verged on pain, she drew her head back.

Her breath steamed on the cold night air. His came hard and fast. Panting, he gripped her tighter while the dark, swirling haze behind his eyes cleared a little. Just a little. Barely enough to see her lick a trickle of red from a two-inch-long incisor.

"You weren't kidding." He shook his head, fighting to clear the fog. "You really do have fangs."

Her only answer was a smile so slow and incredibly sensual that Brett had to battle its erotic pull. Summoning every ounce of strength he possessed, he scowled down at the face turned up to his.

"Lady, you don't need a regular dentist. You need an orthodontist. A good one."

The sharp comment pierced Delilah's sensual satisfaction. Sated from her feeding, she blinked at the man frowning down at her.

Uh-oh. She recognized the wariness in his blue eyes. And the edge to his voice. She should. She'd encountered both often enough in the past century. Sighing, she struggled to swim out of her medicinal soup, amplified now by the hot rush of pleasure this man had given her.

She hadn't drunk deeply. Her blasted tooth was still too sore. She'd be a long time forgiving the idiot who'd eagerly offered his throat, then whipped his head around to see what was happening at precisely the wrong moment! Instead of sinking her teeth into soft, warm flesh, she'd clamped down on his jawbone and broken off the tip of her fang.

She didn't understand why the tooth hadn't healed itself. The rest of her recovered almost instantly from any injury. The only rationale she could come up with was that her retractable fangs had emerged after she'd been turned. They weren't part of the body she'd inhabited as a human. Hence, they didn't heal as quickly as her once-living and now-undead parts.

Whatever the reason, she'd had the devil's own time getting the stupid fang fixed. The first dentist had tripped over his own feet trying to get away when she explained that her chipped incisor wouldn't emerge unless she scented fresh blood. She'd left him passed out on the floor of his office.

The second dentist had shut down his office at noon so he and his staff could party. Not surprising, given that today was the start of the long Christmas weekend. Delilah had used her not inconsiderable powers of persuasion to convince him to reopen for business.

When she saw him weave toward her, however, she'd had serious doubts about trusting him with a drill, much less a syringe. But Dr. Littlejohn had stared into her eyes as she explained about blood scent, succumbed to the force of her will with a goofy grin and obligingly offered his neck.

A half hour later Delilah was out on the street and trying to make it from Denver to Houston in time for her clan's annual conclave. Normally she made the trip in minutes. Seconds. The ability to bound through the night sky like Superman on steroids was one of the advantages of being undead. But whatever Littlejohn had shot into her had screwed up her sense of direction as well as her thought processes.

It was *still* fuzzing her thoughts. She didn't have a clue where she was, but she retained just enough survival sense to know the sudden wariness in the trooper's face spelled trouble for someone with her past and indefinite future.

"Look at me," she murmured, putting everything she had into the sultry command. "Look into my eyes."

His jaw set. Shoulders covered by his brown leather jacket jerked back. When his brow creased under the brim of his hat, Delilah knew she had to work fast to erase the suspicion in his eyes.

"You won't remember thith. You'll vaguely recall feeling happy but you won't know why."

A muscle jumped in the side of his jaw. His blue eyes drilled into her. She couldn't see his hair under his hat, but the stubble on his cheeks and chin suggested it was probably the same dark gold as the bristles.

Delilah's palm itched with the almost overwhelming impulse to stroke his prickly cheek. She could feel his blood warming her icy veins, feel the strength of the arms holding her. As she stared up at his rugged face, her belly clenched with a sudden and completely unexpected desire to lock her mouth on his.

The intensity of the urge, the voraciousness of it, surprised her. She couldn't remember the last time she'd encountered someone who stirred her sluggish veins like this. Ten years? Fifty? A hundred?

She wasn't as sexually active as some in her clan, but she'd taken her share of lovers over the past century. Unfortunately they'd seemed to derive considerably more enjoyment from the experience than she had.

So why hadn't she felt this insidious desire for any of them? Where did this greedy hunger spring from? Both were new and completely unsettling.

It had to be the drugs Littlejohn had injected into her bloodless veins. They'd thrown her entire system out of whack. Weakened her willpower. That much was evident when she yielded to the irresistible urge to raise a hand and stroke the prickly cheek so close to her own.

"You want to take me thomeplace dark, don't you?"

"Yes."

"Where we can be alone."

"Yes."

She felt a small stab of guilt at manipulating him like this. Normally she exuded this combination of sultry and seductive only when she needed to feed. Unlike many of her clan, she preferred willing donors.

But time was running out. She had to go to ground, find a safe place to sleep until she got this garbage out of her system. No way could she plunge into the teeming morass of power politics at the clan gathering with her face frozen and her senses dulled. The opposing factions were too powerful and too dangerous.

"Whath your name?"

He stared down at her, his brow creased, his will battling hers. He was tough, Delilah realized with a mix of surprise and annoyance. Tougher than any human she'd encountered in longer than she could remember.

"Tell me," she commanded.

Still he resisted.

She should have fed longer. Drawn more of him into her. Bent his will to hers.

"Tell me," she murmured, stroking his cheek again. "Who are you?"

"Brett Cooper. Sergeant. Oklahoma Highway Patrol."

He dragged each word out reluctantly, trying to resist without knowing why. Delilah gave him a slow smile, her eyes holding his with mesmerizing power.

"Take me to that motel you mentioned, Sergeant Brett Cooper, Oklahoma Highway Patrol."

He stared down at her so long that she thought she'd finally met someone who could resist her powers.

"I have a better idea," he said at last. "My cabin's only a few miles down this road."

Delilah hid a smile of triumph while she considered the suggestion.

Her clan's annual conclave always kicked off on the winter solstice. The ancient pagan holiday came late this year—the night of December 22nd, which bled into the 23rd—but fit perfectly with the Jewish observance of Hanukkah and the Christian celebration of Christmas. A festival for the undead of all persuasions, her clan leader liked to comment sardonically.

The climax of the opening ceremonies was to have been the merging of two rival clans after centuries of territorial skirmishing. The conclave would end with the selection of a new leader. Delilah, as de facto head of the western band, was duty bound to support her longtime clan chief, Sebastian. She had her doubts, though.

Don Sebastian Diego de la Hoya could be demanding at the best of times, brutal at the worst. He'd died almost five hundred years ago, disemboweled and staked to a barren plain in northern Mexico by the Aztec prince whose family he'd slaughtered. Sebastian undead had lost none of the ruthlessness that had driven him as a conquistador. Delilah would feel his wrath for missing the opening ceremonies, and the full weight of his fury if she didn't support him in the final tally.

So why not give herself a Christmas present? she thought rebelliously, gazing up at the trooper's strong, square chin. Why not spend what was left of this night in pleasure before she endured the inevitable pain?

"Your cabin sounds good," she murmured provocatively. "*Very* good."

CHAPTER TWO

BRETT STEERED DOWN the narrow dirt track leading to his cabin, trying to figure out what the hell had happened two miles back.

One minute he was patting down a possible D&D. The next, he was settling her in the passenger seat of his cruiser and chauffeuring her to his secluded getaway cabin.

Instinct and training had kicked in enough that he'd made sure the 12-gauge Remington shotgun and AR-15 assault rifle racked behind his seat were locked in place. He'd also unclipped his holstered SIG SAUER .45 from the right side of his belt and tucked it on the left side, between his seat and the car door, well out of his passenger's reach. Yet here he was, so eager to get her to the seclusion of his cabin that he could think of nothing else.

He flicked a glance at her. The reflected glare of the cruiser's headlights hitting the frost-rimmed dirt road showed her profile in precise detail. The tumble of auburn hair brushing her jaw. The short, straight nose. The full mouth that looked so red and ripe against her alabaster skin. She had a hand to her left cheek, cradling it in her palm.

"You okay?"

Her gaze swung toward him. Those incredible eyes melted into a smile. "The numbneth ith wearing off. A little."

That's right. Brett remembered now. She'd just had a close encounter with a dentist.

There was more. He knew there was more. There *had* to be, but for some crazy reason the sequence of events between the time he told her to put her hands on the hood of the cruiser and when he'd put the key into the ignition just wouldn't gel.

He'd gone too long without sleep, he decided in disgust. Those six days and nights wading across ditches and plowing through Oklahoma scrub brush searching for Joe Madison had wrung him inside out.

Joe Madison. Aka Joey, Joseph and J. J. Madison. Aka the Christmas Killer.

Brett gripped the steering wheel so hard his knuckles showed white. Acid rolled in his stomach. He'd helped put the bastard away once. Five years ago, almost to the day. Less than forty-eight hours after Madison had ripped his world apart.

Cindy had been just one of his victims. A target of opportunity he'd followed out of a mall jammed with holiday shoppers. Madison had no idea she was engaged to a State Trooper. Or that the entire Oklahoma

Highway Patrol would refuse to stand down until they found Cindy's body behind an abandoned toolshed.

They'd captured her killer the next morning. Christmas morning. After a ticket taker at a toll booth had spotted Cindy's cherry-red Mazda heading west on I-44. Brett had led the high-speed chase that ensued. Madison never knew how close he'd come to being rammed into a bridge abutment.

Now he'd escaped.

An army of Oklahoma law enforcement officers had tracked him for days. The trail led east, then south to Ardmore, where Madison had flagged down a vehicle and left the elderly driver lying in a pool of blood beside the road.

The man's vehicle was found abandoned the next day in a south Texas town—the same day a college coed was reported missing. From there the trail went cold. The betting was the Christmas Killer had taken his latest victim across the Rio Grande into Mexico.

Brett hoped not. He wanted to be there when they cornered Joe Madison. The son of a bitch wouldn't walk away again.

Before he cornered anyone or anything, though, Brett knew he had to get some sleep. His eyelids felt country fried and every bone in his body ached. He'd racked up so many overtime hours during the manhunt and this last double shift that his boss had insisted he stand down for three days. He couldn't wait to peel off his uniform and hit the rack.

So why the devil did his whole body get tight every time he glanced at the woman beside him? He was still trying to figure out that one when the dirt road ended in a small clearing.

The woman—Delilah Wentworth, if that was really her name—leaned forward and peered at the structure just visible through a screen of oaks.

"Ith that, uh, your cabin?"

He had to grin at the doubt buried in the polite question. That was most folks' initial reaction to the cabin he'd built himself, board by board.

"There's more to it than you can see from here."

Delilah caught the smile in his voice and glanced his way. The medication was wearing off. At last! She could feel her tongue again. She could also feel the impact of Officer Cutie's lopsided grin.

It lifted one side of his mouth and crinkled the tanned skin at the corners of his eyes. He looked so human and so delicious. For the second time tonight, she felt desire curl in her belly.

"Hang loose a moment," he told her. "I'll come around and help you. The ground's rough and icy."

He cut the engine and car lights, but she could see him clearly. His bulk was due to the body armor her elbow had thumped against when he'd swept her into his arms. Even without the extra padding, though, he was big and tough. He had to be six-one or -two, and his shoulders strained the seams of his brown leather jacket.

If Delilah didn't know she could send him flying across the clearing with a flick of one wrist, she might have felt a little intimidated. As it was, she simply let herself enjoy the trooper's overall effect while he reached down to help her out.

The moment their fingers connected, his brows snapped together. "Your hand feels like ice. You should have told me to turn up the heater."

There it was again. The frown, followed by the questioning glance that said he was trying to connect dots that couldn't be connected.

"I'm cold-blooded," she said lightly, pulling her hand free from his.

She would have to watch herself with him. From past experience Delilah knew police officers had a difficult time with the idea of the living dead. Police officers and scientists. It was that whole evidence thing. They always wanted proof—physical, empirical, absolute, whatever. She generally avoided them whenever possible.

So where had her inexplicable attraction to this particular police officer sprung from? It could be those broad shoulders and baby-blue eyes. Or the medication so foreign to her system. Or the insidious desire to put off plunging into the seething politics and hostilities of the clan gathering for another few hours.

So for now, for the little that remained of the night, she wouldn't think about Sebastian or the gathering in Houston. Tonight she would work the last of the medication out of her bloodless veins and regain her strength. Preferably in the arms of Officer Cutie.

"Leth go inside."

Nodding, he extracted the weapons from the rack behind the front seat and locked them in the trunk. His sidearm he carried into the cabin.

HE WAS RIGHT, Delilah saw when he ushered her inside. There *was* more to the isolated cabin than could be seen from the outside.

It was built on three levels. A narrow entryway led to a combination kitchen/dining/living room dominated by a natural stone fireplace. A step down led to an open sleeping area that contained an old-fashioned iron bedstead and a rickety nightstand stacked with paperbacks. What looked like a stamp-size bathroom was tucked into one corner of the bedroom.

But it was the wintry nightscape framed by the window behind the iron bedstead that drew a delighted gasp from Delilah.

"Ooooh! How beautiful!"

She saw now the cabin sat on a steep hill that sloped down to a small, irregularly shaped lake. The iced-over lake sparkled under the starry sky, with the moon painting a silver path across its frozen surface. Dark, silent woods crowded the shores. She caught a glimpse of lights on the far side of the lake, but they were too distant to intrude on the wintry stillness and solitude.

"How did you find thiz place?" she asked, enchanted.

Shrugging, he stashed his holstered handgun in a cabinet and fastened the lock. The lock wouldn't keep her out if she wanted in, which she didn't, but she saw no reason to mention that minor fact.

"I wanted to get as far away from civilization as I can on my days off," he replied. "Especially this time of year."

"You don't like all the holiday hoopla?"

"Not particularly."

"What about family?" she asked, curious. "Do you like to get away from them, too?"

"I don't have any family. Hang loose a few moments while I call in. I need to let dispatch know I'm at home." Removing the handheld radio clipped to his belt, he keyed the mike. "This is Cooper with a 10-5."

Static buzzed through the air for a second or two before a female voice responded cheerfully, "Roger, Brett. Have a good one."

"Back at you, Janie." He clipped the radio to his belt again and turned for the door. "I'll prime the generator and bring in some firewood to keep us warm until the heat kicks on. It's cold as a grave in here."

Ha! That showed what he knew.

He should try being buried alive. In a mass grave. With dozens of other victims of the cholera epidemic that had ravaged the country that horrible summer.

Delilah never got an exact count on the dead. She knew there were thousands. Tens of thousands. Only, she hadn't died from the sickness. Instead, she'd sunk into a coma so deep her heart ceased a regular beat and her breathing became so shallow it appeared to stop altogether. Her parents and her fiancé hadn't had much time to grieve. With the sickness so rampant, the graves detail carted off the dead for immediate burial to avoid spreading the disease.

Delilah didn't even want to *think* about coming awake in that reeking pit. Or the suffocating stench of the bodies piled on top of her. Or the primal screams that had ripped from her very soul.

That's where she'd died. Not in her papa's quarters at the Presidio in San Francisco where she first took sick. Not at the post hospital where they'd transported her. Not with her mama weeping at her bedside and the lieutenant she was to marry looking so heartbroken. Oh, no! She had to die in a hole as hot and black as the far reaches of hell.

Then again, if she hadn't been buried in that foul pit, Sebastian might not have found her. He'd been roaming that night and picked up the echoes of her fading screams. Mere moments after she'd breathed her last, he'd dug her out and awakened her. For that,

Delilah owed him allegiance. Obedience. Submission. All of which she would give more willingly if he didn't take such delight in causing pain.

Sighing, she wandered down to the cabin's second level. She didn't need a generator or electric lights to guide her. She could sense like a bat in the dark. Her other senses were similarly enhanced. She heard the trooper crunching over the frost-hardened ground outside well before he tromped through the door with an armload of wood.

"I'll have a fire going in a minute." He stooped in front of the stone fireplace and glanced over his shoulder. "Didn't you say you were thirsty?"

"Mmm."

Did the man have any idea how good he looked hunkered down on one knee, with his leather jacket pulled tight across his shoulders and his gray uniform pants molding his trim rear?

"There's bottled water in the cupboard. I think there might even be a bottle of wine in there somewhere. I wouldn't trust anything else, though, until I haul in some supplies. I haven't been up here in a couple of months."

"Why not?"

Shrugging, he set a match to the kindling. "Work, mostly. Thanksgiving, Christmas, winter roads… They're a bitch…. Sorry. They're tough on travelers. Our accident response calls always peak this time of year."

Delilah was all too familiar with the grim aspects of mortality. She felt a tug of sympathy for the man. He had to deal with death on a regular basis, yet had no family to go home to. No spouse to erase the grim reality of his job, no kids to restore balance in his world.

Like her.

Flames were licking at the logs now. Officer Brett rose and dusted his hands on his trousers. The small roll of his shoulders suggested he was dusting off the grimmer aspects of his profession, as well.

"Thankfully, we have the occasional tornado or prison riot to break up the monotony. When we get *real* lucky, we rescue gorgeous babes in distress."

When his grin flashed out again, all male and incredibly potent, Delilah felt her stomach lurch. The desire she'd experienced out on the road returned with a vengeance.

She felt its bite as the trooper shrugged out of his leather jacket and sent his hat flying toward a chair like a brown Frisbee. His hair was dark blond, as she'd suspected. And that wasn't just body armor straining the buttons of his uniform shirt. Trooper Brett was built.

To her disappointment, his grin faded as he crossed to where she stood and the look she recognized all too well dropped over his face. The cop had returned. Searching. Questioning. Doubting.

"Something happened," he said slowly. "Back there in the road, where I picked you up."

How could he remember? Donors *never* remembered a feeding unless she willed it.

Then again, she hadn't taken that much from him. Just enough to renew her strength and counter the drugs swimming through her veins.

Or so she rationalized as he towered over her. So close she could count the golden bristles on his chin. So near the electricity sparking between them made the coarse, shaggy fur of her vest stand out.

His glance dropped. Frowning, he drew a knuckle over the rough pelt. "What is this? Fox? Lynx?"

"Wolf."

She didn't tell him it had come from a Hunter who'd tried to tear her apart a few years ago. She had other things on her mind at the moment.

Like his lips, mere inches from hers. And his breath, so warm on her cheeks. She went up on tiptoe and looped her arms around his neck, driven by a need that surprised her all over again with its intensity.

His head bent. His mouth came down on hers. She could taste his hunger, smell the sweet, hot lust that rose to meet hers.

"Wait!"

When he wrapped his hands around her upper arms and pushed her away a few inches, Delilah growled in frustration. She came within a hair of throwing him across the room and onto the bed. She curbed the impulse just in time.

"Your pupils are still dilated." He shook his head, self-disgust stamped across his face. "I've done a lot of things I regret, but I've never seduced a doped-up female."

"The buzz is fading." Her eyes held his, inviting, compelling. Her husky laugh rippled on the cold air of the cabin. "What you're seeing is something entirely different."

Still he resisted. Surprised at his stubborn strength, she laid her palms on the planes of his chest.

"Look into my eyes. Look deeply."

She could tell the moment his will began to disintegrate. A flush rose in his whisker-stubbled cheeks. His voice roughened.

"We've got too many layers on," he said, his fingers digging into her upper arms. "Let me shed a few of mine, then we'll start on yours."

She didn't even try to hide her triumph this time. "Sounds good to me."

He yanked at the buckle of his leather belt. The canisters and assorted weapons attached to it thunked as he draped them over the back of a chair.

Delilah's hunger mounted with each second. Her hands eager, she helped him with the buttons of his brown uniform shirt. His Kevlar vest came off next. The white cotton T-shirt underneath molded a very impressive set of pecs. He worked out, she guessed. Regularly.

"Everything," she ordered as he tugged his undershirt over his head. "Your shoes. Your pants. Your small clothes."

His hands stilled. He glanced up, and the hot haze in his eyes cooled a few degrees.

"My what?"

Realizing her slip, she smothered a curse. She couldn't believe she'd used that archaic term for underwear. She worked hard to keep current on contemporary slang and speech patterns. Most of her clan did. Nothing roused unwelcome curiosity like someone spouting ancient Persian or medieval French or, in her case, prim and proper Victorianisms.

The Seekers who searched out the night gathering spots helped in that regard. Fascinated by all things vampire, they were eager conversationalists and even more eager donors. Delilah conversed with them regularly and rarely tripped over her words anymore. Her only excuse this time was the hunger this man roused in her.

She wanted Brett Cooper now as she'd wanted few other partners. *No* other partner, she realized with a small shock.

He wanted her, as well. She could see it in the heat that leaped back into his eyes when she planed her palms over his chest. Hear it in the hiss of his breath. That was all the encouragement she needed to stretch up on her toes and run her fingers over his lips.

When he nudged her hand away and covered her mouth with his, her senses exploded. The logs in the stone fireplace suddenly flamed vivid and bright. The moon glowed incandescently outside the window. She could hear Brett's heart slamming against his ribs, loud and fast.

She reveled in the feel of him against her. His arms locked around her. His skin hot to her touch His erection rock hard and straining against her. She wedged her palm between their hips, slid it downward, gripped his rigid flesh. Before she could get in more than a stroke or two, she felt her belly convulse, low and tight.

Hellfire and damnation!

She didn't know if it was the lingering effects of the medication or the feel of his hot, pulsing flesh against her palm that pushed her to the edge. Whatever the cause, she had only a second of warning. Maybe two. Barely enough time to throw back her head and ride the waves of pleasure that crashed through her.

She wanted to howl like the wolves who hunted her kind. Scream her delight and astonishment that it had happened so quickly. She managed to restrain herself, but couldn't hold back her embarrassment when the incredibly intense pleasure subsided.

Mortified, she mumbled an apology. "I'm sorry. I've never, uh, finished so fast."

"We're not finished." With a wicked glint in his eyes, he tugged her toward the bed. "Far from it."

She would give more than she took this time, Delilah vowed. Much more.

"I've got something for your Christmas stocking," she teased as he peeled off her fur vest and caught the hem of her black sweater.

"That right?"

"Pleasure like you've never experienced before."

He was more interested in getting her naked than anything else at the moment. "Lift your foot."

"Pleasure that only one of my kind can give," she murmured provocatively while he removed her boots.

"Yeah?" he muttered, disposing of her leggings in one swift roll. "What kind is that?"

She stood before him in her bra and bikini briefs. That was one thing twenty-first-century women had all over their nineteenth-century counterparts. Delilah missed her family and the familiar surroundings of her time, but she did *not* miss bloomers and bustiers and corsets laced so tight she couldn't draw a full breath. Not that she needed to draw a full breath anymore. Or any breath at all.

"What kind am I?"

Her skin gleamed pale in the moonlight streaming through the bedroom window. Her eyes smiled into his.

"I'm one of the undead. Some call us night stalkers. Or vampires."

"Right. Okay. Whatever."

He won't remember any of this, she thought as he tumbled her to the bed and dragged down her lacy briefs. But she would. She'd take the memory of his hot skin, his broad shoulders, his flat belly away with her.

And the feel of him! The moist head of his erection thrusting against her hip. The knee wedging hers apart. The fists he buried in her hair to anchor her while his mouth ravaged hers.

His hunger fed her own. She locked her arms around him and took his crushing weight eagerly. Then he began to work his way down her body. He used his tongue and teeth, nipping, kissing, leaving a trail of stinging sensation. Her nipples were already tight and aching when he reached them. By the time he finished, Delilah was squirming with a pleasure so intense it knifed from her breasts to her belly.

Belatedly she remembered her determination to give instead of take.

"My turn."

Rolling over, she straddled his hips. She was wet and ready and eager. So was he. One shift and he was inside her. One thrust and he filled her. Hard. Hot. Pulsing with an urgency that magnified her own.

She searched his eyes, saw only raw desire. Smiling, she bent her head and sank her fangs into his throat. They went in cleanly. No snag, no drag, no pain. The dentist had done his job well. She'd give him that.

Brett went stiff under her. She felt his muscles coil and his hips lift in an instinctive attempt to throw her off. Then he groaned, or she did. Delilah didn't know. Didn't care. All that mattered, all her soaring senses could absorb was the feel of him inside her and the hot, sweet rush of blood that fed her being.

SHE WAS SLICK with his sweat and limp with pleasure when they finally finished.

She curled against him, her back to his chest, her bottom cradled on his thighs. She didn't feel as energized as she usually did after a feeding. Two cataclysmic orgasms and the dregs of the drugs swimming in her system probably accounted for that. But nothing could account for her monumental stupidity in falling asleep in Officer Cutie's arms before she'd blocked his memory.

And before she'd secured herself against the dawn!

She realized her fatal error when she jerked awake an indeterminate time later and found the cabin filling with the gray haze of dawn. With a gulp of dismay, Delilah lunged for the side of the bed, or tried to.

That's when she discovered her right wrist was handcuffed to the iron bedstead. She gaped at the cuffs in utter disbelief until a sudden burst of light whipped her head toward the window.

Her throat went bone-dry. Her skin got clammy. If she'd had any blood in her veins it would have congealed as a ray of dazzling sunshine sliced through the clouds and slanted across the tangled covers.

CHAPTER THREE

BRETT TRAMPED THROUGH the half inch of snow
that had fallen just before dawn. If it lasted until
tomorrow, they'd have one of Oklahoma's rare white
Christmases.

His mind wasn't on the crystalline white, though,
or the sunlight spearing through the hazy dawn. As
he hauled an armload of wood from the rack at the
side of the cabin, his thoughts swirled around the
woman he'd picked up last night.

What kind of whack-job was she? Had he been
hearing things or had she really spouted some cra-
ziness about being a night stalker? A vampire, for
God's sake! With a sore fang yet. Who'd managed to
leave a hickey the size of New Jersey on his neck.

In the bright light of day, he couldn't believe he'd
swallowed her story about some dentist doping her
up. Or that he'd brought her to his cabin instead of
taking her in and requesting an Emergency Detention
Order pending a mental health evaluation. The EDO
would come now, and fast. Christmas Eve or not, the
woman needed help. So did he, if last night was any
indication.

Disgusted, Brett shook his head. His behavior was inexcusable. He had no idea how he would explain his actions to his supervisor when he brought the woman in. He couldn't explain them to himself.

All he knew was that he'd ached for her almost from the first moment he'd pinned her in his cruiser's headlights. Her dark eyes and full, red mouth were imprinted on his brain. Even with all that had happened, the memory of how she'd hooked her legs over his and writhed under...

"Hellfire and damnation!"

The curse cut through the cabin's thick walls, so filled with fury and pain that Brett dropped the firewood and took off on a run. He slammed through the front door, sending it crashing back on its hinges, and felt his heart almost jump out of his chest.

He barely recognized the creature he'd left cuffed to the iron bedstead to prevent her from doing something crazy while he'd dressed and gone outside. She was crouched beside the bed, naked, her lips curled back, her arm almost pulled from its socket. Cursing, straining, panting, she fought the steel cutting into her wrist while she dragged the heavy bedstead away from the window, inch by screeching inch.

Her strength astounded Brett. That bed weighed a ton. He'd had to have one of his buddies help carry it in, and the thing was in four separate pieces then. That she could move it even a few inches blew him away.

"Calm down! Delilah, calm down! The cuff was just for your protection."

And mine, he admitted as he rushed across the cabin. He was halfway to the sleeping area before he caught the stench of burning flesh.

He spotted the smoke a heartbeat later. Thin and gray, it curled from the gaping wound in Delilah's forearm, a few inches from her elbow. Her skin was charred, the muscle below exposed and sizzling.

"Christ Almighty! What did you do?"

"Don't bring Him into it," she snarled, her eyes wild and feral. "Just get these cuffs off me!"

He yanked the key out of his pocket and attacked the lock. The moment the bracelet sprang open, she leaped to her feet and raced for the bathroom.

"I've got a first-aid kit in the car," Brett shouted after her. "I'll put some burn cream on your arm, then we'll get you to a hospital."

He was back within moments, hammering on the bathroom door. It swung open under his assault and flooded the small room light. Delilah was holding her arm under the cold water faucet. She whipped her head up at the intrusion and skewered him with a furious glare.

"Shut the door!"

Brett just stood there, trying to wrap his mind around the fact that the raw, gaping wound he'd witnessed just moments before was now only a patch of blistered flesh.

And even that was healing.

Right before his eyes.

"Shut the damned door!" she shrieked, jerking to one side to avoid the light coming in over his shoulder.

He swallowed, hard, and kicked the door closed. The bathroom plunged into gloom. As his eyes grew accustomed to the dim light, Brett didn't move, didn't speak. He just watched in silence as the skin on her arm grew smoother and whiter.

When every sign of the burn had disappeared, she let the water splash over her raw wrist. Flesh eaten almost to the bone by the steel cuff healed itself, exactly as her other injury had. By the time she grabbed a towel to dry her arm, a cold lump had formed in the pit of Brett's stomach.

"Who are you?"

"I told you! Delilah Wentworth."

Her chin came up. Fire burned in her dark irises, making them appear almost red.

"Tell me, Officer. Is that your standard morning-after technique? Handcuffing women to your bed to keep them there?"

Ignoring the sarcasm, he dropped his gaze to her arm. "*What* are you?"

"I told you that, too," she snapped. "I'm one of the undead."

"Undead. Right."

She tossed the towel aside and shed some of her

belligerence. "Look, I don't have time for lengthy explanations right now. I need to sleep during the day. In here, because this is the only room in the cabin without windows. So do me a favor and use the great outdoors as a bathroom until dusk, okay?"

"Hell, no, it's not okay."

"Please. I really, really need to sleep. The medication...all our activity last night...the fact that you almost fried me this morning... I'm tired, Brett. Exhausted. Totally wiped."

He had to believe her. The fire had gone out of her eyes and her face now had a grayish cast.

"Please," she muttered, dragging another towel from the rack and tossing it onto the floor. "Let me sleep. And close the door behind you!"

Brett reached behind him and fumbled for the latch. He'd figure this out, he thought as he backed out. He had to.

DELILAH BLINKED AWAKE, remembered her terror the last time she'd opened her eyes and came up so fast she banged her head on something hard and cold.

Cursing, she identified the object as the bathroom sink and sank down again. She was safe. Only a small sliver of light showed under the door. Artificial light, which meant it was night or at least dusk.

Okay. All right. She was safe. Somewhere in Oklahoma, she remembered. With Officer Brett. Who'd treated her to two incredible orgasms before tethering her to his bed.

She tried to work up a good mad over that, but the realization that the hard-eyed, suspicious cop had let her sleep through the day kept getting in the way. He must have believed her. Otherwise she would have woken up in a padded cell. Or dead—*really* dead—from exposure to the harsh winter sunlight. The burn on her arm must have forced him into a huge leap of faith. If so, she supposed the searing agony she'd endured was worth it. Barely!

Vowing to steer clear of his handcuffs in the future, she reached for the red plaid shirt hanging from a hook on the door. The warm flannel enveloped her from neck to midthigh. Breathing in the scent of the man who owned it, she rolled up the sleeves and emerged from her dim cocoon.

The first thing that hit her was a combination of scents. Burning logs. Tangy pine resin. New snow and gravy. Rich brown gravy swimming with beef and potatoes.

She tracked the last scent to the kitchen. An empty stew can sat on the kitchen counter, a covered saucepan on the stove's back burner. She couldn't digest regular food, but it could still tantalize her. Shrugging off a twinge of almost-forgotten appetite, she looked around for Brett.

She didn't have to look far. He was sprawled in one of the oversize leather chairs by the fireplace, legs outstretched, ankles crossed. He'd traded his uniform for jeans. Snug, well-washed jeans, Delilah noted as she stepped up to the living area, teamed with a long-sleeved black T-shirt. She had ample opportunity to admire the way both items displayed his muscular torso before he broke the taut silence.

"How's the arm?"

"Good. Fine."

He nodded once. Just once. He was back in cop mode. Hardly surprising, considering how she'd practically gnawed off her arm to escape the sun this morning.

"Thanks for letting me crash in your bathroom."

"Yeah, well, consider it an early Christmas present."

Not that early. Unless she'd slept longer than she thought, this was Christmas Eve. The second of her clan's five-night conclave. She'd missed the critical first night completely.

The reminder made her chest squeeze. If she took off now, right this moment, she might arrive in time to mitigate some measure of Sebastian's wrath. Yet she knew she couldn't leave without answering the questions in Brett's eyes.

"You still can't quite accept what I am, can you?"

"I'm working on it." He dropped his feet to the floor and nodded to the chair opposite his. "Sit down. We need to talk this out."

She owed him that much. Or was she rationalizing, trying to steal just a few more minutes with this man? Knowing it was a combination of both, she sank into the chair. The well-worn leather creaked under her as she smoothed the plaid flannel shirttails over her thighs.

"There's not much to talk out. I lived. I died. I'm living again between worlds."

"I need more than that."

Of course he did. He was a cop.

"What do you want to know?"

"Start at the beginning. Who is…or was…Delilah Wentworth?"

"Ah, there's a question."

She rarely thought about her previous life anymore. Her parents had died long ago. Everyone she'd known then was gone. The woman—girl—she'd once been no longer existed in anyone's memory but her own.

"Delilah Wentworth was a vain, silly miss who grew up on the various army posts her father was assigned to. Fort Sheridan. Fort Polk. West Point. Fort Anderson, in the Philippines. She spent most of her time primping in front of her mirror before waltzing the night away at balls and masques. Her primary—her *only*—goals in life were to marry a handsome young lieutenant, raise a large brood of children and live happily ever after. I got the 'ever after' part right, anyway."

He didn't appear to appreciate her attempt at humor.

"How did you die?"

"In the cholera epidemic that swept the country in the summer of '08."

"In 1908? A hundred years ago?"

"That's right. I'd just turned twenty and had become engaged that very month. Much to my mama's relief." A rueful smile feathered her lips. "I had refused so many offers up to that point that she warned me repeatedly I'd die a spinster. As it turned out, she was right."

"So how did it happen? This 'ever after' business?"

He didn't need the details of the horrific moments she'd spent in a reeking mass grave.

"Sebastian, my clan leader, found me seconds after I took my last breath and shared his essence. I've been a member of his family ever since."

The blue eyes holding hers went cold and hard. She understood why when he raised a hand and tapped the bruise on the side of his neck.

"Is that what you did with me? Shared your essence?"

"No!"

She jumped up, cursing her clumsiness in not making things clearer this morning. He must have been sitting here all day, wondering if he'd joined the legions of the undead!

"I drank from you. That's all. I told you I was thirsty, remember? And you..."

"I thought you wanted water! Coffee! A beer! I didn't think you were going to glom onto my throat and suck out a few pints of blood."

He shoved out of his chair and got right in her face. The ice left his eyes, replaced by fury. Delilah stood her ground. He was big and he was tough, but he was just a human.

"It wasn't a few pints," she countered. "I didn't take more than I needed or more than you could spare."

"Yeah, well, how about asking next time!"

"I *did* ask. And you gave me permission."

"Like hell I did!"

"Okay, I may have blocked that part of your memory. But you were doing your cop thing, getting all inquisitive and suspicious. Like now," she added as his dark blond brows snapped together.

"You can do that? Block my memory?"

"Yes."

"Then why do I remember touching you?"

Anger still burned in his eyes as he wrapped his hands around her upper arms and yanked her against him.

"Why do I remember the taste of you? Your moans when I used my teeth and tongue on you?"

"I, uh, was a little distracted that time."

Too distracted to block the feel of him on her.

In her. All over her. The memory of his sweat-slick muscles and powerful thrusts made her throat go tight.

"I got careless," she admitted. "I've never done that before. With anyone. But I didn't take more than I needed the first time. The second was to give you the same pleasure you'd given me."

The doubt and distrust were still there. They stung more than Delilah wanted to admit.

"If it's any consolation, you made up for those little love bites when you handcuffed me to the bed."

"I thought you were a nut job. I figured I'd better restrain you until I worked an EDO. Emergency Detention Order," he amplified. "I was going to take you in for a mental health evaluation."

"Instead, you almost fried me."

She flipped him a smile that showed she harbored no hard feelings. Not many, anyway.

The cheeky grin only added to the emotions that had churned inside Brett all day. Disbelief. Incredulity. Disgust that he'd let his driving hunger for this woman push him over the line. At her reminder of the morning's events, though, remorse surged to the top of the list. He'd never intended to cause her pain.

"I'm sorry about that."

He slid a hand down her arm, caught her wrist and raised it. The cuff of his shirt fell back to reveal pale, unblemished skin. If he'd needed proof, it was there, right in front of him.

And God knew, he *did* need proof. He'd just spent the longest nine hours of his life. Good thing darkness came so early this time of year or he'd still be sitting in that damned chair, trying to convince himself he hadn't gone off the deep end.

He'd gotten up a dozen times, approached the bathroom door, then turned around. The viciousness of her burn, the miraculous way it had healed, kept playing and replaying in his mind. During one of those endless replays he'd placed a call to his unit and confirmed they'd received no missing-persons report for a woman matching Delilah's description. Nor was there any record of her in the databases the Oklahoma Highway Patrol tapped into.

That's when he'd powered up his laptop. The number of websites out there dedicated to vampires had astounded him. Some were informative, others downright scary.

He'd spent hours cruising the Net, and took a break only long enough to bring in more wood and the groceries he'd stashed in the trunk of the cruiser and almost forgotten. The more Brett read, the more he realized he was about to share his Christmas Eve dinner with a vampire.

Or become *her* Christmas Eve dinner.

"How often do you have to...you know...drink?"

Her gaze dropped to a point just under his jaw. The look on her face was enough to make a vein jump in the side of Brett's throat. He could feel it throbbing as he stared down into her dark eyes.

"Not often," she murmured with a touch of regret.

His vein pulsed harder, faster. "Define *often*."

"Every few weeks if I conserve my strength. Every few days if I engage in strenuous activity." Her gaze lifted. "Like last night."

"Right. Last night." He cleared his throat. "Just out of curiosity, how much of that was me?"

"What do you mean?"

"You've got these powers. You can block memory. You can move beds it took two grown men to haul in, piece by piece. You heal vicious wounds with cold water. What else can you do, Delilah?"

She cocked her head. Her dark auburn hair spilled over one shoulder as a smile crept into her eyes. "Oh, I get it. You want to know if can I make an Oklahoma State Trooper overcome his training and scruples and treat a female detainee to two mind-blowing orgasms."

"Yeah," he drawled, "that's pretty much what I want to know. Although I should point out you weren't technically a detainee."

"I'm happy to inform you, Officer, that you did that all on your own. I merely provided a little incentive."

Brett wasn't sure he believed her. He'd never experienced that kind of unrelenting hunger before. Not even with Cindy. He'd buried his heart with her five years ago. Until last night, he was sure he'd buried all desire for anything except the occasional one-night stand.

Maybe that was why Delilah roused such savage need in him. She'd tasted darkness. She'd survived death. She was the woman he'd lost.

Not in temperament. Or in looks. With her fiery hair, dark eyes and forceful personality, Delilah Wentworth couldn't *be* more different from the shy brunette whose face Brett had to work hard to recall these days.

It was what she stirred in him. A yearning that crossed time. A hunger that knew no physical bounds. He'd wanted her out there, on that cold, deserted road. And again, here in the cabin.

And now.

All he had to do was look into her eyes and the need to hold her, to have her, came alive in his belly. He could feel their pull, see himself in the dark pupils. See, too, the regret swimming in their depths.

"I have to go," she whispered. "I'm late for a meeting of my clan."

He curled a knuckle and brushed it across her porcelain-smooth cheek. "Be a little later."

"I can't. There'll be...repercussions."

A tremor rippled over the surface of her skin, so slight he thought he'd imagined it.

"Thanks for taking me in, Officer."

He couldn't keep her here by force. Much as he wanted to. Yielding with a reluctance that went bone-deep, he dropped his hand.

"Anytime, Ms. Wentworth."

"I'd better get dressed."

BRETT'S UNWILLINGNESS to let her disappear from his life took a sharp spike when she emerged from the bathroom in her cat-burglar outfit. She strutted toward him on those wicked boots, the spike heels clicking on the floorboards. Her black leggings and turtleneck fit her like a second skin. Her hair was a tumble of wine-colored curls. She looked wild and untamed and exotic.

When she shrugged into her shaggy fur vest, Brett was seriously considering clamping the cuffs on her again. The urge was powerful, atavistic and not *entirely* sexual. He hadn't missed that brief tremor when she'd mentioned repercussions. The thought she might be facing danger when she left him ripped a hole in his gut.

"Listen, Delilah. If you need a place to go to ground, a place no one in this clan of yours knows about, you can come here."

"Thanks."

"I'll leave a key outside. There's a loose stone beside the stoop. I'll show you."

He walked to the door with her, trying to think of ways to convince her to stay. One more night. One more day. But all he could do was offer a warning.

"Be careful. There's an escaped murderer on the loose. We think he's gone south, into Mexico, but the bastard has left false trails before."

With a wry smile, she opened the door and stepped into a frost-filled night. "I probably don't have to worry, unless his weapon of choice is a flaming cross or a wooden stake."

"He prefers a knife with a serrated edge. The common kitchen variety. The kind you can pick up in any corner store."

Brett kept his response flat and even. Too flat and even, he realized when her smile edged into a frown.

But before she could voice the question he saw in her face, a high, thin wail cut through the night.

CHAPTER FOUR

"MIS-TER!"

The panic-filled cry reverberated through the woods on the north side of the cabin. Brett whirled toward the echoes, his eyes slitting as he searched the impenetrable darkness. Delilah spun a few degrees to the left and took off.

"This way," she shouted.

"Wait!"

He pounded after her, his gut twisting and his mind filled with the smirking face of the killer they'd just been talking about.

"Dammit, Delilah, wait!"

She flew toward the woods. Literally flew. So fast that Brett caught only a flash of silvery fur before darkness swallowed her. He crashed into the tree line three or four seconds after she had. Every one of those agonizing seconds seared his soul.

Not again. It couldn't happen again.

He didn't think about his service revolver still locked in the cabinet, didn't consider going back for a flashlight. His one, overriding priority was to get to Delilah.

Relief crashed through him when he spotted her. She was down on one knee a few yards ahead. A kid bundled up to his ears in a yellow ski jacket had her arm in a death grip and was yanking on it frantically.

"You gotta come! Now!"

"We will," she assured him. "Just tell us…"

"What's going on?"

The boy's wild, frightened eyes cut to Brett. "My mom's sick. You gotta help her."

Nine or ten years old. Brown hair. Black high-tops caked with mud and dirt. Scrawny build. Bloody scratches on one cheek. The cop in Brett cataloged the details even as he got a handle on the situation.

"Okay, son. Okay. We'll help you. Where is your mom?"

"There." He stabbed a finger toward the faint glow of lights across the lake. "Over there."

Hell! The north shore was only a little more than a hundred yards as the crow flew but completely inaccessible by vehicle from this side of the lake. Brett would have to drive two miles back down the dirt track that led to his cabin, then circle around for another five on a paved county road. Much quicker to shove through the thick woods along the shore, as the kid obviously had.

"We'll go with you, son, but I need to know what emergency medical supplies to bring with me. Tell me what's wrong with your mom?"

"She's all white 'n' sweaty 'n' throwing up. 'N' going to the bathroom. Lots. She said she thinks it was the soy milk she brought from home. That stuff is so gross, but she's always drinking it." His panic poured out on a rush of words. "Now she's lying on the floor all doubled up 'n' the cell phone won't work so I can't call 911 'n' my little sister's crying 'n' I don't know *what to do!*"

Brett dropped a hand and gave his shoulder a reassuring squeeze. "Sounds to me like your mom might have a touch of food poisoning. We'll take care of her. Let me get my jacket and the first-aid kit."

If it was food poisoning, there wasn't anything in the kit that would help, but he grabbed it anyway. He also snatched up a flashlight and his handheld police radio in case he had to call for medical transport. The blue steel SIG SAUER went into the pocket of the camouflage hunting jacket he always kept at the cabin. With an escaped killer on the loose, he wasn't taking any chances.

He was back outside within moments. "Let's go."

The boy whirled to crash back the way he'd come. Brett started to follow, but spun around when Delilah opted for another route.

"I'll go across the lake and meet you at their cabin."

"No! Wait! The ice is too thin!"

He should have saved his breath. With the same

blinding speed she'd displayed earlier, she reached the shoreline in a single leap. A second bound took her almost to the middle of the lake.

A sharp crack of ice breaking rifled through the night and Brett's heart stopped dead in his chest. Then she flew the rest of the way and disappeared into the shadows on the far shore.

"Jesus!"

Whirling again, he raced after the kid. The boy had plunged too far ahead to have witnessed Delilah's acrobatic feat, thank God. He had enough to worry about without adding supernatural beings to the mix.

"What's your name?" Brett asked when he pulled alongside, his flashlight cutting a wide swath in the darkness.

"Tommy. Tommy Hawkins."

"I'm Brett, Tommy."

They pounded through the scrub brush, ducking under brittle branches and dodging stumps.

"You probably didn't see the cruiser parked on the other side of my cabin. I'm a police officer. An Oklahoma State Trooper."

The boy threw him a look of unmistakable relief and hope. "You kin, like, call in a helicopter to fly mom to the hospital?"

"Sure can, if she needs one. So don't worry, okay? Between us, we'll take good care of her."

His first-responder's medical training had focused

more on vehicular trauma, heart attacks and gun-shot wounds than food poisoning. He'd read enough about it to know most forms weren't lethal, how-ever, and that the basic treatment was to repeatedly induce small amounts of fluids into the victim to keep him or her from dehydrating. More serious cases—particularly those caused by foods that had been treated with certain pesticides—could require stomach pumping and intensive care.

Praying that wasn't the case here, he kept his stride matched to the boy's.

WHEN DELILAH RAPPED on the door of the split-level cabin, a timorous young voice called out from inside.

"Tommy?"

The sister. The boy had talked about a little sister.

"No, it's not Tommy. He'll be here in a little bit, though. Can you let me in?"

"Noooo."

It was a small, frightened cry.

"Mama says…Mama says we're never s'posed to open the door to strangers."

"That's right. You shouldn't. But Tommy told me your mama's sick. I want to help her. I'm coming in now."

The dead bolt might have been strong enough to

keep out burglars and bears, but Delilah splintered it easily.

The moment she stepped inside, a barrage of scents assaulted her overly developed senses. The sharp tang of pine from a decorated Christmas tree mingled with the stink of burned cookies. Overpowering both were the odors of vomit and diarrhea coming from one of the bedrooms.

Delilah recoiled, driven back by the memory that sprang into her head. In vivid technicolor and surround-sound, she saw a hospital ward reeking with the same odors. Moaning patients on cots jammed in every corner. Bone-tired orderlies covering the faces of the dead with blankets before summoning the burial detail.

Gulping, she shoved the images out of her head and speared a glance at the youngster clutching a ragged doll's blanket to her chest.

"Don't be scared, sweetie."

The girl popped a thumb in her mouth, her blue eyes wide above the ruffled collar of her pajamas. The candy-apple-red pj's were the kind with footies and decorated all over with Santas and reindeer.

"Tommy and my friend Brett will be here in a few minutes," Delilah told the her. "Just wait right here, okay, while I check on your mama."

She followed the worst of the scents. Her nostrils flared wider with each step, but she made it to the bathroom tucked between the cabin's two bedrooms without gagging.

A honey-haired woman in a pink fleece bathrobe sat slumped on the linoleum, one arm draped over the toilet seat. Beside her lay a crumpled towel and two empty cardboard toilet-paper rolls. At Delilah's entrance, she lifted her head and gasped out a desperate plea.

"Tommy?"

"He's right behind me. He and Brett Cooper. Sergeant Brett Cooper," she tacked on for reassurance. "He owns the cabin across the lake."

The young mother was too relieved to question how Delilah had outdistanced her son and neighbor. Slumping, she rested her forehead on the toilet seat.

"I told Tommy not to go for you. But my darn cell phone doesn't get a signal out here. We couldn't call anyone and Tommy got scared."

"Understandable. You don't look too good."

"I look worse than I feel. The cramps aren't as bad as they were."

Not bad, but certainly not good. That became evident when she stiffened and tried unsuccessfully to bite back a groan.

"Oh, no! Here we go again."

Delilah grabbed a clean washcloth and shoved it under the cold water tap. When the worst of the spasm had passed, she knelt beside the young mother and bathed her face.

"Tommy said you thought you drank some bad milk."

"It didn't taste bad going down. I could tell it was off about five minutes after it hit my stomach, though." She gave a wan smile. "I've been in the bathroom ever since."

"Not the best way to spend Christmas Eve."

"Tell me about it."

The smile slipped, and tears brimmed in her eyes.

"This is the kids' first Christmas since my husband and I split. I rented the cabin from a friend at work. I thought the change of scene would, you know, make it easier on them. Instead I go and scare them half to death."

Sniffling, she dragged the back of a hand across her nose.

"My poor babies. Emma is sure Santa won't find her up here and Tommy is all bent out of shape because there's no TV to play Nintendo on. Now this!"

"Hey, you couldn't help what happened." Delilah scrounged around in the cabinets for a fresh roll of toilet paper. "And the best Christmas present you can give your kids is to kick this thing. What's your name?"

"Sharon Hawkins. That's Emma in the other room."

"Hi, Sharon. I'm Delilah." She shoved the roll at the weepy woman. "Here. Blow."

That produced a watery chuckle. "You sound like me doing my mom thing. Do you have kids?"

"No."

Nor would she, with her body suspended in perpetual half life. Her hair didn't grow, her toenails never needed clipping and she hadn't had a period in more than a hundred years.

"You've got time," Sharon consoled before blowing into the wadded tissue.

More than she knew, Delilah thought ruefully. She wiped the woman's face with the damp washrag again and vowed to get her to the hospital as soon as Brett and the boy arrived to take care of Emma.

"About time," she muttered when Brett finally crowded into the bathroom.

"Yeah, well, some of us have to stick to terra firma. Tommy, why don't you look after your sister while I talk to your mom."

The boy left with obvious reluctance and Delilah scrambled out of the way so he could hunker down.

"Sharon, this is Brett. Brett, Sharon."

Embarrassed, the young mother shoved back her sweat-dampened hair. "I'm sorry Tommy ran over to get you. I told him not to."

"No problem." His blue eyes raked her face. "How are you feeling?"

"Better now. Honestly. I got the worst of it out of my system. Several times."

He laid a hand on her forehead. "No fever. Did you take any medications?"

He'd asked Delilah the same thing, she recalled. Was it only last night? It seemed so much longer.

Of course, that might have something to do with the fact she'd whoozed around in the night sky.

And tumbled down in front of his cruiser.

And ridden him like a wild woman.

And almost chewed off her arm to escape.

"I always carry a pharmacy with me for the kids," Sharon said, jerking Delilah back to the present. "When the cramps started, I popped some Pepto-Bismol."

"We need to make sure you didn't dehydrate," Brett advised. "Think you can keep some water down?"

She looked doubtful but nodded. "I'll try."

He rose to rinse out a pink-coated glass and fill it with tap water. When he crouched down again, Delilah chewed on her lower lip.

"Wouldn't an IV be better?" She met his eyes. "I could get her to a hospital real fast."

"I don't need an IV," Sharon objected. "I'm feeling better. Really."

They had no difficulty translating the distraught

mother's quick protest. She didn't want to leave her kids on Christmas Eve.

"Let's see how this works," Brett said calmly. "Just a few sips at a time," he warned as he held the glass to her lips. "You don't want to throw it back up."

THE WATER STAYED down. Two glasses, drunk very slowly.

Between sips, Delilah helped Sharon change into a clean nightshirt and crawl into bed. As soon as she sank onto the pillows, she called for her children.

Emma rushed in with her blanket clutched like a life preserver against her chest. "Mommy?"

"I'm right here, baby."

The girl started to scramble up on the bed, but Sharon stopped her with a wobbly smile.

"Better not, Em. Mommy's tummy is still a little shaky."

Tommy caught his sister's arm and earned a protesting squcal when he yanked her back. He'd shed his bright yellow ski jacket but still wore a look of worry.

"You gonna be okay, Mom?"

"I am, thanks to you and these kind people." She reached out to grip the boy's hand. "Not much of a Christmas Eve for you and Em, is it?"

"We don't care," he said fiercely, "as long as you get better."

"I will. I promise. I think I'll rest a little bit,

though. Why don't you read "Twas the Night before Christmas' to Em. Or..."

She lifted a pleading gaze to the two adults.

"Maybe you could read to her, Brett, and Delilah could help Tommy pop another batch of cookies in the oven for Santa. The first batch burned while I was, uh, otherwise occupied."

Delilah had never baked cookies in either of her lives. When she was alive, her mama had always employed kitchen help. After she died, there was no point.

"I'm better at reading," she told Emma with a wink. "We'll let the boys do the baking."

Moments later she had curled up on the sofa with a large picture book and the little girl snuggled against her side. The book was well-worn and obviously a favorite. Its front cover opened easily to a page displaying a Victorian-era living room with a humpbacked sofa in deep crimson, fringed lampshades and what looked like a twenty-foot-tall Christmas tree. The scene was so eerily familiar that Delilah had to clear her throat twice before she could begin reading.

"'Twas the night before Christmas, and all through the house...'"

Behind her, Brett and Tommy thumped around in the kitchen. It soon came alive with the smell of cookie dough, nuts and cinnamon. As the tantalizing scents drifted across the room and Emma sucked contentedly on her thumb, Delilah paused in her reading.

For a moment, just a moment, she indulged in wishful thinking. This was what her life *might* have been like. A little girl nestled against her breast. A husband and son performing mundane chores together.

No! She wouldn't go there. It never did any good.

Turning the page, she read on. "'Away to the window I flew like a flash, tore open the shutters and threw up the sash.'"

Emma's head drooped. Her thumb slipped out of her mouth. When she twitched like a sleepy puppy, Delilah eased her body horizontally onto the sofa and covered her with a throw before going into the bedroom to check on Sharon.

"Emma's out like a light. Here, you need a little more water."

"How's the cookie making going?"

"Fine. Think you could handle some tea and dry toast?"

"Yes. And, Delilah?"

"Hmm?"

"Thank you. Thank you *so* much."

"You're welcome."

After preparing the tea and toast, Delilah carried Emma into the other bedroom and tucked her into the lower bunk. Tommy was still worried about his mom and held out until well past midnight. He only climbed into the upper bunk when Sharon insisted he call it a night.

Once she was sure he'd fallen asleep, the young mother swung out of bed and pulled on her fleecy robe. When she emerged from the bedroom, Delilah and Brett were cleaning up the kitchen.

"Sharon! What are you doing?"

"The kids' presents are in the car trunk. I have to finish wrapping them and put them under the tree."

"Brett and I can do that."

"You've done so much already, and I don't want to ruin your Christmas Eve. You must have presents to wrap, too."

"I don't. How about you, Brett?"

She tossed the question off lightly, expecting an equally light response. He'd already told her he wasn't into the whole Christmas scene. He'd also mentioned that he didn't have any family.

"I haven't wrapped a present in five years."

Shrugging, he turned to snag his jacket from the chair, but not before Delilah caught a glimpse of bleak emptiness in his eyes. It was gone when he turned back.

"Toss me the keys, Sharon. I'll get the stuff out of your car."

CHAPTER FIVE

THEY LEFT A mountain of wrapped presents and a still-shaky but very grateful Sharon some hours later.

Brett insisted she keep his cell phone for the duration of her stay at the cabin, because his got service in this remote area and hers didn't. *She* insisted they come back for Christmas dinner later that afternoon.

"Please. Let me thank you for all you've done for me and the kids."

Brett slid a look in Delilah's direction before shaking his head. "Thanks, but you're not going to be up for company or cooking."

"The turkey's already in the fridge, defrosting, and I baked corn bread for dressing before I drank that damned soy milk. All I have to do is chop a little celery and onion, then pop everything in the oven."

Delilah would have given all she possessed to sit down at a table with Brett and the Hawkinses in broad daylight. She'd never regretted her half life more.

"Sorry, Sharon, I need to leave early in the morning."

Like, within the next hour. She had to get to Houston before dawn or she'd end up sleeping through another day on a bathroom floor.

Not that she'd mind. If it weren't for Sebastian and his grab for power, she might seriously consider spending several more days curled up in Brett's bathroom…and several more nights in his bed.

Sharon accepted her excuse with obvious disappointment. "Well, have a safe trip to wherever you're going. And Merry Christmas."

"Merry Christmas."

The night had grown frigid, with the promise of more snow heavy on the air. Delilah didn't feel the bite, but Brett had to hitch up his collar and hunch his shoulders inside his down-filled hunter's jacket.

She walked with him, her keen vision picking out straggling branches and potential obstacles well ahead. She debated for some time whether to ask him about the lost look she'd glimpsed in his eyes. She'd shared the intimate details of her existence with him, but Brett didn't exactly invite questions about his. The lights of the cabin loomed a short distance ahead when she decided to take the plunge.

"You said you hadn't wrapped a Christmas present in five years. Am I getting too personal if I ask what happened to turn you off the holidays?"

He didn't answer for so long she thought he

intended to ignore the question. Then he took her elbow to guide her over a rough patch of ground. His breath steamed on the night air, brushing against her cheek like a warm caress, but his reply chilled her to the bone.

"You remember the escaped murderer I told you about earlier?"

"Yes."

"We dubbed him the Christmas Killer because he liked to strike this time of year. He bragged that all those shoppers coming out of the malls in the dark made for easy prey. My fiancée was one of them."

"Oh, no!"

"It was Christmas Eve. Five years ago. Cindy called to tell me she was going to hit the mall."

The grip on her elbow tightened. Brett stared straight ahead, but she knew he wasn't seeing the welcoming glow of the cabin lights.

"I told her to wait, that I'd go with her when I finished my shift. Then I got hung up working a four-car pileup. So she went alone."

Delilah had existed for more than a century with what-ifs and if-onlys. She knew all too well how bitterly corrosive they could be. Aching for Brett, she accompanied him into the cabin. Once inside, he crossed to the stone fireplace and knelt to add logs to the smoldering embers.

"I've been with the highway patrol for eleven years. I've seen people die in a relatively minor fender bender, others walk away from a vehicle so mangled you couldn't tell the front end from the rear."

He draped an arm over his bent leg and stared into the flames licking at the fresh logs, searching for answers she knew he'd never find.

"I understand that life—and death—are pretty much a crapshoot," he said slowly. "It's one thing to accept that in the abstract, though. Another when it happens to someone you love."

"Or to you."

The low murmur jerked Brett out of his personal hell. Muttering a curse, he pushed to his feet.

"I'm sorry, Delilah. I didn't mean to wallow around in remorse and regrets. It's just… This time of year…"

He hated that it still got to him. Hated, too, that Cindy's face faded a little more with each passing Christmas. He tried to hang on to her, fought like hell to keep her in his heart. But all he had left were fading memories.

"I know," Delilah said softly, as if reading his mind. "It's hard to let go of the past, isn't it?"

She laid her palm against his cheek. Her skin was as cool and smooth as polished marble, her eyes dark wells of understanding.

"You'll forget, Brett. With time. The hurt will go, too."

The hurt maybe. The guilt and regret would stay

with him the rest of his days. But this woman could block them. For a few hours, anyway.

Turning his lips into her palm, he murmured a quiet plea against the cool skin. "Stay with me, Delilah. Just for tonight. Help me forget."

"Are you…" Her voice caught. "Are you sure you know what you're asking for?"

"Very sure." He brought his head around and smiled. "A Christmas kiss."

She couldn't leave him like this, haunted by the ghosts of Christmas past. Going up on tiptoe, she brushed her lips across his. Once. Twice.

THEY MADE LOVE in front of the hearth, stretched out atop the sofa cushions Brett dragged down to make a nest.

The dancing flames warmed Delilah's skin and brought out the fire in her hair. The curtain of shimmering red framed her face as she stroked her hands over his shoulders, his chest, his belly. When she followed each stroke with a kiss, her cool lips hollowed Brett's stomach and heated his blood.

Her hands and mouth and slender, sinuous body pushed everything else to a distant corner of his mind. For that hour, that slice out of time, all he knew, all he wanted to know was Delilah.

She fit under him so perfectly. Her pelvis cradled his hips, her calves hooked around his and her body welcomed him with unrestrained eagerness. He filled her, driving deeper and harder with every thrust. She reciprocated by filling the empty spaces inside him.

But not as she had last night. Or this morning. The pleasure she gave him was every bit as intense. Yet he wasn't consumed by the same mindless, animal hunger. With every move, every thrust of her hips against his, one thought hammered at his mind.

This was Delilah. Exotic, ethereal Delilah. She gave everything she had, along with a gift he hadn't expected.

"You didn't block it," he said when they lay depleted side by side on the cushions. "I'm not going to forget this time, am I?"

"I sincerely hope not." Rolling onto her side, she propped her chin in one hand. "I wanted you to remember tonight, Brett. I certainly will."

"For a while."

He wrapped a silky strand around one finger and tried to ease the inevitability of their parting with a joke.

"Another two, three hundred years and medical science will have made unbelievable strides. I won't stand a chance when compared to those hot, twenty-third-century studs."

"I won't argue the advances in medicine, but I doubt it will produce anything to compare with you, Officer Cutie."

"Stay with me, Delilah."

The plea came from deep inside him. He didn't understand how this woman had worked her way into his heart so swiftly and so completely, but she had.

"Tonight. Tomorrow. Next year. Forever."

"I can't," she whispered.

"Because of this meeting of the clans? Why is it so damn important?"

"We're...we're in the middle of a monster power play. Sebastian, my clan leader, already controls most of northern Mexico and the southwestern U.S. But he wants more. More territory, more wealth, more power. I bring the support of the Colorado band. Sebastian needs me at this gathering to back his claim over those of his rival."

"So you're—what? Some kind of a super-delegate?"

Her mouth curved, but the smile didn't reach her eyes. "I *wish* it could all come down to a vote."

Passages from some of the gorier websites Brett had called up earlier this afternoon leaped into his head. He couldn't suppress sudden, bloodcurdling visions of rival vampires tearing out each other's throats or dousing their enemies with flaming oil.

"So don't go. Don't put yourself in the middle of it."

She rested her chin on his chest and sighed. "The problem isn't just Sebastian. It's us, Brett. My 'forever' isn't the same as yours."

"I'll grow old and die, and you won't. Is that what you're saying?"

She nodded, digging the tip of her chin into his chest. "I had to watch that happen to everyone I loved. My parents. The lieutenant I was betrothed to. My friends. It tore me apart. Every time."

Just as it would to watch him die.

As soon as the thought formed, Delilah knew she'd committed the unthinkable. She'd fallen more than a little in love with this man.

He wasn't like the Seekers, so morbidly fascinated with her kind that they searched out night gathering spots and offered their throats like bleating sheep. Or the disbelievers, so terrified of anything and everything they couldn't understand.

Brett was…himself. Suspicious, wary, slow to trust. Yet he'd accepted her for what she was. *Wanted* her, despite what she was. Delilah would have given whatever was left of her soul to do as he asked and stay with him for another day, another night. She would not, however, forfeit *his* soul. Sebastian would rip out his throat if he found her here, in this man's arms.

"I have to go," she whispered, dropping a soft kiss on his mouth.

Their second farewell of the night, she thought as she gathered her scattered clothing. The first had been reluctant on both sides, but this one was harder. So much harder.

She'd assured Brett he would forget. In time. But would she?

Trying not to dwell on what they might have had in a different life, Delilah tugged on her leggings and sweater. She was zipping up her boots when a cackle of static cut through the stillness in the cabin.

"Sergeant Cooper, this is Dispatch. Do you read?"

Brett crossed to the jacket he'd tossed over the back of a chair and fished his radio out of the pocket. "Ten-two, Dispatch. What's up?"

"The major needs to talk to you."

A male voice replaced the woman's.

"We just got a call via the hotline. That 4532 we've been hunting is in your area."

"The hell you say!"

A feral light leaped into Brett's blue eyes. For a startled moment he reminded Delilah of the vicious hunters who preyed on her kind. She had no idea what a 4532 was, but from the look on his face, its days were numbered.

"The hotline caller owns Larry's Gas-'n'-Go," his major related. "It's a convenience store about…"

"Ten miles from here. I know it. I buy groceries and bait there."

"This guy Larry told us a man stopped to ask directions to the lake. Said he recognized Madison from the news coverage of the escape."

Madison! The name jerked Delilah's head up.

That was the escaped murderer Brett had warned her about. The one who'd killed his fiancée.

"When Madison asked for directions to the lake, Larry remembered you were the one who took him down five years ago. He figured the bastard is out for revenge."

"I hope so."

The low growl raised the hairs on the back of Delilah's neck. And they said vampires were scary!

"What's he driving?" Brett bit out.

"A late-model white Ford pickup, Texas plates, first two digits L-1. It was reported missing a few days ago. I've got two units headed your way and more responding. They're thirty minutes to ETA, but your friend Larry bought us some time by giving Madison directions to the north end of the lake instead of south, to your cabin."

Brett went still. "He sent Madison north?"

"He says there's a vacant cabin at the north end. He figured Madison would think it was yours and…"

"The cabin's not vacant, Chief! A woman and her two kids rented the place for the holidays."

"Hell!"

"Her name's Sharon Hawkins. She's got my cell phone. Call her! Now! Tell her to bundle the kids in the car and…"

He stopped, gave a vicious curse and shook his head.

"No good. The cabin is accessed by a one-lane

dirt road, just like mine. She might meet Madison coming in. Tell her to stay put."

His gaze sliced toward Delilah.

"I'll have someone there before you get off the line with her."

"Who?"

"No time for explanations. Just call Ms. Hawkins. Tell her we're heading over there."

He cut the transmission and dug into the other pocket of his jacket. His eyes were flat and cold when he pulled out a blue steel pistol and turned to Delilah.

"You ever fire a semiautomatic?"

"No, but I don't need a gun."

"This guy's vicious."

"He can't hurt me." She made for the door in swift, long strides. "Not unless he burns the cabin down around my ears or happens to have a sharpened stake handy. But I can hurt him. Bad."

And she would, she vowed as Brett popped the truck of his patrol car and pulled out his assault rifle.

"I'll go across the lake," she told him. "I'd carry you with me, but I haven't fed tonight and I don't have the strength."

"Go." He jerked his chin toward the woods. "There's a shortcut. It'll take me to the county road Madison has to go down to get to the north shore. I'll try to cut him off before he gets to the cabin."

If he hadn't already.

Driven by a mounting sense of urgency, Delilah nodded.

"I'll take care of Sharon and the kids. You—" She grabbed the front of his jacket and hauled him close for a swift kiss "—take care of yourself."

As she leaped toward the frozen ice, instincts older than time surged through her veins. She could count on the fingers of one hand the number of times she'd yielded to their primal pull. Each time, every time, it was kill or be killed.

Tonight, her instincts screamed, was one of those times. If Madison showed his face anywhere in the vicinity, if he tried to harm anyone, he would die.

IT WASN'T THE Christmas Killer who attacked her just as she reached the far shore, however, but her seething, vengeful clan leader.

CHAPTER SIX

HE CAME OUT of the night with an animal roar and a blast of frigid air that sent Delilah flying backward.

She crashed down on the ice, hitting so hard that it shattered like thin glass. Black, icy water knifed into her eyes, her mouth, her lungs. Gasping, she scissor kicked toward the jagged hole in the surface. Another powerful kick propelled her out of the frigid water and onto the shore.

"Damn you to all the fires of hell, Sebastian!"

He stalked toward her, his boots trampling the snow. He was short but heavily muscled. His upper lip and chin bristled with the short, pointed beard of a conquistador, and his eyes blazed with fury.

"Hell is exactly where you'll spend the next century, you ungrateful bitch. A very painful, very private hell of my making."

Shaking with a fury that matched his, Delilah shoved wet hair out of her eyes. "I'll take whatever punishment you prescribe…"

"Yes," he snarled, "you will."

"But not now!"

"You dare to dictate to me? *Me!*"

His eyes burned a fiery red. Whipping out an arm, he lashed her across the face. The blow would have separated a lesser mortal's head from his shoulders.

In Delilah's weakened state, it did damage enough. Her head snapped back. She staggered and almost fell into the lake again. Starbursts of pain burst behind her eyeballs. She blinked away the blinding agony to find Sebastian stalking toward her again.

"Do you forget who pulled you from that reeking pit?" he raged. "Do you forget who turned you?"

"No! How could I?"

"You owe me your allegiance. Your obedience."

She cast a desperate look over his shoulder at the cabin nestled amid a stand of bare, leafless trees.

"You'll get both, Sebastian. I promise. Just let me…"

The sharp crack of rifle fire cut her off. She froze, dread flooding her veins, as a second shot followed the first. Then another, and another, in such rapid succession she knew that was Brett's assault.

The shots still reverberated in the icy air when a thunderous boom split the night. A second later, a fireball leaped above the distant tree line.

As Delilah flew back across the ice, she knew her strength was failing. Fast!

Any other time, she would have leaped alongside Sebastian and arrived at the scene of the explosion the same time he did. Instead she bounded up several seconds later.

She found him surveying the flaming wreckage of a white pickup with an avid gleam in his eye. Nostrils flaring, he sorted through the suffocating stink of burning gasoline and rubber to pick up the scent of blood.

"Two fresh kills. Both still warm," he added with visceral satisfaction. "We'll feed well tonight."

"No!"

The scream ripped from Delilah's throat as she searched around the leaping flames with frantic eyes.

She spotted Madison first. He lay sprawled in the scrub brush a dozen yards away. His lips were pulled back in the rictus of death. Blood pumped sluggishly from bullet holes in his head and chest.

Fear hammered at her with steel fists. She whirled in a full circle, searching the woods, the road, the heavy underbrush. When she saw the figure slumped against a tree just off the road, his assault rifle resting across his thighs, relief burst inside her with the same blinding intensity as the pain she'd endured just moments ago.

"Brett!"

She dropped to her knees beside him. The explosion had singed his brows and blackened his face. It had probably thrown him through the air, too, and slammed him into the trees. She didn't see any visible wounds, but he could be concussed or have internal injuries.

"Brett, can you hear me?"

Teeth clenched, he lifted his eyes to hers and ground out a hoarse question. "Did I...get...him?"

She glanced over her shoulder, saw Sebastian feeding on Madison's bullet-riddled body.

"You got him."

"Didn't...shoot to kill. Tell them...I took the front tire...out first. He skidded off...the road. Jumped out. Started shooting. Tell them...I had to...return fire."

"You tell them!" she said fiercely, her eyes frantic as they searched him from neck to knees. "Where are you hurt? Brett, where are you hurt?"

Grunting, he shoved the assault rifle aside. Only then did she see the pool of blood at the jointure of his hip and thigh. The ground beneath him was dark and wet with it.

If she hadn't been so weak, if the burning oil and rubber hadn't overwhelmed her senses, she would have scented his blood right away.

"Bullet...hit the...femoral...artery," he got out through gritted teeth.

Too high on his hip for a tourniquet, she saw with a fresh swell of panic, and too deep to stop the pulsing jets of red. All she could do was whip off her vest and wad the fur against his wound.

He grunted again when she applied pressure. His shoulders slumped lower.

"Hold on, Brett! Please, hold on! Your boss said help was on the way. They'll be here any second."

His eyelids fluttered down. Hot blood seeped through the fur and drenched her hands.

"Brett! Look at me!"

The effort it took for him to open his eyes again ripped her into small pieces. One glance at his dilated pupils told her she couldn't save him. He was in shock and not even her powers could counter the loss of blood.

"Stay with...me," he whispered. "Tonight. Tomorrow. For...ever."

The last word was so faint Delilah wasn't sure she'd heard it right. Did it mean what she thought it did? Did he really want to live in darkness? With her?

"Do you want me to turn you? Make you one of us?"

She got her answer when he groped for her hand and drew back his lips. The agonized ghost of a grin stabbed her through the heart.

"You're...in *my* blood, Delilah. For...ever."

"Brett, are you sure? Brett?"

He didn't respond. Couldn't. She heard his heart flapping like a wounded bird inside his chest. The beat was erratic. Wild. Slow. Wild again.

Then it stopped completely.

She curled back her lip. Fangs bared, she swooped down.

Just as quickly, she jerked back. She didn't have enough strength to awaken him. If she drank from him now, the beast within her would take. Just take. Not give.

"Sebastian!"

He raised his head. Fresh blood dripped from his fangs. His eyes glowed with savage gratification.

"Sebastian, I need you!"

He arched a dark brow. A sardonic smile curved his lips. "Do you?"

"I haven't fed in several days. I can't turn him. You'll have to do it."

"*Have* to?"

He was playing with her. Batting her between his paws like a cat with a frantic mouse. All the while Brett's blood seeped into the frozen earth.

"Just do it! Please! I'll go back to the conclave with you. I'll support you. I'll tear out your rival's throat, if you want me to. Just turn him."

He sauntered over and stroked a hand over his pointed beard. "Why should I do as you request? What is this man to you? A friend? A lover?"

"More than a lover."

Delilah knew she was handing him absolute power over her. Knew, too, he'd exploit it in every way he could. She'd deal with that later.

"He's one I could share the darkness with, Sebastian. The only one I want to share the darkness with."

The smile he gave her held equal parts of evil and triumph. "You'll owe me for this, you know?"

"I know."

"Very well. Move away from him."

CHAPTER SEVEN

HEAT SEARED BRETT'S entire body.

He felt it engulfing him, pouring through him. Like molten lava, it burned everything in its path. His spine arched. His tendons corded into tight knots. Still the fire devoured him, searing his soul.

At its worst, he thought he heard someone calling to him.

Delilah!

He couldn't see her but he could hear her. Blinded by the swirls of blazing red, he reached for her.

SLOWLY, SO SLOWLY, the heat cooled. Degree by infinitesimal degree, the flames retreated.

Hours passed, maybe days. Brett was wrapped in a dim coolness when his mind reengaged. Fighting through the haze, he searched for an explanation of the conflagration that had almost consumed him.

The truck. The explosion. He remembered bullets thudding into the white pickup. Hitting the gas tank. Not *his* bullets. He had better aim than that.

He'd shot out the rear tire. He was sure of it. The

blowout had sent the vehicle skidding off the road. Brought Madison leaping out of the cab.

Madison.

A snarl ripped from Brett's throat. His lids flew open. He jerked upright, his eyes wide and searching for the vicious murderer.

Instead he saw Delilah hovering over him, her face illuminated by the faint glow of a lamp and a smile trembling on her lips.

"It's about time you woke up."

"You…? You okay?" he rasped, still gripped by the memory of Madison's murderous gunfire.

"I'm fine."

"Sharon and the kids?"

"They are okay, too."

He slumped in relief and glanced around to get his bearings. He was in a bedroom. An unfamiliar bedroom. Stretched out in a four-poster bed with a sheet as smooth and cool as silk draped across his hips.

"Where am I?"

"Houston."

"How the hell…?"

He broke off, slammed with another burst of memories. He'd taken a hit. A bullet to the groin. He could remember the shock, the pain. Remember, too, Delilah pleading with him to hang on.

Shit! He'd bled out. Right there in the road. Brett knew it, but still had to ask.

"I died, didn't I?"

"Yes," she said softly.

Thinking it was one thing. Hearing it confirmed was another. His mind reeling, he wrestled with the idea of his death and apparent rebirth.

Delilah watched him, saying nothing. She'd been there herself, a hundred years ago. She knew exactly what emotions were tearing through him right now.

Finally Brett lifted a hand and rubbed his neck. If she'd bitten in and sucked out whatever life had been left, he couldn't feel it.

"Did you…? What do you call it?"

"Awakening. We call it an awakening. Or turning. I wanted to, but I didn't have the strength. Sebastian did it for me."

"Sebastian, huh? I'll have to meet this guy."

"You will. Probably not tonight, though. He's just consolidated his leadership of the western clans and is still at the enclave, laying out his new ground rules. This is his house, by the way. We brought you here to give your body time to turn."

Her eyes searched his, desperate for reassurance.

"It's what you wanted, isn't it?"

"Yes."

"I was sure that's what you were trying to tell me." Relief added a giddy note to her voice. "I couldn't turn you…correction, I *wouldn't* turn you against your will. But I wanted to. You have no idea how much."

"Yeah, I do."

Brett closed his fingers over her hand. To his surprise, energy flowed down his arm, infusing him with badly needed strength.

"In those last seconds, when I sat there with my back to that tree, I knew I was dying. And all I could think of was you. Your mouth. Your eyes. Your loopy smile when you were still punchy from your visit to the dentist. I wanted all of that, Delilah. All of you. Forever."

She sniffed, then gave a hiccuping laugh. "It's a good thing I can't cry. You'd have me bawling right now."

"I'd rather have you naked."

The energy flowing through him was incredible. He'd never felt so powerful. Or so hungry for a woman.

This woman.

"I don't know what you call this craving I have for you," he said, "but I'm here to tell you it's like nothing I've ever felt before."

Laughter poured out of her, as bright and delighted as her luminous eyes. "It's love, you idiot. At least I hope it is."

"Vampire love?"

"Love, period."

"Yeah, well, let's try it out."

He intended to tumble her down beside him. He couldn't believe it when his tug spun her across the sheets and almost dumped her onto the floor on the opposite side of the mattress. She caught herself just in time and came up grinning.

"Easy there, cowboy."

"Jesus H. Chri…"

The sudden punch to his stomach muscles left him wide-eyed and gasping.

"That's one of the things we don't do," Delilah informed him ruefully. "It's an old taboo. One that goes back to the times Christians were fed to the beasts. Our kind got a bad rap over that."

"Wh…" He slicked his tongue over his lips and waited for his gut to unkink. "What else don't we do?"

"You'll learn, in time."

Brett drank in the sight of her, her hair falling over one shoulder, her smile bright enough to light the room.

"Please tell me having vampire sex isn't on the list," he begged.

"Definitely, certainly, assuredly *not!* As I'll demonstrate when you think you're strong enough for vampire sex."

Brett had to grin. "If every male felt the way I do now, Viagra would go off the market tomorrow."

With a joyous leap, Delilah bounded off the bed and tore at her clothing. She'd lived, breathed and

oozed terror through her pores during Brett's pro-
tracted awakening. He'd lost so much blood and Sebastian had toyed with her for so friggin' long that
she'd begun to believe the transformation wouldn't
work! But he was awake now, his skin as cold as hers
and the desire in his eyes every bit as hot.

Still she tried to curb her hunger when she joined
him in the bed Sebastian normally reserved for kings,
queens and other heads of state. After giving him the
power he craved, Delilah supposed she now qualified
as royalty.

Brett didn't buy her attempt at restraint, though.
With a low growl, he rolled her over and positioned
himself between her thighs. His hungry gaze roamed
from her face to her breasts and back again.

"Do you have any idea how beautiful you are?"

"I'd say we're well-matched."

She planed her hands over his powerful shoulders,
his chest, his lean hips. Her palms slid to his buttocks.
She felt the taut muscle flex, felt his sex probe her
sensitive flesh. She opened for him, joyfully, and
shuddered in ecstasy when he thrust into her.

"Very well matched," she gasped.

REALITY CAME WITH the sound of a door thudding
shut downstairs.

While they were here, shut away from the frenzy of
the conclave, Delilah had been able to keep thoughts
of what would come next at bay. But Sebastian would

have informed the clan about the latest awakening and his plans to induct the new recruit into their midst.

With the sound of his footsteps heavy on the stairs, Delilah knew it was time to warn the inductee.

"There's a ceremony, Brett. A ritual pledging of allegiance." Easing out of his arms, she pushed upright and tucked the sheet around her breasts. "It can be brutal."

"Now she tells me."

His lazy reply suggested he wasn't worried. She swallowed, remembering her own induction and tried to prepare him.

"Sebastian was a Spanish conquistador. He marched through the Yucatán with Cortés and helped destroy the Aztec empire. He…he knows a number of ways to inflict pain."

"That right?"

"That's right."

"Yeah, well…" His grin came out, cocky and confident. "I'm guessing your boy Sebastian never came up against an Oklahoma State Trooper."

The footsteps grew louder. Delilah's stomach twisted into knots. She wasn't afraid for herself. She was prepared to take whatever her clan leader threw at her. But Brett…

He refused to share her worry. Throwing off the sheet, he rolled to his feet and held out a hand.

"We're in this together, Delilah. No one, not even

a throwback to heavy-handed Spanish conquerors, can change that now."

She put her hand in his. Their palms joined, cool to the touch, yet fired by the unshakable bond blazing between them.

"You're right," she got out on a shaky laugh. "Sebastian's never come up against an Oklahoma State Trooper. Neither have I, for that matter. Until you."

"So stop worrying and kiss me. Then we'll take on this ferocious clan leader of ours."

"Together," she echoed, falling into his arms.

"Forever," he promised, covering her mouth with his.

* * * * *

THE VAMPIRE WHO
STOLE CHRISTMAS
Lori Devoti

ABOUT THE AUTHOR

Lori Devoti grew up in southern Missouri and attended college at the University of Missouri-Columbia, where she earned a bachelor of journalism. However, she made it clear to anyone who asked that she was not a writer; she worked for the dark side—advertising. Now, twenty years later, she's proud to declare herself a writer and visits her dark side by writing for Harlequin Nocturne.

Lori lives in Wisconsin with her husband, her daughter, her son, an extremely patient shepherd mix and the world's pushiest Siberian husky. To learn more about what Lori is working on now, visit her website at www.loridevoti.com.

I grew up on a dirt road where many people dumped their unwanted pets. These animals would arrive at our home covered in mange, mats and with wounds too horrible to describe here. I can remember the tears in my father's eyes when he had to put one such animal down because its injuries were too great to be healed. I also remember the appreciation and love the ones we could help showed when my mother bathed them, fed them and found them homes— or took them into our own.

I dedicate this novella to The Humane Society of the United States and everyone who has ever taken time out of their lives to help a hurt or deserted animal. Hugs and good homes to all...

CHAPTER ONE

THE SNOW WHIRLED round and round, like tiny tornadoes. Twirling flakes found their way past Drystan Hurst's collar and the hair that brushed his shoulders, the icy bits making it onto his bare skin. He didn't shiver, didn't bother to brush them away—his attention was too focused on the woman standing in his adoptive mother's window.

The white lights of the Christmas tree shone behind her, revealing her form, lithe as a dancer's, and the shape of her hair, a mass of curls he knew framed an almost elfin face.

Aimee Polk, the all-night-drugstore clerk who had stood between a suicidal boy and seven hostages, had begged the boy to take her in their stead, had by all accounts talked him out of the mass murder he'd planned.

Aimee Polk, who'd been sprayed with the boy's blood when he'd turned the gun on himself, had been caught on film as she stood there shocked, sobbing, mourning the loss of the boy who seconds earlier had threatened to take her life.

The media had gobbled it up.

And the Myhres had gobbled her up.

Maureen Myhre, Drystan's adoptive mother, had seen an opportunity and sprung on it. Maureen's son, Ben, was up for governor and Aimee was a media magnet. Maureen had wasted no time in seeking out the girl. Probably convincing her, like Maureen had convinced Drystan at one time, that she cared—in his case loved him, like a son.

He hissed, lifted his upper lip, revealing dagger-sharp fangs. How that story had changed once he'd messed up, been a kid, stupid but still worthy of love. And nothing he'd done afterward, not even saving her precious Ben at the cost of Drystan's own mortal life, had changed her lie to truth.

Drystan had avoided the Myhres, their constant plays for press and this town, for ten years.

Maureen Myhre had left him for dead in an alley. Pulled Ben, whom he'd saved, from the scene, then called the police, claiming Drystan, not Ben, had been trying to score a fix…. She was worried.

How unfortunate for her, a vampire had found Drystan before the police, turned him before he could fully bleed to death there in the cold.

He'd stayed away for ten years, but he was back and ready to make the Myhres pay.

AIMEE POLK SLIPPED off her silver flats and curled her legs under her body. Across the room, her soon-to-be mother-in-law touched a waiter's arm and pointed toward Aimee. Within seconds, a full champagne flute was pressed into Aimee's hand. Even though the dry champagne wasn't her favorite, Aimee accepted with a smile and took a sip. She preferred something sweeter, but knew whatever vintage Maureen Myhre had chosen was far more expensive than the sparkling wine Aimee used to buy on special at the drugstore where she had worked.

She let out a sigh and glanced around the living room filled with people she would never have dreamed of meeting, much less mingling with only a few months earlier.

How her life had changed in just one short year.

"Are you enjoying yourself?" Her fiancé, Ben, slid onto the couch next to her. In navy dress pants and a V-neck sweater he managed to look classy and relaxed. Even in a silk dress that Maureen had hand-selected for Aimee, Aimee felt neither. She ran a hand over her hair.

Ben slid his arm behind her back, giving the appearance of closeness without quite making contact. Across the room a photographer raised his camera. Ben leaned a little closer and tilted her chin up with one finger. Staring into her eyes, he murmured, "With the light behind you, the world will swear I'm marrying an angel."

Aimee shook her head. "I'm no angel." Angels didn't lose their charges, didn't stand by helpless as they blew their brains out.

"You'll never convince them of that." Ben nodded toward one of the invited paparazzi, pulled her closer as the photographer snapped the one-millionth picture of the evening. "They have you on film talking down that killer, convincing him to let those people go."

"He wasn't a killer," Aimee murmured and gripped the stem of her champagne flute tighter.

"Because of you." Ben squeezed her hand.

Because of her, Kevin was dead. "He was only seventeen," she said more to herself than Ben. "Who knows what he could have become?"

"A mass murderer?" Ben shook his head. "Seriously, Aimee, the kid was a loser. Destined for the needle. That bullet just saved the taxpayers hundreds of thousands of dollars in court fees."

Aimee flinched; she couldn't help it. Ben's words were callous, but he was a good man and his family had power. Power she could use to make up for her mistake, for costing Kevin his life. If she had to endure a few callous, even hurtful, words here and there, it was no more than she deserved.

Still, she couldn't help pulling into herself a little.

To her surprise, Ben noticed. "Tired?" He took the champagne flute from her fingers. "No more of this, then. Can't have you nodding off at your own engagement party."

The spark of elation Aimee had felt when Ben asked if she was tired faded. "How much longer?"

Ben laughed, his gray eyes carefully scanning the people around them. "It's only ten. If you're going to be a politician's wife, you're going to have to become a bit more of a night owl."

At that moment one of Ben's legislative aides came over and interrupted. Seizing the opportunity, Aimee murmured a few polite noises and excused herself, wandering back to the mansion's wide front window. She pulled back the curtain and stared out into the night, at the still-falling snow.

It wasn't the hour she found exhausting but the people. As a daimon, an intermediary between heaven and earth, Aimee could feel humans' needs and not just physical needs, but emotional and spiritual, too.

And the room behind her teemed with them. Needs buried so deeply beneath desires—for money, power, esteem—that Aimee was sadly confident she was the only being in the room who truly recognized them.

How did humans manage to concentrate so thoroughly on petty passing desires that they never fulfilled their true needs? How could someone confuse the need for love with the desire for power?

Aimee had never understood humans, doubted she ever would. And that was why she couldn't be a daimon any longer. Couldn't risk losing another soul that was entrusted to her.

Instead, she would marry Ben, be a good human wife, working behind the scenes, using the human power he would bring her to help others, and she would block out the incessant calling of lost souls around her. She would not try to save them, not a one.

As if on cue, something glimmered from beyond the window. A shadow darker than the night surrounding it. So dark, so filled with sorrow, Aimee could feel it pulling at her, calling her.

Without thinking, she pressed her hand to the cold glass, leaned forward until her breath formed a circle of fog blocking her view.

"Do you see something?" Maureen's voice cut through the haze that had enshrouded Aimee. She jumped as if struck, pulled her hand from the glass.

"No. Nothing." Curling her fingers into her palm, she turned her back on the window, on the being that waited outside still calling...

THE NEXT EVENING, Aimee was back at work, her Cinderella night behind her. She ripped open a cardboard carton and began unloading books onto a rolling rack. It was after ten and her shift as a hospital aide had just started. She would work until six, checking in on patients who couldn't sleep, read to them, chat, do whatever she could to take away their emotional pain.

She had taken this job a week after Kevin had killed himself. She couldn't stand going back into the drugstore where she'd worked for almost a year, made friends. The blood was gone, but the energy, the emotion left by his drastic act, hung like dark clouds under the fluorescent lights.

Besides, she'd only taken the job because she was his daimon. She'd known some event of significance in Kevin's life would happen there—known she needed to be there as much as possible, too. And she'd been right, the most significant event in anyone's life, their death, had struck there, but she had been of no help, not to Kevin.

A thick tome tumbled from her fingers onto the floor. The hardcover binding split on impact. She bent to retrieve it with shaking hands, then ran her index finger down the crack. Broken, like Kevin. But unlike the book, Kevin couldn't be repaired, not anymore. At the morose thought, tears welled in her eyes.

Pressing her lips together, she shoved the book back into the box. *Enough.* She had to get herself together. She'd already faced that she was a failure as a daimon, couldn't be entrusted with one being's life. Instead she was going to forget what she was, had been, concentrate instead on doing the small good deeds she could handle, and once she and Ben were married, on using his family's influence to do even more.

But she would not play guardian angel. She would

not be arrogant enough to believe she had the power to save anyone.

"Aimee, you in there?" A knock sounded on the door, then the door edged open. "Did you find the new—" Erin Schelling, another aide, stood in the doorway, a small carton tucked under her arm. "You did. Good." She held out the box.

With a smile, Aimee took it. "The MP3 players." She quickly tore open the box and pulled out six brand-new players.

"I have to say having the future wife of a state legislator on staff has increased the quality of our donations." Erin crossed her arms over her chest and leaned against the door frame. "Although I doubt that's all of it."

Aimee frowned. "What do you mean?"

With a laugh, Erin plucked one of the players from Aimee's fingers and pulled off its plastic covering. "I mean you. People have a hard time telling you no. They'd probably open the doors to Fort Knox if you asked nicely enough."

"I don't…" Aimee began.

Erin waved a hand. "As long as you're on our side it's all good in my book, girlfriend." She placed the player beside the others Aimee had stacked on the cart. "Might want to go by Mr. Belding's room first. He was asking about you, and…" Her voice dropped. "I heard the doctor talking to his daughter in the hall. Doesn't sound like he'll be going home. They're sending him to some nursing facility. They're telling him tomorrow."

Aimee stood. "But his dog. She's all he talks about."

"I know." Erin dropped her gaze. "Listen, I gotta go. Just wanted to give you a heads-up." She pursed her lips. "Go see him."

When Erin was gone, Aimee finished loading her cart and angled it out of the small room. For the millionth time, Aimee wished she had real powers, powers that would let her heal Mr. Belding, let him go home to his little one-bedroom house, his favorite chair and his dog. But all she could do was listen, hold his hand—just be with him.

It wasn't enough.

"Aimee," one of the nurses called. "There's a guy looking for you. I sent him to the waiting area—but you know he really shouldn't be up here this late. I'm not sure how he made it past the guards."

With a nod, Aimee deserted her cart and hurried to the waiting room. When she and Ben had first started dating there had been a number of such incidents, but the guards had never let anyone past their station.

At the threshold of the waiting area, she stopped. Standing with his back turned to her was a large man, over six feet tall with dark hair that skimmed broad shoulders. Kevin had worn his hair long, pulled back in a ponytail more often than not, but still the sight of a man with hair longer than the norm stopped her for a second.

As if feeling her gaze, the man turned.

It was then, when she could see his eyes, that she knew how he'd gotten past the guard.

Magnetism, hot and strong, like arms of molten metal wrapped around her, pulled at her.

She sucked in a breath, her eyes widened. Unable to move, she just stood there, struggled to conquer whatever had taken hold of her emotions. The man took a step forward, then faltered, too. His eyes flared.

Energy seemed to pulse between them.

Aimee lifted a hand—to protest…reach out to him…she didn't know what, but with the gesture her daimon skills clicked in. Her eyes widened more. The magnetism was still there, wrapping around her, caressing her, warming her, but there was more— something she was sure he was incognizant of—a vortex of hurt and need that threatened to suck her off her feet, send her flying toward him.

With stiff legs she staggered to a chair and braced her hands on its back. "Who are you?" she asked.

CHAPTER TWO

THE BLONDE ANGEL caught Drystan off guard. It wasn't her elfin beauty; he'd seen that on TV. It wasn't the shock, verging on horror, that pulled at her features as she stared at him, asked who he was.

It was the hunger that roared through him as soon as he'd turned—the burning need to be near her, touch her...feed off her. He bit down on his lower lip, let his fangs puncture his flesh, his own blood filling his mouth.

She couldn't see what he was doing. His actions, his fangs, everything that would identify him as one of the undead was hidden by his beguilement. She, like the guard downstairs and the nurse who'd barely cocked an eyebrow when he had asked for Aimee, could only see what Drystan wanted them to see—a human male, no more intimidating than a three-year-old child.

The bitter taste of his blood brought him back under control, reminded him why he was here.

"Drystan Hurst. I work for *City Brides*. We hoped you'd agree to be our featured bride next month."

"Drystan?" She frowned. "I've heard that name before."

He cursed under his breath. It hadn't occurred to him to give her a false name, but he hadn't thought his ex-family would have mentioned him, either. It had been ten years since his "death." Ten years the Myhres had spent eliminating his memory. Even his headstone had been removed—and it hadn't borne his true name. He hadn't learned it himself until after his death. He'd been Drystan Doe until twelve when the Myhres took him in. Then he'd taken their name with pride—ignorant weak child that he'd been. Just like the fragile woman standing in front of him.

He laughed. "It's not an uncommon first name— at least not around here. A lot of people in this area have roots in Norway." He tilted his head. "But you know that. You're engaged to a Myhre."

"Yes, I am." Her fingers clamped onto the red, padded back of the chair in front of her.

"So, will you talk to me?" He ran his tongue over the tip of his fangs and took a step toward her.

She retreated, not physically, but emotionally… or…he couldn't put a name to what she had done. She had been there one moment, energy just out of his reach, like he could hold out a hand and stroke the welcoming warmth that surrounded her. Then the bubble had contracted, pulled close around her, robbing him of…something.

"It doesn't have to be here, if you're busy." He said

the words, but his mind sent a different message, his beguilement working overtime to convince her she had nothing else to do, could waste whatever time he needed.

"That…that would be good." Her eyes were wide, gray, almost silver from where he stood. She gestured toward the hall from where she had entered. "I have rounds, people who expect me."

Already moving forward to take her hand and lead her to the small couch a few feet away, Drystan stumbled to a stop. "Of course you do." His brows lowered.

"Maybe tomorrow, in the afternoon? At your office?" Her hands, which had looked tense earlier, relaxed atop the cushion, and she tilted her head to the side, exposing a length of smooth, pale skin.

A throb of desire knocked into Drystan. He curled his thumbs over his fingers until he could feel the strain in his knuckles. "Tomorrow," he repeated verbally, but his thoughts were saying *now*.

She nodded her head, as if relieved. "If you have a card, you can leave it at the nurse's desk. I can call you when I wake up—after shift I usually go home and sleep a bit, but I'll be up by two. Will that work?"

Of course it wouldn't work. She was supposed to meet with him now, listen to everything he had planned to put into her head, then scamper back to the Myhres and wait until the time was right for her to humiliate them in the most public manner possible. "Six would be better," he replied. The sun would set by five, giving him time to be fully prepared for his next meeting with this puzzle of a woman.

"Six," she repeated, pursing her lips. "Fine, at your office?"

He thought quickly. "It will be closed. How about…" He named a restaurant that was private and comfortable with serving mixed company—alive and undead. He reached into his pocket and pulled out a card. "In case you need to get hold of me." He held the card between two fingers, willing her to take it, and to believe the words she would see printed there.

She held up one hand. "I'm sure it will be fine. I really have to go now. Until tomorrow." With an unsure smile she hurried from the room.

Drystan waited until he heard the wheels of her cart squeak down the hall and through a set of swinging doors before dropping his cloak of beguilement.

The question she'd asked when she'd first appeared echoed in his head. *Who was he?* He wasn't sure he knew the answer right now, but more important, who was she? What was she and would he be able to bend her to his will? Would he be able to get her to do as he wanted, and if he couldn't, what would he do next? How far would he go?

Aimee walked away from the waiting area as quickly as her feet could carry her without breaking into an all-out sprint. Once through the swinging doors that led to the H hall where Mr. Belding was staying, she slumped against the wall and let her pounding heart and spinning thoughts slow.

What was Drystan Hurst? He wasn't human, that much was sure. No human could hold the darkness Drystan did and function.

Another daimon sent to check on her? Daimons served as intermediaries between heaven and earth, but not all had the same purpose as Aimee. Some served a totally different role—to tempt, not help, humanity.

Could that be what Drystan was? Was he here to tempt her? To punish her for turning her back on her calling?

The doors swung open beside her. Aimee grabbed her cart and jerked it out of the way. It banged into the wall, knocking a line of books onto the floor.

The night nurse, who had directed her to the waiting area and Drystan, bent to help retrieve the books; between her fingers was a white business card.

"That guy left this for you." She held out the card.

Aimee stared at it, her hands glued to the books she'd just rescued from the linoleum. "What is it?" she asked.

The nurse frowned. "A business card." She glanced

at Aimee from the corners of her eyes. "Are you okay?"

Aimee laughed and began shoving the books back on her cart. "I meant what's it say?"

Her brows still lowered, the nurse flipped the card around so she could read it. "Drystan Hurst, Features Editor, *City Brides,* then there's a phone number and address." She held out the card again.

Aimee pretended not to notice. "Have you heard of them?"

"City Brides?" The nurse pulled back, something flickered in her eyes, then slowly as if not sure of her words, replied, "Of course. When my cousin was getting married she bought every copy."

"Is it monthly?" Aimee asked. She was sure she had never heard of the magazine.

"I think…yes." The nurse nodded. "It's monthly." She seemed relieved with her answer, like she'd been under great pressure to get it right. She dropped the card in Aimee's lap and stood. "Word of advice, though."

Aimee pulled her gaze away from the white card-stock to look at the nurse.

"Don't let your fiancé catch you with him." She nodded to the card. "Even if it is innocent. There was something about him…" She shivered. "He has *bad boy* written all over him. I may have trouble sleeping." She pushed against the swinging door with her hip and shot Aimee a wink. "In a very, very good way."

Alone, Aimee twisted her lips to the side and considered the card. It had passed through the nurse's hands before getting to Aimee. That had to have diluted any energy Drystan had left on it. She carefully placed her fingers on the top and bottom edges, so her skin made as little contact with the card as possible. A tiny shadow of energy pulsed against her finger pads, so tiny she wouldn't have given it a passing thought if she hadn't met Drystan, witnessed the strange pull he had in person.

She blew a puff of air from between her lips, shook her head at her wayward thoughts.

What had she been expecting? Even if Drystan was a daimon, sabotaging a business card was hardly daimon style.

Feeling more secure, she gripped the card firmly, letting the pads of her thumb and forefinger both press against the cardstock, then she closed her eyes and concentrated on amplifying the energy she'd been hiding from seconds earlier.

Darkness hit her first. So dark, so lacking in hope she wanted to step inside the pit, soak all the sorrow she felt emanating from that card inside her…make it disappear.

But, she reminded herself, she had made the choice. She would no longer let herself be a daimon.

She had to keep her resolve, couldn't let the pull

of this energy so opposite of her own lure her. Still, even with the thought pounding in her head, the need to neutralize what she felt coming from the card, to convert it to light, was almost overwhelming.

But she couldn't. Her daimon skills had failed her and her charge before. She wouldn't make that mistake again. Let the powers in heaven assign someone else, someone who wouldn't fail.

But—she stared down at the black print—there was so much need there, even in this tiny two-by-three-inch card. If such a small sample was so full of darkness, how much did the man himself contain?

CHAPTER THREE

DRYSTAN HID IN the shadows, willed his beguilement to hide him completely. He'd delivered his card to the nurse, then pretended to leave, but instead he'd gone searching for Aimee. Her resistance to him was unprecedented. She didn't know him, had no reason not to believe whatever he suggested.

To his knowledge, that was the only way a human could resist beguilement—if they already knew him, already had expectations of him. Even then it might not work, but to be honest, he'd never risked it, never approached anyone from his past. When he first rose, he hadn't wanted to see the distaste in their eyes, had been afraid he'd weaken, turn back into the little boy deserted by his mother, run.

He was over the fear now, had no need to hide, but he still hadn't approached the Myhres. He didn't want them on guard; he wanted to surprise them, shock them, when he delivered his revenge.

The squeak of wheels sent him sinking deeper into the shadows of an unoccupied nurses' station. Aimee swept by, her brows lowered in thought. She stopped outside a door a few feet away, smoothed her scrubs and took a deep breath. With a smile that would melt the polar ice caps, she backed into the door, pulling her cart behind her until it set half in the hall and half in the room.

Wrapping himself in illusion, Drystan followed her steps, stopping so he was hidden behind the door. If anyone looked his way they would see nothing more disturbing than a janitor taking an unauthorized break. If Aimee looked his way...Drystan had no idea what she might see.

Luckily, the soon-to-be Myhre seemed completely caught up in conversation with the room's occupant.

"I found you a new mystery, Mr. Belding. You want me to read some to you?" Drystan could hear the smile in Aimee's voice. It made him ache inside, in his core.

An older man's voice rasped a response. Aimee made some kind of soothing sound deep in her throat. Drystan felt himself moving, being pulled closer by nothing more than the promise of relief he heard in Aimee's tone. She murmured again. Drystan stopped by the open door, his fingers curling around the wood. He closed his eyes, soaked in the energy emanating from her. Her voice...it was like a gentle hand wiping away a tear or a kiss on a child's hurt knee.

The man spoke again. This time Drystan could make out the words.

"They're putting me away, you know. No reason to lie. I'm old and I'm dying. Doesn't make me stupid."

Drystan peered around the door's edge. An old man lay on a hospital bed. He was pale and shriveled, dry, like a leaf minutes before it crumbled to dust. And he was right; he was dying. The scent clung to him, but it wasn't thick yet. The man had months, maybe years with today's science, before he succumbed. But the smell was there, the moldering scent of death.

"You know I wouldn't lie to you." Aimee rested a paperback book she'd been holding on the edge of the bed.

"So, when are they shipping me off? How bad are we talking?" The man jerked on the plastic tube that protruded from his nose.

Aimee pulled his hand away and adjusted the tube herself. "Better?" she asked.

He grunted. Aimee's hand drifted from the old man's face to his hand. Slowly she slipped her fingers inside the curve of his. Drystan could see the old man relax, see anxiety leaving his body, disappearing like mist.

The man took a deep breath through the tube, then stared at Aimee so intently that Drystan almost came around the door to protect her. "You have to save her," he said. "They'll kill her. Soon as they decide for sure I'm not coming back, that I won't know what they did to her, they'll kill her. And that will kill me." A tear appeared in the corner of the man's eye and he fell back against the pillow, like the life had been jerked out of him.

"You don't know that." Aimee's words were soft, and filled with worry.

"I do, and so do you." The man stared at the white tile ceiling above his bed. "I know it seems strange, but that dog is all I have. She was a stray, you know. Meant to give her to the pound, but when I took her down there, I made the mistake of carrying her back to the cage for 'em. I tried to shove her in, but I couldn't do it. She wouldn't let me do it." He lowered his gaze back to Aimee. "Never saw a look like that on a dog. Terrified. She was terrified I was going to leave her, and I just couldn't do it. Swore to her I never would, that I'd make sure she was always taken care of, loved." The man sniffed, and fidgeted with the tubing again. When his hand dropped, there was moisture rolling down his sunken cheek. "Everybody deserves some love." He turned his head to face Aimee; there was pain in his eyes, real, unmistakable pain. Drystan blinked at the realization.

"Don't make me break my word," the man finished, his voice no more than a whisper, then turned his hand palm up. Without a word, Aimee slipped her hand into his. As the man's fingers closed over hers, Drystan took a step back.

The man loved his dog with such intensity it was staggering.

Drystan had never had a pet. Foster care didn't really allow for keeping an animal and Maureen Myhre didn't believe in them, claimed she was allergic.

What would it be like to love something with the thoroughness this man loved his dog? Or be the recipient of such love?

Drystan couldn't imagine.

Behind him the cart began to move—Aimee leaving the old man's room.

"I'll do what I can," she called, but softly, more to herself than the man.

Quickly, Drystan disappeared back into the space behind the door, concentrated on blending into the wall.

Aimee paused, glanced around, her gaze darting around the hallway, but her eyes never focused on the space where Drystan stood. Finally, she shook her head slightly, thinned her lips and continued down the hallway.

When she was gone, Drystan stepped around the door, stared into the now-dark room. The man mumbled in his sleep. Unable to understand him over the hissing of whatever machine the man was connected to, Drystan stepped farther into the room.

The man's lips moved. Still unable to make out the words, Drystan bent closer. The man mumbled again, another spat of words Drystan couldn't make out, then two he could. "...help me." The old man's eyes flew open and his hand reached out, grasping Drystan's wrist. "Help me," he said again.

The man stared at Drystan with no fear in his eyes. At first Drystan was shocked, then he realized the old man was asleep, talking in his sleep, most likely remembering Aimee, asking for her assistance, not Drystan's.

The man's eyes closed and his grip lessened. Drystan pulled the man's fingers away from his wrist, started to drop them onto the bed, but without realizing he was going to do it, without understanding why, he gave the man's fingers a tiny squeeze first, then gently laid them on the generic hospital sheet.

Help. Love. The old man wanted the impossible.

IT WAS ALREADY dark. Aimee would be late for work if she didn't hurry. Twisting the leash she'd brought in both hands, she stared at the closed door of Mr. Belding's one-bedroom home. His daughter had told him a college student was watching his house and Garbo, his Toto-like dog. But while the college student was present, the dog wasn't, and according to the fresh-faced girl, the animal hadn't been there for three days.

Three days. That was two days before Mr. Belding's doctor had told his daughter, Carol, that he didn't think Mr. Belding would be able to make it on his own.

It was possible his daughter had taken the dog to

her house, but... Aimee moved the leather leash to one hand and shoved the other hand into her pocket to pull out her cell phone. She flipped open the lid—five-forty. She had twenty minutes to make it to work. She'd been called in early tonight. Another aide had forgotten a birthday party and begged Aimee to cover for her.

Aimee had been more than happy to help out, especially because it gave her a perfect excuse to avoid Drystan. She tilted her head to the sky and took a deep breath through her nose. The reporter, or whatever he claimed to be, scared her.

She had gone to sleep this morning thinking of him, remembering the darkness that surrounded him. She'd awakened a few hours later with him still on her mind. So much need. She had never encountered such a void before.

A void. The shadow she had seen outside the Myhres' two nights earlier. Had that been Drystan?

Her phone chirped, reminding her that she was due at work—almost past due. With one last glance at the house, she shoved the leash into her bag and hurried to her car.

Tomorrow she would find Garbo, think of a way to find out what Drystan was, *and* how she could permanently avoid him.

DRYSTAN LEANED AGAINST the metal-and-rock sculpture that decorated the entrance to the hospital. Aimee had stood him up—or at least not called. Normally this would have shocked him, but with her response to him, or lack of one, last night, he realized he would have been disappointed if she had fallen so easily.

Beguilement was easy, less messy than hunting, but it was also less fulfilling. Until Drystan had met Aimee, he hadn't realized how much. Since awakening he'd prowled around his condo, waiting for her call, hoping she wouldn't, wanting an excuse to search her out himself—to be the aggressor.

And she'd given it to him; she'd ignored him.

He had never been happier.

With his thoughts on Aimee, his concentration slipped, the web of deceit he'd wrapped around himself slipping with it. A mother who was headed his direction with two school-age children in tow ground to a halt. Her eyes lit on him and rounded with recognition of what he was—a threat to her, her family, everything she loved.

He smiled, letting his fangs show for just a fraction of a second, then snapped the beguilement back in place. Ignoring her children's cries of complaint, the young mother jerked them closer, and abruptly changed her path, hazarding traffic rather than walk past him.

An older woman, seeing the mother drag her children off the sidewalk and onto the street, made a judgmental grumbling noise. His disguise again snapped in place, Drystan shrugged and shook his head in apparent agreement.

He was watching a group of interns grumbling among themselves over steaming paper coffee cups, thinking of signaling one, luring her to a spot behind the massive sculpture and relieving her of a pint or two of blood, when he felt the mood around him shift—lighten.

Aimee, an oversize leather bag slung over her shoulder, stepped out of the parking garage and into the crosswalk. Her head was down, her feet moving quickly. But even in her obviously harried state, the world seemed to lighten around her.

He watched her, willed her to look up and see him.

As if pulled by a string, Aimee's head lifted and her wide gaze met his. He felt the tiny exhaled "Oh" in the center of his chest, an anticipatory tightening, a flicker of something light and filled with promise he hadn't felt since he'd heard someone—the Myhres—wanted to adopt him.

The feeling, he reminded himself, couldn't be trusted. Still, he couldn't completely cut off the disturbing trickle of joy that wound through him as Aimee continued on her course toward him.

"You didn't call," he said.

Her hair was as wild as it had been the night before. Curls that would give under his hand, spring back when he removed his touch—the kind of hair that always look tousled, like she'd just left her bed, but innocent, too.

"I had to work early." She gestured to the building behind him, then twisted her mouth to the side. "Why are you here?"

"I figured something like that happened. The all-night angel wouldn't just stand me up."

"Don't call me that." Her words were firm, almost terse. Drystan raised his brows.

"Please," she amended. "I don't care for the name." Sadness touched her eyes.

Silence fell over them—Drystan unsure what to say. He should jump on this opportunity, take advantage of her melancholy, break her. He opened his mouth, determined to tell her the Myhres didn't care about her, how they would use her for political gain, then discard her if she faltered even one step. Instead, to his surprise, "Are you okay?" came out.

She seemed as surprised as he was. A smile curved her lips, so sweet and full of hope, Drystan wanted to step closer, to soak the warmth he could almost feel radiating from her into his soul, store it for the cold days…years to come.

"People don't usually ask about me," she replied. Her gaze was on him now, fully, as if despite the beguilement he carefully held in place, she could see him, really, truly see him, and she wasn't repulsed.

"I'd like to know about you," he said, and he wasn't lying. What had started as a game, a way to cause the

Myhres embarrassment and suffering, was quickly morphing into something else.

The thought scared him.

"For the magazine, that is," he added.

The light in her eyes lessened. "The magazine. I don't know. The Myhres...that is..."

"I'd show you a copy before it ran, of course. We're a bridal magazine, not a supermarket tabloid."

"Well—"

A kid on a skateboard slid down the concrete lip that separated the road from the statue they were standing next to. Without thinking, Drystan wrapped his arms around Aimee and jerked her out of the teen's path.

Anger swarmed over him. His beguilement gone, he jerked his head to the side and hissed at the delinquent over Aimee's head. In his arms Aimee flinched. He pulled himself back together, snapped his beguilement in place and stared down at her.

Her eyes were huge, her lips parted. "What are you?" she asked.

But Drystan barely heard her question. Warmth had radiated from her body into his. Her heart beat against his chest, so quick, so alive, while he was so slow, so close to dead. It was like walking into spring after years of barren winter.

He pulled her closer, wished they weren't separated by layers of heavy coats and clothing. His hair fell forward across his cheeks. People passed them, brushing along with hurried steps to get out of the cold, but neither Drystan nor the woman in his arms moved.

"What are you?" she whispered again.

He stared at her parted lips, full but unstained by lipstick, just a slight sheen that glimmered at him, invited him.

"What do you want me to be?" he asked, then before she could reply, he lowered his head and caught her lips with his. His fangs scraped over her lips, pulling but not piercing her flesh. He cupped her face in his hands, holding her head so the temptation to bite down, to suck in the sweet taste of her blood, didn't overwhelm him. What he was doing was bad enough. He already knew she was resistant to his powers. He might not be able to make her forget this.... She might run....

But she didn't, at least not at that moment. Her bag slipped from her shoulder onto the ground and her hands crept up his chest until her fingers curled around the lapels of his coat and she held him almost as tightly as he held her.

Drystan stroked the soft inside of her mouth with his tongue. Sweet, almost as sweet as he knew her blood would be. His groin hardened. She rubbed against him. He started to pull back, afraid the feel of him would startle her out of their embrace, but she clung to him, pressed her pelvis against his, shyly, but still there.

A groan escaped from his lips and was devoured by their kiss.

People were staring; he could feel their gazes on them. With a swish of his arm, he raised a veil around them, caused snow to spin, blinding anyone who glanced in their direction.

He was running his fingers over her cheek, dipping them down the curve of her neck, when a chime sounded, breaking the fog that surrounded them, bringing him back to reality.

Aimee pulled away. Her eyes looked heavy and unfocused, her lips bruised. Drystan could feel the quick beat of her heart, see her chest rise as she took in a breath. His own heart felt leaden in his chest. The muscle still worked like it had before he'd turned, beat like any other, but what he was feeling now... he'd thought this was in his past. Fear, pain, loss, he was used to, expected, but hope...love...those he hadn't felt for years. He didn't want to feel it now.

She blinked at him and he waited for her to ask again what he was, to jerk away, for her face to crease with horror at what she'd done, and with whom. But she just stared at him, pressed two fingers to her lips, then slowly pressed them to his.

"I need to go to work," she said, softly, almost apologetically. She bent to retrieve her bag and a cell phone. As she pulled the phone free, a leather dog leash fell to the ground. Drystan scooped it up.

"You have a dog?" he asked to divert his mind from the emotions swirling through him.

She shook her head. "A patient. I was trying to help him out."

"Trying?"

Her fingertips skimmed his palm as she took the leash.

She smiled, but her eyes were sad. "It's important. I'll try again."

Her answer was incomplete, but Drystan didn't ask her to explain, didn't need to. She hadn't found the old man's dog. Drystan's gaze drifted toward the hospital, to the window of the old man's room.

"About…this…" she started.

Drystan grabbed her hand, pressed his fingers into her palm, let his thumb sweep over the fine bones of the other side. "Forgotten." He paused and with his other hand, tilted her chin so she stared into his eyes. "It's forgotten. Nothing happened between us. You didn't even see me, just realize you *need* to see me, want to talk to me—that you trust me, will believe everything I say." He pulled a breath into lungs that needed no air, felt his powers thicken, wrap around her.

Her eyes widened, dilated. He nodded; her head followed the up and down movement of his and he knew that it was done, that the kiss that had warmed him, made him forget how cold the world could be, had in her mind never happened.

CHAPTER FOUR

AIMEE DIDN'T KNOW what Drystan had done or tried to do. She'd felt magic wrapping around her, felt it weave through her, confusing her.

She pressed a hand to her forehead. What had happened? She had seen Drystan; she knew that… or thought she did. The entire encounter was like a vivid dream, the kind that wakes you in the night and takes minutes to clear from your head, to convince yourself it *was* just a dream.

But her visit with Drystan was the opposite. Something was working inside her, trying to make her think it *hadn't* happened, but she knew deep in her soul that it had.

"Aimee…" Andrea, the nurse on duty, called from behind the counter. "Can you stop by Mr. Belding's room? His daughter left a couple of hours ago. They… talked." Her lips thinned. "He isn't doing well."

Aimee shoved her cart back into the closet and hurried to the older man's room.

DRYSTAN WATCHED AIMEE from the shadows for any sign his suggestion had taken hold. Once she'd arrived on her floor, she had gone to a closet to re-trieve the cart filled with books, then slowly began to push it down the hall. Every few steps she stopped, a confused look on her face.

His suggestion taking hold or some totally unre-lated problem she grappled with?

He'd almost decided his lurking would tell him nothing when a nurse said something to her and she raced off.

He, of course, followed.

When she paused outside the same room where he had spied on her last night, she took a deep breath and closed her eyes for a second before placing a smile on her lips and stepping inside.

The old man was propped up on his pillows, a distant look in his eyes.

"She sent Garbo to the pound," he said. "Sending me there, too."

Aimee squeezed his hand, but didn't say anything. At first Drystan was surprised that she would just sit there and let the old man suffer alone, but then he realized that was what the man needed, a listening ear, one that wouldn't judge, but just be there for him. Must have been the role his dog played before.

Besides, anything she said would be nothing but platitudes. The old man was being sent away from the life he had known, the things he had loved. He was in the last stages of his human life. There was no way around it. No way to make the journey easier…

except maybe not having to feel like he was taking the trip completely alone.

And that was why Aimee sat there, just holding his hand.

DRYSTAN LEFT THE hospital and prowled the city. He was restless; some feeling he couldn't pin down gnawed at him. He roamed, trying to shake the unsettling notion that there was something he should be doing, something he'd left undone, or maybe something he needed to undo. Finally, unable to relax, he found an upscale restaurant, one that would never have admitted him as a human, and stalked inside.

He sat in the back alone, sipping wine and pretending to eat. Across the room a woman sat with a date, both dressed to seduce—he with success and she with sex. Drystan watched them for almost an hour, stewed over the iniquities of life—the haves dining on filet and dressed in silk, the have-nots scrambling for change to buy a fast-food burger and pulling someone else's cast-off coat around their shoulders.

Life was horribly unfair, always had been. Luckily Drystan was no longer victim to the iniquities that ruled human existence. He could make his own rules now.

The woman dabbed at her carefully made-up lips with a white linen napkin, uttered a few polite noises, then slid from behind the table—headed to the bathroom.

Drystan waited a few seconds, watched her sway her hips as if to some inaudible blues tune, then dropped his own napkin onto his full plate, and stood to follow.

She was waiting for him when he turned the corner—or might as well have been. She stood in a dark alcove, her cell phone flipped open, her fingers already pushing numbers. Without saying a word, he slipped the phone from her fingers and snapped it shut.

She was ready for him; he barely had to extend his powers for her to fall against him, her hands kneading his chest, like a cat preparing its bed.

He stroked her hair away from her neck, whispered against her skin—even grazed his fangs over her throat. She smelled expensive, unattainable, exactly what he hungered for, or thought he did.

Her body felt good against his; her curves were soft, her skin supple. Everything was right or should have been. He murmured against her throat, preparing himself as much as her for what he was about to do, but as his lips were about to touch her flesh, his fangs to puncture her skin, he paused.

He wasn't hungry for her blood. Didn't need it to survive, at least not right now.

He only had to feed once a week, could even stretch that. So why was he here, doing this? Violating this woman? Yes, she would walk away happy with no memory of what he had done, but still he was using her, like he'd been used—and with no higher mission to justify his act. The flash of conscience hit him unawares, angered him.

He pulled back his lips, a hiss escaping between his teeth.

He tried to shove the unwelcome tussle with morals aside, but the thoughts continued to roll through his mind.

He didn't need this woman's blood to survive— he wanted it to forget. Blood, taking it, tasting it, made him forget…made the pain he'd carried all his life subside, at least for a while. And tonight, after being so close to Aimee, seeing her comfort the old man, knowing all that was left for the old human was pain, loss…Drystan's own pain had surged back tenfold, like the sea reclaiming a beach. He stared at the length of white skin the woman laid bare before him.

Morals be damned. No one had worried about morals when he'd been left beaten in an alley close to death. They'd chosen to hide his body rather than risk exposing the Myhre family to unsavory press. Left him where a vampire found him, fed on him, turned him into this. Drystan curled his upper lip, snapped his teeth together.

He did need this woman's blood, like an addict needed a fix. He bared his fangs, prepared to bite.

An image of Aimee with her hand wrapped around the old man's filled his mind.

With a curse, he shoved the woman away. She teetered on her heels, blinked up at him with her eyes vacant, no sign of hurt, or dismay, just a blank void—like the hole that was Drystan's life. With a snap of his fingers next to her ear, he jerked her from the spell, murmured something about her date and her need to hurry back to him, then turned on the ball of his foot and stormed from the restaurant.

IT WAS AFTER midnight. The squat brick building in front of Drystan appeared empty, but it wasn't. Drystan could hear the heartbeats of dozens of lost souls inside, desperate to escape, desperate to be loved. He approached the door, still not believing he was here, doing what he was about to do. He could lie to himself and say it was part of his game, that it would get him closer to Aimee, but gaining her trust wasn't what brought him here tonight.

He knocked on the door, not expecting an answer, but choosing to try a mundane form of entry first. To his surprise, a male voice yelled out to him. "Closed. You got an emergency, call the Vet Line. It's posted on the door."

A white sign with red block print hung from the door, just as the voice claimed, but Drystan didn't bother reading it. Instead he pressed a palm against the wood and whispered to the voice inside, urged the man to open the door.

He could feel a moment of resistance, the man

starting to step away, then halting before shuffling close again. Drystan redoubled his efforts, making up for the wooden door separating them, cutting off at least some of his powers.

The sound of a lock twisting followed and the door swung open. A man dressed in unitarian gray and holding a bucket stared out at Drystan.

With a smile Drystan stepped inside.

AIMEE SAT IN the small break room, a tuna sandwich untouched in front of her. Mr. Belding's despair clung to her, like smoke after a night in the bars. She'd tried to lighten his mood, to pull the sadness from him, but the facts of his life were too set, too real. His life was ending. There was no way to change that, nothing that could make that fact go away.

Yesterday, he'd seemed better, stronger, but today he'd had time to face the changes, completely grip that his life as he had known it was over, that his dog was lost to him.

His dog. If only Aimee had been able to find her. If only she could have told him she was okay, safe. But the shelter had been closed, and she hadn't wanted to make promises she might not be able to keep. What if she told him she would save his pet, then went to the shelter tomorrow and found her gone…dead?

Aimee shoved the sandwich away. What kind of daimon was she if she couldn't even bring a few minutes of peace to a dying old man?

She'd been sitting there another ten minutes or so, when she heard voices outside the door arguing.

"Who authorized it? Are you sure it's okay? Did someone ask him for paperwork, something?"

The voice that answered was low, confused. "I don't know. He must have had something. I know everything was in order…it had to be."

Curious and done pretending to eat, Aimee dropped her dinner into the trash and walked into the hall.

A nurse and doctor stood outside. The doctor frowned and placed her hands on her hips. "Did he give you something?"

The nurse shook her head. "No, but I know it was okay, and it made Mr. Belding so happy."

Mr. Belding. Not waiting to hear the doctor's response, Aimee rushed to the older man's room.

Her soft-soled shoes padded over the floor, quiet—too quiet to warn the visitor in Mr. Belding's room he had an audience. Still, the man, his broad back to her, tensed. Then as she stood there, her breath coming quick from her race down the halls, he relaxed, leaned forward and placed a small white dog on the bed.

For seconds, Aimee forgot to breathe, just stood there staring at the scroungy-looking mongrel prancing atop the bed.

"Garbo." Mr. Belding leaned forward into Aimee's view. His outstretched hands shook, as if he was afraid the dog that was leaving tiny black footprints on the otherwise white sheets wasn't real, might disappear. He grabbed the animal under her front legs and pulled her close—until her nose touched his.

"How'd you..." the older man began, but as the dog began to wiggle from tip to tail, snuffling her nose over his face, he let the words fade—started talking to his pet instead.

Pulled forward by the scene in front of her, Aimee stepped into the room. The good Samaritan still stood with his back toward her. She reached out, wanting to meet the man who had succeeded where she had failed, to thank him.

Before her fingers could brush the material of his dark coat, he turned, and she found herself staring into the fathomless depths of Drystan Hurst's eyes.

AIMEE WAS IN the room. Drystan had sensed her, felt his spirit lifting as she'd come to a stop outside the door. He turned before she could touch him, not sure what she remembered of their earlier encounter, not sure what he would do the next time her body made contact with his.

Her eyes widened when she saw his face. "Drystan, I..." She raised her hand, palm up, and gestured to the bed, and the reunion taking place there between Mr. Belding and his dog. "How'd you..."

Drystan. She'd said his name, hadn't had to search for it—just knew it. The realization brought a second of joy. Then recognizing where his thoughts were going, the weakness he was exposing, Drystan curled his fingers into a fist and steeled his mind against the softness that threatened to take over when he was around her.

If she remembered his name so easily, what else did she remember?

"Mr. Belding's an old friend. I was at the pound today, looking for a pet for my niece. She's turning two." He smiled, the lie flowing easily from his lips, reassuring him he was still in the game, not being sucked in by whatever strange softening power Aimee seemed to hold. "When I saw Garbo, I knew it had to be some kind of mistake. So, I paid her fee and brought her right here."

"But it's…" Aimee glanced at the clock "…after midnight and this is a hospital. How did you—"

Drystan shrugged. "I'm good with people." He pulled a dog cookie from his pocket, held it up to the little mutt. Garbo let out a happy yap and plucked it from his fingers. "Dogs, too." He smiled, willed Aimee to accept his words.

As he did, Mr. Belding made a sound, calling the dog back to him. Aimee opened her mouth, to ask another question Drystan assumed, but as she watched the old man murmur and coo to his pet, she let out a breath and all tension seeped from her body.

"Thank you," she said.

A warmth crept over Drystan, made him smile

somewhere deep inside, somewhere hidden, somewhere long dead or so he'd thought.

"That isn't enough." Aimee placed her hand on his sleeve. He could feel her fingers through the heavy wool, had to fight to keep from placing his hand on her back, pulling her close.

"What can I do to thank you?" she asked, her face tilted to his, her eyes free of all guile.

Just twenty-four hours earlier, he'd known the answer as well as he knew his own name, as surely as he knew why he hated the Myhres, would do anything to destroy them. But as he looked into her eyes, saw the sincerity, the gratitude for something he had done—he found himself at a loss for a reply.

She smiled and squeezed his arm with a quick pressure of her fingers. "The interview. I'll make time for it tomorrow. You can ask me anything. I'll tell you anything."

But would she do anything? Would she help him exact his revenge? Would she leave Ben Myhre at the altar?

Drystan stared into her impossibly bright eyes, felt the longing being near her seemed to bring. The void inside him had never felt bigger. He placed his hand on top of hers. She gasped and the light in her eyes flickered.

She started to tug her hand away, but, almost desperate in his need to touch her, he held fast.

Suddenly he realized destroying the Myhres

wasn't enough. He needed what he felt when Aimee was near, needed to touch her, needed *her*. She made him feel alive, more alive than he'd ever felt—even before joining the undead.

She tugged again, pulled her fingers free, wrapped the fingers from her other hand around the one he'd held—stared at him—uncertain, wary.

He knew the look, hated it. She was afraid of him, saw him as different, beneath her. The spot that had begun to warm inside him cooled, died. He might think he needed her, might want her, but she could never want him, accept him—no one could. Maureen Myhre had done him one favor by teaching him that.

Now he had to hold that truth close, keep from letting the magic Aimee wielded cloud his mind and keep him from seeking his revenge: destroying the Myhres and anyone who stuck by their side.

CHAPTER FIVE

AIMEE WAITED OUTSIDE the restaurant, her pashmina shawl, a gift from Ben, pulled tightly around her. It was a little too cold for just the wrap, just like it was a little too snowy for her three-inch heels, but Aimee had fallen victim to vanity—a vice she had never had before ignoring her daimon calling.

Chewing on her lower lip, she stroked the cashmere. It had been four months since she had walked away from being a daimon, had started ignoring the almost constant peals that chimed inside her head—a soul in need looking for his or her personal daimon—but in the past few days, she hadn't heard a single chime, not even a hum.

No nagging from her daimon conscience, and now falling victim to one of the most basic of human failings—vanity. Could she actually be turning human? It was what she wanted....

"Aimee." Drystan Hurst stepped beside her, his head brushing the scalloped edge of the restaurant awning. Snow dotted his black coat. Without thinking, Aimee brushed the flakes from the wool.

Drystan, his hands covered in leather driving gloves, captured her fingers and stared down into her eyes.

"Are you this solicitous with everyone?" His tone was light, but there was an intensity behind his gaze that made her want to pull her fingers away, like she had last night. This time she left them in his grip, tried for a light tone to match his.

"Hazard of my job," she replied.

"I didn't realize hospital aides took their roles so seriously."

There was a sharpness to his words and Aimèe wondered for a second if she was supposed to take offense—if that would be the normal human reaction. But then he smiled and rubbed his gloved thumb over the backs of her knuckles.

"I doubt they all do. I think you may be...special," he added then leaned down.

Her breath catching in her throat, Aimee edged forward on her toes. Snow covered the tips of her kid-leather pumps, icy water leaked in through the keyhole design that decorated their tops; she ignored the tiny discomfort, ignored everything except Drystan.

"Well, I guess we should get inside." Drystan dropped Aimee's hand, stepped away so suddenly she teetered backward. Seeing her predicament, he placed a hand on her shoulder to steady her, but his touch was impersonal, cool.

She flipped the end of her shawl over her shoulder,

hiding the flutter of disappointment that washed over her, tucked her hand into the arm he offered and let him escort her inside.

The restaurant was full, but after a few earnest words with the maître d', Drystan guided her to a table.

"I've never been here." She glanced around, avoiding Drystan's eyes, and tried to slow her heart, which seemed to be skittering inside her chest. The maître d' had taken Drystan's coat and her shawl. As Drystan walked to his chair, she looked up, took advantage of his turned back to study him. His dress shirt hugged his body, showed off the V shape of his tapered waist and broad shoulders. Candlelight danced on the table. He pulled out his chair, and caught her gaze for a second, his eyes seeming to flicker with the flame. A shiver danced over Aimee's skin, made her wish she'd kept the wrap, had something to pull around her, hide behind.

"Really? Your fiancé never brought you here?" The question should have been innocent, but the words seemed to fall between them, land on the table like stones, hard and unyielding.

At the mention of Ben, a mantle of guilt settled over Aimee.

She pinched the stem of her water goblet and stared at the ice cubes floating inside. She had no reason to feel guilty. She hadn't specifically told Ben she was having dinner with a reporter, but if she had, he would have been thrilled—which was why, she told herself, she hadn't bothered. Besides, a feature article would be the perfect wedding gift. Maureen Myhre had been perfectly clear that media coverage was of utmost importance—more important than the wedding itself, if Aimee read the older woman correctly. Which, of course, she did.

Aimee sighed. How she wished she didn't always read others' motivations so clearly. She'd like just once to be blindsided by someone's nature—surprised. Maybe that was why she'd agreed to this dinner. Drystan was a puzzle, a void of dark need but with a strange light that seemed to flicker in and out, like a flame struggling to come to life.

She looked up; Drystan's gaze was still on her. "Ben and I don't go out much—at least not to restaurants."

"Oh." Drystan laid his hand on the white linen cloth, his fingers curled toward the table.

"What?" she asked. His gesture had been dismissive, as if her response were to be expected and pitied.

"Doesn't it bother you that your fiancé doesn't take you out, just the two of you?"

Something began to wind around Aimee, something she couldn't see or hear, but could feel—a coaxing that made her body want to sway, her mind want to agree. Her head started to nod, then, realizing what she was doing, she frowned and focused on Drystan's question. "I don't mind," she replied.

In fact she preferred it. She and Ben hadn't spent a great deal of time alone yet. Once she actually married Ben, she would have to, and she'd face another problem, one she hoped wouldn't bother her once her daimon life was completely in her past. Physical intimacy without love was a lie to Aimee. Daimons didn't lie. As far as Aimee knew they were incapable of it—even daimons of the dark.

Of course, daimons of the dark probably didn't see the human act of sex as a declaration of anything. Just another base desire to use against humanity.

If Drystan was a daimon, was that how he saw it? She touched her fingers to her lips. She had wanted to kiss him outside. Was that why? Was he using daimon powers against her?

"But you have to admit…" he placed his hand over hers, curled her fingers into his palm "…this is nice."

His fingers were cool against hers—too cool for a human, but not unpleasant, actually to Aimee quite the opposite. She hooked her fingers around his, let warmth pass from her body into his.

The exchange was tiny, warmth, nothing more, but it made the daimon inside Aimee lumber from forced sleep. Made Aimee want to flood Drystan, body and soul, with light, hope, love—but she couldn't. That's what she had done to Kevin—unharnessed the almost desperate love she felt, her hopes for what he could become—and he'd staggered under the weight. No more able to bear that burden than the ones life had already given him. Yes, he'd seen what he was doing was wrong—not the solution—but rather than taking time to assess, to rethink, he'd taken the quick way out...pulled the trigger.

Aimee jerked her hand away, broke contact, then stared at her menu, refused to glance up at the man she couldn't quite read, who scared and intrigued at the same time.

AIMEE PULLED HER hand so quickly from Drystan's that even with his vamp senses he didn't have time to react, but he felt the loss—her hand warming his... and something else, something sliding from her to him, making him feel...safe.

He fisted his hand on the table. Safe. It was a ludicrous thought. Of course he was safe. He was a vampire—who did he have to fear?

"It's good not getting to be alone with your fiancé doesn't bother you," he murmured, hoping to bring their conversation back where it had been, to find an opening to drive a wedge between Aimee and the Myhres. "He certainly takes you enough public places." He picked up his glass, took a sip of water. "Of course, now that I think of it..." he frowned "...all those places are political, aren't they?"

Aimee glanced up, gazing at him with the clear

beauty of her eyes—innocent, sweet. "He's a state legislator."

"Who wants to be governor," Drystan added.

"Yes." Aimee gazed at him, her face open, expression frank, as if waiting for him to continue.

"That doesn't bother you?" Drystan dropped his hand to his lap, balled his napkin in his fist.

"That he wants to be governor? Why should it?"

She seemed sincerely confused now. A line formed between her brows and she blinked as if truly struggling to make out his meaning. "There are much worse ambitions, and being governor…that could be good, no, great. Think of all the things you could influence, the people you could help."

"You want to be married to a governor?" Drystan felt as though he'd swallowed a lead ball. Despite the happy glow that surrounded her and her work at the hospital, Aimee wasn't the angel he'd thought her to be. She wanted the same things the Myhres wanted—power, influence, a political office for her husband if not herself.

She dropped her gaze to the base of her water goblet, twisted the glass back and forth on the tablecloth. Then, without warning, she looked up. "Is that wrong? To want to do something that would give you real power? Power to help people like patients who don't fill their prescriptions because they can't afford it? Or mothers who have to choose between shoes for their kids and a mammogram? Is that wrong?"

Drystan swallowed, his mouth suddenly dry. If anyone else had been asking him these questions, he'd have known they were attacking him—and been justified. His tone had been laden with accusation and judgment. But Aimee still had that same damn look of receptiveness, like she truly wanted to hear his opinion. Was what she was doing wrong?

He wanted to yell *yes,* to tell her nothing could justify marrying into the Myhre family, that the quest for power no matter the motive behind it was wrong, hurtful. He wanted to hurt her, make her cringe and agree to stop her plans. He opened his lips. "Not wrong. Not wrong at all."

Her lips curved into a smile, lighting her face, her eyes, the space around them. Drystan's annoyance with his own honesty faded before it could even materialize as a frown.

"I don't think you could do anything wrong," he murmured. "Not intentionally."

Her smile disappeared; the glow behind her eyes dimmed. "Intentions don't matter. Outcome does."

And that was it. The conversation was over like someone had sliced through a phone line. Suddenly, desperately, Drystan wanted to bring the joy back to her eyes.

He placed his hand on the table, not touching hers, almost afraid to touch hers.

"Intentions do matter—a lot." If Maureen Myhre had taken him in, trotted him out at every media event, but her intentions had been true—to share something with a boy who needed a family, who needed love—would he have wandered off the path? Would he have acted out in a ridiculous attempt to gain her attention?

Perhaps. But he wouldn't be able to blame her then, wouldn't hold the hate that festered inside him.

"Sometimes," he continued, "intentions are everything."

There was sorrow in her eyes now, deep and intense. Drystan pressed his fingers into the linen, felt the lines of the cloth, stopped himself from grabbing her hand, telling her everything would be okay—he would make it okay.

"Intentions didn't save Mr. Belding's dog. You did. I intended to help him but failed."

"But I wouldn't have saved him, if I hadn't seen—" Drystan stopped the flow of words. He'd almost given himself away.

"Seen what?"

It was too much, he'd come too close. The conversation was getting them nowhere—or nowhere Drystan wanted to go. It was time to up the stakes, to take Aimee somewhere he could work on her alone—before *his* intentions were lost, before he fell under her spell and forgot who he was, what had been done to him.

He placed his hand over hers, captured her gaze with his and began to weave a cloak of beguilement around them. He'd take her back to his apartment, work on her, make her see the cost of marrying into the Myhres was too high, that she could help others without selling herself...losing her soul.

AIMEE BLINKED, tried to focus on where she was, how she'd got here. She was in an apartment, sitting on a couch. Her palm rested on the seat next to her...cool to the touch, leather. She blinked again, her mind processing this bit of information. The room was dimly lit, one lone table lamp given the job of illuminating the entire space. Music floated around her, soft, sultry, something with lots of horns and a seductive beat.

Not the type of music Ben, who preferred the dramatic sounds of opera, would have chosen or the jarring rap Kevin had cranked in his rusted-out compact.

All in all the place was peaceful, tempting. The kind of place that made her want to kick off her shoes and let herself slide down the cushion, just lean back and relax, forget everything bad that was going on in the world, everything she couldn't fix.

She closed her eyes, considered for a second letting the apartment win her over, ignoring the nagging thoughts that said she shouldn't be here, but a ping stopped her, caused her to sit up straighter, look around.

The place was an illusion, a snare. Underneath

its calm exterior lay a history of dark emotions. No amount of music, stylish furniture or dim lights could hide that from her.

Whoever lived in this apartment must seethe with anger, malice and hate for the disturbing imprint to be so clear. She edged forward on her seat, strained to see past the lamp's small ring of light into the nearby kitchen.

Someone very troubled lived here.

And she wasn't alone.

CHAPTER SIX

AIMEE WAS STIRRING.

Drystan had flooded her with every strand of beguilement he could pull from his body, from resources he didn't know he had, and now he was paying the price. He placed two wineglasses on the granite counter with shaking hands, started to grab the unopened bottle of merlot he had already pulled from the wine rack, but instead reached into the refrigerator for another bottle. One of the bottles he got delivered secretly to his home every Sunday night.

He jerked the cork from the glass neck, started to tip it over his glass, but with a curse pressed it to his lips instead. Blood, thick and heady, rolled down his throat. Even unnaturally cold, straight from the refrigerator, he could feel it moving through his system, renewing his depleted energy stores.

The slight crunch of Aimee shifting on his leather couch alerted him she was now awake, aware, but he couldn't face her yet. He pressed his palms onto the countertop, took a step back and let his head hang for just a second between his outstretched arms. The muscles in his back pulled, relaxing him.

The couch crackled again. His gaze darting from the door to the bottles, he picked up the chilled bottle and filled his glass halfway. After filling Aimee's with merlot and topping off his own with the wine, he picked up the glasses and strode into the living room.

"I brought your wine."

Aimee stared at him with round eyes. For a second, he thought his ploy had failed, then she pulled in a breath and slowly collapsed back against the leather sofa.

"Red? I don't usually drink red," she said.

"That's why you wanted to try it." He leaned down, let his fingers brush hers as he handed her the glass. The contact was tiny, but he hungered for it. A zap of electricity shot through him as his skin touched hers. He turned away to hide the flash of desire that knifed through his body.

"Your apartment is nice." She took a sip of the wine, then slid it onto the table next to her. "Funny, I don't remember coming here." Her gaze was on the glass, her body still.

"I'm sure. You weren't feeling well. My apartment was close. Seemed a better solution than sending you off in a cab." He took a drink, letting the red liquid linger on his palate for just a second.

"Oh," she responded.

He waited, willed her to accept his words.

"I have Garbo now. She couldn't stay at the hospital."

Her sudden change in topic threw him off balance. He held his glass to his lips, inhaled the scent of blood and fruit, bought time to translate what she had said.

"She's a wonderful dog," Aimee continued.

"The old man..." Drystan set his glass onto the floor. "Will he get to see her again?"

Glancing around the room, it took Aimee a second to answer. When her eyes found his, they glowed. "I talked to the people who run the home his daughter found for him. He's leaving for there tomorrow. They said as long as she behaves herself and no one complains, Garbo can visit as much as she wants."

"No one will complain." Drystan would make sure of it.

"No, I don't think they will."

A moment passed between them. Drystan smiled, content, happy....

He shook himself, sat forward in his chair. What was happening? He was slipping...almost as if Aimee were the one with powers...the power to lull him into forgetting who and what he was, the rejection that had made him into this. He clenched his teeth together, focused.

"The wedding's only a few days away now. Are you getting nervous? Any second thoughts?"

Aimee swirled her wine, seemed to be admiring

how the red clung to the side of the glass, then slowly rejoined the rest. She looked up, cocked her head. "I don't think so."

"Really?" Drystan waited, but she shook her head and set down her glass again. He took a sip of his wine/blood cocktail, both to cover his frustration and to gain strength, then asked, "You haven't known the Myhres that long. Does that bother you? Aren't you worried there are skeletons they might be hiding?"

She pursed her lips; doubt flitted behind her eyes. "Is this for your article?"

The article. "Yes. No. I'm just looking for a new hook. Everyone's heard the 'official' story. I'd like to hear something new, personal." He tapped his fingers on his thigh, wished he'd thought this through more. He'd imagined telling her his story, the horror in her reaction, then her agreeing to his plan. Or if that failed, her falling for his beguilement. Unfortunately neither seemed likely at this stage. For whatever reason he was having a hard time working the conversation around to the Myhres' betrayal of him. And while he'd managed to confuse her enough to get her to his apartment, he doubted he could pull on his powers sufficiently to send her on her way convinced she should dump Ben at the altar. It was still days until the wedding. After witnessing her resistance to his spells, he couldn't risk that the beguilement would hold that long.

"Ben had a brother. His name was Drystan." She

angled her neck, caught Drystan's gaze, a spark of recognition in her eyes. "I knew your name was familiar."

"The drug addict?" Drystan reached for his glass. She'd turned the conversation for him, and suddenly he wished she hadn't. "I've heard about him. Are you saying he's their skeleton?"

"Perhaps. Maureen doesn't talk about him, but Ben has mentioned him."

"Has he?" Drystan feigned disinterest, but his fingers pressed against the stem of his glass. With a crack, the stem snapped.

His vamp reflexes saved the drink, his hand cupping to catch the bowl of the glass, the stem falling onto the wood floor with a clatter.

Aimee's eyebrows lifted.

"Must have been cracked."

"I guess." Aimee's gaze stayed on the glass's base until it finished its trip rolling across the floor, stopping at her feet. Drystan expected her to pick it up, but she just stared at it, almost as if she were afraid of the one-ounce fragment of glass.

"I think Ben misses him," she added.

"Really?" The question was sharp.

Aimee's gaze shot to Drystan's face, tried to capture his, but he evaded her, staring at a point just left of her head instead.

"I've heard the Myhres didn't treat him very well while he was alive. Used him for media coverage—

'look and see how generous the Myhres are, taking in the poor, discarded child of a drug addict.' But at the first sign of trouble, of teenage rebellion, they turned their backs on him, did their best to make sure everyone knew he wasn't a Myhre, not really."

"I hadn't heard that version."

Drystan was sure she hadn't. No one had, no one but he and the Myhres knew the truth. He swallowed the last of his drink, stood and set his glass on the table beside Aimee, ignored it as it rolled back and forth, dangerously close to falling onto the floor and shattering.

He moved to bend over her, his hands on the cushion behind her, trapping her.

"Teenagers, tough as they act, can be fragile. But when this boy needed love the most, what did the Myhres do? They turned their backs on him, walked away."

"Loving someone isn't enough. It won't save them." Aimee lowered her face, stared at the wineglass still balanced on the edge of the table beside her, then she snapped her gaze to his, pressed her palm to his chest, over his heart. "They have to love, too—themselves, even the people they think don't love them. Do you think this boy did that?"

Heat poured through Drystan, but not from anger. Understanding. She was making him understand another side of things, a side he didn't want to understand. He could feel himself weakening, listening to her, as if her hand pressed to his chest, the heat pouring from her, was melting his resentment.

He pulled back, broke the contact. Placed his own cold hand where her warm palm had been seconds before.

As he moved, she stood; there was intent in her eyes, purpose. "What happened to this boy…man, he was grown when he died…was tragic, but how do you save someone bent on destruction? How do you make someone love himself?" Her hands fisted at her sides. Lines of stress showed in her neck.

She was angry, but Drystan was angry, too, had gone too long holding this anger inside, sharing it with no one.

"Do you know how he died? Not the official story, the real one? You haven't heard that. He wasn't the one looking for drugs. He'd given that up years before. No, it was the golden boy, your understanding fiancé. He went looking for a high, ran into a bad group instead, was almost killed—would have been if this Drystan hadn't shown up, pulled sweet, ignorant Ben from that pit of greed and desperation he could never understand, had never experienced before. No, sweet Ben, the rich child, who was handed everything in life, playing at being a bad boy, saved by his worthless white-trash adopted brother.

"That's the real story. Sound anything like the story you heard? I doubt it, because the Myhres left

Drystan holding the drug deal, twisted what happened to protect Ben, let the world think Drystan was the problem, got what he deserved.

"But they had no choice, now did they? Ben was alive. Drystan was dead. Why shouldn't he offer one final sacrifice? Like his life wasn't enough. Not for the Myhres." Disgusted, with himself, the Myhres and Aimee for getting him to spill the poison that had been swirling through his veins for a decade, Drystan started to turn, to run away and hide until he could regain control, bring himself to face her again, but she grabbed him by the arm.

"I'm sorry." And she was. Drystan saw it on her face, felt it in how her fingers pressed into his skin—firm but gentle—as if sharing strength rather than attempting to use it to hold him.

He'd done what he'd hoped or started the process. She'd softened to him, seemed receptive to anything he wanted to tell her now, but all thoughts of swaying her, of convincing her to publicly denounce the Myhres fled from his head. All he could think of was how good it was to feel her touch, to see the understanding in her eyes…and how much he wanted… needed more…from her.

He placed his hand against the curve of her jaw, ran his thumb over her cheek. Her lips parted. He waited for her objection, unsure what he would do when she did. Stop himself or try to pull from his depleted reserves, force her to forget Ben for just a few hours, force her to let Drystan pretend he was something he wasn't—loved.

SO MUCH HURT. That was all that Aimee could think about—the pain rolling off Drystan. The daimon she had shoved into a dark corner inside her wanted to open to him, sop up the dark emotions inside him like a sponge, but she couldn't, knew from her experience with Kevin it would do no good. It might even make matters worse.

You couldn't "fix" a human; they had to do that themselves. Still… She turned her head, pressed a kiss to the palm that caressed her cheek.

He stiffened, shock flashing through his dark eyes—darker than she remembered them being. Then in one forward motion, he pulled her to him and pressed his lips to hers. Something sharp grazed her lower lip, but before she could pull back, analyze what it was, his tongue found hers and her body began to react in the most human of ways.

Daimons didn't mix with humans—not like this. It was…frowned on. Aimee shoved the thought away, let her hands slip onto Drystan's shoulders, feel the strength there, the way his muscles moved under his blazer as he pulled her even closer.

Need. He needed her. Nothing could be more seductive.

His lips left her, trailed down her neck. She tilted her head, enjoyed the feel of his mouth pulling at her skin. Something sharp dragged against her throat; her hands tightened on his shoulders and the sensation was gone. Drystan murmured something under his breath, against her skin.

His hands moved to her hips and he pulled her pelvis to his body. His erection pressed into her. She knew what it was, what it meant. She'd seen what the bad humans did in the pursuit of lust, but now caught in the web herself, she couldn't pull away. Instead she wanted to push forward, discover for herself everything being human meant…wanted to discover it with Drystan.

Her hand lowered almost by its own accord, skimmed Drystan's chest, paused to press against his breastbone, feel the slow but steady beat of his heart.

She knew what she was doing, about to do, was wrong, both as a daimon and a human. Daimons didn't mix with humans, not like this, and humans didn't cheat on their fiancés. Wrong. She was about to do something morally, undeniably wrong.

The thought should have stopped her, but strangely it thrust her forward. Doing everything right hadn't saved Kevin, hadn't made her the perfect daimon. She couldn't see how it would make her the perfect anything. Perfection didn't spring forth fully developed like Athena from Zeus's forehead. Perfection was created, bit by bit, mistake by mistake.

Maybe doing something wrong was the first step

in learning how to do right. Aimee's hand continued its descent until it rested on Drystan's groin, until she could feel the hard pulse of him beneath her palm.

CHAPTER SEVEN

THE SCENT, TASTE and feel of Aimee almost overwhelmed Drystan, made it hard to keep his vampire nature hidden, to keep him from plunging his fangs into the blue vein that lay just beneath her porcelain skin. He wrapped his hand around her cascade of curls, pulled them from her throat, brushed his lips up and down the column of her neck. So tempting. So hard to resist.

Her hand was on his stomach, her fingers curling into the white cotton shirt he wore, nails scraping against the material. He licked his lips, willed his mind to slow, not to slip.

Everything about this moment was impossible. He wanted to remember it, savor it.

Then her hand moved, dropped until her fingers pressed against his sex, caressed the hard rod, the visible sign of his need. He almost bit her then, did let his fangs nip against her skin, enough that a tiny taste of blood made its way into his mouth.

Sweet, sizzling…like exploding candies he'd eaten as a child, but better, so much better. One tiny taste wasn't enough—only made him want more.

Her hand began to move, unzipping his pants. He shrugged out of his jacket, let it fall to the ground. As his erection sprang forward into her hand, he pulled back, tilted her face to his and stared into her eyes.

"Do you want this?" he asked. Suddenly it was important he knew she was choosing this as clearly as he was. He might make her forget this encounter later, but for now he needed her to want it, to want him, as much as he wanted her.

She answered by rising on her toes and pressing a gentle kiss to his lips. Then slowly, surely, she slipped each button of his shirt free, pushed the material away and skimmed her fingertips across his chest—traced each line of muscle, every ridge and indentation.

His sex hardened more with each pass of her fingers, his fangs seemed heavy in his mouth. He had never wanted anything more than he wanted this woman.

He unzipped her dress, watched as she let it slip forward, revealing her breasts as it folded slowly onto the floor. She wore nothing but a bra and panties underneath, no hose or slip to block his view. She stepped out of the circle of fallen silk, her heel catching on the cloth, but her eyes never leaving his face.

She was giving him something, he could feel it, was unsure what it was at first, then it hit him. She trusted him, believed he wouldn't hurt her. He started to pull away, knowing that was a lie, that this time

together could only end in pain—as all things ended
with Drystan—but she grabbed both his hands in
hers, held them palms up, her thumbs resting on
top.

"Do you want this?" she asked.

Damn his soul to hell, he couldn't lie, not about
this. He pulled his hands from hers, thrust them into
her hair and pulled her face to his. "More than I've
ever wanted anything."

MAKING LOVE WITH Drystan was no simple physical
act. Body parts touching, nerve endings reacting, it
was all there—but there was more. Aimee ran her
hands down Drystan's chest, let her warmth flow
into his body, breathed in as he blew out, devoured
the darkness inside him. It wouldn't change who he
was or have a lasting effect. She wouldn't lie to herself and say that it would, but for now it felt good,
fed the bit of daimon still inside her, made her want
more. And Drystan had more, was a never-ending pit
of darkness, longing—a truly lost soul who needed
Aimee as much as she needed him. She wanted to
change to pure spirit and seep inside him, be inside
him—closer than two humans ever could be.

But only a daimon who accepted her powers could
do that, and Aimee didn't, wouldn't. But she would
make do with the next best thing. She kicked her
dress to the side and slipped her thumbs under the
elastic of her bra. It was time to get closer—past time.

Her body tingled with the need, outside; inside all of her screamed for Drystan's touch, for the feel of his bare skin against hers.

His hands clasped her face, pulled her mouth back to his. The sting of something sharp piercing her lip almost jerked her from the moment, but then his tongue lapped away the pain, and she could think of nothing but Drystan, his scent, his touch—she pulled her mouth from his, ran her tongue down his neck—his taste. She had never felt so alive, so *in* the human body she normally only occupied.

She wanted to experience more, to feel more.

She grasped his pants and shoved them out of her way. Drystan moved with her, as if he could read her mind, as if they shared the same thoughts. He stepped forward, while she clung to him, her fingers digging into his shoulders, her breasts pressed to his chest. The backs of her knees hit the couch and he slipped an arm behind her, lowered her onto the cushions.

The leather clung to her heated skin, the smell of it mingling with Drystan's scent, forming a masculine mix that Aimee pulled into her lungs, wished she could bottle and keep forever.

She ran her hands up and down Drystan's now bare back. He leaned down, skimmed her neck with his lips, his palms finding her breasts. She arched into his touch. Her breasts were heavy, and his touch cool—nothing could feel better.

Except...he lay atop her, his weight pressing

her deeper into the cushion. Her legs inched apart, his thigh falling between hers. Anticipation coiled inside her. Then his erection pressed against her. She tilted her hips, parted her thighs until the tip edged inside.

Her breath caught in her throat. Then Drystan murmured against her ear and guided his erection inside her.

Aimee's back curved again, this time angling her pelvis toward Drystan, urging him to go deeper, faster inside her, but despite her almost frantic need, he moved slowly, letting her body stretch, letting her feel every inch as he edged inside her.

His lips found her breasts; his tongue swirled the aching tips. Aimee's hands dropped to her sides, pushed against the cushions. So many sensations were pulsing through her, she didn't know what to do, how to react.

"Relax, enjoy," Drystan murmured. "Forget everything."

All tension left her hands, arms, her mind leaving only the growing feeling of tautness spiraling inside her, where Drystan's body met hers, slid in and out. Drystan nipped at her breast, pulled the nub in between his teeth and rolled his tongue around it. Aimee grabbed his sides, held on to the firm muscle. So much sensation… She shifted beneath him, ran her fingers over his chest, then leaned up, grabbed the skin on his neck between her teeth and nipped him back.

Drystan stiffened, then a growl rolled from his throat, his pace quickened, his body moving in and out of Aimee's until she felt her spirit slipping, leaving the human body assigned to her and floating overhead, hovering. This wasn't supposed to happen. She was supposed to have given up this ability by turning away from her daimon self, but being with Drystan, experiencing his touch, accepting his darkness... Below her Drystan continued his movements; her body reacted by tightening around him. Aimee could feel the patter of her heart, his teeth grazing her skin. Her spirit was separate, but still connected—the best of both.

His pace became even quicker now, and Aimee, not wanting to miss anything, forced her spirit back down to the couch, into her body where she could feel everything, miss nothing no matter how small. His hands slipped behind her buttocks, tipping her upward, increasing the depth of each thrust. Aimee's breath came out of her chest in tiny pants and her body began to tighten on its own, without her control.

She gripped Drystan's sides, dug her nails into his flesh. His mouth dropped back to her neck, his lips caressed her skin. Even as he moved inside her, brought her body to the edge, he seemed tense, holding something, a piece of him back.

"Let go," she whispered, to herself and Drystan. He thrust again, and her body reacted, released and tightened and released again until she felt herself propelling upward, back out of her body, her spirit swirling overhead in a kaleidoscope of human and daimon senses—one almost indiscernible from the other.

As she twirled there, caught in an eddy of emotion, she felt a sharp prick at her neck, the undeniable pain of something sharp sliding into her skin…her neck… her vein, and even before the next wave of euphoria hit, she knew what Drystan was, how he held such darkness.

The man she had made love to, who made her feel both human and daimon, made her appreciate both, was not a dark daimon as she had feared, but he wasn't human, either.

No, he was the one being who could do the impossible—walk the earth alone, without even his own soul for company.

He was a vampire.

DRYSTAN HAD RESISTED as long as he could, denied the hunger that raged inside him, but at Aimee's whispered words, her permission to release what he was hiding, to relax, be himself, the dam had broken. He'd punctured the skin of her throat, taken the first tiny sip of her blood and known he was lost. No matter if she followed through with her plans, married Ben or left him at the altar as Drystan prayed, Drystan would never be the same, his world would never be the same.

Because this time, if...*when*...Aimee left him, he'd be alone, more alone than he'd ever been in his life.

Aimee stirred beneath him, stiffened. For a second fear lanced through him, fear that his beguilement had failed, that she realized what was happening— what he was—that she would shove him away, look at him with disgust and dread. But as quickly as he had noticed her movement, she relaxed again, tilted her head farther to the side, baring more of her neck, ran her hand up his chest until her fingers brushed his throat, her nails scraped his skin.

Her blood filled his mouth. Sweet but light, it crackled through his veins, through his heart, warmed him more than a roaring fire. His sex, spent just minutes earlier, began to stir, desire for this woman who wasn't his, never could be, building again.

He wanted her sexually, spiritually, completely. He drew another mouthful of her blood, let it slide down his throat. Aimee moved again, rubbing her breasts against his chest. Her fingers stroked the side of his neck, gentle, soothing, telling him everything was okay, would be okay, and for that moment Drystan let himself believe her. He shoved aside all doubt and hate, shoved aside everything except being with Aimee...being accepted, feeling loved.

He swallowed hard at the last thought, but as Aimee's fingers shifted from his neck to his side and the pressure changed from stroke to knead, as her breath fell faster from her lips, in sharp pants, he forgot his doubts and pain, was pulled back into what was happening.

Her thighs parted beneath him. His lips still on her throat, her blood still winding through his body, he took her again, slipped inside the warm welcome of her body. She tightened around him; he groaned from the pleasure, his mouth pulling away from her neck as he did.

Aimee moved again, her lips parting to let out a murmur of objection mixed with heavy gasps. She grasped his head, pressed his mouth back to her throat.

He stared at the woman in his arms. She was enjoying his feeding, perhaps as much as he. The exchange didn't repulse her, at least not now in the midst of their passion. He *could* relax, be with her in every way, not hide who or what he was…at least for right now.

With the realization soaring through his body, he placed his mouth on her neck, let himself truly relax, enjoy the taste of her blood, the surge of energy he seemed to get as it trailed through his body. Her hands grasped at his chest and she quivered beneath him—as if the act of taking her blood alone was enough to bring her to the brink.

And suddenly Drystan was there with her—just knowing she was getting such pleasure from him excited him more than any sex act alone ever had. He increased his pace, his mouth never leaving her neck. Together their bodies began to shake, their muscles tensed, then relaxed and tensed again, until Drystan could hold on no longer and he exploded inside her. Her head flinging back, her back arching, Aimee clung to him as no one had ever clung to him before, and just for a second as her orgasm swept over her, Drystan felt something lift him up and away...away from his body and any pain he had ever known.

IT WAS DAWN and Aimee was alone, or might as well have been. Drystan, her vampire lover, was dead, and would stay that way, if the tales she had heard were true, for at least another eight hours, when the sun started to edge down past the horizon.

She placed her palm over his bare chest. His heart, which she had heard beating only a few hours earlier, when she was pressed against him marveling at what had passed between them, was still, cold, lifeless— just like a corpse.

He was a corpse.

How did it feel to have your heart start and stop each day? To feel your life drain away over and over? That alone would pull most humans down into a dark mire of emotion, but Drystan...his darkness was deeper than that, reached farther back into his mortal life.

Drystan, she realized, was the adopted son of Maureen Myhre—Aimee's future brother-in-law. Which meant his stories at dinner were true, or at least true to Drystan. Who knew what the Myhres' side of things might be?

Aimee lay down, her cheek pressed against Drystan's cold chest; a tear leaked from her eye, dropped onto his skin. Drystan's reality was so much worse than Aimee had imagined—for him, for her, for the two of them.

She stayed there another hour, just to think and to be with him. She'd betrayed Ben. She'd known she was doing so last night, when she gave in to the physical need to be with Drystan, but now alone in Drystan's apartment, lying on the bed next to him, she realized how complete her betrayal had been. She had slept with another man; that alone would be unforgivable in most human relationships. But Ben didn't love her, he was marrying her for purely political reasons.

He didn't love her—but he had loved his brother.

No matter Drystan's doubts, Aimee was sure of it. So not only had she slept with another man, but that man was Ben's brother, a brother he thought dead, for whose death he blamed himself.

How would he react to knowing his brother was alive, that he could speak to him?

She stroked Drystan's cold chest. But she couldn't tell Ben, couldn't let him know Drystan's secret—because that would mean betraying Drystan, too. Once again, intending to or not, she'd interfered with humans' lives, stood on the brink of possibly destroying someone.

Her mind whirling, she walked to the bedroom, but paused at the threshold. A king-size bed complete with oversize pillows and a down comforter dominated the room.

A bed for a man who never slept.

Why bother? Another wave of sadness swept over her. Maybe his way of clinging to his past humanity?

Lore said vampires lost their humanity, their souls—that because of this they couldn't enter a church or touch a cross. That would certainly explain the void she felt inside him.

Aimee pulled the cover off Drystan's bed, then walked back to the couch, the blue comforter trailing behind her. Carefully, she tucked it around him and brushed a bit of hair away from his brow.

He was beautiful and…she leaned down, kissed his unmoving lips…he was Drystan. The lore was wrong; he had a soul. She wouldn't feel like this if he didn't.

But he was still lost in his darkness, and as she had told him last night, no one else could save him from that. No matter how she felt, how much love she had to give, he had to save himself.

So, Aimee, the daimon…human…she was unsure what she was anymore, couldn't stay with him, had to leave, had to let him sort things out on his own. Had to, in the face of her own actions, sort things out for her own life.

She had tried being daimon, then, having failed that, tried being human. Now it appeared she was failing there, too. She couldn't tell Ben that Drystan lived, couldn't choose Drystan over Ben.

All she could do was run away from them all, leave them all behind and let them sort it out for themselves…but she knew deep in her heart she couldn't do that, either.

CHAPTER EIGHT

IT WAS DARK and cold. Normal for Drystan's first waking moments, but this time his hands groped around him, searched for something...someone... For some reason this time he didn't expect to be alone...but he was.

He sat up, let his mind come to full awareness.

He was alone. Aimee had left. He should have expected that, but he hadn't. Deep inside, even while in his vampiric coma, death, whatever this curse put him through each day, some bit of hope that this time he'd awake to a gentle touch, a smiling face, to Aimee, had stayed alive.

He should have known better.

He shoved aside the comforter that covered his chest and stood. He started to move toward his bedroom to retrieve clothing for the night ahead, but his feet tangled in the cover he'd just tossed aside. He stopped, stared down at it.

A cover. He bent and retrieved the tangled mass. Something so simple, but it told him last night hadn't been a dream and, more important, that Aimee hadn't run from him in horror. No, after he'd passed into unconsciousness, she'd stayed at least long enough to find this comforter and tuck it around him.

At least for a while he hadn't been alone. That was worth something.

He balled the covering in his hands, wished he'd known what she was doing at the time. If simply asleep, he might have felt her touch, realized she was close, but as a vampire after dawn he was dead to everything, literally.

He strode to his bedroom, tossed the cover onto his bed and pulled slacks and a shirt from his closet.

She hadn't left scared. Had she even realized his state? He shoved his arms into sleeves and began shoving buttons through holes. No. She couldn't have. If she had, she would have thought him dead, called 911.

So, what did that mean? She'd tucked the blanket around him, but not tried to wake him, not got close enough to realize he was dead, albeit temporarily. Or maybe he looked more alive than he thought. He'd never actually seen a vampire after the day coma hit. Maybe the sight wasn't as disturbing as the reality felt.

Either way he had slipped by not beguiling her before the sun rose. He had used his powers some while he fed, but he'd still been drained from getting her to come to his apartment at all, and he'd seen Aimee's resistance. He couldn't count on the little power he'd used on her to keep her from realizing what had happened.

He had to find her, see what she remembered.

See which meant more—the comforter tucked with care around his body or the fact she was missing now.

AIMEE PULLED BACK the heavy curtain and stared out into the street. It had been dark for hours. Drystan would be awake by now. Was he looking for her? What would she do if he came for her?

"Aimee, would you like some brandy?" Maureen Myhre paused on her way through the living room. "I usually have a glass before bed."

Aimee dropped the curtain and studied the older woman. Was she the monster Drystan made her out to be? Aimee resisted the urge to reach out with her daimon powers and see. She already knew the answer; she'd analyzed Maureen and Ben when she first met them, before allowing herself to be brought into their world.

Maureen Myhre was ambitious, blinded like so many humans by the drive to succeed. The carefully coiffed matriarch had forgotten exactly why she needed that success in the first place, forgotten about love, had let power overshadow it.

She wasn't evil. She was human.

Aimee sighed. "No, I'm fine. Thanks."

Maureen took a step, then stopped. "Is everything

okay? There isn't something you need to tell me… someone from your past…a reason you asked to stay here until the wedding?"

"I told you my lease was up." Not a lie. Aimee never had a lease. It was up the day she moved in. The landlord just let her stay as she wanted.

"Yes, it's just…" Maureen placed pale hands on the back of the couch. Her arms were stiff, tension showing in her shoulders. "It was so sudden. You hadn't mentioned…"

"I'm not much of a planner." Aimee tilted her head, smiled, a sad tilt of her lips, she knew, but all she could manage. "I hope that doesn't bother you. A governor's wife probably needs skills I don't have."

With a flick of her wrist, Maureen brushed the comment aside. "You have other assets." The line that had formed between her brows faded for a second, then reappeared. "So, no one from your past? Nothing you need to tell me before the big day?"

Aimee's hand found the curtain, held on to it for support. "No, no one from my past."

DRYSTAN WAS BACK at the Myhre house. He'd hoped he'd never have to return here. He had hoped he'd done enough to convince Aimee she didn't belong with these people, but when he'd gone to the hospital looking for her, he'd learned she'd taken the rest of the week off—to prepare for her wedding.

Then at her apartment, he'd discovered something

even more disturbing. She had let the place go and was living with the Myhres permanently.

Despite his best efforts. Despite their lovemaking and the feeling he'd had while with her last night, she was still going through with it. She was choosing the Myhres over him.

And despite all that, here he was standing outside the Myhre house, hoping he'd see some sign that none of what he'd heard tonight was true. That Aimee would see him standing here and rush out, tell him all of it was lies.

AIMEE'S FINGERS TIGHTENED around the draperies. Drystan was there—outside in the snow. He'd come. She'd hoped he would, that maybe, just maybe, enough had passed between them last night that he would come here to find her, that once here he would have no choice but to face the demons that haunted him, face his past and his adopted family.

She waited, watched for some sign the dark void she knew was Drystan planned to approach, to knock on the door. But he didn't move, not even when a truck swerved on an icy patch, came within inches of bumping onto the curb where he waited. He just stood there like a statue, unmoving...uncaring.

The curtain tumbled from the rod above Aimee's head, torn down by the force of her grip.

"Aimee? Are you all right?" Maureen again, a tumbler of amber liquid in her hand. She'd been watching Aimee all night, pacing past the door to the living room under one pretense or another. "Oh, the curtains." Maureen hurried into the room, slid her glass onto a walnut side table and bent to pluck a corner of the heavy drapery off the floor. "What happened?"

Her gaze back on the dark spot she knew was Drystan, Aimee didn't reply.

Maureen picked up the fallen curtain and peered out the window. "Is someone out there? Should I call the police?"

Forcing a laugh, Aimee took one end of the curtain and began folding it. "No, I was just watching the snow. I thought I saw an animal moving around out there. Maybe it was Santa!" She smiled and hoped her joke would take Maureen's mind off calling the police.

"Oh, it was probably that dog you brought here." Maureen patted the curtain, which now hung folded from her arm. "I let her out. That's okay, isn't it?" Doubt flitted behind the older woman's eyes. "I've never had a dog. She won't run off, will she?"

This time the smile on Aimee's lips was real. Maureen was falling for Garbo. The little creature might be better at daimon skills than Aimee.

"Maybe I should go look for her." Maureen started to turn. Aimee jumped forward and grabbed her arm.

"No."

At the shortness of Aimee's tone, Maureen frowned.

Aimee inhaled, relaxed. "You're ready for bed. If she doesn't come back soon, I'll go look for her."

After a few seconds more of reassurance from Aimee, Maureen left. Aimee turned back to the window and Drystan. With the curtain down, the only thing shielding her were the ivory sheers. And with the tree lit behind her and his vampire vision, he could surely see her standing here, had watched her exchange with Maureen.

Maureen. Aimee had panicked when the woman had mentioned going out into the snow...out where Drystan waited. Aimee had hoped Drystan would come here, and by being here, be reminded of his human past, find something inside himself that let him forgive the Myhres and accept himself. But he hadn't. He was still a dark void of pain, nowhere near healed.

Would he have hurt his adopted mother? Aimee didn't think so, but she hadn't thought Kevin would turn the gun on himself, either.

Something moved in the darkness, a flash of white pelting across the ground. Aimee shoved aside the sheers and pressed her hands to the glass. Garbo. The little dog was in the front yard, heading for the street, heading for Drystan.

A CHILL CLAWED its way over Drystan's body, gnawed at what was left of his spirit. Aimee was watching him from inside the Myhres', but had made no move to acknowledge him. She'd stood for minutes talking with Maureen. An icy rod had shot through Drystan's center when he'd seen the woman whom he had once thought loved him or at least cared about him.

Seeing her now next to Aimee made this all the more real, Aimee's rejection all the more hurtful. Anger vibrated through Drystan's body. How he wished the Myhre matriarch would step past that heavy wooden door, out into the night. He had never faced her, never made her face what she had done to him. Maybe it was time. Maybe her terror when she saw him would be reward enough.

His hands balled into fists at his sides, his fingers curling so tightly into themselves his knuckles popped.

Liar. He clenched his jaw, forced his eyes away from the window. He was lying to himself. He didn't want Maureen Myhre to come out her door, didn't want to face her. If he had wanted that, he could have done it ten years ago—easily wreaked his revenge as soon as he arose, killed her. But he hadn't…because somewhere deep inside, he knew she had been right, that he was nothing but a white-trash boy unworthy of saving, unworthy of love. His mother had been an addict. One of his only memories of her was holding her stash when the police raided the bar where she "worked." He'd given it back to her as soon as they left—known even at that young age what it did to her, but helped her. Then when he got old enough, he'd gone down the same path.

Since that last night, one question had never stopped swirling through Drystan's mind.

If Drystan hadn't existed, if Ben had never met him, would the golden boy have become involved with drugs? Or was it, like Maureen claimed, Drystan's fault?

Drystan cursed his weakness, forced the questions back into the cranny where he kept them hidden. Maureen *was* at fault. He couldn't forget that. If she had shown him real love, he wouldn't have done what he did, and Ben wouldn't have had Drystan's condemnable example to follow.

He should stop with the pretense, face her...kill her. His face contorted, his beguilement dropped. If anyone had stood near they would have seen the monster that he normally kept hidden from himself, everyone. Lips pulled back, fangs obvious, his face changed when in such a rage. He knew it, hated it. The transformation, ease of it, was undeniable proof of the demon that lived inside him—that had since birth. But tonight he would embrace him, and finally let this demon Drystan do what people like Maureen would expect.

A siren sounded in the distance, an accident somewhere. The demon Drystan embraced the sound. It was an ugly night—matching his mood. Soon more sirens would be called, here, and Maureen would get the news coverage she craved—too bad she wouldn't be alive to enjoy it. He turned back toward the house, one foot moving out, ready to take the first step.

But Maureen was gone. Aimee stood alone in the window. Her body angled to the side, her face closer to the glass.

She was searching the darkness for something. Even under the control of his devil, Drystan's heart caught, stalled his steps. Just as quickly he realized her gaze wasn't on him, it was closer to the house, scanning the front yard. His gaze followed the line of hers.

A small white form zigzagged across the lawn, almost invisible against the backdrop of snow. Drystan stepped back, unsure what he saw. Then a tiny yelp broke through the night and he was hit from the side by twenty pounds of wiggling, damp dog.

AIMEE'S FINGERS FLATTENED against the glass. Garbo had run into Drystan, stood dancing on her legs now, begging him to pick her up—but Drystan had changed. Sometime in the last few minutes while Aimee had been focused on Maureen, then Garbo, Drystan had changed. The darkness that lived inside him had grown, morphed into something monstrous, carnivorous, devouring every speck of goodness and humanity that was left inside her vampire lover. He practically glowed with malevolence, like a pressure cooker heated past its limits, ready to explode.

His dark figure stooped, picked up the tiny white dog. Aimee heard a yelp. She shoved her body away from the glass with enough force that the seal holding the pane popped, then hurried toward the door, tripping over her own feet.

If he hurt the little dog, it would be Aimee's fault for coming here, for praying he would follow her, finally face his past.

If he hurt Garbo, another piece of Aimee would die, and worst of all, so would the little piece of hope that still struggled to survive inside Drystan.

CHAPTER NINE

DRYSTAN HELD THE squirming creature in his arms, his mind fighting to make sense of what was happening. The demon inside him said to toss the animal aside, or use it, drain it like other vampires did when desperate for blood—to send a message to whoever owned the animal that the streets weren't safe at night, that nowhere was safe. They should hide, cower inside their mansions. The money and love they'd poured into their little pet couldn't protect it.

He grabbed the animal by the scruff of the neck, pulled its face up to his, snarled. Black eyes glistened back at him, confused.

Drystan lifted his lip, ready to snarl again, and the creature whimpered, the first signs of fear appearing in its eyes. Doubt slivered through Drystan. The hand holding the animal began to shake; the dog began to shake, too. And suddenly he saw what he was doing, saw Garbo staring back at him, quivering, her body curling into itself.

Drystan's nostrils flared. He pulled the tiny dog to his chest, cradled her there and murmured reassuring noises in her ear. She whimpered again, but softer, and slowly her struggling ceased. Still he could feel her tiny heart beating hard and fast against his chest.

What was happening to him? Where was his control? He'd spent the ten years since his rising focused, never allowing himself to get too angry or happy, building a life filled with apathy. Now in the past three days his moods had swung maniacally. He didn't know himself, was afraid of which Drystan would appear next.

A column of light split the night, grew wider. He blinked, realized it came from the Myhre house. Aimee stepped onto the front porch. Her feet were bare, her arms wrapped around her. The warmth of her called to Drystan as strongly as it had the night before, stronger, but he dropped his head, stroked the little dog in his arms. "She's looking for you," he whispered. "Not me. She doesn't want to see me, and I can't see her…not now." Maybe never.

Aimee took a step toward the snow-covered walk, but stopped as he bent, placed Garbo on the ground. The little dog stood for a second, her neck twisting back and forth as if unsure what to do.

"Go." Drystan gave her a nudge, then pulled his beguilement around him and disappeared into the darkness.

THE NEXT DAY was the eve of Aimee's wedding— the day before Christmas Eve. She woke to Garbo snuffling at her face, nudging Aimee with her nose. The dog was safe. Drystan had lowered her to the ground last night, then disappeared, faded until Aimee couldn't discern his dark form from the night around him.

She was getting married in less than two days and all she could think of was Drystan. However right or wrong it was, she wanted to be with him.

A failure as a daimon and a complete mess as a human. What was she going to do?

She sat on the edge of the bed, one hand scratching Garbo's head, the other resting on the satin comforter. She ran the pads of her fingers over the smooth material—so different from the plain cotton cover that she had draped over Drystan.

She couldn't save Drystan. She knew that, had seen how close he'd come last night to sinking into a darkness from which he would never return—but she couldn't walk away, either. Despite the short amount of time she'd known him and all the things she didn't know about him—she loved him.

So what did she do? She couldn't marry Ben, she realized that now—probably would have realized it even if Drystan hadn't come into her life. She didn't love him and he didn't love her. By letting him marry her for all the wrong reasons she would be cheating him out of the life he could have, the love he could find.

But what did that mean for her? She couldn't save

Drystan, but couldn't be with him the way he was, either.

"I've kind of made a mess of things, haven't I?" she asked the dog, who stared up at her with a sad kind of wisdom. "Drystan needs to face his past, and his future. It's the only way he'll be whole." The dog shoved her nose into Aimee's hand, flipped it. Aimee started to stroke her back, but the dog stood, shook, then plopped down beside Aimee, her gaze steady, encouraging.

Aimee's hand dropped to her lap; she started to stand, but her knees bent beneath her. "I've made a mess of things. No one can fix it for him. He has to face his past and accept who he is," she mumbled the words. The dog stayed in place, intent. With a light laugh, Aimee looked up, stared at Garbo. "Maybe you are a daimon."

Then she walked to the closet and began pulling on her clothes. She had a lot to do in very little time.

DRYSTAN TAPPED HIS fingers against his glass. He was the only occupant of the busy bar's patio. He'd come here tonight thinking he'd relieve the feelings churning inside him by targeting some coed or bored female executive, luring her into one of the bar's many dark crannies, enjoying her blood, her hands on his body.

But despite the many curves that had brushed up

against him, hands that had flickered over his arm, eyes that had caught his over a lifted glass, his body had been unmoved, his hunger unstirred.

He didn't want these women—not for sex or blood. He didn't want anything right now except Aimee. She had become an obsession—an even greater one than revenging himself on the Myhres.

He took another sip of whiskey. It rolled down his throat, cold and tasteless. He gripped the glass, squeezed until he knew it was within seconds of cracking. Even a twenty-one-year-old bourbon couldn't warm him anymore.

A door opened behind him; music and the smell of cigarettes spilled out. Public smoking was illegal here, but like so many things, like Drystan escorting the occasional guest into a dark corner, the owner ignored it. Drystan set down the glass, followed the swaying steps of a group of twentysomethings with his eyes, but he didn't move to stand—had no interest. He picked up the glass, slammed it against the metal tabletop, felt it shatter in his hand. He shoved his palm into the fragments, grinding them into smaller pieces, dust. The tiny shards fell onto the ground, sparkling in the bit of light that leaked from the bar, but Drystan's palm was barely touched, just little black bubbles of blood, like old oil. As he watched, the skin underneath healed. Even the physical pain was fleeting. How could his body feel pain when his spirit was so glutted with it?

He stood then, not sure where he would go, what he would do, only knowing he was tired of spending every night alone with only the occasional pretense of closeness with another living being. As he dusted the last of the glass from his palm, pushed the chair back against the table, he saw her—Aimee standing under the streetlight, her white coat reflecting the light, her hair forming a halo around her face.

And damn his weakness, his heart leaped and his hands began to shake.

HIS PAIN WAS thick tonight, darker than Aimee had seen it, but thankfully the monstrous cloud she'd seen engulf Drystan last night was missing. Guessing he frequented the same place night after night, places where the clientele knew vampires were real, she'd gone first to the restaurant where they'd had dinner. A waiter had suggested this bar. He'd looked at her sideways, and she'd known he thought she was some kind of groupie, a vamp tramp as she'd heard them called. She'd let him think what he liked. It didn't matter. Nothing mattered but finding Drystan, trying one last time to get him to let go of the hate, pain and resentment of his past. It was the only thing that would save him, the only way they could be together.

Drystan hesitated, his hand opening and closing as if checking his grip. She pulled her lower lip into her mouth, bit down and waited. She had nothing to say, not yet. If he wouldn't come to her, wouldn't give that much, then her cause was lost, Drystan was lost.

DRYSTAN COULDN'T BELIEVE she was there. He blinked, waited to see if his eyes were fooling him, if she was some kind of vision, a mix of the swirling snow and the three glasses of bourbon he'd consumed tonight. But Aimee didn't disappear, didn't turn away. Instead she leaned forward as if about to approach, then stopped herself, her lip disappearing into her mouth.

Her eyes were huge, her arms wrapped around her body. She was unsure, afraid. Just like he was.

Without letting his mind form another thought, he shoved the table out of his way and strode off the patio, into the circle of light where she stood.

Once close to her, he didn't know what to say and he felt foolish. "You left your apartment."

She nodded. "I had to."

It wasn't an answer, not to the unasked question that hung between them, but for now Drystan let it lie. Did she remember everything that had happened between them, their lovemaking? Had it been as real for her as it felt to him? "I was looking for you."

She didn't reply, kept her hands on her arms.

"For the article," he added, suddenly afraid he'd misread everything, that what he'd felt the previous night hadn't been real, that without meaning to he'd spelled her into wanting him, into making love. He *had* played with her head only a little earlier. That could have left her weak, easy to sway to desires he was too weak to keep hidden.

She curled her fingers around the lapels of his coat, rose on her tiptoes, then pressed her lips to his, and all questions, all thoughts evaporated from Drystan's mind. His hands found her waist and he let himself relax, believe...again.

But then, with no explanation, she stepped away. Her hands stayed on his chest, but her body was an arm's length away. He could feel the cool air where she had been. She smoothed his coat, stared at the button in the middle of his chest, then put another step between them, turned on the ball of her foot and walked away.

Drystan stared after her...stupidly...no words coming to his mind. She couldn't be leaving, couldn't be going back to the Myhres'. She had found him, searched him out, hadn't even taken the time to explain...to let him know what she knew or had figured out.

She was leaving him, like his father, his mother... the Myhres. Like everyone he had ever dared trust.

Anger bubbled inside him. He wouldn't let it happen—not this time. She had to come with him. Had to choose him. He could make her. He would make her.

AIMEE COULD FEEL Drystan approaching—a pulse of angry energy pounding closer and closer. She sighed, her shoulders curving under the weight of what this meant.

He hadn't let go of the anger inside him, not yet. Couldn't come to her with just love, instead let anger and resentment drive him.

How far would he let it take him? She slowed her steps until she could sense him right behind her.

"Aimee." He stepped in front of her. She let her body jerk as if surprised by his appearance. "You need to come with me. You want to come with me."

The air seemed to thicken around them. The world past Drystan disappeared, as if they were standing in complete darkness, a dim light shining on only them.

The intensity in his voice increased. "Come with me."

Her hand began to lift. She stared at it, surprised by its movement.

"You don't want to marry Ben. You never did. You can stay with me until the wedding is past, or…" He paused, seemed to think. "You can call the media from my apartment. Get everything out in the open."

Ben. The name ripped through the fog that had settled around Aimee. This wasn't about Drystan wanting to help her, *wanting* her. It was about his revenge on the Myhres. Her hand ceased its movement. And this feeling, this urge to do what Drystan said, to believe and trust him, it wasn't coming from her own brain. She shifted her gaze, stared at Drystan's lips, saw for the first time the fangs that protruded slightly beneath his upper lip.

They didn't turn her off, didn't detract from his attractiveness in any way, but seeing them so clearly told her his powers, whatever hold they'd had before, no longer worked on her. From now on, anything that passed between them would be totally of her own free will, under her control—but Drystan wouldn't know. There was no better test, no better way to discover how guided he was by hate, how much, if any, love still survived inside the pit of darkness and anger that too often seemed to swallow him whole.

She let her hand rise, let him take it in hers, and when he whisked her away in a whirl of twirling snow and shifting realities, she didn't murmur a concern. She went with him, a placid look on her face, and a hole in her heart.

WHEN THE WORLD settled down, Aimee was back in Drystan's apartment, his bedroom this time. He hadn't bothered pausing in the main room, exchanging words. And Aimee was glad, she saw the desire burning in his eyes, knew that at least was true, and she felt it, too. No matter what happened tonight with Drystan, she wasn't going to marry Ben. She would figure out some way to let him down easy, to keep the wedding that wouldn't be from damaging him with the media. She wasn't worried about his heart; love had never been in play, not between her and Ben.

So tonight she would be with Drystan, get the need to feel his touch out of her system. Tonight she would think about the now—because later she might have to say goodbye.

They pulled clothing from each other's bodies as they walked, Aimee moving backward, her hands on Drystan's body grounding her, keeping her from stumbling. His kisses tasted of vanilla and oak, sweet and earthy. She fell back on the bed, sinking into the comforter she'd placed around him two nights before. He fell beside her, pulled her flush against him, then rolled so she lay naked on top of him.

He started to say something then, but she pressed two fingers to his lips. She wasn't ready to hear him speak, to feel she needed to reply, too. Once she started talking she was afraid the words would tumble out, her daimon half would force her to say everything she was thinking, ruin this moment, perhaps their last together.

His lips closed and he watched her, expectant. She ran her fingers from his mouth, down his chin, his neck, to the little hollow at the base of his throat. She replaced her fingers with her lips, pulled skin into her mouth, nibbled.

His hands tightened on her back, found her buttocks and began to knead.

She pushed herself up to stare down at him. Her breasts swayed, her nipples brushing against the hair on his chest. Her fingers curled toward his skin, her thighs parting, inviting him.

He pushed her farther upward, found the tip of one breast and pulled it into his mouth.

She could feel his erection, pressing against her, close to the opening between her thighs. She edged herself down his body until the tip nudged into her, slipped a little inside.

A gasp escaped her lips. He grasped her buttocks, keeping her in place, his sex barely held by hers, his lips on her breasts, his teeth grazing her skin. Aimee wanted to claw at his skin, to force him to release her so she could plunge downward, feel the full length of him inside her.

Instead, he reached lower, slipped one finger along her folds, found the nub that was hidden there, circled it until Aimee's back arched, and her body tensed.

Her lips parted, her breath coming in pants. Drystan circled the nub again, allowed his erection to inch farther inside her. Her body began to quiver, her muscles to clench, and with no warning, without him fully inside her, her spirit begin to slip, but this time she bit down, forced her daimon soul to stay in her human body, to experience this orgasm as a human, with Drystan. As the waves hit her, she held on to the comforter beneath them, twisted and pulled until the material billowed around them.

Finally, as the last spasms passed, she collapsed. Drystan removed his mouth from her breast, lowering her until her head rested on his chest. He stroked her back, his fingertips tracing every bump of her spine.

Her heart slowed and her fingers began moving on their own, making lazy circles in the hair on his chest. His hand moved to her hair, his fingers weaving through the mass of curls until he reached her scalp. She sighed, a smile tilting her lips. She'd never felt so relaxed, so at home.

He lifted his other hand, skimmed his fingers over her side. Goose bumps tingled across her skin. She shivered, a pleasant shake of awareness, of her body and his. She turned her face until her lips pressed into his chest, swirled her tongue over his skin, tasted him.

He tasted of salt and smelled of soap, both very human, even though she knew he wasn't…not any longer. She swallowed the lump that formed in her throat at the thought. Things couldn't be simple for her, for them. No, Drystan had to be a vampire, a creature of the night, ruled by darkness, lost in his own pain.

She shoved the thoughts aside, determined not to think of them again, to keep this time special.

She raised her leg to Drystan's waist, pulled herself higher on his body until her mouth found his, then she kissed him, putting every bit of longing she had into the act.

CHAPTER TEN

AIMEE'S LEG WOUND around Drystan's waist. Her breasts brushed against his chest. He held her lightly, almost afraid gripping her too tightly would wake her, end the dream he'd created for himself.

So what that she'd tried to walk away? So what if she came with him only because he made her, beguiled her? Right now he only cared that she was here, with him.

Her lips met his, covered his with a need, a yearning that almost matched his own. Her tongue slipped inside his mouth. He met it with his own, guiding her away from the sharp point of his fangs. He hadn't fed since he'd been with her two nights before, hadn't felt the need, at least not physically, but with her here, her scent engulfing him, her heat beside him, he could feel the hunger growing.

His body thrummed with it. He flipped her over, beneath him, his weight pressing hers into the down cover. She pulled her lips free, stretched her neck as if inviting his bite, as if she knew what he wanted and welcomed it. It was too much for him to resist. He murmured to her, to himself, to whoever brought this woman to him, and trailed his lips down her jaw, her neck.

He lay there a second, listened to the speeding thump of her heart, the rush of blood through her veins. He could hear it, smell it; all that was left was to taste it.

She bent her head farther to the side, exposing the artery. He pressed his lips against the spot, felt the even but rapid jump of her pulse. She squirmed, her hands moving to his lower back, finding the indentation at the top of his buttocks and stroking, encouraging. As her fingers drifted lower, moved to the front, to his almost painful erection, he couldn't resist any longer. He pulled back his lips and plunged his fangs into her throat.

Bliss, sweet and sure, swept over him. Her blood was just as he remembered it, or was it better? Had it been this fresh? This full of light and hope? He could feel it rushing through his body, warming him, changing him, making him think just for a while everything was okay—he was okay.

Her fingers wrapped around his erection and he groaned against her neck; never before had he had a partner who participated so fully in both acts, blood and sex. Aimee gave where others only took—took the thrill of bedding a vampire, experiencing the bite. The few humans who knew about vampires, who hung out at the bars looking for them, saw him as a novelty, something to experience and move on.

Even though he took their blood, and experienced an orgasm, it was really all about them—their thrill, their walk with danger.

Yes, he occasionally cornered an unknowing, sated his thirst, but he never combined that mind control with sex. Using it to take the blood, playing vampire puppeteer in that way, felt wrong. To use the skill for sex was unthinkable.

But with Aimee he hadn't had to, she'd come to him willingly. She hadn't known he was a vampire, but she hadn't turned from his bite, either, and she was back with him tonight. He'd brought her to his apartment, but hadn't beguiled her into sex. That was a choice she'd made freely—or so he'd thought. Was he somehow controlling her without knowing? Had she not realized what had happened the last time, did she not realize it now?

He needed to ask these questions to know what she knew, but as she moaned beneath him and rocked her hips upward, he tamped them down, let himself go.

Her fingers moved along his shaft, guiding him, but caressing him, too. His muscles tensed, nothing but will stopping him from plunging inside her, thrusting in and out. Her thumb flicked over the sensitive tip of his erection, swirled like his tongue had swirled over her nipple, like his tongue did now over the puncture wounds on her neck. She shivered, moved her thumb faster, then placed the head of his shaft against her folds and lifted her hips once more.

Drystan cradled her in his arms, pressed a kiss to her ear, then lowered his mouth back to her neck and plunged inside—fangs and shaft, blood and sex, beautiful, natural—meant to be.

In and out he thrust, slow despite the pounding need to move fast, to reach the peak he knew waited. Her blood zinged through his body, increasing his excitement. Her fingers clawed at his chest in long, strong strokes, mimicking the in-and-out movement of his body inside hers.

Finally, she began to quiver in his arms; he knew her release was upon her. He increased his pace, let himself go, felt her tighten and relax around him, felt his body tighten and relax, as well. Then just like two nights earlier, his spirit shifted. His consciousness left his body, drifted overhead, but this time Aimee was with him, holding him, wrapping around him, keeping him warm, surrounding him with an emotion he'd never felt before, not this pure, this intense—love.

She loved him, and as they floated back down together, as the dawn crept closer, he realized he loved her, too.

IT WAS ALMOST dark again, and Aimee was still with Drystan, had stayed with him all day. She'd watched him this morning, held his hand as he stiffened, as the light in his eyes faded, as he died. She couldn't think of it as anything else, realized now after witnessing the flash of panic in his eyes, he couldn't, either.

It was a horrible fate, worse than anyone who knew of vampires realized.

Just thinking of it, tension ran through her body, her hands stiffening, her fingers forming claws. She wanted to scrape away the cocoon of death that had enveloped him, pull him back to the living—but she couldn't. He was a vampire; nothing she could do, not even as a daimon, could change that.

His eyes were closed now. He'd shut them before the state hit, kept them closed as the light crept up the horizon. She ran a finger over his brow, his closed lid.

Kevin's death had almost killed her, had driven her away from being a daimon, from herself. Could she stand spending night after night with Drystan, watching him die dawn after dawn? She slipped her hand into his, squeezed his fingers—he didn't respond, not even a reflex.

A tear worked its way into the corner of her eye. If Drystan couldn't change, couldn't give up his hate for the Myhres, accept who he was, could she walk away, could she leave him to face this fate alone?

Neither choice seemed possible. Both almost physically painful.

But it wasn't her choice to make. She wanted to be with Drystan, but she couldn't carry his burden alone—he had to let go of some of it himself. If not, their life together would be haunted, by his hate, and her worry—that one day he would make the same choice as Kevin, or return to the monster who waited outside the Myhres' last night.

She couldn't do that to him or herself.

As the sun crawled from the sky, Aimee curled her body next to Drystan's and waited. At midnight she was supposed to be getting married. She had a thousand things to do to prepare, but she wouldn't leave Drystan until he awoke. She'd seen him die twice now. At least once she wanted to see him come back. She prayed the process held some joy that made the other bearable, something that made the altered state more trade than loss.

And she had to talk to him, had to tell him what she was doing and why, had to give him the chance to talk her out of it, to show her there was still some light left in his soul.

Then she had to go to the church, face Ben—whether with Drystan by her side or alone was yet to be determined.

DRYSTAN MOVED HIS fingers, first just a tiny wiggle of the last joint, then bending and unbending the digits, reminding his body how to move. It had become a ritual for him to start with the slightest flicker of movement. Then as his courage increased, as he became sure that yes, once again he was alive, he'd open his eyes and eventually sit up. But tonight something was different.

Tonight he wasn't alone.

Until just two nights earlier he had dreaded waking like this, realizing someone hovered near him while he lay at his most vulnerable. But after falling into his catatonic condition with Aimee by his side, he realized how much he hungered for a companion, to enter and leave the darkness with the hope that only having someone, Aimee, with him could provide.

"Drystan?" The pressure of her hands was no more than a whisper on his chest. His lips tilted in a smile. Her fingers slipped into his and he squeezed, a silent thank-you for staying with him, for being with him, even though he knew she'd had no choice; he'd given her no choice.

"Are you a…" she leaned closer, her breath falling across his face "…awake?"

He knew she'd changed the word at the end, been thinking *alive*. Now he knew how he looked when out. The same as how he felt—dead, cut off from everything, even his own mind.

He opened his eyes, stared up into hers. She smiled then, a slightly sad tilt of her lips, but still a smile. Her hands moved to his face, and she stroked his cheek. He stayed still, stretching the moment, the only pleasant awakening he could ever remember.

Finally, he sat up, reached for her, but she placed a hand on his chest, stopping him.

"Are you okay? Do you need to do anything?" she asked. A tiny line of concern darkened the space between her brows.

He leaned in, rubbed his nose against the line, pulled the smell of her into his lungs. Waking to her, holding her, made him happy. Again he tugged her toward him. Again she stopped him.

Her body was tense, her face wary.

Seeing how she watched him, Drystan grew wary, too. Slowly, he lowered his arms, let her pull away.

"I'm fine."

She seemed ready to say something, but stopped.

That's when he realized he owed her an explanation. She'd stayed with him through the day, had no choice in the matter. He'd sealed the apartment as soon as they entered it, disabled the phones, and before he'd gone completely under he'd put a spell on her, too, forced her to sleep by his side. Could he do that every night? Change her so she lived the same nocturnal existence he did?

So, she hadn't sat here all day thinking him dead, but still she had obviously been awake before him. She deserved some kind of explanation.

"I'm fine," he repeated. "I'm a—"

"Vampire." She pushed herself off the bed, turned her back on him and stared at his dresser where a digital clock glowed the time, 8:00 p.m.

Her shoulders were square and pulled back. She was upset. He could understand that, was surprised she hadn't run screaming at the door, wasn't standing there beating on it now—surprised but also happy. He swung his legs over the side of the bed, placed his bare feet on the floor.

She glanced over her shoulder at him, picked up a discarded shirt and jeans and tossed them beside him.

"You know," he said. His voice dropped. Despite the fact that she seemed under control, not panicked by her discovery, he couldn't stop the uncertainty that filled him. What did she know of vampires? How did she even know they existed? Would she see him as others saw vampires, as the monster he sometimes became?

She turned. "I also know you're Ben's brother, and why you sought me out."

His mouth twisted to the side. Ben. Somehow he'd forgotten for a few blissful hours that she was his adopted brother's fiancée, forgotten that their relationship, whatever it was, was based on lies—his lies. But that didn't matter now. It was Christmas Eve—the night scheduled for their wedding—and she was going nowhere.

Somehow despite all odds, he'd come out on top, he'd ruined Maureen Myhre's plans and got Aimee for himself. He smiled and reached out to touch her, concentrated on bringing her mind back to him, away from where she was supposed to be, to whom she was supposed to be marrying.

He'd deal with the missed wedding later. Plant seeds in her mind for her to repeat to the media, but for now he just wanted to enjoy being with her.

She stepped back.

His hand fell with a thud to his lap.

"You can't control me, Drystan." There was no judgment in the words, but still they hit him with the force of a slap. "I didn't stay here today because you made me. I didn't come here last night because you put thoughts in my head. And I know you think the door is locked, that I can't escape, but it isn't true—not for me."

She held her hands out to her sides, palms tilted up, middle finger and thumb curved slightly together, like some medieval picture of a saint or...an angel.

His nostrils flared. It couldn't be. She couldn't be. Angels didn't exist.... Of course, most people didn't think vampires existed, either.

"I'm a daimon—or was." She frowned, seemed to lose her concentration for a second, then took in a breath and repeated herself. "I'm a daimon." This time as she spoke the words the air around her began to shimmer, tiny rays of light shooting from her body, outlining her.

"A *daymun*." He said the word like she had. He'd never heard the term, not in relation to anything he associated with Aimee.

"I'm a light daimon. There are others. I was assigned to Kevin."

"The boy at the drugstore," Drystan murmured, not knowing where this was going, not sure he wanted to know. Had Aimee been assigned to him? Had she been playing with his mind, trying to convert him from his vampire ways? His jaw hardened. As if his life was that simple—as if this state was something he chose.

"Are you here to judge me?" he asked. He snapped the jeans straight, then began jerking them on. "Or fix me? People have tried both before." He pulled the shirt over his head, shoved his arms through. "They've failed."

"I'm not here to judge you or fix you." Her words were quiet, the glow around her softer now, pulsing, soothing. "You came to me, remember?"

"Maybe." He took a step back, leaned against the wall. "Or maybe some cosmic puppeteer arranged that, too, planted a seed in my head."

She blinked and her arms started to drop, then resolve flashed through her eyes, and she straightened her neck, pulled her arms back to their angelic pose. "Daimons don't make people do things. We don't mess with free will—any choice you make is your own."

Drystan's jaw jutted to the side. He didn't want to believe her, wanted to call her a liar, but he couldn't. Angry with himself and wanting to be angry with her, he shoved himself away from the wall and strode toward the bedroom door.

"I'm not staying," she called after him. "I'm going to the church."

He ground to a halt, his palm smacking into the wall beside the door as he did. Without turning around or even looking at her, he replied, "Are you?" She said he couldn't hold her, but he had no proof of that. She had stayed with him since last night. Why would she have done that if his powers didn't hold her?

"Do you want me to stay?" she asked.

Drystan pulled back his fist, started to pound it into the wall, then slowly, his muscles tensing with the effort, uncurled his fingers, laid his flat palm on the drywall instead. "Would I have kept you here if I didn't?"

A sigh, heavy with sadness, greeted his response. Behind him, Aimee moved—the energy in the room shifting as she came closer, close enough he could have spun, pulled her into his arms. But he didn't— wouldn't let himself. She'd lied to him, used him. He wasn't sure for what reason yet, but he wouldn't let her see his wounds, wouldn't stand here and admit to needing her, to needing anyone. He'd been taken in again. This time would be his last.

"You're hiding," she said. He could feel her hand rise, feel energy warm like a heat lamp flowing from her palm, over his back. She was within inches of touching him, and he wanted that touch as much as he had wanted anything, but he stood still, refused to let his body arch toward her.

"How am I hiding? Because I only come out at dark? You know I have no choice in that. Because I didn't search out the Myhres after I rose?" He kept his voice low, controlled, but felt the vibrations as the sound left his chest, knew she could probably hear the anger he was trying so hard to contain. "Maybe I did it to save them. Maybe I knew that if...when...I faced them I wouldn't be able to stop myself. That the vampire in me would truly break free. That I'd kill them."

She dropped her hand. Angry as he was, caught up as he was, he still mourned the loss, had to concentrate to not lower his chin to his chest.

"I don't think you're hiding from the Myhres. I think you're hiding from yourself."

He spun then, ready to confront her, but as he did, she disappeared. He spun again, faced the main room. Aimee stood with her back to the door, one hand resting on the top of the leather couch where they had first made love; the other was tucked behind her.

"I love you. I need to tell you that, but I can't save you. I can't keep you from hiding in hate. I tried that with Kevin and failed, learned that lesson the hard way. If I stay with you, I'll be your crutch, something to keep you from having to face who you are, good or bad, to forgive, accept, move on."

He took a step into the room, his gaze on her arm where it curved behind her. "I don't want to move on."

"I know." She pulled her hand from behind her back, held it out showing it was empty. "Not everyone is out to get you. Not everything you can't see or don't understand is bad. If you believed in yourself, forgave yourself, you'd see *that*." She turned, placed her hand on the knob. "I want to be with you, but I can't, not unless you forgive yourself, accept yourself—good and bad. If you can shrug off those ghosts, I'll be at the church."

"The wedding—"

"Is scheduled for midnight. That gives you time to think things over. I can't give you any more. If I do, I'll weaken. I can't let myself do that. It's tonight or never."

She didn't want him to come. She'd set things up so he couldn't come. He laughed, a dry sound like leaves crumbling. "Vampires can't enter a church."

Her back tensed, her hand tightening around the doorknob. "Being a vampire doesn't change who you are, not if you don't let it. If you give up the darkness, leave it behind, the doors will open. Goodbye, Drystan." The space where she stood began to sparkle, her voice to fade. Drystan held a hand in front of his eyes, shielding them from the light. When he looked back she was gone.

CHAPTER ELEVEN

AIMEE STOOD ON the other side of Drystan's door, her palm pressed to the wood. No sound came from inside. What was he doing? Why wasn't he already following her?

She waited another five minutes, before lowering her head and heading down the hall. He would realize the good still inside him, give up the resentment that he'd gathered around him like a protective cloak. He had to and he had to do it by midnight tonight.

As Aimee had stood before him, declared herself a daimon, she'd realized she *was* a daimon. She couldn't ever be human. She might have failed with Kevin, but she'd done her best at the time, and one failure didn't mean she would fail each time. No, it meant she knew more now, that she would be better next time.

And as she'd stood there, she'd heard the peal again, the call of a soul that needed her guidance, a hand to hold as it struggled to stay on the right path.

Her threat of midnight was real. One minute later and she'd be gone, off to help her new assignment.

Leaving Drystan was hard—would be hard no matter what—but to leave him still like this, lost, wandering... That would haunt her as much as Kevin's death. Kevin only sank into the darkness once. Drystan went there every dawn.

She rubbed her hand over her forehead and forced her steps to quicken. The Myhres were waiting for her. No matter Drystan's decision, she knew now she wouldn't...couldn't marry Ben. He deserved an explanation.

DRYSTAN SAT IN his chair, a glass of the bottled blood in his hand—warmed this time. He held the liquid in his mouth, let it slide down his throat. The raised temperature of the drink did nothing for him, the blood did nothing for him—didn't zing through his body like Aimee's had, didn't warm him, make him feel anything except the monster he was.

He picked up the glass and strode to the kitchen— threw the stemware into the sink. Glass and blood splattered up the sides, onto him. His hands gripping the edge of the sink, he lowered his head between his arms and took in deep heaving breaths. Breaths he didn't need—but the human action usually calmed him, made him feel somewhat in touch with his human past.

This time it did nothing.

He didn't understand Aimee, didn't understand himself, or the thoughts pinging through his head.

Aimee was some kind of angel, some being of light. He was a vampire and she'd known it. How long? All the time? Had she been playing with him? But why? Why lower herself to be with him—then leave him?

He wanted to scrape the slivers of glass out of the sink and fling them in again. Instead he gripped the counter's edge tighter, took deeper breaths, tried to think.

She'd said he needed to let go of the resentment, to love himself or some other do-gooder babble. Like he had done this to himself, like he, the victim, was to blame.

With a curse, he spun, grabbed the half-empty bottle of blood from the counter and stormed back into the main room.

Sitting in his chair, drinking the blood straight from the bottle, he made his mind slow, thought about what he wanted, what he'd wanted all along.

Revenge.

Aimee was right. It was time to stop hiding from what he was. He was a vampire. Time to show the people who helped make him into one exactly what they had created.

He had planned on giving the media a show. They were at the church now, gathered, waiting. What better time to step out of his coffin? What better time to take down the Myhres? To exact revenge as only a vampire could?

THE CHURCH WAS empty when Aimee arrived. Determined to find Ben before the media appeared, Aimee had hurried from room to room, even called out, but nothing except her own voice greeted her back. Finally, she'd gone to the library—the room assigned to her, the bride. Someone had been here. Her white lace ball gown and the wreath of white roses that were meant for her hair hung next to a full-length mirror. The scent of roses pulled her closer. Her hand reached out, caressed the lace.

"Aimee, are you in there?" The door edged open and Maureen Myhre slid sideways into the room, as if a crowd of people pressed around the other side of the door struggling to see in.

Aimee jerked her fingers back, curled them into her palm.

"Get dressed." Maureen pointed at the dress.

Aimee stepped backward, into the dress. "Is Ben here? I need to talk to him."

"After you're dressed. We're going to do pictures before the wedding."

"But—" Aimee could feel the blood draining from her face. She had to talk to Ben. She had to tell him she couldn't marry him. She couldn't tell Maureen— not before Ben.

"I know the old wives' tales—bad luck and all that. Bad luck will be if you don't get that dress on in the next five minutes. I have Andrew White from the *Journal* waiting on you two. If we want a picture in tomorrow's paper, it has to be now."

"I need to talk to Ben."

"After you're dressed." Maureen strode across the room and began pulling the gown from the hanger.

Aimee stood by, unsure what to do. If she ran from the room, looked for Ben again, she could easily run into the reporter instead.

But… She stared at the dress Maureen now held out for her. If she put it on, let the interview happen, was she compounding her sin?

"Aimee?" Maureen gave the heavy material a tiny shake.

Praying this would work out somehow, Aimee shrugged off her shirt and pants and stepped into the gown.

SPOTLIGHTS SHONE ON the white brick church, illuminating the building like the crown jewel in a princess's tiara. Black limos, expensive imports and media vans lined the street outside.

Aimee was inside that church, marrying Ben. Drystan braced his feet, clenched his fists at his sides. The blood he'd swallowed earlier churned in his stomach, refused to digest.

A wide staircase curved up toward massive double doors. Twin white crosses constructed of roses hung on the doors.

Drystan placed a foot on the step, his hand on the

cold metal railing. He was here, he was going in. He was going to… His mind drifted, the blood in his stomach hardened, seemed to weigh him down.

Why was he here? What did he want? How would humiliating the Myhres, killing them, even, solve anything? Would it bring Aimee back? Would it bring him the life he'd always wanted?

His legs bent beneath him. He sat on the cold snow-covered steps and spread out his fingers, pressed them into the snow. Someone should have cleared this. If Drystan were marrying Aimee, had everything Ben was about to have, he wouldn't have allowed any detail to go unnoticed. He would have spent the last three months making sure every little aspect was perfect.

But Aimee didn't mean anything to Ben, not like she did to Drystan.

The thought should have made him angry, given spark to the rage he'd somehow lost as he traveled here from his apartment, but it didn't. Not this time. This time he just stared at his fingers resting on the snow, thought of how if Aimee's hand were there beside his, the snow would melt, the cold would go away, Drystan's pain would melt.

But it wouldn't go away, hadn't. The small chip of resentment and anger he kept tucked inside him at all times had prevented that. Aimee had given him everything he had ever wanted, but it hadn't been enough. He'd still clung to old hates, still plotted to get even.

How could a daimon, an angel, love someone like that? How could he love someone like that? He raised his head and stared at the sky. Big fluffy snowflakes began to fall, landing on his face. He closed his eyes, let them cover his lids.

He had a choice to make. He could cling to the hate and resentment that he'd carried with him since childhood or he could let it go, take responsibility for his choices—accept what had happened in his past and move on. Let himself love and be loved—let love be more important than anything else.

Moisture leaked into his eyes. He reached up to brush it away, then paused. *Into* his eyes. The snow on his face was melting. He pulled up the hand that had been lying on the snow, flipped it over. Beads of water clung to his palm—snow melted by his body, his warmth.

He folded and unfolded his fingers, unable to grasp what was happening, then reached up and pressed his fingers against his upper teeth. The fangs were still there. He was still a vampire.

For a moment, he sank back, then slowly his spine straightened. He was still a vampire, like he was still Drystan. Maybe that was the point—accepting, not hiding, not trying to change what he couldn't.

He stood, his hand back on the railing. It felt colder

now…the difference between his warming body and the icy metal more obvious.

All that stood between him and Aimee were two cross-covered doors, and Ben, the brother who thought Drystan was dead. Squaring his shoulders, he walked up the steps. At the top he paused again. The brass doorknob shone against the dark wood.

His hand shaking, he reached out and wrapped his fingers around the cold metal.

THE VESTIBULE OF the church was dark as Drystan stepped inside. Thick carpeting covered the floor, the smell of candles filled the air, and everything was perfectly still, perfectly quiet—no lightning bolts searing him to ash, no avenging angels dropping from the sky, swords drawn to pierce him through the heart.

A holy water font, carved in marble, hung on the wall. Drystan wasn't Catholic, had rarely entered a church before his rising, but the belief that he couldn't, that he was cursed, had been yet another burden to add to all the others he carried.

Holding his breath, he dipped two fingers into the font, then out. Water dripped onto his shoes, made little round dark spots on the carpet, but that was it—the extent of the chaos.

Aimee was right. Becoming a vampire hadn't made him evil. If he was a monster it was because he allowed himself to be one, let the anger make him into one.

He took only a moment to let the realization sink in, to accept that he had made the choices that led him to where he was, that while perhaps the Myhres could have also made different choices, ultimately he had created his destiny.

A chime sounded from inside the sanctuary. Leveling his shoulders and raising his head, he held his gaze steady. Unashamed, he strode toward the closed doors. He had a wedding to stop.

THE DOORS GLIDED open on oiled hinges—not a whisper to alert the occupants of the chapel of Drystan's arrival. His heart thumped in his chest. This was it, the moment he'd dreamed of, but now his goal was so different. He was going to stand exposed for the world to see, for the Myhres and Aimee to see.

No more hiding, from them or himself.

The room was dark, lit only by flickering candles. At the front near the altar holding a candle of her own stood Aimee, dressed in a billowing gown of white with a ring of roses peeking from her hair. Beside her was Ben, another candle in his hand.

Drystan was too late. They were lighting the unity candle which stood waiting on the altar. The ceremony was over. Aimee was married.

A hollow ache began to build inside Drystan's chest. He reached for the door before it could fully close, trap him in here with Aimee and Ben, the people sure to start clapping, the joy that would never be his. But as his fingers hit the wood, he stopped. He was running, hiding again. He'd sworn to himself he would stop. If he could face this, he could face anything. If he didn't face this, it would, like every other pain he'd experienced in his life, fester and grow, twist his spirit, make him back into the monster he had just conquered.

He turned, faced the sanctuary.

Aimee had moved, was halfway down the aisle, but she was alone, the lit candle still in her hand.

"You came." The flame bounced up and down in her hand, like she was shaking, excited, nervous.

"I… It's almost twelve. I'd thought…" She stopped, looked over her shoulder. Ben stood unmoved, stiff, his gaze locked on Drystan, all color drained from his face. "I told Ben a little, but not everything. Not how…" She let the words trail off again.

Drystan's muscles seemed to have locked up, his voice to have left. He forced his fingers to let go of the door, his arm to drop at his side. He made his gaze flow over the darkened pews, ready to see shock, fear even, but there was nothing—the pews were empty.

"Is it over? Where is—" he gestured to the empty church "—the media? Maureen didn't…"

At his mother's name Ben took a step forward.

"She's holding court in the reception hall. It's behind the church."

Aimee was beside him now, the candle glowing in her hand. He could see the detail of her dress, the lace that covered her bodice, the tiny pearls stitched along the top. "You're beautiful," he murmured. He couldn't stop the pain inside him, but he clenched his jaw, refused to let it take over.

"So are you." She ran her hand down his arm, her touch soft, her face filled with disbelief. "You're different."

"Not so much." He pulled back his lips, showed her his fangs.

"Not there. Here." She placed her hand on his chest, over his heart.

Her touch hurt; to have her so close and know she couldn't be his hurt. "I…I hope you and Ben will be happy," he said.

"Ben?" Her lips stayed parted, her gaze darting to the side where his adopted brother still stood stiffly next to the altar. "We didn't get married. We called off the wedding, managed to convince the media it was all a stunt to get their attention, to get them to listen to Ben's new plan to help youth like Kevin who have no one, who turn to drugs as an escape.

"The church was already set up for the wedding." Aimee waved her hand around, gesturing at the candles. "Ben and I were just cleaning up, and waiting, hoping you'd come." She licked her lips, seemed about to say something else, but Ben took a step forward.

"I told them my story...our story." The candle in Ben's hand bobbed with his words. "Mother wasn't happy, but once it was out, she had no choice but to go along, to act like it was our plan from the beginning. By the time they leave she'll have convinced them and herself it was her idea all along." He laughed, but it was a nervous sound, made Drystan want to look away.

Then everything Ben and Aimee had said sunk in, and he did look away—back to Aimee. "You didn't get married?"

She shook her head. Drystan smiled, grabbed her then. "You didn't get married." Hot wax from the candle dripped onto his sleeve. He ignored it, ignored everything but Aimee.

But something was wrong. She wasn't smiling, didn't look like she shared the joy racing through Drystan's body. "No, but there's something else I have to tell you."

He dropped his hands, let her pull away. She was going to leave him. He stepped back, turned to face the wall. It was too much, this roller-coaster ride she'd put him on.

"I don't want to leave...you know that, but I don't have a choice. I told you, I'm a daimon. I have to answer the calling. Someone needs me."

He needed her.

Her hand landed on his shoulder; he ignored her touch, fought to stay under control, not to slip backward.

"I'd stay—" The church bell began to strike. Panic washed over Aimee's face. "I want to stay. Believe me. I love you." As the bell continued to toll, her voice grew faint. Realizing he couldn't let her leave like this, couldn't let their last seconds be lost in his anger, Drystan spun, reached out for her, but as the bell struck twelve, she faded and was gone.

IT WAS DARK and cold when Aimee materialized. She was on a street somewhere, a street she didn't recognize, not that she would recognize much through her tears. She swiped the back of her hand across her cheek. The lace on her sleeve scratched her quickly numbing flesh. She glanced down, surprised to see she still wore her wedding gown.

What kind of soul needed a daimon in a wedding gown?

Unable to process that she had lost Drystan, given him up to follow her duty, she staggered forward. Her slippered feet slid in the snow; her hip knocked into a Dumpster she hadn't seen in the dark. She glanced around, saw no one and let herself succumb to a moment of weakness, let her knees bend and her body sag to the ground. She sat there, her body hunched, her chin pressed to her chest, and took in heavy breaths of cold night air.

In the distance a car door slammed. Voices murmured. Aimee reached out and pressed her hand against the brick wall beside her, tried to gather the energy to stand, but she couldn't—not yet. She dropped her hand, kept her head down and said a silent prayer that the voices would pass by, that neither belonged to her new charge—not yet. She couldn't meet him or her yet.

"This was it? I was so out of it…" a male voice spoke softly. "It's still a bad neighborhood. After you died, nothing was done, not that I know of."

"I know." A new voice, deeper. Aimee could hear emotion running through it…sadness, resolve. Something inside her stirred, recognition. The voice belonged to her charge. She had to get herself together, face him. She sucked in a breath, pressed her hands to her face and willed herself under control.

"Aimee?" The second voice, the voice of her charge.

Aimee blinked, a new recognition rolling over her. She looked up, her fingers curling into the skirt of her gown, her heart thumping so hard she could hear nothing else.

Standing in front of her, his shape silhouetted by headlights that shone at his back, was Drystan.

In two steps he was beside her. His hands reached for her waist, and he pulled her off the ground.

"I thought I'd lost you," he murmured against her hair. "But you're here. You're here."

Aimee was trembling, her hands shaking so badly she could barely wrap her fingers around the lapel of his coat. "How? You're…you're my…"

"Yours. I'm yours and you're mine, and I'm never letting you go. Do you hear me? No matter what. Nothing can make me let you go." His hands were in her hair and his lips on her mouth. And finally, Aimee realized what had happened, that she had made the right choice, that she could be a daimon and have Drystan, too. That he was her reward, and that he was right, nothing would ever separate them again—nothing.

She laced her arms around his neck, met him, kiss for kiss, and held on, just like she planned on holding on, forever.

* * * * *

SUNDOWN
Linda Winstead Jones

ABOUT THE AUTHOR

Linda Winstead Jones has written more than fifty romance books in several subgenres. She has won the Colorado Romance Writers Award of Excellence twice, is a three-time RITA® Award finalist and, writing as Linda Fallon, won the 2004 RITA® Award for Paranormal Romance. Linda lives in northern Alabama with her husband of thirty-four years. Visit her website at www.lindawinsteadjones.com.

For Danniele Worsham and Marilyn Puett,
"Children" I never thought to have.
May your futures be bright!

CHAPTER ONE

THE UNDERLYING THRUM of heartbeats. Tempting scents and primitive urges denied. It was a night like thousands—tens of thousands of others.

Abby stood behind the long, polished bar of her place, wiping down a beer mug until it shone like the row of gleaming glasses lined up behind her. She studied the customers, subtly keeping an eye on them much in the way a mother hen might, though no one who knew her well would mistake her for such a caring creature. On the other side of the room a number of round tables arranged around a small dance floor were populated by a mixture of vampires and humans, regulars for the most part. Things were quiet tonight, as Tuesdays often were. Friday and Saturday would be another story; weekends around here were rarely what anyone would call quiet.

The vampires here were, of course, acutely aware of the humans in their midst. Thirsty as they were, tempted as they might be by the scent of fresh blood and living flesh and the gentle, steady thudding of a dozen heartbeats beneath warm skin, they were not allowed to hunt within ten miles of Abby's place, and they were expressly forbidden to ever take the life of one of her customers. She was the oldest in town, and they respected—and even feared—the strength that came with centuries of survival in an unfriendly world. There was no official hierarchy, no appointed position. She was the strongest among those who gathered here, and so she led.

Abby did her best to show those of her kind who would listen that it wasn't necessary to take lives in order to survive. She wasn't tenderhearted and she didn't have any special fondness for humans, but logic drove her to be cautious and to convince others of the necessity. The existence of vampires was best served if there wasn't a constant stream of dead, bloodless humans to explain away. Besides, why kill when you could drink your fill, touch a weak mind and make your donor forget, and continue to live in one place for many years without fear of being discovered? Only the stupidest, the most out of control, killed their prey.

The humans who imbibed and talked and laughed in Abby's bar had no idea that they drank next to monsters, the stuff of fantastical nightmares. That was as it should be. Most of them lived in the neighborhood, mortals blind to the fact that some of the other customers in their favorite bar never actually drank the whiskey or beer placed before them. They didn't think it odd that the two groups never mingled, that there was an invisible but impenetrable wall between them. Instinct kept them from making friendly gestures toward the vampires; innate self-preservation prevented them from asking too many questions. They drank, sometimes too much. They paid, they laughed, they left the day's troubles behind. And they listened to Remy's music.

Remy played piano on the raised stage, his fingers moving with the ease brought on by more than two hundred years of practice. The piano itself was nothing special—it had been bought at a discount from a retiring piano teacher—but in Remy's hands the beat-up upright became special. Jazz was his favorite style, but in the hours the Sundown Bar was open to the public—to the living—he played to the crowd. Country and classic rock, for the most part, but always with a touch of the jazz he loved. No one played "Blue" quite like Remy, and he could bring the house down with "Sweet Home Alabama." At the moment Remy was using the surname Zeringue, but like Abby, he changed his last name often.

Abby had lived in a lot of different places over the years. Big cities, small towns and villages, mountain-top cabins, a cave—though not for very long—and an isolated farm or two. Budding Corner, Alabama, was a midsize town, large enough to keep her business profitable, small enough that the place wasn't overrun with rogue vamps, who usually preferred the anonymity and massive feeding ground of a large city. Here the air was clean, which was a comfort for her sensitive nose. The days were quiet and the residents were into easy living and minding their own business. What more could she ask for?

When the door to the windowless bar opened, almost every head in the room turned to see who was entering—no different from any other time that door swung in. Abby cursed beneath her breath, though the man who entered was a regular himself and she should be used to seeing him by now. Since Stryker had moved to Budding Corner a few short months back he'd stopped by her place almost every night, sometimes for a few minutes, other nights for hours. Abby wasn't bothered by cops. She paid her bills; she adhered to health codes and ABC regulations to the letter; she was very careful to do nothing that might call attention to her.

But this particular cop had been hanging around too often and too long. Detective Leo Stryker was observant—unlike the other humans in the room, unlike the large majority of the humans Abby met. There was something about him that made her nervous.

And he kept asking her out. On a date.

As Stryker approached the bar Abby grabbed a bottle of Jack Daniel's. Jack and Coke was his drink, and he never had more than one. Two on a really bad night a couple of months ago, but for the most part when his one drink was done and she turned down his always-charming offer of a date, he headed out the door. Leo left alone every time, even though more than one customer had made it clear that he didn't have to go home without a companion. He could get lucky in the parking lot night after night. But he didn't.

She placed a glass on the bar where Leo always sat, but he waved her off. "Nothing for me tonight," he said, taking his badge out and unnecessarily flashing it for her. "I'm here on official business."

Abby didn't allow her concern to show. Official business could be as simple as a patron parking their car where they should not, or a sign improperly displayed, or maybe one of her human customers was up to no good and he wanted to ask questions about that human. She smiled at him; he did not smile back as he usually did.

Leo took his usual bar stool and leaned onto the bar. If she was warm-blooded and into dating, she'd definitely accept his invitations. For a mortal he was quite handsome and well built, with medium-dark blond hair cut fairly short, but not severely so, expressive blue eyes and a strong jaw. His neck was thick and muscled and she could smell it from where she stood, a good four feet away. He had to be at least six foot two, a good twelve inches taller than she was, and he was a big guy—big arms, broad shoulders, large hands. Her mouth watered. It was the scent that got to her most strongly. She clenched her fists behind the bar, so he couldn't see her reaction. She was rarely so tempted, and it bothered her that this human had become something akin to a weakness.

It was past time for her to feed from a living, breathing human being with a heartbeat and deliciously warm skin, but she'd be an idiot to drink from an overly observant cop, no matter how tasty he smelled, no matter how pleasing he was to the eye. Besides, it wasn't as if she was about to break her own rules about tasting the customers.

"Do you know a girl by the name of Marisa Blackwell?"

"Sure," Abby said, momentarily relieved. What on earth could Marisa Blackwell have done to get herself into trouble? Marisa was a regular, a quiet, pretty young girl who seemed harmless enough. Still, looks could be deceiving. Abby herself was proof of that. "What did she do?"

Leo's expression hardened. "She got herself murdered, and her roommate says the Sundown Bar was her last stop."

LEO WATCHED ABBY for a reaction, as he always did when he questioned anyone concerning a murder. The news of Blackwell's death seemed to make Abby angry. She wasn't visibly shocked, she didn't cry or shake…but she was not unaffected.

"I'm so sorry," she said softly, her voice reaching inside him and grabbing, as it always did. "What happened?"

"It wasn't a natural death, I can tell you that much." He wasn't about to explain to her, or to anyone else, that the victim's blood had been drained from her body, that the pretty girl's throat had been practically torn out. He couldn't explain yet what had happened, but he didn't want to alarm anyone. If that tidbit hit the newspapers and the television news, there would be hell to pay. Budding Corner's only newspaper was a thin weekly filled with the escapades of the mayor and city councilmen, as well as a shitload of recipes and letters to the editor, and the closest television station was in Huntsville, so maybe he could keep the details quiet for a while. "Do you remember who she was with last night?"

Abby's eyes narrowed. Even though he was here on business tonight, he couldn't help but note—not for the first time—that she was a striking woman. Beautiful, yes, but the world was filled with beautiful women. This one was somehow different, and he'd known it from the first moment he'd laid eyes on her. Abby Brown had long, dark hair, pale green eyes, a body that wouldn't quit and a face that would've been at home on a statue of a goddess. Her plain, white, button-up shirt gaped when she moved just so, revealing a tiny little bit of swelling cleavage, but not so much that she was flashing the customers in order to get better tips. The sight was very nice, after a long, crappy day.

But what called him to her went beyond her looks.

She was smart, she was savvy and she kept secrets. He knew it; he felt it in his bones; he saw it in her eyes. And dammit, he wanted to uncover every one of her secrets—along with what lay beneath that plain blouse and whatever else she wore. She was partial to longish skirts that offered no more than an occasional flash of calf, on the rare occasions she stepped out from behind the bar.

He kept asking her out and she kept turning him down. For many divorced men that rejection might be traumatic. Abby's refusals were never brutal, but there was a certainty in her eyes and in her voice that would've warned most men away. Far, far away. Leo intended to keep trying; he was known for his patience and persistence, and he wanted this woman. One of these days he'd wear her down. A woman like Abby would be worth a little trauma and a bruise or two to his ego.

"She came in with a friend of hers," Abby said, answering his question. "Alicia, I believe."

"Yes," Leo responded. "We spoke to Alicia this afternoon."

Abby stared a hole through him. "Then why did you ask me who she was with?"

"I'd like to know if Alicia remembers last night's events correctly."

Abby leaned into the bar, bringing her face closer to his—but not close enough to suit him. She breathed deeply, once. "Detective Stryker, be honest. You want to know if one of us would be so foolish as to lie to you."

He couldn't help but smile a little. "There is that. And how many times do I have to tell you to call me Leo? I've been in here damn near every night for the past three months." When he'd moved to this little podunk town and taken a job as an investigator with a department much smaller than the one in Birmingham, he'd taken a cut in pay and had traded his very nice condo for a ramshackle rental house at the edge of town, a house he kept telling himself was only temporary. It had been worth every sacrifice to get away from his ex and all the reminders of the years they'd spent together—good and bad. Finding a woman like Abby here had been a nice little bonus, or would be if she'd give him the time of day.

The woman he'd been fantasizing about for months had never stared at him quite this way. Her eyes met his and held them, and he could swear he felt that gaze to his soul. It burned a little, it invaded, and he couldn't help but squirm.

"The two girls came in together," she said, her voice smooth and sensual. "As they often do. They had margaritas, two each. They were approached by two men who are not regular customers, young men I would guess to be in their midtwenties, who brought them each another margarita. Around ten in the evening, Marisa left. Alone. Alicia left an hour or so later in the company of one of the gentlemen.

The other stayed awhile longer. I'm afraid I didn't get their names, and they paid cash."

That wasn't much more help than Alicia's story that the guys' names were Jason and Mike, no last names offered or asked for, and they were simply "traveling through." Alicia had taken Mike home with her, but where had Jason gone?

"Did you often see Marisa and her friends here so late on a work night?"

"Sometimes," she responded in a smooth voice.

"I don't suppose either of those men is here tonight." Leo turned on his bar stool to survey the room, knowing what her answer would be. He recognized everyone here.

"No," Abby said as Leo watched the cocktail waitress Margaret, a blonde who was almost as beautiful as her employer, serve a tray of bottled beers to an appreciative table. Every man there took a moment to study Margaret's nicely displayed cleavage or long legs, depending on their body part of interest. She didn't seem to be offended, but then, if you dressed that way it wouldn't make much sense to be easily offended by open appreciation.

"You seem to have a good memory," he said to the woman behind the bar. "Think you can provide a description for a sketch artist?"

"I can do better than that."

He spun around to face Abby once more. "How's that?"

She cocked her head slightly and it seemed that for a moment there was no one in the room but the two of them. Leo held his breath; he almost forgot why he was there.

"I'm a bit of an artist myself," Abby said. "After we close up tonight I'll draw the men as I remember them."

"Thanks." He leaned into the bar, wishing he could order a drink and stick around and just look at her for a while longer. She could certainly make a bad day better, if she put her mind to it. But tonight he had work to do. Marisa Blackwell's was the first murder in Budding Corner in seventeen years, and folks were excited. They were also worried. It hadn't been your normal robbery murder and it sure didn't look like your everyday domestic violence. Much as he wanted a drink, he wouldn't consider himself off duty until this case was solved. "Can I pick the sketches up in the morning?"

Abby smiled at him, but there was no warmth in her expression. The smile, like everything about her, was cool and controlled. Man, how he would love to make her lose control. How he wanted to discover the secrets beyond the cool exterior. "I'll stick them on the front door of the bar in the morning and you can pick them up at any time."

"I'd rather collect them from you, in case I have any more questions."

"That's not necessary, is it?"

He leaned over the bar. "I really don't like the idea of the sketches out in the open where anyone could snag them. It'll be best if I take them straight from your hand. Over lunch?"

Was that a smile? Maybe.

"If you must collect the sketches directly from me you can pick them up tomorrow night. We open at sundown, as you well know." She gestured to the red-and-gold neon sign behind her. The Sundown Bar. It was fine to have a gimmick, but wasn't this taking things too far? Her insistence in not opening until after sunset had made the summer days too long, and he was glad autumn had arrived and the nights were now a bit longer.

"We need those sketches as soon as possible. Is there any chance…"

Abby offered a hand over the bar, palm up. The fingers were long and pale and slender, and she wore no jewelry. No ring, no watch or bracelet. He was too old to be tempted this way, especially when he was working, but he had an almost uncontrollable urge to grab that hand and lick the palm. Just once.

"Do you have a card?" she asked, as he ignored the hand she offered. "I'll call you if I get the drawings finished sooner and wish to meet you earlier in the day."

"Sure." He fished a card out of his jacket pocket and laid it in her hand. The tips of his fingers brushed her palm, which seemed oddly cool. She'd been handling ice and cold bottles, he reminded himself as he stood, nodded and reluctantly headed for the door.

WHEN THE DOOR had closed behind Leo, Abby dropped the card he'd given her in the trash can at her feet. She'd have to wait until 2:00 a.m., when the human customers would be forced to leave, and then she'd interrogate her vampire friends and patrons. Surely none of them would be so foolish as to not only feed upon but also kill one of her customers, but she'd plucked a vision from Leo's head and she knew Marisa had been attacked at her throat. A human might've attacked her there, but the wound he had remembered so vividly indicated a vampire, a vicious one—and if a vamp had done the deed it was likely he or she had been here. Like called to like, and besides, after two in the morning she served blood. This was the only place for two hundred miles or more that a vamp could order a pint. She served pigs' blood for the most part, which tasted like crap if it wasn't warmed properly. She had become an expert at preparing a safe, easy meal. Pigs' blood wouldn't entirely satisfy a vamp forever, but oftentimes it was enough.

Killing the customers was against Abby's rules, and though she was not the biggest or the physically strongest vampire in the world, or even in the country, she was the oldest and most powerful for hundreds of miles. At more than four hundred years old, she had powers those who flocked to her had not yet developed. The other vamps were drawn to her; they respected her; they obeyed her. Many newer vampires came here to learn from her, either sent by their makers or drawn by instincts they had not yet perfected and yet could not reject. She helped guide them to control, to hone whatever powers they'd been given. It was only through control and strength that a vampire could survive. The weak were lucky to last a year.

Her undead customers and students would tell her the truth of what had happened to Marisa, and then she could help Leo with those portraits.

But not before sundown tomorrow. She could very easily get the sketches done before dawn and leave them at the bar door, but if he insisted on taking them from her hand he would have to wait. She'd only told him she'd consider meeting earlier to get him off her back.

The hours after Leo left passed quickly, and Abby busied herself cleaning up behind the bar. She might've spent some of that time in her office, taking care of the tedious paperwork that went along with owning a business. But she remained behind the bar, keeping an eye on her customers, wondering if one of them was a murderer. As the hour grew late the human patrons left, one or two at a time. The vampires watched those remaining humans very closely, willing them to leave, waiting for the moment when they could have the bar to themselves. Those few lagging customers began to instinctively realize that they were not wanted. They squirmed. Now and then they glanced with trepidation to the silent and too-still group that remained. Remy's repertoire changed from country tunes to pure jazz, his fingers flying over the keys with inhuman speed. By one-thirty there wasn't a human left in the place.

Margaret locked the main entrance after the last mortal patron departed, and then she turned to blatantly admire the piano player. The sole barmaid in this establishment was a young vamp who listened intently to Abby's lessons. She did her job well, but had an annoyingly obvious crush on Remy, a crush she didn't even attempt to hide. The piano man continued to play, but the tune he switched to after the last of the humans had gone was softer. Gentler. The notes drifted through Abby's blood, and if she was not so angry she'd take great pleasure in the tune.

The vampires who remained looked at Abby expectantly, waiting for her to fetch the blood and warm it properly. This was what they'd been waiting for, after all. A safe feeding. Nourishment. The blood they craved.

Instead of going to the back room for the pigs' blood, she walked around the bar and confronted them all. She lifted a single hand and Remy instantly stopped playing. The sound of the last note hung in the air for a moment, reverberating.

"One of my clientele has been killed," Abby said, her voice even and cold. She looked from one face to the next, searching for a clue. She couldn't see visions from the minds of those like her, only from humans, so the thoughts of her vampire customers were black to her. She searched for signs that one or more of them had recently fed well on human blood, but they all looked hungry. They were all anxious for the pigs' blood, twitching with need, in some cases. If one among them had drained a woman last night that would not be the case. Unless he or she was a very good actor.

It was Charles who looked expectantly from face to face. "We're all here, so you must be talking about a human. What's the big deal? They don't exactly have a long shelf life."

Charles could see snippets of the near future, when he put forth the effort. Usually he misused his gift to choose the mortal women who could give him what he wanted—easy sex and nourishment. He hadn't killed, though, at least not to her knowledge. Charles, with his long, fair hair and pretty face, had been handsome as a human and was even more so as an immortal. The life agreed with him; he embraced it.

And he was annoying her. "Short *shelf life* or not, it is against the rules to kill my customers."

He lifted his hands in easy surrender. "Just saying, boss."

"It couldn't have been one of us," Margaret argued. "I mean, why? We have food aplenty, thanks to you."

Remy nodded his head in agreement. "No one here would dare, Abigail." With his Cajun accent he made the statement sound easy, nonchalant. But there was a fire behind his eyes. Did he believe what he said? His eyes met hers, but she couldn't decipher any alternate meaning there.

But they had a point. It was a relief to be able to believe that whatever had happened to Marisa had not originated here, in her place. As Charles had pointed out, all of her regulars were present tonight, each and every one of them, and they were anxious to be fed. Remy, Margaret, Charles, Gina, Dalton—a dozen more. So, had a rogue vampire killed Marisa or had a human done the deed?

Humans could be as deadly and merciless as any monster.

She knew *that* all too well.

CHAPTER TWO

AFTER THE VAMPIRES had been fed they peeled away from the place, one by one, or two by two. Abby cleaned, allowing Margaret to help for a little while before she sent the blonde on her way. When the bar was in good shape, ready for the next day's business, Abby left by the rear door. A very short walk from that back door sat a small, eight-unit apartment building that wasn't much to look at. It was boxy and faded, as plain as any structure could be. She owned it. For now, that sad-looking beige building was home. Upstairs she'd knocked out a couple of walls and had converted the entire second floor into a very nice place. The building might not look like much on the outside, but beyond those walls the rooms were not at all ordinary. Margaret and Remy each leased an apartment downstairs, and the other two units were usually rented out to a vamp passing through. A couple of times she'd leased to humans, but they never stayed very long. They didn't know what was wrong with their new home, but their instincts warned them to get out. And they did.

She hadn't taken three steps away from the back door when an unexpected voice startled her.

"I don't suppose you have those sketches yet."

Abby spun around. Leo Stryker stood in shadow, but she should've sensed him there the moment she'd opened the door. The news of Marisa's murder had her rattled. She never got rattled these days. The fact that a human could surprise and even unnerve her was annoying.

"No, I don't." She gathered her composure. "I believe I told you I'd have them for you tomorrow."

The detective stepped out of the shadows. "You did. I just thought I'd take a chance. It never hurts to ask."

"Have you been waiting all this time?" she asked, realizing as she voiced her question that if he'd been here for hours, so close, she would've known it. She would've felt his presence.

Leo shrugged his shoulders. "After I left here I went to the office for a while. I did a bit of research online, read the medical examiner's report for the umpteenth time, and studied crime scene photographs I'll never be able to get out of my head. I was on my way home, passing by the Sundown Bar, and something just…pulled me in."

Marisa's murder was indeed important to Leo, but when he'd turned into Abby's parking lot he had not had murder on his mind. Murder was his business; he'd come here for the purpose of forgetting that nasty business for a while.

They were alone in the dark, without Remy's music, without the rumbling conversation and laughter of a room full of people—and vampires. It was easy to reach into Leo's mind and see what he really wanted, what he always wanted. Her.

"Why me?" she asked.

"Those sketches…"

"You're not here to ask me about the sketches," she interrupted. "You're not here to investigate Marisa's murder at all."

In the darkness she could see Leo much more clearly than he could see her. His eyes were lively. His face was friendly and determined at the same time, if that were possible. Had she unknowingly done something to draw him to her? She could and had mesmerized human males in order to get what she wanted and needed from them, but she had *not* used her influence on this man. If only she could use her sway to make him disappear, to repulse him…and then the truth hit her. She could do just that, could've done it at any time over the past three months, and yet she hadn't. She didn't now.

"I want to know why you won't go out with me," he said. "There's not another man, I know that."

"How could you possibly know there's no other man in my life?"

"You live alone, and there's never any guy hanging

possessively around you at the bar. I thought for a while maybe you and Remy had a thing going, but I've seen you two together and you don't act like a couple. You're good friends, I suspect, but there's not a hint of jealousy from either one of you and you rarely touch. Besides," he confessed, smiling gently, "I asked Margaret."

The last thing she needed was a cop taking an interest in her. If he started asking questions, if he got too curious, she'd have to move from this place long before she was prepared to. She liked it here in Budding Corner; she liked her home and her business, and while there was always another home and another bar down the road, she liked this one and wanted it to last. How was she going to get rid of Leo? The truth was disturbing; she didn't want to hurt him. She would *not* hurt him.

But if he learned what she was…

"Lunch," he said. "That's easy enough and really can't be considered romantic."

"No."

"A picnic by the lake," he suggested, undaunted. "More romantic, I suppose, but totally innocent."

Abby took a step toward Leo, drawn by his scent and his throat and his heartbeat and the arousing images in his mind. She was a vampire, but she was also a woman, and occasionally she was beset with a woman's needs and desires. It was a weakness to crave more than blood from a man, and yet she did crave. Humans were food, they were occasionally suitable for entertainment, they were pets, at best. What she was experiencing at this moment went against everything she taught, everything she believed. To become too closely involved with humans meant the very real possibility of exposure. Knowing that didn't make her want Leo any less.

"Innocent?" she said. "I do not think you want innocent from me."

His heart rate increased. She heard and felt it. He blushed, a little, the blood rushing into his face. And lower.

"Tell me what you really want," she whispered as she stopped directly before him. Her hand rose and rested lightly on his chest. Beneath the jacket and shirt and tie she felt his lovely heartbeat. She leaned into him, rested her cheek on his shoulder, moved her lips toward the throb in his throat, testing her own control. "You don't want lunch." A need she had not experienced in a long time sprang to life in an unexpectedly strong way. There was no bar between her and Leo now, no audience of humans and vamps watching. Her own body never throbbed, not in the way it once had, but so close, so very close, she felt a growing and urgent need to take what she should not from this man who was so eager to give it. "You don't want to take me on a picnic. You don't want lunch. This is what you want, isn't it?"

Abby kissed Leo's throat gently. She could almost

taste the blood that raced beneath his skin, and she craved it. She had not yearned so desperately for the warmth of human blood on her tongue in a very long time; she took a taste when she could and she enjoyed it, but she did not yearn. And now she was overcome with excitement and craving and desire. She was being swept away; she was losing control. This was like being new and desperately hungry, but she *did* have control and she exercised it now.

Leo wrapped his arms around her and moved her—danced her—into the deeper shadows at the back of the bar. He took her head in his hands and kissed her, and she let him. It had been a long time since Abby had been kissed, and she liked it. She'd missed this sort of touch, the loss of control, the soaring passion. The kiss was more powerful than she remembered any kiss being, more moving and arousing as their lips moved in a magnificent rhythm.

She tasted Leo's tongue as it speared into her mouth. He was so warm he felt hot to her, and she knew that to him she would feel cool. Did he like her cool skin or did it repulse him? Did he think it odd or was he already beyond rational thought? He did not kiss like a man who was repulsed. Whatever restraint he'd been exercising was gone, and the images in his mind came fast and furious. They were chaotic and powerful and primitive, and she knew without question what he wanted.

"You want to be inside me," she said, her lips still touching his.

He didn't respond verbally, but his mouth found her throat and he suckled there as he pushed her skirt high with the intention of removing her panties, only to discover that she wore none. She felt his response and it moved her; his passion, his need rushed through her, as well as through him. They shared a fine, lightning moment of desire and need that wiped away everything else. She lowered the zipper of his trousers and reached inside to touch him, to free him.

Blood flowed to his penis, making it hard and hot, and she wanted it in a way she had not wanted anything for a very long time. She craved the heat and the connection, she wanted the pleasure she'd denied herself for a very long time. She trembled with need.

So did he.

In one smooth motion he lifted her, and she wrapped her legs around him. A muscular man, he did not stumble under her weight or prop her against the wall, but held her steady without any additional support. She liked that he was strong, in body, as well as in heartbeat and desire. He was a fitting partner for a strong woman who had been without male companionship for so many years she could not begin to count them.

Clutching one another, close to coming together

and yet enjoying the delicious anticipation of what they knew was to come, they kissed again. Leo's tongue speared into her mouth and Abby rocked her hips, bringing him closer, teasing them both, reveling in the unexpected desire he had brought to life within her.

Leo suffered a troubling thought, an image that flitted through his mind, unwanted but important. She soothed his fears without waiting for him to adjust his stance and fumble in his wallet for the condom he thought he needed.

"I can't have children," she whispered.

That news came as a relief to Leo, as he did not wish to pause what had begun. Unable to wait any longer he pushed inside her, filled her, pumped into her hard and fast. The sensation of being joined was startling and sharp and wondrous and warm, so warm. She had forgotten the intensity of the pleasure of sex; she had forgotten the sheer force of the urges that drew a man and a woman together. She rode him as hard as he pushed into her, hanging on, reveling not only in the physical sensations but in the images in his head. At this moment she was not a teacher, not a leader. She was just a woman taking pleasure from a man. Completion teased her and she slowed, not wanting this moment to be over too soon.

She felt Leo throughout her body, she felt him completely, in an intense rush of pleasure that usually only came to her when she took blood. If she could have both...oh, if she could have both...

With that thought Abby came, the orgasm washing over her with unexpected ferocity. She cried out, she shook, and unable to control herself she lowered her mouth to Leo's throat. A kiss, a lick, and then, as he found his own release, she extended her fangs and bit down.

Blood poured over her tongue, and she tasted not only that warm, nourishing blood, but the power of Leo's pleasure. They were joined entirely, in mind and body, by blood and by lust. He pounded into her and she sucked at his throat, drawing his life into her, tasting all that he was. The world he lived in was filled with colors and beauty and life. She felt that life, she smelled and tasted it.

Leo took a couple of unsteady steps and rested her body and his against the back wall of her bar. He gasped; he panted; he did not release her as she continued to feed. One more sip, one last gulp. And then one more.

Abby felt the weakness that washed over him and she jerked her head away, removing her fangs from his delicious throat. She leaned in for a lick that would cause the wound to heal quickly, but she couldn't allow herself more than that. What had she done? Instead of enjoying a taste she'd latched on and taken nearly twice as much as she should've. If she'd had less control she might've drained him while he was still inside her.

His breath came hard, he shook a little, but he held her. This was what he'd dreamed of, she knew. He'd fantasized about just such an encounter, but she wondered if he'd ever expected they would end up here, like this. She certainly had not. Tempted to distraction by a human. How awkward.

Abby knew what she had to do. For Leo, this encounter could not have happened. She would remember him for a very long time, perhaps forever, but he had to forget it all. It was easy enough. All she had to do was look into Leo's eyes and push at his mind, and he'd forget. The conversation, the kiss, the sex… the fact that she'd drunk from his throat…the fact that he wanted her at all…all gone.

"You're amazing," he said, his voice husky. "I always knew you'd be amazing, I knew it from the first time I saw you. Now that I have you I'm not going to let you go. Take me home with you."

"No."

"Then come back to my place. It's pretty much a shithole, but…"

"I can't."

"I want you again," he said, his voice all but growling.

And she wanted him, much more than she should. She'd tried to turn his mind away from such thoughts, but perhaps that was impossible while they were still joined and shaking. An incredible thought crossed her mind. Could she keep him for a while? Could she make Leo a lover? Feed from him gently, take the pleasure he offered her, be not alone? With a human? Romantic bonds among vampires were not unknown, though they were fairly rare. Sexual partnerships were much more common, but they did not normally last more than a hundred years or so. And here she was actually considering forming such a bond with a mortal man?

What a terrible idea. In a completely illogical way she wanted Leo to forever remember what had happened here tonight, she wanted him to remember *her*, but if he did then he'd show up night after night, and she would not be able to resist him. At this rate she'd end up killing him within a month.

"Put me down," she said.

He did, reluctantly, and when she stood before him she took his face in her hands and looked him in the eye. She stared well past the eyes, into the heart and soul and mind of him. Without words she commanded him to go home, to take a shower and wash the scent of her off his skin. She ordered him to go to bed and forget what had happened. Reluctantly, more reluctantly than she liked, she commanded him to forget the way he wanted her.

This man was too tempting for her to keep, even for a little while; he was the kind of man who could ruin the orderly life she'd made for herself.

LEO PULLED INTO the driveway of his rented house, foggy-brained and exhausted. He glanced at the clock on the dashboard before turning the key and shutting down the engine. Where the hell had the night gone?

He stumbled a bit on his way to the dark front porch, but quickly regained his footing. Should've left a light on, he supposed. Hell, he was exhausted, and the days to come weren't going to be any better. He was determined to catch the man who'd killed Marisa Blackwell. No one should have to die that way. He was far from perfect, as his ex-wife had been so fond of reminding him, but he did his job well. Maybe he occasionally forgot a birthday or brought the job home with him, but he was who he was, and he couldn't always leave that at the door. Catching bad guys and locking them away was his calling. Once he got his teeth into a case he didn't let go. With that thought he instinctively raised a hand to his throat.

Inside the house he dropped the case file on a table in the hallway and headed for the bathroom, craving a hot shower as if it would wash the stink of the day off him. He stripped unconsciously, bathed quickly and stepped out to dry himself off. His mind went to Abby Brown, as it too often did, and he realized that there was no reason for him to be so obsessed with her. She'd made it clear she wasn't interested, so he'd move on. The world was filled with women and Abby Brown wasn't any more special than any other. He might as well just give up where she was concerned.

He crawled into bed and closed his eyes, and right before he drifted off his mind took a sharp turn. Abby Brown was special. She was the kind of woman who was worth fighting for. And he was willing to do battle for her.

ABBY HADN'T BEEN inside her apartment long when someone knocked gently on the door. Not Remy, she knew from the hesitant knock. Certainly not Leo, who should be sound asleep by now, dreaming of other, more suitable women. She answered the door to find Margaret in the doorway. The pretty girl looked over Abby's shoulder as if she expected to see someone there.

"I'm alone," Abby said.

"Oh. I was sure I smelled a man." She looked at Abby and her eyes went wide. "But that's none of my business. That's not why I'm here."

"Why *are* you here?" Abby stepped back and gestured for Margaret to enter.

"I'm worried about what you asked us about tonight." Margaret wrung her hands. "The poor dead girl who was in the bar last night, Marisa. I hate to think that maybe one of us killed her."

"So do I."

"I mean, she was human, but she was pretty nice most of the time. She left good tips. Most of the young girls don't leave good tips at all."

Abby sighed.

Margaret sat on Abby's long, sunset-colored sofa. The reddish-orange was bright, a flash of color in a world where to watch the sun set was impossible. The young vamp didn't need to rest, not anymore, and yet there were times Margaret seemed to forget that she was no longer human. In time, all that was left of her humanity would fade, and she'd be happier for it. Not yet fifty years old, Margaret was still learning.

"It could've been another human, I suppose, and if a vampire did the deed he could've been, you know, passing through. But I was wondering, if there's a rogue vampire, won't he come to us eventually? Won't he be drawn to us the way Charles and Dalton were?"

"Possibly."

"He could just as easily kill one of us, couldn't he?"

"I suppose he could, but no vamp, no matter how hungry he might be, would feed on another vampire if there was any other choice." Immortality and invulnerability did not go hand in hand.

"But some vamps do…"

"Our blood is cold," Abby said sharply. No vampire should have such fear as this one did. "It would nourish but would not be particularly tasty. Vampires only kill other vampires when there's a feud of some kind, a slight or an insult."

"But vampires do sometimes feed on one another during, you know, sex."

"That's different."

"I know." Again, Margaret fidgeted.

"Don't worry," Abby said. "If a rogue comes to us, he comes. He or she, I should say. However, if the vampire who killed Marisa Blackwell is truly rogue he's already moved on to another town and another victim." The creature who'd sucked Marisa dry wouldn't come to Abby's place hungry for pigs' blood.

"I hope you're right. I wouldn't want anyone to get hurt, especially not Remy."

Abby had to fight to contain her smile. "Remy can take care of himself."

"Yeah, he can." Margaret dipped her head. "Okay, I know I shouldn't say anything, but I admire you. You're my hero, really you are, and to see you take up with a human, it breaks my heart, it truly does."

"That's none of your business," Abby snapped.

"I know that, but I had to warn you. I'm not the only one who sees the way Leo Stryker looks at you. Charles commented on it tonight, right before he left. He said it wasn't fitting for a vampire in your position to be so soft on a human. Using them is one thing, but to truly be friendly just never works. Maybe Charles is jealous, I don't know, but he doesn't like that cop at all. And unless you scrub the smell of him off your skin I'm not going to be the only one to know that you've taken it a step further." She looked up and wrinkled her nose slightly. "He's not like the others, the humans who are so easy to manipulate. We all see it, so surely you do, too. I like it here. I don't want to leave, not yet. If you end up killing a cop we'll all have to disappear in the night, and that will cause a stir. That was the first lesson you taught me. Be invisible, you said."

"I'm not going to kill Stryker."

"How can you be sure?" Margaret fidgeted on the sofa. "The first guy I slept with after I turned, I swear, I couldn't help myself. I sucked the poor fella dry before I knew what I was doing, and it was so damn *good*. I thought I'd do better the second time around, but it didn't work out too well. Not for him, at least. That's one of the reasons I'm determined to confine my romantic relationships to those of my own kind, from here on out."

Meaning Remy, of course.

Abby walked closer to the blonde on the couch. "I am not a fledgling who can't control myself. I have no intention of killing anyone, least of all a cop, nor do I intend to let him, or anyone else, get too close." She leaned down and placed her face uncomfortably close to Margaret's. "And my personal life is none of your concern."

As soon as Abby backed away, Margaret jumped

up and headed for the door. "Sorry. I really do have the best of intentions. I think you and I could be friends eventually. We have so much in common, after all."

Abby had friends across the world, but none so young or naive as this one.

When Margaret was gone, Abby stripped off the clothes that still smelled of Leo, only to discover that she herself smelled of him even more strongly. In this one instance, Margaret was right. Leo was different.

CHAPTER THREE

LEO WOKE WITH a killer headache. If not for the fact that the murder investigation was so new, he'd call in sick—and he never took a sick day. Lying in bed, barely awake and trying to still the pounding in his head, he wished he could get the image of the dead girl out of his mind. He'd seen the bodies of murder victims before, but they hadn't been anything like this one. Marisa Blackwell had been mutilated, she'd been ripped apart. Swear to God, it looked as though someone had chewed her up and spit her out.

Headache or not, he had people to question today, and he'd be picking up those sketches from Abby Brown. If the sketches were crap he'd bring an ABI sketch artist into her bar and they wouldn't leave until she gave a decent description. Budding Corner didn't have much of a police force; much of a police force wasn't called for, on most occasions, but the Alabama Bureau of Investigation had made their resources available for this case. In a couple of days, ABI investigators would arrive to take over the case, if he didn't solve it before then. As much as he appreciated good help, Leo wanted the murderer in custody before someone arrived to take the case away from him.

In spite of the details of the gruesome case that filled his thoughts, his mind turned to the pleasure of seeing Abby Brown again. Why the hell did he so look forward to spending time with her when she'd made it clear she didn't want to have anything to do with him? A niggling thought teased him. She wasn't worth the trouble. She really wasn't all that good-looking or special or tempting. There were better women out there, women who would give him the time of day. A moment later he rejected those thoughts. The divorce had messed him up more than he'd realized, that was the only explanation. He'd been newly single for two years, transplanted here in this small town for a little more than three months, and instead of getting on with his life he'd gotten fixated on a woman who'd made it clear he was *not* her type.

Why was he so certain she was wrong about that?

Messed up or not, he wasn't waiting until tonight to get those sketches. He knew where Abby lived, after all.

His rented house, the one he kept telling himself was temporary even though he'd made no attempt to find another place, had two small bedrooms and one ancient bathroom. Still, there were a couple of benefits to the place. While he remained in the city limits, barely, the house was remote. He'd never lived in such a quiet place, and he was discovering that he liked the silence. On this crisp autumn morning he heard a few birds, a chirp that might be a chipmunk, and now and then he heard the wind rushing through the trees that surrounded the house. Peaceful moments had been few and far between before his move to Budding Corner.

One other benefit was that the shower had great water pressure. He stood beneath the spray for a long time, letting it pound his face and chest as he thought about the day to come. This morning he had paperwork to take care of, calls to make to the state forensics lab and to the ABI, and there were a couple of Marisa's friends he still wanted to talk to. After that, he was going to drop in on Abby Brown. He smiled. She wasn't going to like him showing up unannounced, but that was too bad. He had the high ground, here. This was a murder investigation, after all.

Logic made Mike and Jason the prime suspects. If Marisa had been drugged, strangled, beaten, raped or any combination of those sad possibilities, that's where he'd concentrate his investigation. But there was something about the way Marisa had been murdered that screamed of more than the usual sickness. Something darker. He was going to pursue the two men Marisa and Alicia had met in Abby Brown's bar, but they weren't the end of the investigation. They were just a small part of it. What had made Marisa Blackwell tick? Why had she spent so many work nights at a—apologies to Abby—seedy bar? Marisa had a job answering phones in a small car dealership, so her mornings started early enough. Alicia's hours at a downtown boutique were more flexible, but still, these girls had jobs. If Mike and Jason had been the ones to kill Marisa, why had Alicia gotten off without a scratch? No, there was something else going on.

Leo drove past the Sundown Bar on his way to the station. The neon lights were off; the parking lot was empty. His eyes shot to the building where Abby lived. It wasn't much to look at, but he was in no position to make judgments in that regard.

The police station was located in one of the newer buildings in Budding Corner, but it wasn't much to look at, either. It was as square and boxy as the blustery mayor, and had about as much personality. The people who worked there were nice enough. They were dedicated to their jobs, if not the most brilliant among law enforcement. They were good, down-home folks who were well-intentioned, but not exactly what anyone would call razor sharp.

Maybe that was why Leo hadn't made any but the most casual of friends in the past three months. He didn't fit in here; he wasn't one of them. In fact, he felt most at home in Abby Brown's bar. What did it say about him that he was most comfortable in the company of a woman who was a constant source of rejection?

He dismissed Abby Brown from his mind as best he could, and set about working the case. When it came to his personal life he wasn't particularly sharp himself, but when it came to asking questions and separating the truth from the bullshit, he was a star.

WHEN THE DOORBELL rang, Abby ignored it. Now and then people got lost, or a man in an unattractive uniform made a delivery to a wrong address. Eventually whoever it was would go away. She was nicely settled on the long reddish-orange couch that dominated the great room where she spent her sleepless days. Since she was alone, and since her skin was so sensitive, she didn't bother with clothes. Why should she? True, her flesh was all but invulnerable, as long as she stayed out of the sun, but with her heightened senses came an increased sensitivity to touch, to the flow of fabrics across her skin. The caress of silk, or of a properly used hand, was heavenly. The rasp of coarse material or an unskilled touch was bothersome.

Her incredible sensitivity also made sex beyond pleasurable. Until last night, she'd denied herself. How would she continue to deny her urges when the memory was so sharp?

This apartment was her haven. When she wasn't

in the bar she spent most of her time in this great room. There was also a huge bedroom she rarely used—which at this moment seemed a real pity—and a fabulous kitchen that was a waste of space. There were also two largish guest bedrooms. Not that she had many guests, but she knew vampires all over the world and some of them, a rare few, she called friends. It didn't hurt to be prepared for company, even if she only had a guest every fifty years or so. One never knew when a friend might show up looking for sanctuary.

When she'd remodeled she'd had to keep reselling in mind, since she couldn't stay in one place for more than fifteen years or so—and that was lucky. More than one bedroom was called for with that in mind, as was the kitchen.

The doorbell rang again. Persistent sucker.

This great room was filled with bookcases heavy with books, a large wide-screen HDTV and an expensive CD player, along with an impressive collection of CDs and a sleek, new laptop computer. She didn't sleep and couldn't go outside while the sun shone, and she had to have some way to pass the daylight hours. Too bad she couldn't keep Leo around for entertainment. The idea made her smile. Think of the ways they could pass the day if she had him here.

Her smile faded. If she didn't kill him. It was too late for those thoughts, since just last night she'd nudged him away from her, mentally. He wouldn't find her attractive any longer. He likely wouldn't bother to come into the bar at all, once his investigation was over.

The doorbell rang again, and this time it was followed by a deep voice she recognized. "Come on, Abby. I know you're in there. Time to wake up, sleepyhead. I need those sketches."

In a huff she leaped from the couch, grabbing a silky length of decorative fabric in swirls of red and orange and hot pink. She wrapped the soft fabric around her body and stepped to the door.

"Go away!" she shouted.

There was a short pause before Leo said, "No, I don't think so. I've talked to everyone I can without those sketches. Come on, it's almost three in the afternoon. You can't still be asleep."

She knew what angle the sun would be at, this time of day, this time of year. There was also a large silver maple right outside the door, still fully leafed even though September had arrived weeks earlier. Opening the door would not be painful or dangerous as long as she stayed away from the threshold. With a surge of anger she swung the door in to reveal a tall, too tempting, much-too-curious man.

"What do you want?" she asked, taking care to keep the door more closed than open and to keep herself away from any creeping sunlight.

"Sketches."

"You can collect them tonight," she snapped.

Leo looked her up and down, taking in the length of fabric that covered the parts of her that had to be covered for minimal decency's sake and not much more. The same sorts of mental images she'd caught from him last night reappeared. His mind was not entirely on solving his case. Dammit, he should not be thinking of her this way. She'd done what she could to persuade him to forget his obsession.

"Aren't you going to invite me in?" he asked casually.

"Do you need an invitation?"

"I'm a cop, Abby. Yes, I need an invitation. Please?"

She sighed, stepped back, and allowed the door to swing farther open. "Come in, Detective Stryker."

IN HIS ENTIRE life, Leo had never seen anything as tempting as Abby Brown wrapped in a length of thin, colorful fabric. And, quite obviously, nothing else. The fabric clung to her curves, it gaped in interesting places. It barely covered her ass. If he had even a little bit less control he'd be drooling.

Why was a woman like this one alone? Instinctively he glanced toward a door that might—or might not—lead to her bedroom. *Was* she alone? Or did she keep her secrets well?

"How well do you know Remy Zeringue?"

Her eyebrows arched slightly. "Remy? I've known him for years. Why?"

"Marisa's friends say she had it bad for Remy, and a couple of them think they might've been meeting on the sly."

For an instant Abby looked alarmed, and then the telling expression passed. Too late. She was surprised by that tidbit of information.

She recovered quickly. "Remy never mentioned Marisa, though he is a bit of a flirt, I suppose, and I can't say he's never taken a female customer home. You're welcome to ask him about it tonight, of course."

"I stopped by his place downstairs," Leo said. "He didn't answer his door, either." A thought he didn't like occurred to him. What if the piano player was here? What if Remy Zeringue was in the bedroom, the reason Abby didn't have on a stitch of clothing? He'd watched them together and had dismissed the idea that they might be involved, but too many women were suckers for a long-haired, brooding musician with a Cajun accent who called every woman he met *chère* or *darlin'*. "Mind if I look around?"

Abby gave him an unfriendly smile and gestured with her hand. "Be my guest."

She gave him the nickel tour. The apartment, or rather *apartments,* sprawled. The rooms were large and nicely furnished. She liked red and orange, apparently, but there was one nice-size guest room decorated in teal and green and blue, and another was dominated by shades of lavender. In every room the windows were entirely covered with heavy drapes. Not a hint of sunlight broke through. There was enough artificial light to illuminate the rooms well, but it was odd, not to have at least one window opened on such a pretty day.

The master bedroom was huge, dominated by a neatly made king-size bed covered with a silky red bedspread and dotted with orange and hot-pink pillows in various sizes. There was no Remy, no sign of a man at all, in sight. The framed oils on the walls were nice, florals featuring poppies and roses, an autumn scene filled with flame-leafed trees. He was staring at that one when he noticed the initial in the bottom right-hand corner. *A.* Nothing else, just an ornate, flourishing, *A.* When he glanced around again he noticed that all the paintings were signed the same way. *A.*

"Yours?" he asked, gesturing to the paintings.

"Yes."

"You're good."

"Thanks to years of practice," she responded coolly.

She didn't look old enough to have had years of practice at anything. The information he had on Abby Brown listed her as twenty-eight, but she could easily pass for a college student. Her skin was perfect, if pale, her light green eyes bright, her body fine, petite and still curvy… He shouldn't go there.

"Do you suspect that Remy killed Marisa?" Abby asked softly, and though she tried to hide it, he heard the pain in her voice.

"I don't know," Leo said. "I hope not."

"Why?"

"Because he's your friend and it'll hurt you if he's the one."

She looked to be genuinely surprised by his answer. "You should not care about my feelings. I'm nothing to you, as you are nothing to me."

The words were unusually formal and harsh, but he didn't think it was Abby's intention to be hurtful. She spoke her mind plainly. She was logical and a little confused. He had a sudden and vivid image of Abby laid across her bed, the bright silky fabric around her, beneath her, but not covering her. He could see, so clearly, his body and hers coming together. Hell, he could almost feel her around him, as if the sensation of entering her were a memory, not a fantasy.

"I wish you would not do this to me," she whispered.

"Do what?"

"I'm strong, stronger than you know, but I am not as strong as I should be."

"Who says you have to be strong?"

She didn't answer, but walked to him, dropped

the fabric that was all she wore, and without a word began to undress him.

"I'm working," he said halfheartedly. "Nice as this is, I really should…"

"You really should be quiet and help me get these clothes off," she said as she pushed his jacket to the floor. "They are in my way."

Leo wasn't a complete idiot. He did as he was told.

Abby's hands were cool and insistent. Her long, dark hair was loose; it fell across her cheek as she glanced down to unbuckle his belt and unfasten his pants, hiding her expression from him. Was she as anxious as he was? That appeared to be the case. What the hell was happening?

He was a fool to ask questions when everything he'd wanted from Abby Brown was happening right now. Her hands were quick and gentle, her face revealed her hunger for him. Naked and needful, she looked oddly delicate, and he wanted nothing but to give her everything she wanted of him, and more. She wasn't shy; her hands were everywhere. She even licked her lips as she peeled away his clothes.

He was so caught up in the moment he almost forgot about the condom in his wallet. With a jerk of his hand he reached for his pants, but Abby's surprisingly strong fingers on his wrist stopped him from moving too far. And then she pulled him onto the bed, where they both bounced gently and his body pressed to hers.

"You don't need it," she whispered. "I cannot have children and we are both healthy."

"How do you know I'm healthy?"

She arched beneath him, wrapped her legs around his hips, brought them closer together. "I know," she said softly, "because I have powers beyond those of normal human beings. I can see into your body and your soul, I can see who you are and right now what you want and what I want is the same."

"Kinky," he said. "I like it." And she moved against him and wiped out every thought.

Her skin was cool and smooth and perfect. She smelled like cinnamon and sex and vanilla. Cookies. She smelled like cookies. He kissed her shoulder, wondering if she would taste as sweet as she smelled. His lips lingered on her perfect flesh. No, she didn't taste like cookies; she tasted like woman.

He was so close to being inside her it was driving him crazy, but he waited. For months he'd dreamed of this moment, and now that he had Abby wrapped around him he wasn't going to rush; he wasn't going to waste this opportunity. He smoothed her hair away from her face and kissed her throat. She gasped, moaned in pleasure. She responded intensely to his touch, and he liked it. He wanted to make her his in every way. His hands skimmed over her body, stopping here and there to explore and arouse.

Abby moved like a snake, undulating against him, rubbing her body against his, bringing them closer to the end. He'd pursued her for months and she'd denied him, but now that they were here it seemed she had less patience than he did. She caught her breath in a sigh of intense pleasure and wanting. She threw her head back and arched her spine. Maybe he was willing to be patient and take his time, but she obviously was not.

He pushed inside her, filled her, eased the ache that had been driving him crazy since she'd opened the door and presented herself to him barely covered by that length of brightly colored fabric. He'd thought of having her in just this position a thousand times, but even his imagination hadn't been as remarkable as the real thing. There were times when he'd thought he'd never get what he wanted from her, never be so close. Now here they were, like a dream come true.

She was oddly cool, inside and out. Her skin, her lips, the inner muscles that quivered against him, all were without the expected heat, as if she were made of gentle frost over silk. No sensation could compare to the delicious combining of his heat and her chill. He was lost in her and there was nothing but the two of them and the pleasure their bodies reached for. She kissed his chest...what the hell, was she biting?...no, no, it was just a kiss. A fervent kiss. As she kissed him her body grew warmer; the chill of her skin subsided, her hips moved faster, more insistently. She stole every thought from his head, until there was nothing but her body and his and the need that drove them.

She came hard, with her lips still latched to his chest, her legs tight around him, their bodies joined... and while she quivered he gave over, too.

They lay spent on her bed, silent but for the sound of his breath. The woman beneath him seemed to make no sound at all, no raspy breathing, no pounding heart. If he didn't know better he'd think she was entirely unaffected.

Nothing had ever drained him so. Abby kissed his chest, she licked him there. Her head was tilted so he could not see her expression, and he wanted very much to see her face.

"I should like to keep you," she whispered.

He bent his head and kissed her shoulder. "I would very much like to be kept."

"Would you, truly?"

"Yes."

She rolled him onto his back with surprising quickness and ease. "I have not shared myself with anyone for such a long time," she whispered. "I crave the sharing as much as the sex, as much as the blood."

Leo's body tensed. "The *blood?*"

She was above him, now, as he had once been above her. Her eyes bore into his and he felt an invasion, as if her gaze was a physical thing that pierced his eyes and traveled into his brain. "You cannot move."

Leo attempted to gently push Abby away and roll from the bed, but she was right. He couldn't move. His limbs were frozen. Had she drugged him? And if so, how? He hadn't drunk or eaten anything since entering her apartment.

But there had been the sting when he'd thought she was biting him. Did she have a needle in this bed? Had she drugged him with a muscle relaxant? Hell, he had the worst taste in women!

"I won't hurt you," she said, and as she spoke she smoothed back a strand of hair at his temple. "When this day is over I will make you forget, but for now…I swear, there is something about you that makes me feel lonelier than I ever have before, something that compels me to cling to you, to tell you the truth of who I am."

"Who are you?" he asked, still confused but no longer afraid. Her words and her voice—and more important her eyes—spoke of loneliness and fear and a need for something he himself craved. Someone to cling to. Though the situation was confusing and should be frightening, he could not be afraid of her. Besides, if she'd meant to hurt him she could've done so by now.

Abby shook back her long, thick hair, and then she looked him in the eye. Softer this time, without demand, without that feeling of invasion. "I was born

Abigail Smythe in 1543. My memories of that time are not clear, but I know I was a farmer's daughter on a spot of land in the north of England, who grew to have a passably pretty face and a pleasing manner, both gifts from my mother. My life was simple. I suppose it was happy enough, though to be honest it's hard to remember, after such a long time. It's as though that girl was someone else, someone distant, and yet I realize that foolish, weak girl was me.

"When I was fifteen my father arranged my marriage to an older man who was important in the community. I thought he was quite something, but of course now I know he was nothing more than what today would be called a big fish in a small pond. Mr. Bailey, though nearly as old as my father, was a good and attentive husband until it became clear to him that I was not going to give him the sons he desired. Two of our children were stillborn, both girls, and when I was nineteen I gave him a strong, beautiful daughter. The delivery was difficult and I almost died. After Merry was born I did not conceive again."

Leo knew when people were lying to him; it was part of his job, hell, it was a part of who he was. Everyone had a tell or two, when they were spinning a lie, and he could spot them from a mile away. From all he could see, Abby was not lying. Impossible or not, she believed what she was telling him. Still...

"This is not..."

"Possible? I assure you, it is. Listen to me, if you please." She turned her head to gaze toward the heavily curtained window. "The final years of my human life are more clear in my memory than those that preceded them. I was as happy as could be expected, considering that my husband despised me and would on occasion beat me when he found himself longing for the son I could not give him. I had my daughter, a lovely, sweet girl, and I never had to worry about food or shelter. All in all, my life was fine."

Leo felt a surge of anger. Her story was fantastic, it was unbelievable, but there had to be some truth to it, somewhere. "He beat you?"

Abby ignored his question. "When I was twenty-three years old, a young mother and a reluctant wife, a scourge came to our village. People died horrible deaths in the night, and their dry, bloodless bodies were left in the streets for all to see when the sun rose. There was panic, as you can imagine. Town meetings were held frequently. Mr. Bailey was always present at those meetings, of course, as he was a leader in the community. We were told to be vigilant, to be suspicious of everyone, even those villagers we thought we knew. We were warned to be especially cautious at night, as that was when the killings occurred, and not to allow anyone into our homes."

He saw the pain in her eyes; he felt it as if it were his own, as if they remained connected in a way that went well beyond sex.

"But how can you say no to a traveling priest who arrives at the door, hungry and looking for shelter from the rain, just past dark? How can you turn away a human being in need?" She looked him in the eye. "I did not turn him away. I invited him in, even though my husband was not at home. In a matter of moments the priest who was not a priest at all rendered me immobile, as I have done to you, and I watched as he broke my daughter's neck and drank every drop of her blood. When that was done he turned to me. I begged him to kill me. I did not want to live without my child. Merry was all I had in my life that was good, and I could not continue on without her."

Her voice dropped. "The creature did kill me, but he didn't allow me to remain dead. He brought me back as a vampire, like him. I think if I had not asked him to kill me he would've left me alone, he would've allowed me to remain dead."

Perhaps realizing, or at least suspecting, that he did not believe her, Abby smiled. Two fangs appeared, sharp canines elongating and growing more pointed before his eyes, transforming what should've been a pretty smile on a beautiful face into a demonstration of terror.

And he believed. How could he not? The truth was right before his eyes. "Are you going to kill me?"

"No." The fangs retracted as quickly as they had grown.

What she'd told him was impossible, incredible, but he had no choice but to believe. Beyond the truth he knew, another world existed. A dark, hidden, terrifying world where creatures he'd thought to be mythical existed. Considering some of the nasty murders he'd seen during his career, he couldn't be shocked. He was surprised, however, that Abby was a part of it. She wasn't evil. No matter what she said, he saw who she really was and there was nothing to fear. "What happened next? How did you survive?"

Abby cocked her head and looked at him as if she were confused by his question. Maybe she was just taken aback that he wasn't begging for mercy or shrinking away in horror. "I was crouched in the corner, holding the body of my child, when Mr. Bailey came home. He didn't realize what had happened, of course. When he saw us there he thought I'd somehow killed Merry. As if I would've ever..." She shook her head quickly. "Mr. Bailey rushed toward me. He raised his hand to strike me as he had a thousand times. But this time, I fought back. I pushed against him as hard as I could and he flew across the room. I followed him, angry and grieving and hungry in a way I did not understand. My husband screamed when he saw my face and realized what I had become. He pleaded for mercy when I threw him to the floor with a newly discovered strength. While he cried I pounced upon him and I went for his throat. I drank every drop of Mr. Bailey's sour, old blood, and I liked it." She looked him in the eye. "I am a monster, Leo."

He could not argue with that statement, not if what she told him was true. "Did you kill Marisa Blackwell?"

She shook her head. "No. I haven't killed anyone in a very long time. I can survive quite well on pigs' blood, and by occasionally feeding on humans and then making them forget, as I made you forget last night."

"Last night I..." He got no further before the memory came rushing back, perhaps because she allowed it to return to him. A really great kiss, a quick coupling in the shadows...and more, apparently.

"Other vampires, younger ones, don't always have such restraint. They either kill randomly or subsist on animal blood until they learn to control their strength and their needs. I serve pigs' blood in my bar after hours. I teach those who wish to learn how to survive without giving in to their monstrous urges." Her green eyes went paler than usual, losing almost all their color, for a moment. "It's not as if we can allow people to disappear night after night, it's not as if we can feast on the humans around us and continue to thrive. We do not die easily, but we can die. We can be hurt. It is not in our best interest to make our existence known, and that means keeping the body count down no matter how thirsty we might be. In the name of survival we learn to deny ourselves what we most want, as I have denied myself you, until now."

Four hundred years was such a long time. How many people had Abby killed, before she'd learned the control she spoke of? Was she truly a monster behind the face that had enchanted him? Would a monster "most want" a bond with a human, a connection she confessed she had denied?

"What happened to you, after you changed?" he asked.

Abby dipped her head almost demurely, though he knew she was anything but demure. Long, thick, soft hair hid a portion of her face from him. "My little village was entirely wiped out," she whispered. "There was no one left to tell the tale of what had really happened, so the travelers who found the remains of the carnage blamed the deaths on a terrible disease and burned everything. The vampire who did all the killing survived, of course, as did I and a couple of other fledglings. The others he turned did not last out the year. They weren't strong enough."

"What happened to the creature that killed your daughter and all the others?"

Her eyes narrowed, and he saw in them a hatred that would bring most men to their knees. "I learned a few years later that he called himself Callosus. He was ancient then, a power among powers. He survives still, I know it. I swear, some days I'm sure I can feel him close by, other days…nothing. One day I will find him, and when I do I'll take his head, even if it means losing my own in the process."

He should not believe a word of Abby's fantastic tale, but he did. In the face above him he saw the woman and the monster, the tragedy and the slaughter and the heartache. He saw her heart and the gruesome fiend she was…had been…could be.

He should be terrified, but he wasn't. It occurred to him with more than a touch of humor that Abby Brown, no matter what she'd done, couldn't be much more of a bloodsucker than his ex-wife….

"Why are you telling me this?"

"Because I like you," she said, "even though I should not. You make me feel lonely, when for the past two hundred years I have been more than happy enough to remain alone, to rely on no one but myself, to be solitary in all ways. It's too dangerous to get close to anyone or anything. Every few years I change my last name, though I keep the name Abby or Abigail. That's not much, but it's all I have left of who I once was and I am loath to let it go entirely. I have been content. I have not killed—I've tried to live my life simply, with no complications, and now… and now here you are, a complication of the worst sort."

Beyond the sad and horrifying story, behind the fangs and the assertion that she was a monster, Leo saw something more. He saw the woman he'd been drawn to from the beginning. She was real. Not exactly as he had believed her to be, not as simple or ordinary, but still, she was real and she was here and there was a reason for this confession.

"You're telling me all this because you want my body," he said wryly.

"In more ways than one," she responded. "The sex is fabulous. I'd forgotten how powerful a man and woman coming together in the name of pleasure could be. And I swear, I want to suck on every vein in your body."

He could not stop the mental image that formed in his mind. "Every one? Have at it."

"Don't be flip," Abby said, slightly angry, still more sad. "It simply can't be. For a few nights, maybe even a few years, perhaps we could make it work. But I would always have to hide the truth from you, feed on you and hope I don't feed too much, take away the memories you cannot keep..."

"I don't want you to take away my memories."

"I know." She caressed his face. She looked into his eyes in that way she had, and suddenly he could move again. He had control of his body once more. Any sane man would leap from the bed and run like hell, but instead Leo took Abby into his arms. He should not believe what she'd told him, but he did. He should be afraid, but he was not. If she'd wanted anything from him that he wasn't willing to give she could've taken it last night, or when he'd shown up at her door. She could've taken him up on any one of his invitations during the past three months and while they were alone she could've done whatever she'd pleased with him.

For now, at least, she didn't want anything other than what he most craved.

Her skin had grown cool again and he tasted it with relish. Not as she had tasted him, to the bone, but still, he feasted.

CHAPTER FOUR

REMY MET ABBY at the door to the Sundown Bar at opening time. He wouldn't start playing for an hour or two, but like her, he was tired of hiding in his apartment. He stood behind her and took a long breath. "Abigail, darlin'," he said, his Cajun accent heavy, even after all his time away from the city where he'd been born—both in body and as a vampire, "you smell like police."

She sighed, unlocked the door and stepped inside. "I showered." Twice.

"He's not just on you, he's in you. He's in your very cells and he's in your veins. Are you sure this is a good idea?"

First Margaret and now Remy! "It's my life to do with as I please." She glared at him. "It's not like you can criticize. You take up with humans all the time."

"Not policemen." He shrugged his broad shoulders. "Well, policewomen would be more my type, if I were so foolish."

She spun on him. "Marisa Blackwell? For goodness' sake, Remy, she was little more than a child!"

His expression was suddenly solemn. "She was no child, I assure you. And since you are so obviously wondering, I didn't kill her."

"You screwed her and fed on her. How am I to know you didn't get carried away and take it all?" Goodness knows she'd been tempted enough to take every drop of Leo's blood.

"I did not," he said softly. "Believe me or don't."

The door swung open and the first of their human customers arrived. There was nothing more to be said, not until much later. "Swear to me," she whispered.

Remy's expression didn't change. "Believe me or don't. I do not beg or swear."

LEO WAS STRANGELY tired, but he didn't let up as the afternoon turned into night. None of the usual suspects made any sense at all in Marisa Blackwell's case. She hadn't been robbed. She didn't have anything other than the most casual ex-boyfriend. She wasn't into drugs. Her frequent evenings at the Sundown Bar were her only evidence of a wild side, that and her affair with Remy.

She'd told several of her friends about him, though her family had never heard the name. In their eyes she was a sweet, untouched, virginal angel. He didn't bother to disabuse them of that notion, and wouldn't unless it became necessary for the case.

Remy or the elusive Mike and Jason? Someone

he had missed entirely? A sociopath passing through town? This case wasn't nearly neat enough to suit him.

In many ways, the piano player was the only suspect that made any sense to Leo. Still, he had no proof and he didn't want Remy to be the one. He wasn't sure why and it didn't matter what he wanted. Between Remy Zeringue or a serial killer—or killers, if that was Jason and Mike's game—with no motive other than "she was there," he'd take Remy any day.

At least tonight he'd get to see Abby when he went by her place to collect the sketches. He'd meant to do that this afternoon, but had never made it over that way. He must be coming down with something. Instead of going to Abby's place and insisting on collecting those sketches she'd promised him, he'd… well, he wasn't sure how he'd gotten so sidetracked, but hours after he'd left the station he'd woken from a long, mind-numbing nap in his car, parked behind the Dollar General Store on the main drag.

He couldn't afford to get sick now, and he had to look beyond Remy. Until he tracked down the men who'd been with Marisa and her friend Monday night, he couldn't settle on anyone as the sole suspect. Some sort of proof would be nice, and at the moment he had none.

He was suddenly assaulted by a craving for cookies.

ABBY FURIOUSLY WIPED down the bar, ignoring the stares from humans and vamps alike. She was moving a touch faster than was normal for any human; she knew that and still she couldn't make herself slow down. Let them stare; she didn't care. Her mind was spinning and her body was tense, tight, on fire. It was probably no coincidence that Remy was playing a haunting version of "Crazy" at the moment.

Remy—and others—had often encouraged her to take up with a human or humans in a sexual way. Many vampires kept ignorant mortals as sexual partners, treating them as if they were pets. Abby had dismissed the notion, claiming it was a weakness to need anything from a human beyond blood. She needed no one, least of all something—someone—as fragile as a man.

Her craving for Leo should be satisfied by now. She'd sampled his body and his blood all afternoon; she'd enjoyed pleasure and warm sustenance and even laughter. The bed she never slept in had become a haven for one fine afternoon. And then she'd wiped Leo's mind of their interlude and sent him away.

Abby was now acutely sensitive to Leo, thanks to the blood she'd taken in. When he pulled into the parking lot, she felt his closeness. She knew, before he opened the door to the bar, that he was confused by the missing time and weakened by the loss of blood. And all she wanted was to hold him, take him into her body again, and taste his blood. Just a drop. That would be enough, for now.

Maybe.

Leo smiled wanly as he walked toward her. Every vamp in the place, every one, watched Leo with too interested eyes. Were they made curious by his reaction to her, or by her reaction to him?

"Do you have those sketches?"

"Yes." She reached under the bar and pulled out two pencil drawings of the men she remembered seeing with Marisa and Alicia. Not that they would do him any good. The more she picked from Leo's brain concerning the murder, the more certain she was a vamp had done the deed.

"Thanks." He took a stool, ran fingers through his hair, and reached for the sketches she offered. "Wow, these are great. I didn't know you were such an artist."

Abby's heart broke a little. Just hours ago he'd admired her paintings. After sex, explanations he'd miraculously accepted and sex once more, he'd asked about the artwork in her bedroom. She'd told him when and where she'd painted them, and what her life had been like at the time. As she'd shared that part of her past, she'd realized that in her most productive years, artistically speaking, she'd been alone. Entirely, completely alone, existing cautiously from one meal to the next, filling the long hours with paint and canvases and strangers who would never remember that they'd met her.

Naturally, Leo remembered nothing of the conversation, which was the reason she'd felt so free with him. If she were so foolish as to have sex with him again, she'd have to tell him once more that she could not have children so he did not need the blasted condom in his wallet. For him, sex with her would always be the first time. There could never be anything resembling a meaningful relationship between them—as if that was possible for any vampire.

"I'm not really an artist," she said. "I dabble. You look beat. How about a nice, tall glass of…"

He stopped her with a raised hand. "On duty."

"Orange juice," she finished with a smile.

He grinned. "Probably not a bad idea. I feel like I'm coming down with something." He studied the drawings. "I fully intended to drop by your place this afternoon and see if these were ready, but I didn't make it." He frowned; wrinkles in his forehead creased. She wanted to soothe him, to explain that he wasn't losing his mind. If she got too close she'd have him back in her bed, and this time she might not let him go.

"I have the oddest craving for cookies," he said. "I don't usually have much of a sweet tooth, but man, I'd kill for a sugar cookie right now."

In the old days she might've chained Leo to her bed and taken what she wanted until she tired of him, and then she'd make him forget everything and release him after he was so dazed and damaged that he no longer appealed to her. These days people did not go missing without causing a stir, especially not a cop. More's the pity. He was so incredibly special and different. She had never known another man like him.

Abby steeled her spine. She was beginning to sound like a human, weak and sentimental, instead of approaching Leo as if she were the monster and he the victim. Did monsters love? Not that she had seen. There was loyalty, in some cases. There was occasionally companionship or friendship or an alliance formed for the sole purpose of self-preservation. But that was not real love. It was part of the price she paid for immortality, for strength, for gifts that no human could ever understand.

Sadly, she realized that she couldn't stay here much longer. Looking at Leo she knew that too well. He would always be a temptation, and she could not afford to be tempted. As soon as Marisa's murder was solved, she'd make arrangements to move on. If she disappeared now, without cause and a modicum of preparation, he would surely consider her a suspect. It wouldn't do for him to chase after her.

"I need to talk to your piano player," Leo said. "Did you know Remy was seeing Marisa Blackwell?"

"No, I didn't. Are you sure?" He'd told her the news this afternoon, but of course he didn't remember.

Remy wasn't above taking a woman home, sleeping with her and taking what he needed, but like Abby he was old and powerful and had control of his needs. He would never kill to take the blood he required; it was simply unnecessary. He said he hadn't killed Marisa, and she took him at his word. If vampires had souls—and Abby was conflicted about that question—then Remy's was one of the good ones. As long as he had his music and a string of women for sexual entertainment and blood, he was content. He had no reason to kill.

Unless something had broken and he'd lost control. A day ago she would have thought that impossible. Now she had to wonder.

"He doesn't take many breaks," she said. "Can it wait?"

"I suppose." Leo sipped at his juice. She wished she had some decent food to offer him, something to help build back the strength she'd sapped this afternoon, maybe one of the cookies he craved, but all she had was a jar of pickled eggs. Even if she didn't gag at the thought of real food, pickled eggs wouldn't appeal to her at all. There were peanuts, and she casually placed a bowl near Leo. She didn't want him to think she was mothering him, but the man needed some protein. He almost immediately honed in on the nuts, munching, watching the crowd, keeping an eye on Remy—and on her. It was unnerving.

Once again Remy started playing "Crazy."

When Abby couldn't take it any longer she put Margaret in charge and headed down a narrow hall to her office. The room was no better than a glorified closet, and she didn't spend any more time here than she had to, but at the moment it was a place to hide. Vampires shouldn't hide from anyone, least of all an easily influenced human male whose only appeal to her was in his penis and his blood. He was ordinary. He was replaceable. Everyone was replaceable!

But like it or not there was more. She would never forget the way he'd looked at her as she'd spilled her guts about her past, her making, who she was. He'd forgotten, but she had not. Even though she had used her power to immobilize him, even though she had revealed herself as a monster, he'd felt sympathy for her. Not pity; she hated pity. But he had been moved. He'd cared.

And she was an idiot for allowing that to matter.

She felt him coming down the hall, but she didn't hide or run, as she could've. Instead she sat on the edge of her desk and waited. When Leo appeared in her doorway, she attempted a smile.

"What's wrong?" he asked.

"Nothing."

He didn't believe her, that was obvious, but didn't

press the issue. "So, when are you going out with me? You can't keep saying no."

"I can," she said gently.

"You don't know me well enough, is that it? Okay, here I am in a nutshell. Thirty-one years old, former homicide detective, current catch-all detective in a podunk town where *usually* nothing much happens. Divorced, no children, no family living close by so I'll never subject you to Sunday dinner with a brother or a cousin or my mother. They're all many, many hours away from here, which is best for all concerned."

"Leo, I…"

"I believe in Jack Daniel's, college football, and I suppose I must believe in love at first sight because I have not been able to get you out of my mind since the first time I walked into this bar."

She did not have a heartbeat to race, but she felt as if her stomach clenched, as if her insides turned to cold stone. "Maybe that's just lust at first sight."

"Maybe," he conceded. "At this rate I'll never find out."

Abby took a deep breath, not because she needed to breathe, but because the action itself was calming. Yes, she had to leave Budding Corner as soon as possible. If necessary she'd find Marisa's killer herself, turn him over or dust him, depending upon his species, and then she'd be able to get out of town and away from this tempting man.

"Would you kiss me?" she asked.

The request took Leo by surprise, she could tell by the expression on his face. "Here and now?"

"Here and now." Perhaps she could not have everything, but that didn't mean she could take nothing at all.

Leo walked into the room with a steady, strong stride. All she could take was a kiss, but she wanted to leave him something to remember. If she took any more blood she might kill him; and she couldn't have sex with him without being driven to take a taste. But a kiss...a kiss wouldn't hurt anyone, and when she disappeared he would have that kiss as a pleasant memory.

And so would she.

It was a test of her strength, to kiss him and take nothing more, but she was strong. She was powerful. She could do it.

Abby sat on the edge of her desk; Leo placed his hands on either side of her and leaned in. As far as he knew this was their first kiss, but he didn't hesitate. His mouth took hers, and she reveled in his warmth and his taste. More than that, she got lost in the emotion of the kiss, the power of connection, even of love, of not being alone in this small world where time flew past and had no end.

Leo's arms gradually and gently worked around her and she stood, pressing her body to his. His hands were in her hair, his heat enveloped her. She did not want the kiss to end, but nothing lasted forever. Nothing.

His hands settled on her hips, slipped around to her backside and pulled her close so she could feel his response. Perhaps instinctively he knew this wasn't a first kiss, maybe he knew her body and his were meant for one another.

Finally, he ended the kiss with a sigh. "You have to go out with me now."

"Maybe tomorrow."

He jerked away from her. "Really? You're not yanking my chain?"

She had such a hard time keeping up with all the new slang and phrases, they changed so fast, but this one she knew. "I am not yanking your chain."

"Lunch?"

"Dinner. I can let Remy and Margaret run the bar for a couple of hours."

"Hot damn." In spite of his exhaustion, he gave her a true smile.

"I have to go back to work."

"Me, too. When can I talk to your piano man?"

She'd been so caught up in the kiss, she hadn't realized that the piano was silent. "Sounds like he's on a break right now."

"Good. Let's get this over with." Leo allowed her to lead the way down the hallway. Everyone, human and vampire, was watching as they walked into the bar from the back room. Remy was nowhere to be seen. Neither was Margaret. One of the regulars, a human who was in the bar at least four nights a week, had taken over behind the bar and was doing an acceptable job, but Abby was furious.

"Where did Remy and Margaret go?" she asked hotly.

"They left a few minutes ago."

"Together?" Leo asked.

"No." An older man who sat in the corner, as usual, responded. "Remy skedaddled, and Margaret took off after him. You know how that girl loves her some Remy."

"I gotta go." Leo leaned down and gave Abby a warm peck on the cheek. "I'll see you tomorrow night." And then he was gone.

After the door closed behind Leo the bar seemed horribly empty and silent. No music, no laughter from bubbly Margaret. Everyone stared at Abby, and she couldn't blame them. The vampires were surprised that she'd taken up with a human, and the humans had never seen her with a man before.

Abby relieved the customer who'd taken over the bar; she polished a glass that did not need polishing. Where would she go next? Up north, she supposed. Perhaps for a while she'd stay in a place even more isolated than this one. No more caves, no more farms, but there were many places in this big country that were basically off the map. There was also

Europe, but it wasn't quite time to head back in that direction.

Though she craved time by herself, time to plan for what might come next, she didn't stay alone for long.

Charles hadn't been in Budding Corner more than a month. He'd gravitated here looking for a peaceful way of life, hoping to learn the control required for a long existence. It wasn't love of a weaker species that made him cautious. Like her, he wanted to exist as peacefully—and invisibly—as possible. He was a pretty boy, with blond hair almost as long as Remy's and amber eyes that had once been dark brown. He had a dry sense of humor but didn't say much. Everyone liked him well enough.

Most vampires had some sort of power that was revealed to them as they came to terms with their new bodies and minds, and Charles was no exception. He saw snippets of the near future, but had not as yet learned to control his power. He was young, still, not much more than seventy years old. Visions came and went, most of them of no concern to an immortal who had no love for the humans. The women he dallied with meant no more to him than the carton a human's milk might come in. He kept them alive, he drank from them carefully without ever revealing who and what he was, but to him they were containers. They were necessary.

"Got yourself a human, I see," Charles said.

"That's none of your business," Abby snapped.

"They are handy," he said, not taking the broad hint. "I remember sex from before the change, and it was pale in comparison to a vampire's experiences. There's nothing at all wrong with having sex with a human, but I suspect you're looking for more from our local detective." He shook his head.

"What do you want?"

Charles shrugged his shoulders, obviously unconcerned. "I just had a vision and it concerns your new friend. I thought you might want to know, but if you don't…"

"Tell me!"

Charles shook his long, pale hair and gave her a tight smile. "All right. The next time you see your cop boyfriend, he'll be dead."

CHAPTER FIVE

LEO PARKED HIS car in front of his crappy rented house at the edge of town, turned the key to shut off the engine and stepped out, a too thin manila folder clutched in one hand. The night was dark, tree limbs overhung the dirt drive, and his place was so isolated there wasn't another house in sight. He'd thought Budding Corner would be temporary, but since Abby had kissed him…maybe it wasn't temporary after all. He couldn't very well bring her here. She deserved better.

He'd hoped to catch Remy in the parking lot or in his apartment, but had had no luck. For now he'd take another look at the case file, hoping to see something new before the ABI came in and took over. Come hell or high water, he would talk to Remy Zeringue tomorrow.

She was sitting on the front porch steps. He didn't see her right away, since the front porch light was burned out.

"Abby?" How had she gotten here so fast? Why did she look so worried? She stood slowly, and he was shaken by the certainty that something was wrong.

She looked different. Something was off. "What are you doing here?"

"I missed you," she said, whispering. Didn't exactly sound like her voice, but then he was tired, and it was late, and nothing was as it should be.

"How did you get here so fast?"

She walked toward him. The usual white blouse and long skirt were damn near painted on her, showing him every curve, every tempting swell. "Shortcut. I ran."

Dressed like that? "But…"

"Don't ask so many questions." She smiled, and he relaxed. "You know what I want."

He knew what *he* wanted, but Abby had never shown much interest in him, until tonight when she'd asked for a kiss and accepted his invitation for a date. When she relented she really relented. Nice.

She walked into his arms, and he quit asking so many questions. Abby was here. He'd be a fool to question that.

She was cool. She squirmed against him as if she could not get close enough. He loved the feel of her, but something was wrong; she didn't smell right. Abby always smelled good, sweet and clean and tasty. At the moment there was something sour about the way she smelled, something wrong. He was about to release her when she lifted her head and kissed his throat. She licked the side of his neck, and he went very still, enjoying the sensation. Maybe the sour smell was coming from the woods; that couldn't possibly be Abby. She took the folder from his hand and dropped it to the ground. He didn't care. Pages fluttered. A gentle wind caught Abby's sketches and took them away.

And then she bit him. He felt her teeth sinking into his skin, the sharp bite of invasion. Too late, he heeded the warning, he heeded the smell. He tried to fight her off, to push her away, to get her the hell away from his throat, but even though she was tiny compared to him, she was stronger than he was, much stronger, with arms and jaws like steel. She held him in place with incredibly, impossibly strong arms while she sucked on his throat. She gurgled; she slurped his blood, and Leo felt the life draining from him. His knees went out, but Abby held him up. His eyes rolled back in his head, and his entire body shuddered. She slammed him to the ground, her face buried in his throat as she sucked the life from his body. He smelled his own blood, as well as the stench that came from her skin. In the midst of the violence a fleeting but coherent thought crossed his mind. Was this the way Marisa Blackwell had died? Had Abby, the woman he had fantasized about and dreamed about and kissed, torn Marisa's throat apart and sucked out her blood? Impossible...and yet here he was.

Dark hair covered his face, blocking out the night's

gentle light. Right before everything went black that hair turned to blond.

A trill of laughter that was not Abby's filled the night.

ABBY RAN, following Leo's trail, drawing on the connection she had formed with him when she'd drunk his blood. With a vampire's grace and unnatural speed she all but flew, a blur in the quiet neighborhoods, and then beyond, where the homes were far apart and the trees grew thick. Dogs barked. The cool night air washed over her, and she listened, trying to find Leo's heartbeat among all the rest.

There it was. Too slow, too unsteady. A thump. Seconds later another thump. And then...nothing.

She did not stop but continued on. All was quiet. Too quiet. If she'd been able to shed tears, tears would've come. Amazingly, she found she was capable of experiencing deep sorrow, still, after all this time. It hurt. Leo Stryker was a good man and she should've been able to save him.

If she hurried, perhaps she still could.

She ran into the side yard of a small clapboard house, his house, her eyes on the two forms in the dark driveway. Leo lay on the ground, motionless. Dead, as Charles had said he would be. Margaret stood over him, licking her lips, laughing.

"Why?" Abby screamed as she rammed into Margaret and spun the vampire who was warm with Leo's blood back against his car. The metal of the driver's door crunched and crinkled beneath Margaret's weight and Abby's force.

The young vampire laughed. "You're asking me why? Hypocrite. You didn't leave me much. He was barely an appetizer."

"I could've loved him." The words Abby spoke surprised her with their power and their truth.

"He was going to tie Remy to Marisa's death," Margaret argued. "I couldn't allow that."

"Remy can take care of himself!" Abby glanced down at Leo's body, so cold and still and pale. It was wrong; he should be alive and laughing and flirting. He should be on the trail of a killer who'd broken the rules of his world, rules he had sworn to keep. She didn't want to believe it was possible but she had to ask, "Did Remy kill Marisa?"

"Yes," Margaret said. "And no." The young vampire shimmered, and instead of Margaret pinned to Leo's car it was Remy.

Or at least, the form appeared to be Remy until it spoke.

"He was sleeping with her," Remy's body with Margaret's voice said. "Night after night after night. I don't mind that, really, because I knew he was feeding from her. Pigs' blood will do in a pinch, but it doesn't compare to human blood fresh from the donor. But he started to like the twit too much, and I couldn't have that. We're going to be together, Remy and I, as soon as he comes to his senses."

Abby slammed Margaret against the car once more. The figure shimmered, and once again she appeared in her true form. A beautiful monster. "You finally found your gift, I see."

"I did. And isn't it a doozy?" Margaret smiled. "This is really going to come in handy." The vamp's gaze remained steady. She was not afraid—and that was a mistake. "You don't teach the fledglings that to take all the blood from a human is so exhilarating," she said. "I've tried to adapt, as you have, but I always remembered what it was like in those wonderful, free, early days. When I took the last of Marisa's blood, I was washed in a flood of power. I felt her life inside me, I knew everything, I felt her love for Remy and her confusion that he had killed her, because of course she saw what I wanted her to see, just as your Leo saw you in his last moments."

It infuriated Abby to know that with his last breath, Leo believed that she'd killed him. She didn't have much time to make amends for that. But first she had to handle the current problem. She couldn't release Margaret. The young vamp had tasted the power of taking a life and she'd liked it too well. There would be no stopping her now, and with her newly discovered gift of illusion no one was safe. No one. A young vampire's unstoppable hunger would bring the human world, Leo's world, on a hunt, and Abby would be at the center of it all. Even rogues practiced some restraint, some caution. Margaret would not.

Margaret was tough, and recently fed, and in the midst of finding her own powers. But she was not as old and strong as Abby. She seemed to finally remember that, as Abby raised her right hand and allowed the nails there to grow into five-inch razor sharp claws that curved upward.

Realizing what was about to happen, Margaret shimmered once more. To Abby's eyes it looked as if Leo stood before her, alive and mortal and beautiful. "He loved you, you know." Margaret's voice coming from Leo's mouth was wrong. "Until the end, when he thought you'd ended him, he loved you. He wasn't even sure why, the love was just there. Humans are silly that way, I suppose."

Abby ignored the face before her and remembered Margaret's form, and where Margaret's heart would be. With a cry that was loud in the night her blade-fingers sliced into Margaret's chest. So damaged, so violated, the young vampire could not maintain her illusion.

Abby grasped the dead heart within Margaret's chest and ripped it out.

Even though it did not beat, without the heart the vampire could not survive. Margaret looked at her own heart, she screamed, and then she and the heart turned to dust and a sudden night wind took it all.

Abby dropped to her knees beside Leo. His face

was pale as death. It *was* death. He had not been dead long, there was time, but still, it was a risk. Only the strongest could survive being turned, and some were different after the change, as if who they had been inside did not survive. If the man she loved wasn't present in the monster she created, would she be able to end him as she'd ended Margaret?

With the nails she'd used to rip out Margaret's heart, Abby sliced a vein in her wrist. Blood dripped, and she quickly led that wrist to Leo's colorless lips. "Drink, love," she whispered. "There is life in my blood. Take it. Drink it. I swear, I don't want to live in a world without you in it."

Drops of blood hit his tongue, those drops seeped through his mouth, down the throat. After an agonizingly slow passage of minutes his heart beat once, weakly. Only Abby could hear it. It beat again, and a few minutes later again. His eyes snapped open and that heartbeat stopped with a final thud.

For a moment he was terrified of the face above him, and Abby understood why. For all Leo knew she had been the one to kill him. But she watched as his expression changed. Terror, suspicion, confusion, then relief. "Blonde," he said hoarsely. "Not you."

"Yes, dear," Abby said sweetly. "Blonde. Not me."

"You smell like cookies. She smelled like death."

"Cookies?"

He nodded weakly.

"Leo, darling, I want you to drink something."

"Drink what?" he asked, still ignorant to what was happening, to what he had become.

"Me," she said, lying beside him and placing her wrist against his mouth. "Drink of me."

Leo instinctively latched his mouth to her wrist and suckled there. Gently at first, and then harder. He was starving, and did not know how or why. A basic survival instinct urged him on, forced him to drink long and deep. They lay on the ground entangled, joined in a new way. He took too much; she did not care, not even when she passed out.

Abby had not slept in more than four hundred years; she had not needed sleep. But then this was not sleep, it was oblivion, a result of the loss of blood. Eventually, Leo slept, too, when he had drunk his fill. She knew he slept because he joined her in her dream world. They were together in her mind and soul, and in his. They were linked. She would never again return to an existence where she was alone. In her dream she clung to him. Though she had only recently discovered the depth of this bond, she knew that to be without it would be worse than death.

Hours after she'd passed into oblivion with his mouth at her wrist, she woke slowly to find Leo on top of her. He kissed her healed wrist, licked her throat, rubbed his body against hers. Already he had discovered a vampire's enhanced sensitivity, and a new urge drove him. Without a word he pushed her skirt up, over her hips. With insistent hands he spread her thighs, he touched her intimately, his fingers dancing on and inside her. He freed himself and filled her quickly, thrusting inside her as if that connection was as necessary for him as the blood with which she'd given him life.

She came almost instantly, sending yet another cry into the darkness of the night. Her body shook; she trembled in an entirely human way, and yet she did not think it a weakness. Leo's movements slowed. He was still hard, still moving in and out of her in a fine, easy rhythm.

"Everything has changed," he whispered.

"Yes, love."

"I see, even though it is dark. I see you with a startling clarity, and you are more beautiful than you have ever been. For a while I was gone, gone from everything, and then I woke with your scent in my nostrils and when I touched you I found you warm. Not cold, as you have been in the past, but warm."

"I will always be warm to you now."

"Yes. Nothing has ever felt so incredible, so right. I'm inside you, you're inside me. I do not know where one of us ends and the other begins."

"We are one," she whispered, knowing it to be true. Beyond the physical joining of bodies, to the pit of their souls—if they had souls...

He moved faster, harder, and then he, too, came.

Leo lifted his head and looked down at her. He

had already found his vampire eyes, and he saw her very well. "Abigail Smythe."

"You remember."

"I remember everything now. I see everything."

"I could not let you go," she whispered. Would he hate her? Would he hate what he had become when he understood fully how his life—his existence—had changed?

"I could never hate you," he said gently.

"You read my mind."

"Did I?"

A vampire who found his gift so quickly could only be a very powerful one. Then again, perhaps it was only her mind he could read, since they were so close. No, more than close, they were one being sharing two bodies. She had tasted his blood; he had tasted hers.

It was time to run again, to make a new home, to change her name, but this time…this time she wouldn't be running alone.

LEO PACED ABBY'S apartment, still amazed at the vividness of the colors around him, still childlike in his wonder at all the sensations being a vampire afforded. Abby had him on pigs' blood for the time being, with an occasional nip of her blood, when the time was right. She wasn't certain he could control himself with human blood in his mouth. Not yet. With his strength he would be unstoppable; even

Abby couldn't best him, and she was pretty damn strong herself. She would teach him control, she said. The strength that had come with the change was incredible, and the sex was so good he was amazed he and Abby ever left their bed.

The case of Marisa's murder had been solved, though no one beyond the vampire community could ever know that justice had already been served. He'd presented the case to the ABI, along with a sharp gardening tool which would explain away the wounds at Marisa Blackwell's throat. A lot of people knew Remy had been seeing Marisa, and just as many people knew that Margaret was crazy jealous. A convenient statement from Abby's follower Charles indicating that he'd seen the two women together less than an hour before Marisa's death sealed the deal. A manhunt was on; they'd never find her, as there was nothing left to find.

He and Abby—and all the others, he assumed—would be leaving town, soon. He'd be able to explain away the fact that he went to the station after dark for only so long, before his coworkers started getting suspicious. Maybe there wasn't a Sherlock Holmes among them, but they weren't complete idiots, either.

Abby was still afraid, now and then, that he would hate her for turning him. He not only read her thoughts, he was washed in the emotions she claimed not to possess. Love and fear, guilt and joy, need and trepidation. Behind a stoic face she experienced them all, and he experienced them with her.

"We're going to be together forever," he said as he caught a snippet of a thought filled with doubt.

Though Abby's gift had never before allowed her to access a vampire mind, she was often able to see into his. Words and images, stray thoughts, every day that link grew stronger and clearer. When it was complete and eternal, as he suspected it soon would be, she'd have no more doubts.

She looked at him from across the room. When they were alone she didn't like clothes much, so she'd wrapped herself in that length of soft cloth that was sometimes draped across the back of her sofa. "You don't yet know what a very long time forever can be."

"Marry me."

She laughed in surprise. "Vampires don't get married!"

"Why not?"

"Because as I already said, forever is a *very long time*." She squared her shoulders. "Besides, can you imagine a bitter divorce between two immortals? It's best to just let a relationship run its course and then, when the time comes, move on."

He crossed the room to stand before her, looking her in the eye so she would have no doubts about what he had to say. "I love you. I'm not going anywhere. I suspect forever will not be long enough where you're concerned."

The strength that came with his new body was taking some getting used to, as was the speed. He actually had to make an effort not to move too quickly in the presence of humans, or to display his strength. But with Abby, he had to hide nothing. He picked her up now, as if she weighed nothing, and held her close as he very gently tasted her throat. The fabric she'd had wrapped around her body fell away. And in that moment, forever seemed very fine.

EPILOGUE

THE SUNDOWN BAR, located on a county road in northern Wisconsin, did a brisk business with hunters, vacationers and a handful of locals, especially on Friday and Saturday nights. During the week the human crowd was sparse, but the vamp crowd didn't change. Every one had followed Abby when she'd left Alabama. Where else were they going to get properly prepared pigs' blood and the company of their own kind? Where else could they get instruction from a powerful elder? The building had changed, the weather and the people had changed, but what went on inside the Sundown Bar had not changed much at all. Remy played piano, usually sticking to the jazz he loved. Abby waited tables. Leo tended bar. There was a small but very nice apartment on the second floor, where they made their home for now.

Outside, a thick December snow fell, blanketing the ground. The human customers often talked about Christmas coming. The presents, the food, the traveling. Over the river and through the woods…

To the locals the owners of the new bar were Abby and Leo Johnson. He'd wanted to choose a more exotic surname, but with the blasted Internet you couldn't be too careful. The more common the name, the better. In the interest of distancing themselves from what had once been, Leo had accepted that he was going to spend his life being a Johnson or a Smith or a Jones or a Brown. He really didn't care what anyone called him, as long as he had Abby beside him. If anyone ever got too close to the truth, they likely wouldn't even be able to keep their given names—in public, at least. A worry for another day.

The police chief in Budding Corner hadn't been too pleased when his newly hired detective left, running off with a local bartender in a flurry of scandal and leaving the pursuit of one Margaret Harris—who would never be found—to others.

It had been a couple of months since they'd left Alabama, and there was still much to be done to tie up the loose ends. Leo called his family now and then, but he knew he couldn't ever see them again. If they saw his face they would know he was different. His eyes were a lighter shade of blue, his skin was smoother and paler. He looked slightly different; just enough that the people who knew him well would notice. Even if he could hide his strength and speed, those who knew him would be able to see that he moved differently. He could make his voice sound the way it once had, but he had to work at it. Yes, they would know he was not the Leo Stryker they knew and loved. A part of them would fear him, no matter how familiar he tried to appear.

One of these days he'd fake his death, he supposed. He hated to do that to his mother, but it was preferable to the truth—for her, at least. It had been hard enough telling her he wouldn't be home for Christmas this year. This Christmas, every holiday, every day of his existence to come, would be spent with Abby. Only Abby.

Abby's rules about munching on the customers still stood, and everyone knew it. No hunting within a ten-mile radius. But now and then the two of them made a trip to Milwaukee or Chicago and enjoyed a night on the town. Humans were weak-minded and easily swayed, he'd discovered, and damn, they tasted good. He and Abby could hook up with another couple, take a bit of blood—enough to sustain and gratify, but not enough to kill the donors—and then they'd leave the couple alone, with no memory that they'd ever met Abby and Leo Johnson or Smith or whatever.

Thanks to Abby he had never killed. Maybe he would, someday, if he had no other choice, as Abby had had no choice but to kill Margaret—a twisted vampire who had discovered joy in taking lives. He had enough human left in him to disdain the idea of unnecessarily taking a life. For now.

Now and then Abby asked him if he missed being human, but in truth there wasn't much to miss. Cherry pie, which now tasted like cardboard. Jack and Coke, which tasted like piss, these days. Cigarettes. He no longer had to worry about the health risks and they tasted like old socks. Didn't that just figure? Sunshine, which would instantly burn his skin like acid and would kill him if he stayed in the light long enough. Or so he'd been told. He hadn't worked up the nerve to test that particular lesson.

And yes, he did miss his family. They'd been a pain in the ass at times, but he had loved them. He loved them still, but they were better off not meeting the creature he'd become. In time, he wouldn't miss them at all, Abby told him. Already, his memories of them were fading. He knew who they were and he did care, but his memories of them were as if through murky, distorting glass.

Other than occasionally missing those things, which he could certainly live without, he was content. He passed his nights tending bar with Abby at his side, and his days in a thickly curtained suite of rooms decorated in shades of red and orange and the occasional hint of pink. They made love and read and danced. Naked. Abby was teaching him to paint. Maybe in a hundred years or so he'd be a decent enough artist, but he didn't think so.

Maybe he should take up the piano.

He'd discovered a new talent, since the change. Abby was surprised, but pleased, that he had found this new power so quickly. She considered it a sign of great strength, and great strength equaled survival. In the same way that she could see into the heads of humans when she so desired, he knew when they were telling the truth and when they were lying. Even something as simple as a "No, honey, that dress doesn't make you look fat" sent his radar pinging. Unlike Abby's gift, his was just as effective on vampires as it was on humans, though the signals themselves were different. A lie was a lie, no matter who told it. Abby thought it was hilarious, since he'd been a cop in the old days, that he was now a walking, talking lie detector.

He'd never caught her in a lie. He didn't expect he ever would.

It was a busy night, and Abby had her hands full with a table of thirsty hunters. While she took their order she looked at him and smiled.

Love you. She thought, and he heard the words as if she had spoken them, just for him.

Love you, too.

Remy played a lightning-fast version of "Take the A Train." The vampire customers put their heads together, whispering as they waited for the humans to leave so they could claim *their* time and enjoy their late-night sustenance.

Leo didn't feel like a monster, though he knew there were those who would disagree, if they knew the truth. As long as he could love, he wouldn't feel like a monster in the truest sense. As long as Abby loved him, she was much more than the stuff of nightmares. Together they were better than they had ever been apart, no matter what the cost.

One of these days, she was going to marry him. She'd come around. As she said, forever was a long time.

Abby walked to the bar with the hunters' orders in hand. With a nod of her head she signaled to Charles, who'd been filling in now and then and doing a decent enough job. Leo tossed his bar towel down and followed Abby toward the door, in sync with her, following her lead without conscious thought. As she opened the front door one of the hunters called out, "You two better grab your coats! It's cold out there!"

Abby smiled at him. "We won't be long." Then she closed the door behind her, and hand in hand, they walked out into the parking lot, into the snow. Leo lifted the hand Abby did not hold and let a few snowflakes land there. "It's not cold at all. Feels like a whisper of rain, only lighter. A mist off the water, maybe."

"Close your eyes."

He did.

"Feel the fall of snow on your face."

He did.

"It's a little like sunshine," Abby said. "If you use your imagination, you can almost feel as if you're standing on the beach on a summer's day."

She had often asked him if he missed human things, but he had never asked the same of her. He did now, as they stood in the snow and imagined another place and time.

"There have been moments," she said, after a short, thoughtful pause. "I used to occasionally miss apples, and the sun on my face, and even the release of shedding tears. There have been times when I missed the beat of my own heart, and good dreams and the feel of waking up in the morning and stretching out sleepy muscles." She looked up at him and her mind joined with his.

But I don't miss anything any longer, because now I have you and I can ask for nothing more from this existence. Kiss me, Leo, kiss me in the falling snow.

He did.

* * * * *

NOTHING SAYS CHRISTMAS LIKE A VAMPIRE
Lisa Childs

ABOUT THE AUTHOR

Lisa Childs has been writing since she could first form sentences. A Halloween birthday predestined a life of writing for Harlequin Nocturne. She enjoys the mix of suspense and romance. Readers can write to Lisa at P.O. Box 139, Marne, MI 49435 or visit her website at www.lisachilds.com.

CHAPTER ONE

SIENNA BRIGGS STOOD alone beside her grandmother's casket. Twinkling lights, wound around pine boughs, reflected back from the shiny surface. Her hands trembled against the lid as she closed it, hiding her grandmother's beautiful face. "Goodbye," she whispered into the silence, the funeral home empty but for her. "Tell Gramps Merry Christmas."

The elderly couple had loved the holidays, and each other, so much. They would be so happy to be together again. Sienna blinked back tears, refusing to feel sorry for herself over being alone. Nana had made Sienna promise to celebrate Christmas. Of course, at the end, her grandmother had said a lot of things that hadn't made much sense. Had to have been the drugs talking....

Maybe the painkillers had been the reason she'd insisted Sienna keep the ring. She stared down at her right hand, and the finger onto which Nana had slid her engagement ring the day that she had died. The diamond twinkled more brightly than the Christmas lights. Sienna had wanted to bury it with Nana, but the older woman had been adamant that Sienna wear it—on her right hand until she met the man who would slide it onto her left hand.

"You will meet him," Nana had promised. "You'll meet the man who loves you with all his heart."

"Yeah, right…" The last thing Sienna expected to find under her tree this Christmas was a man. A pile of bills, an eviction notice, probably, but not a man. Chuckling to herself over Nana's romantic notions, she turned away from the casket, and collided with a tall, hard figure. Her hands trembled as she lifted them to his chest to brace herself. The heat of his body penetrated his black silk shirt, warming her palms and making her skin tingle.

He lifted his hands to cup her shoulders. His deep voice was a low rumble as he warned her, "Careful…"

"I thought everyone had left," she said. Even the funeral director had gone, with instructions to pull the door shut behind her and it would lock. The holidays were fast approaching, so he had probably wanted to get home to his family.

So this strange man wasn't an employee of the mortician, and he was too young to have been a friend of Nana's. Yet something about him was eerily familiar. The deep-set dark eyes, the finely chiseled features and the black hair that hung just past his broad shoulders—all of it struck a chord in her memory. Especially the small diamond-shaped scar near the cleft in his chin.

Her heart hammered against her ribs, and fear cracked her voice as she asked, "Who are you?"

"I think you know," he challenged her.

Beneath her palm, his heart pounded hard. Realizing she still touched him, she curled her fingers and pulled away her hands.

"I'm sorry." She shook her head, her mind muddled with confusion and exhaustion—and his distracting nearness. "I don't know you."

But a thought, buried in the dark recesses of her mind, tugged at her. Sienna refused to recall the dark memories, though; monsters lurked with those memories, threatening to hurt her. Again. That was why, even at twenty-seven, she still slept with the lights on.

He didn't release her, his fingers holding tight to her shoulders. "Don't be sorry," he said as if it didn't matter, yet something about his tone suggested that it did. "It was a long time ago."

She jerked from his grasp, suddenly very aware that they were all alone…except for the dead. "Don't pretend to know me when you don't."

"Sienna…"

She shivered. He knew *her* name. But he could have learned it from reading her grandmother's obituary. "Who are you?" she asked again. "Or should I ask *what* are you?"

He sucked in a ragged breath. "What do you mean?"

"I know you're a con man."

A muscle twitched just above the line of his tightly clenched jaw as anger and pride flashed through his dark eyes. "Sienna—"

"Don't waste your time with me," she advised him, "I have nothing for you to con me out of." Only the ring.

He caught her hand in his, but instead of reaching for the diamond, he wrapped his fingers around her wrist where her pulse leaped with a rush of heat and adrenaline from his touch. "I am not a *con* man."

"I don't expect you to admit that you are," she said with a short laugh. "You won't even tell me your name and how you know me."

"I don't have time to explain," he said with a glance over his shoulder.

Sienna couldn't see what he was looking at; he was so much taller than her, his shoulders so broad, that she could see nothing but him—his handsome face, his muscular chest straining the buttons of his silk shirt. Over the shirt and jeans, he wore a long wool jacket—open, as if the cold outside didn't affect him at all.

"You're going to have to trust me." He stroked his thumb across the leaping pulse point in her wrist.

She swallowed hard, but her throat remained dry with nerves and a sudden rush of desire. How could she be attracted to a man she just met and who frightened her so much?

In protest of her attraction as much as his command, she murmured, "No…" She tried to tug free of him again, but he held her with his dark-eyed gaze and his grasp.

Then he pulled her closer so that her breasts pushed against the hard wall of his chest. "Once I get you out of here, I will tell you everything."

She shook her head, trying to break the connection between them. "I'm not going anywhere with you. Let me go!"

He tightened his hold and slid an arm around her back, so she couldn't escape him. "I can't. I came here for you, Sienna. I'm going to save you."

I'm going to save you…

The words reverberated inside her mind. And she flashed back to big hands reaching out of the darkness for her, pulling her from the twisted metal that was all that was left of her parents' vehicle. Staring deep into those compelling dark eyes of his, she remembered now where she had seen him before—when she was seven and had become an orphan.

She grimaced as the old memories pummeled her; the screech of metal as the car struck the guardrail, sparks flying. Then the crunch as the rail broke, and the car tumbled down the hillside, end over end. The screaming—her mother's screams and hers…echoed inside her head.

She shook her head, trying to wake herself from the nightmare. The pain, the fear, the darkness…

it was all too much. She clutched at him, pleading, "Make it stop…"

He leaned forward, his mouth nearing hers as if he intended to kiss her. But before his lips touched hers, it stopped. *Everything* stopped.

JULIAN VOSSIMER CAUGHT her, as her body went limp against his, and he lifted her in his arms, holding her close to his madly pounding heart. Her head settled into the crook of his shoulder and neck, her breath warm and whisper-soft against his skin.

His blood pounded in his veins, not just over the imminent danger she was in—but because of the danger she had put him in. The danger of falling for her.

She had become such a beautiful woman. Her hair, the same honey tone as her skin, bore shimmery streaks of sunshine. Her eyes, although closed now, were a bright blue that had glistened with the tears she'd fought as she told her grandmother goodbye. Those tears had been the only hint of her grief, of mourning. The visitation room for her grandmother was decorated with red and white poinsettias, lights, pine boughs and a Christmas tree. Instead of traditional black, Sienna wore a red dress in soft velvet that hugged every curve of her tempting body. But he didn't intend to seduce her; his only intention was to protect her. Yet had he actually hurt her? Or had she fainted just from fear?

If she was this afraid now, what would she be when she learned what he really was?

"She's fine," he assured himself. For now. But if he couldn't get her to listen to him, she wouldn't be fine. She would be as dead as her grandmother.

Balancing her slight body in one arm, he grabbed up her purse and jacket from a chair in front of the casket. He found her keys then draped her coat over her before slipping out a back door to the parking lot. He couldn't have witnesses who could identify him as the man with whom Sienna Briggs had disappeared.

And she had to disappear, in order to save her life.

Her breath escaped in white puffs into the night air, and snow drifted down, falling in wispy flakes onto her beautiful face. The flakes melted and slid down her skin like tears. He suspected she had shed a lot of tears in her life. She had lost so many people she loved.

Because of Julian. Guilt twisted his gut. If only…

But he could not change the past. He could only affect the future. And he had to make sure she had one. He wouldn't be responsible for taking that away from her, too.

Julian pushed the button on her keys, so that the lights on a small SUV flashed on and off while the locks opened with an audible click. He had to take her car, too, so no one would realize from where she'd gone missing. But would anyone realize she was missing?

Few people had showed up tonight to pay their respects to her grandmother, or offer their support to Sienna. She seemed so alone now, as if she had less than when he'd pulled her from that wreckage almost twenty years ago. Regret joined his guilt.

"I'm sorry..." he murmured as he pulled open the passenger's door and settled her limp body onto the seat.

He should have warmed up the car; her skin chilled, the snowflakes no longer melted on her face, but clung to her lashes. Suddenly light flashed, momentarily blinding Julian as fire sprang up around the vehicle. He hadn't moved fast enough to protect her.

"No!" he shouted. "Leave her alone!" But he didn't want her alone, he wanted her with him.

A woman stepped out of the smoke, her eyes burning as brightly as the flames—with hatred and madness. "Vossimer, step back..."

Ignoring her order, Julian reached through the flames and gathered Sienna back into his arms. Clutching her close, he wrapped his coat around them both. "I'm not going to let you kill her..."

"She has to die," Ingrid Montgomery argued. "I was there. I heard her grandmother tell her the secret."

"The woman was terminally ill." As Ingrid knew

since she had posed as a hospice nurse. "Sienna won't believe what she heard."

"If she'd seen this, she would." Ingrid pulled a picture from the pocket of her cloak. Across the space separating them, Julian recognized a young version of Sienna's grandmother and himself. "She'd realize you aren't human."

"You don't know that," he insisted. "Burn the picture, not her. She won't repeat what her grandmother said."

"Like her grandmother wouldn't repeat the secret? You can't trust humans," the woman said, the pitch of her voice rising to the level of a hysterical scream. "You can't trust them. You know what happens…"

Not as painfully as she knew. "Ingrid—"

"If we don't kill her," the woman persisted, "more of *us* will die."

Julian shook his head. "She's already suffered enough. I won't hurt her."

"I figured you were too attached to her," Ingrid said, "so I brought reinforcements."

Her *reinforcements* stepped from the shadows, but the darkness remained part of them, buried deep in whatever was left of their souls. He glanced at the three men, all big and burly and more than willing to do Ingrid's bidding.

Anger coursed through him, vibrating in his voice as he shouted, "Stay back!"

"Let her go and you won't get hurt," Ingrid negotiated. "I'll clean up your mess for you."

"She's not my mess—"

"She's too much to you," Ingrid said with a snort of disgust, "and she's too dangerous for the rest of us. You know the rule—no human can learn the secret of our existence and live. She must die, Julian. Now."

"She's not a threat—" he turned to the men who inched closer to him "—to any one of us."

"That's not what your grandfather says—that's not what he sees," Ingrid reminded him.

Julian's heart clenched with dread. "My grandfather…" That was why Ingrid had posed as the hospice worker, to make sure Carolina Briggs died. Orson Vossimer had threatened to order her death long ago—not because of what he suspected but hadn't been able to prove she knew—but to reclaim their family honor. "He's behind all of this?"

Julian wasn't surprised; he was *sickened*. How long could the old man hold a grudge?

"Your grandfather's worried about you," Ingrid said. "He believes you've lost your objectivity, that your pity for the little girl she once was has clouded your judgment. All grown-up, she is a threat to you, but you can't see it."

He could see—and feel—that Sienna Briggs was all grown-up now. But a threat? Probably. He would admit that only to himself, though. He shook his head again. "I'm not going to let you kill her."

Ingrid's reinforcements eased closer to him and the flames that still lapped around the burning vehicle.

"You're going to have to kill me first," Julian threatened, "and I don't think that would make my *grandfather* very happy."

Ingrid gasped, as if shocked by his ultimatum, and her men halted their approach, uncertain how to proceed.

Julian took advantage of their indecision. Clutching Sienna more tightly in his arms, he leaped and launched them into the sky. The falling snow, cold and hard, struck his face as he propelled them higher.

The flames rose, licking at the sky and nipping at Julian's heels. But he flew, cutting through the thick black air. Even though the reinforcements, spurred on by Ingrid's shouts, chased him, he was too fast and too motivated. He outdistanced them with ease until not even a wisp of smoke reached him.

Sienna shifted in his arms and murmured, as if she was regaining consciousness. She had already been out so long. Perhaps exhaustion, more than fear, had caused her to collapse. He tightened his grip, so that she wouldn't slip from his hold. He had to get her to safety—had to return her to land before she awakened. She had been frightened of him *before*— he couldn't risk her awakening during flight. If she fought him...

If she fell...

Instead of saving her, he might wind up being the one responsible for her death…as he was responsible for other deaths.

CHAPTER TWO

SIENNA'S EYES OPENED—to total blackness. Panic pressed against her chest, and a scream burned in her throat, escaping in a mere gasp of breath.

"Shh," a deep voice murmured. "You're all right. Everything's fine." Flames flickered as he lit candles. The soft light illuminated the room.

The bedroom. Sienna lay on a soft mattress, a brown suede bedspread pulled to her chin. The drapes, drawn across the windows, were also brown and so thick that they blocked any hint of moonlight or streetlamps. The candlelight didn't dispel her panic as her fear increased. "Wh-where am I? Where did you take me?"

"Home."

She glanced around at the plaster walls that stretched ten feet to a coffered ceiling. An ornate chandelier hung from the center, but only the reflection of the candlelight shimmered in the crystal and leaded glass.

She shook her head. "This isn't my home."

"This is *my* home."

"Your bed?"

He nodded, his black hair skimming across his broad shoulders. He'd ditched his jacket and wore only the black silk shirt now, pulled free of the waist of his dark pants. Several shirt buttons had been opened, revealing the sculpted muscles of his chest.

Sienna shivered.

"You're still cold?"

Her fingers trembling, she lifted the blanket and peered beneath. She still wore her clothes, but the red velvet dress had twisted, the hem tangled around her hips. "You—you didn't undress me…"

"Did you want me to?" he asked as he settled onto the bed next to her, his hip pressed against hers.

"I— Of course not," she replied. And she tried to shift away, but he stretched his arm across her and planted his palm atop the blanket on the other side of her, trapping her in the bed—her face just inches from his. She tried to ignore his closeness and tried not to stammer as she demanded, "I want to know why—how—when you brought me here."

He opened his mouth, as if he intended to answer at least one of those questions. But Sienna needed to know something else first, so she put a finger across his lips. "Who the hell are you?"

"My name is Julian Vossimer."

The name meant nothing to her. But the man did—if he really was the one she remembered from that old nightmare. Yet everyone had told her that

that had been just a dream, her mind playing tricks on her...like Nana's had been playing tricks on her at the end.

"I don't understand," she said, "why I'm here."

"We need to talk, Sienna," he said, his deep voice lowered to a soft whisper. "I have some things to tell you, some things you need to hear."

"I remember."

"What?" He tensed. "*What* do you remember?"

The memories didn't surge back like they had, violently, at the funeral home. They were just *there* now—like she was just *here* with him. It hadn't been a dream or a trick of her mind, no matter what anyone had tried to convince her.

"I remember that night," she said, "that you were the one who pulled me from the wreckage." He hadn't just pulled her, though. He'd had to manipulate the twisted metal, wrenching it apart before he'd been able to get her free. Maybe she had dreamed that part because no man was capable of such strength. Since he had saved her once, she shouldn't fear him now. "I guess I owe you...my life..."

A muscle flinched in the deep crease of his lean cheek. His face was all sculpted planes and hard lines that tempted her finger to trace and touch. Did it matter what else he was, or why he'd brought her here?

"You're my hero..."

The muscle jerked again as he shook his head. "I'm no hero."

"Did you bring me here to hurt me?" she asked, but she already knew that he hadn't. If she'd felt she was in real danger from him, she would have started fighting to escape him. It wouldn't make sense for him to have saved her all those years ago to hurt her now.

"No," he answered her, his dark eyes serious and sincere. "I brought you here to protect you."

"See, you're my hero," she said. Maybe it was his eyes—those deep-set dark eyes that pulled her into his soul. Maybe it was the attraction, quivering inside her, that she'd never felt as intensely for another man. But she leaned forward and lifted her face to his. Her lips skimmed across that diamond-shaped scar on his chin before she kissed him.

His mouth moved against hers as he took possession of her. His lips parted hers, and his tongue slipped inside, tasting her. He eased her back onto the pillow and followed her down.

Sienna had never been kissed as thoroughly. She slid her hands into his hair, tangling her fingers in the silky black strands as she clutched his nape. But he pulled away, breathing so heavily that his chest pushed against her breasts.

"I'm not cold anymore," she murmured. But then reality intruded, reminding her that she didn't know this man. Not really. She had only a child's exaggerated memory of the man who'd saved her life. This same man, who appeared not even a day older, although nearly twenty years had passed. She shivered again.

"You're not?"

"I'm scared," she admitted. Scared of the feelings he drew out of her—feelings she'd promised herself she would never risk experiencing. She'd already lost too many people she cared about; it was easier to stop caring.

He said nothing, just continued to stare at her with that molten dark gaze.

"This is where you're supposed to tell me that I have nothing to fear," she prodded him.

"I can't."

"No, because then you wouldn't need to protect me." She reached up and traced the line of his jaw to the scar on his chin. "Why do you need to protect me?"

Did he know about the mounting debts? Did he pity her for having no one and nothing left?

He stared down at her, his conflict apparent in his dark eyes. "I thought I needed to protect you from… from something else…but now I think I need to protect you from me."

A smile twitched at her lips. "I don't need protecting from anyone," she assured him. "I can take care of myself. I've been taking care of myself for a long while." Except for that night, when he'd pulled her from the twisted metal of what had once been the family sedan.

"For a long while, you've been taking care of everyone else," he said. "Your grandfather. Your grandmother."

How did he know so much about her? How did he know that she had cared for both her grandparents through long illnesses? Both had died from cancer. "Have you been watching me?"

All these years…

"I know you," he claimed. "I know that you haven't taken care of yourself."

"I said that I had…that I can…"

He shook his head. "You were so focused on your family that you didn't take care of yourself. I don't think you know how."

"Of course I know how."

"When have you ever done something for yourself?" he asked. "Something just for you?"

She slid her fingers back into his hair. "This. You. This is the first time in…" Forever that she remembered thinking only of herself, thinking only of her pleasure. Not her pain. And she had no idea why. Remembering who he was had brought all that pain crashing back, the force of it so strong that it had rendered her unconscious. But now, in his bed, in his arms, desire held that pain at bay.

She knew it would come crashing back again with the reality of all that she had lost and with how alone

she was. But in his bed, in his arms, she wasn't alone.
And she wanted that feeling to last. She wanted nothing to do with reality for the rest of the night.

She pulled his head down to hers and kissed him
with all the passion burning inside her. His mouth
opened as he sighed her name, and Sienna slid her
tongue across his bottom lip. And across the line of
his teeth which was even but for the point—the sharp
point of an incisor. Yet it was longer than a mere
incisor and sharper.

Like a fang.

And she realized why he had not aged a day since
he'd rescued her. The man was immortal. The man
was not a man. *He was a vampire.*

SHE KNEW.

The minute her tongue had brushed across the
tip, his fang had distended. Usually he could control
it—usually he could control his passion. But not with
her.

Not with Sienna kissing him, her fingers running
through his hair, clutching at it to hold his mouth to
hers. But then she pulled back and shoved her trembling hands against his chest, pushing him away.

Her eyes, wide with horror, stared up at him, and
she stammered, "You're— You're a…"

She couldn't speak the word aloud, but then neither could he, for so many reasons.

"Sienna, you're upset—exhausted. You're not

thinking clearly," he tried to convince her. "You need to rest."

"I need to leave," she said, her voice steady now and her hands stronger as she pushed at his chest.

He wouldn't budge, refusing to ease up. Instead he lowered his body more heavily onto hers, holding her down. She wriggled beneath him, her hips grinding against his erection as her breasts pushed against his chest. He groaned and closed his eyes until she stilled. Her breath, ragged with fear and exertion, blew hot against his throat.

"Let me go," she pleaded.

He shook his head. "I can't let you go."

"Yes, you can," she implored. "You saved me once. No one else would have found the car. I would have died—if you hadn't come along when you had…"

Guilt wound around his heart, clenching it. He'd seen the car crash, but light had been breaking through the night sky, the sun rising. And he hadn't been able to get to her then—not without risking his own life. He'd had to wait until darkness fell again. He'd had to leave her alone, for hours, with her dead parents—scared, possibly hurt. He would never forgive himself. And if she knew, neither would she.

"I'm saving you now," he insisted, "by keeping you here. If I let you go, you won't survive." As she had survived all those hours alone in the tangled car wreck. She was in infinitely more danger now than she'd been then.

"I told you I can take care of myself," she reminded him. "I don't need you…"

He was afraid that he needed *her;* his body ached and throbbed with desire for her. A desire more powerful than he'd ever felt before…for *any* other woman.

Her slender throat moved as she swallowed and added, "…to protect me."

"You have no idea of the danger you're in."

She stared up at him, fear still widening her eyes. "I think I do…"

"You can trust me. I would never hurt you." Intentionally. But inadvertently he already had. He lifted his hand to her face, cupping her cheek in his palm. Then he skimmed his thumb along the curve of her delicate jaw. Her skin was so silky. He lowered his head, his lips just brushing her throat as he breathed deeply, inhaling the sweet scent of vanilla and the sweeter scent of her blood.

Hunger burned inside him, hunger to taste her.

She shuddered, as if able to read his mind. And maybe she could. Her grandmother had certainly had that gift. She'd known things he hadn't told her, things he hadn't admitted even to himself. He hadn't loved her; he'd only wanted her for her beauty. She'd been right to deny him. Sienna was even more beautiful than her grandmother and probably just as smart if not smarter. No doubt she would deny him, too.

"I won't hurt you," he said again, as he stared into

her eyes, willing her to believe him. Willing her to trust him even though he wasn't entirely certain he could trust himself—with her.

Her eyes dilated, the pupils eclipsing the glittery blue. "This seems like a dream," she murmured. "I must be just dreaming…"

"What do you dream of?" he wondered.

"You…" Her breath caught, quivering in her chest. "I dream of arms reaching out, pulling me to safety, holding me close. I dream of *you*…"

"Sienna…" He didn't deserve the gratitude he glimpsed in her eyes. He was no hero.

"I didn't think you were real," she admitted. "Everyone told me that I must have made you up, but they had no explanation for how I'd gotten free. No human could have twisted apart that metal. But nobody was around when they found me by the side of the road. So I began to believe them, to believe that I'd only imagined you." She lifted her hands to his face, her fingers trembling as she traced his jaw. "But here you are, and I'm still not sure you're real."

"I'm real…" And desire had driven him beyond his guilt and regrets. He caught her hands in his and turned his face, nuzzling her wrist. Her pulse leaped beneath his lips, racing.

"But you're a…" She shook her head. "I didn't think Nana was lucid when she told me about…" She swallowed hard, the creamy skin of her throat rippling. "I thought it had just been the drugs making her talk crazy…"

So Ingrid hadn't been lying. Sienna knew… *things*…no mortal could know and live.

"Hell," she scoffed, "maybe I'm the one who's crazy. Before I woke up—here—I had the strangest sensation as if I was flying…" She released a shaky sigh. "Or floating…"

"You're not crazy, Sienna," he assured her. But *he* was for thinking he could save her. Because now, knowing for certain that she'd learned about the Underground Society, there was only one way he could do that.…

"Yes, I am," she insisted, "because even knowing what you are, I want…" She pressed her lips together and closed her eyes, as if willing the words back, or herself somewhere else.

"What, Sienna?" he asked, his heart pounding hard and fast. Maybe he wasn't so crazy after all. "What do you want?"

She opened her eyes, and along with her fear, he glimpsed the fascination. And desire?

Her voice whisper-soft, she admitted, *"You."*

CHAPTER THREE

PASSION BURNED IN his eyes—brighter than the flickering candles. And Sienna wished she could take back her admission, scared of his reaction and hers. This…man…had some kind of unnatural hold on her. His dark gaze drew her in, hypnotizing her into forgetting what he was…and the danger he posed to her.

She shook her head, her hair rustling against the satin pillowcase. "I didn't mean it…"

"You didn't mean to *say* it," he astutely surmised. "But you meant it. I can see it in your eyes, in the flush on your skin. You want *me*."

Even knowing it was too late, that she was in too deep, she shook her head again and hotly denied, "No!"

"Liar," he accused, his low voice vibrating with a sexy chuckle.

Julian Vossimer with his long, silky hair and hard muscled body epitomized *sexy*. And Sienna was powerless to resist her attraction to him. As he had accused her earlier, it had been a long time—too long for her to remember—the last time she'd done something just for herself. But making love to him...

Did she dare?

Taking the choice from her, he rolled off her and left the bed. She must have imagined the passion in his eyes. While she wanted him, he didn't want her.

Standing beside the bed, he stared down at her—his dark eyes still aglow. And his fingers went to the buttons on his shirt. First he undid the cuffs, then the rest of the buttons down the front, parting the silk to reveal the sculpted muscles of his chest.

Sienna swallowed. His masculine beauty as the candlelight bathed his skin made her lose her breath. She found her voice, although raspy and weak, to ask, "What are you doing?"

His lips curved into a slight, wicked grin, and he reached for his belt, unclasping and pulling it free of his dark jeans. "I'm coming to bed..."

Then the jeans, and his boxers along with them, dropped to the floor. And Sienna's jaw dropped, too. Her mouth fell open and she gasped. His erection jutted from lean hips and heavily muscled thighs—so thick and long. When once she'd been so cold, now her skin heated—burning—but before she could push back the blanket, he jerked it off her.

He reached for her next, his hands shaking slightly as he wrapped them around her upper arms and lifted her to her knees on the soft mattress. "Try to tell me you don't want me now," he challenged her.

The lie caught in her throat, choked with desire. She couldn't…resist him. She slid her hands over his chest, and his heart pounded against her palm—in perfect rhythm with the frantic beat of hers.

"You're so arrogant," she admonished him. But not without damn good reason.

Could any woman resist him?

The glow dimmed in his eyes for a moment, as if he'd taken insult at her comment.

"I'm sorry," she murmured.

"You're not the one who has cause to be sorry," he told her.

Not yet. But would she if they made love? Would she live to regret what she'd done? Would she live at all?

He must have glimpsed the fear in her eyes, for he stroked his thumb along her jaw again. "Don't be afraid," he said, "I won't hurt you."

She already hurt, aching for his touch—for his kiss. For the possession of his body. She stared into his handsome face, mesmerized by his dark gaze. "Julian…"

He leaned over her, lowering his mouth until just a breath separated their lips. "Do you want me?" he asked.

She slid her hands up his chest, muscles rippling beneath her palms, and tunneled her fingers through his thick, silky hair to grasp his nape. "You know I do..." She pulled his head down so that their lips met.

The kiss was feather-soft and nearly innocent. Then she opened her mouth, and his tongue slid across her lower lip, stroking the sensitive flesh before dipping inside to taste her. Innocence fled as he made love to her mouth, his tongue driving in and out, sliding over hers.

His fingers knotted in the fabric of her dress. Then he dragged it up—their lips parting as he pulled the velvet over her head then dropped it to the floor. His breath shuddered out as his gaze traveled over her body, over the bits of scarlet lace covering her breasts and the curve of her hips.

"You're beautiful," he praised, the words a raspy groan of appreciation. "So beautiful..."

It wasn't the first time she'd been told, but it was the first time a compliment had affected her so that her nipples hardened, pushing against the thin lace, and heat rushed through her, burning between her thighs. She swallowed down a whimper that tickled the back of her throat.

But then he touched her, with just his fingertips, gliding them over her shoulders, along the ridge of her collarbone to the curve of her breasts. And the whimper slipped free even before those clever fingers reached the aching points of her nipples. When he touched them, sliding his fingers back and forth over the lace, she moaned and arched her neck.

Fear flickered to life. What if he took that gesture as an invitation to bite her?

"I won't hurt you," he repeated, his voice raspy with passion, as if he'd read her mind. His hands moved, sliding around her back to the clasp of her bra, which he undid. Then he pushed the straps down her arms so that the bit of lace fell away—leaving her breasts naked to his touch.

He cupped the mounds. And he kissed her lips again, deeply, as he gently massaged her sensitive flesh. Her nipples pushed against his palms, and she arched again—needing more from him than kisses.

His mouth broke from hers, and she panted for breath as his lips slid down her throat, his tongue flicking over her leaping pulse before moving lower. He traced the curve of each breast before closing his lips around one aching point. His tongue flicked across the sensitive tip.

She cried out and shuddered, a mini-orgasm rippling through her, dampening her panties. "Julian," she panted his name now, aching for more pleasure. Her hands moved, sliding down the rippling muscles of his back to the curve of his buttocks. She raked her nails over the taut skin. And now she pleaded, "Julian…"

He shook his head, his lips tugging at her nipple. Then he lifted his head. "Not yet..."

"Now," she begged, "please..."

He pushed her back then knelt on the mattress, between her legs. His hand shaking slightly, he tore the lace from her hips then lifted her thighs to his shoulders. He skimmed his mouth along the sensitive skin of her inner thighs, making her quiver, before kissing her intimately. His tongue stroked over her cleft before slipping inside and tasting. A moan of pleasure slipped from his throat.

Tears stung Sienna's eyes at the exquisite torture. Pressure built inside her, more intense and painful than she'd ever experienced. "You're hurting me," she murmured. "I'm hurting..."

But his fangs only pressed lightly against her swollen mound as his tongue dipped deeper inside her. His hands moved—one to a breast, which he molded, the other to the most sensitive part of her. His thumb pushed against the nub, breaking the pressure free inside her as an orgasm slammed through her.

She screamed, the pleasure tearing her apart. But then he moved, his mouth sliding over her navel, up her ribs to the tip of a breast. His lips tugged at the nipple as the tip of his erection pushed through her wet curls.

She wrapped her legs around his lean waist, her fingers sliding down to his butt again to clutch him to her. She stretched, trying to accept him, as the pressure built again. He was so big—so thick—that her skin burned. Then he slid so deep, he touched her where she'd never been touched. Pleasure exploded, so intense that she fought to retain consciousness. "Julian!"

"Sienna!" he shouted her name, as if he, too, were shocked by the power of their passion. He thrust, driving deeper and deeper.

She clung to him, matching his frantic rhythm. The pressure wound tight inside her then exploded again, shattering her as she came even more powerfully than before.

He tensed, every muscle rippling, his skin slick with passion. He threw back his head, the tendons in his neck jutting out, as he uttered a guttural groan. Then he pumped his orgasm inside her, filling her as he came. His body shuddered as, finally spent, he clutched her in his arms and rolled to his side.

Sienna stroked her hands across his broad shoulders and through his hair, as if trying to soothe him, even as her own heart beat madly from an exertion that was not just physical. What the hell was she doing? Had she not only made love with a vampire, but fallen in love with him, too?

"Julian..."

The voice called to him out of the darkness. Not Sienna's voice. She slept in his arms, her head on his chest—almost as if she trusted him. But he didn't deserve her trust.

"Julian!" Impatience sharpened the masculine tone. And he recognized his telepathic *caller*.

"Grandfather," he answered the summons, speaking the words only inside his head.

"You foolish boy," Orson Vossimer berated him. "You think you can hide her from me?"

Boy. No matter the centuries Julian had existed, to his grandfather he would always be a boy. Never a man.

"You don't know where we are," he called the old man's bluff. He'd been careful to let no thought of their whereabouts pass through his mind—the mind his grandfather had always been too easily able to read.

"I will," Orson vowed. "Soon. You better fix this before we find you. I'm tired of cleaning up your messes, boy."

Julian winced. "You're overreacting. Just like before..."

"And just like before, you're too arrogant," his grandfather reprimanded him, "and too careless. You're not just endangering yourself, but everyone else in the Underground Society."

"She's no threat and you know it," Julian challenged him. "Just like her grandmother was no threat."

"And her father?"

Julian sucked in a breath. "You didn't need to—"

"Save the Underground from an inevitable massacre?"

"You nearly killed a little girl," Julian said, his arms contracting around Sienna's sleeping body. His fingers tunneled through her silky blond tresses.

"If she had died, it would have saved you from making another mess," Orson said with none of the regret and guilt that haunted Julian. "Like you're making now."

"She's not a mess."

"You're the mess, boy," Orson said, "and I can't keep bailing you out. You're a liability the Underground can't afford."

"None of this is about the Underground," Julian surmised. "This is about the Vossimer name."

"You've dishonored the family," Orson admitted. "And by hiding her away, you've done nothing to restore the honor."

"So I'm a liability to the Vossimers, as well as the Underground?"

"A liability neither can afford."

Julian shuddered. He'd always known the old man barely tolerated him. But hate him? "Are you threatening me?"

"I'm cautioning you to do the right thing."

"Your definition of right and mine are completely different."

"We've been at odds for years," Orson admitted.

"That's your problem. You won't listen. Maybe it's time you stop being a problem."

Julian had no doubt now. Not only would Sienna lose her life if they were discovered, he would lose his, too. There was no changing his grandfather's mind.

"You have one option, Julian."

Orson Vossimer giving him an escape? "So what is this option?"

"*You* have to kill her."

"That's not an option. As long as I live, Sienna won't die," he vowed.

"Then make her one of us," Orson advised. "One of the undead."

"It's not that easy." To make her undead, she would have to risk death. She would have to trust him completely, and he'd never turned a human before. Even though he'd already determined it was his only way to save her, he didn't trust himself to not accidentally kill her. And if he couldn't trust himself, he couldn't expect her to trust him, either.

"It's quite simple, son," Orson insisted. "Turn her or you'll both die."

"She still may die," Julian pointed out. And he'd be the one who'd personally killed her. Was that what his grandfather counted on?

He received no reply. Orson had severed their telepathic connection. And Julian would have to work to block his grandfather's return to his mind. He couldn't be found yet—not until he had time to earn Sienna's trust. His heart clenched as he admitted to himself he wanted more than her trust. He wanted her love.

He muffled a snort of self-derision. He was the fool his grandfather thought him if he actually believed he could earn anyone's love. His own parents hadn't wanted him and Orson had only taken him out of family obligation and honor. And while many women had wanted Julian over the centuries he'd lived, none of them had actually loved him—not enough to want to spend eternity with him.

He focused on Sienna, studying her beautiful face as she slept. She turned, arching her neck against the pillow. He leaned forward and nuzzled the delicate skin of her throat, breathing in the sweet fragrance that was her very spirit.

If he were smart, he would forget about her trust and her love, and he'd take her now. He'd take the choice away from her and turn her into what he was. Undead. But if he failed, she'd die....

CHAPTER FOUR

A SCREAM BURNED Sienna's throat when she opened her eyes to blackness. As memories rushed back, panic pressed down on her chest, making it hard for her to breathe. She had been trapped under twisted metal, shut in darkness even during the day, for hours before Julian had pulled her from the wreckage. Ever since then, she'd suffered an anxiety attack any time she was in the dark again.

She forced herself to take slow, deep breaths, and steadied her racing pulse. As she calmed down, she noticed the blackness was not complete. Flames, from candles burned low, flickered faintly—dispelling tiny circles of night.

She didn't need light to know that she was alone. Julian was gone. She lifted a hand to her neck. Running her fingertips around her throat, she noted no puncture marks—no sticky blood clung to her skin. He'd kept his word; he hadn't hurt her. Yet. Could she trust him?

She lifted the blanket, and cool air rushed over her bare skin. *She was naked.* Despite the room's low temperature, heat suffused her body—with embarrassment and vestiges of the passion he'd drawn from her—from her soul. She'd never responded to any man the way she had to him.

But he wasn't a man—at least not *just* a man. He was so much more. More than she could handle.

Hands shaking, she jerked the sheet from the bed and wrapped it toga-style around her. Her eyes adjusted to the darkness now, she searched the hardwood floor around the bed but could not find her dress. So she opened the doors of the antique wardrobe, but only a few men's shirts hung from the rod. She dropped the sheet in favor of one of the shirts, thrusting her arms into the long sleeves and doing up the buttons. The tails reached nearly to her knees, and she had to roll back the cuffs several folds in order to see her hands.

She continued her search through the drawers of an antique bureau, finding only a few boxer shorts and socks. From the sparse furnishings, she would guess this was not his primary residence. Where had he brought her?

Fumbling around in the faint candlelight, she found some thick drapes, but when she drew them back, she revealed only more aged brick wall. No window. No escape but for the door. Before she rattled the knob she knew it would not turn. A lock held it closed, trapping her inside. And him out?

Could she believe him? Was he only intent on protecting her? Or seducing her? Since he'd already done that, he didn't need to keep her. Unless his body, like hers, ached for more….

Her knees weak, she returned to the bed and sank to the edge of the mattress. He hadn't caused her reaction; it wasn't desire for him making her weak and vulnerable. It had to be hunger. He wasn't wrong— she hadn't been taking care of herself much lately.

Actually, she hadn't taken care of herself at all. If she had, she might not have fainted in his arms and wound up trapped in a dungeon—albeit an elegant, romantic one. The darkness spurred her panic again, but she fought it back, refusing to let fear control her. She couldn't let him—and her desire for him— control her, either.

She had to find a way out. Noticing the bedside table she had yet to search, she yanked open a drawer. Despite the candle burning atop the table, she didn't have enough light to see inside so she had to fumble through the contents. She pulled out a phone charger but could find no phone, only some papers she held near the candle to read. Take-out menus for restaurants in the downtown Zantrax area. The city in Michigan, which was even larger than Detroit, was hours from the suburban town where Sienna had lived with her grandparents.

How long had she been out that he'd had time to bring her here? Had he drugged her? Was that why she, who was always so cautious with men and especially with her heart, had made love with him so soon after meeting him?

Yet it wasn't soon. She'd known him a long time. And despite what he was, he was still her hero. Or he had been. She wasn't sure what he was now, nearly twenty years after pulling her from the wreckage. A photograph slipped from between the menus and fell picture-side-up on the tabletop. Faces peered up at her from the yellowed snapshot. Familiar faces. Julian's handsome face and one that was eerily similar to hers, but the picture was aged. The embracing couples' vintage clothing and the antique car behind them, that was at least sixty years old, dated the photo.

Her grandmother and Julian had had a relationship? The thought churned in her empty stomach, and she pressed a hand over her mouth. Her palm held in the gasp that escaped when the door rattled open. She caught just a brief glimpse of the hall before he closed the door with his back, his hands busy with the tray he carried.

"You're awake," he said, his voice rough with a trace of disappointment. He'd pulled on just his pants, leaving his heavily muscled chest and arms bare.

"Yes..." She swallowed hard, fighting down the instant desire that he inspired in her. "I— I'm awake."

"And unharmed," he told her, his lips curving into that wicked grin again. "I told you I wouldn't hurt you."

She nodded, agreeing that he'd said the words, but she still wasn't convinced he would honor his claim. "Why did you bring me here?" she asked. "To seduce me?"

"I'm not sure who seduced whom," he teased her as he settled the tray onto the mattress. Fresh fruit overflowed a bowl; frothy whipped cream filled another. Champagne bubbled in flutes.

She gestured toward what he'd brought her. "I think it's pretty clear…" That he wanted to seduce her again. She crossed her legs, trying to fight the pressure that was already building inside her.

He shook his head. "No, it isn't…" He leaned forward and skimmed his fingers along her jaw. His voice low with awe, he murmured, "You are so beautiful…"

She lifted the photo she'd found and held it next to her face. "I look like my grandmother."

He didn't even glance at the picture, his mesmerizing gaze intent on her face. "You're even more beautiful."

Nana had always claimed the same thing; Sienna couldn't see it, as she studied the old photograph again. She only saw Julian's arm wrapped possessively around her grandmother's slender shoulders.

"Were you…" she choked on the word, but finally managed to utter it "…lovers?"

"No," he said, his voice firm with sincerity. "She was already engaged to your grandfather when we met. She would not betray him—no matter what I offered her."

"Immortality," she said, remembering the rambling story Nana had told on her deathbed. "I thought it was just the drugs talking…"

"If only it had been," he remarked, "if only I hadn't been so arrogant…"

He had every reason for arrogance. He was more handsome than any man she'd seen before—even on movie screens. "So you did…offer her immortality?" she asked.

"I never actually said the words…"

"But Nana knew," Sienna realized. "She just knew things. Grandpa said she had a gift." A gift Sienna wished she'd inherited so that she might be able to reveal Julian's true intentions.

"I wish my grandfather had believed that." He pushed a hand through his long hair, tangling the glossy strands. "But he didn't believe mortals have gifts."

"So he's a…?"

His mouth lifted, again, in that wicked grin. "You still can't say the word."

She still struggled to accept that she was awake, that she wasn't dreaming the whole thing…especially making love with him. The intensity of passion and pleasure…that had to have been a dream. But even now, the attraction simmered between them, causing her skin to tingle and her pulse to quicken. And he hadn't touched her again except with that dark gaze of his. "Everything seems so unreal," she admitted. Especially him and her attraction to him.

"I'm real," he assured her, as if he'd read her mind. "And to answer your question, yes, all Vossimers are."

Vampires.

DESPITE ALL THE trouble his arrogance had caused, Julian had to know, "Is that why your grandmother turned me down?"

Sienna's blue eyes sparkled with amusement. "Her rejection stung?"

Regrettably that was all it had done. At least if he'd loved her, all the tragedy that had followed wouldn't have been so senseless.

But Julian had never loved anyone. Maybe he wasn't capable—none of the Vossimers he knew had been. His parents had abandoned him to his grandfather when he was just a child. And Orson Vossimer hardly oozed affection. The man had always considered Julian a burden. Maybe Julian's problem was that *he* just wasn't lovable himself.

Sienna must have picked up on his thoughts for she leaned forward, her hand on his forearm. "Did you love her?"

He shook his head.

"That's what she chose over you," she explained. "Love."

"Over immortality?"

"She didn't regret her decision, not even at the last." Her face paled as if she was about to faint again as she added, "Not even when she was suffering so much..." Her skin cancer had metastasized, spreading to all her organs.

"I'm sorry," Julian said, covering her hand with his. "I'm sorry she had to suffer." His grandfather, who could not only telepathically communicate, could also sometimes predict the future. Julian suspected that was why Orson had let Carolina Briggs live as long as she had—because he'd "seen" her suffering. "That must have been horrible for her... and you."

She nodded as tears shimmered in her beautiful eyes.

"Here," he said, gesturing toward the tray, "I brought you something to eat."

The tears dried, and the amusement returned. "And champagne. Are you trying to get me drunk?"

He'd brought the champagne to celebrate...when she agreed to become his bride. But for once his arrogance deserted him. While her grandmother's rejection had only stung his pride, he worried that Sienna's might hurt more. He couldn't ask her yet—not until he was certain of her answer.

And her love.

While he wasn't convinced he could love, he was confident that...if he had time...he could make her think she loved him. Then, by the time she realized, like everyone else had, that she didn't really love him, it would be too late.

If only Orson and the rest of the Underground would give him the time....

"I'm not trying to get you drunk," he assured her. "I'm trying to take care of you."

"And I told you I can take care of myself."

From the dark circles beneath her eyes and the thinness of her slight body, he doubted it. So he reached for the tray and held up a strawberry to her lips.

Instead of continuing to argue her self-sufficiency with him, she opened her mouth and sank her straight, white teeth into the ripe berry. Juice squirted out and trailed over her chin, down her throat.

His heart slammed against his ribs as his hunger overwhelmed him. He had never wanted to taste anyone with the urgency he wanted—*needed*—to taste her. He pulled the berry away and replaced the fruit with his lips, pressing them to the sweetness of hers. Her mouth opened again, her tongue sliding across his lip to touch his. The kiss wasn't enough to satisfy his hunger. He slid his mouth over her chin and down her throat.

Her fingers clenched in his hair, and she shivered. "Please...don't hurt me..."

"Never," he promised, even though he feared it was a vow he would eventually have to break. His fingers shook as he fought the buttons free on the shirt she wore—*his* shirt. Possessiveness gripped him, filling him with satisfaction. She was *his*. He parted the shirt then pushed it from her shoulders. His breath left his lungs in a ragged sigh. "You are so beautiful…"

Despite her thinness, she had generous curves. Full breasts, dark pink nipples tilting up from the honey-hued mounds. Soft hips sloped from a tiny waist. He skimmed his fingers down her sides, over her silky skin. She shivered again.

"You're cold," he said, cursing the fact he'd had to hide her here—underground. Even if he wasn't hiding her, he'd have to stay here…as the sun was bound to rise soon. Consignment to life in the dark, that was the curse of his existence. Could he ask her to share it?

She shook her head. "I'm not cold."

But he lifted the tray from the mattress, setting it atop the bedside table where she'd dropped her grandmother's picture. He hadn't kept it all these years to remember Carolina Briggs; he'd kept it to remember his own foolishness in asking anyone to become his bride.

When he reached for the blankets to pull them over her naked body, she caught his wrist, her nails nipping at his skin. "I'm not cold," she repeated, "I'm hungry."

Before he could retrieve the tray, she reached for the snap of his pants. A laugh rumbled first in his chest, then his throat. The vibration eased his urgency, calming his anxiety over their predicament. He hadn't laughed in so long.

Then she planted a palm against his chest and pushed him back on the mattress, and his laughter ceased, the tension and urgency returning to his body with painful intensity. But it wasn't fear driving him; it was passion.

"Who's the seducer now?" he asked, his words turning to a groan as she unzipped his fly and released his straining erection.

First she slid her fingertips down the length of him. Then she leaned over and ran her tongue over his engorged flesh. He tangled a hand in her hair, holding her to him as she closed her lips around the aching tip of his penis.

"Sienna!" Her passion surprised him. But her generosity should not have; she'd obviously grown used to putting others' needs over her own.

He couldn't take advantage of her. So he pushed her back, refusing to take the pleasure she offered with her mouth. And he made love to her body, kissing every inch of sweet skin. When his fangs scraped across a sensitive point, like the tip of her breast, or the dip of her navel, she moaned. If he bit her, he knew she'd enjoy it, but he didn't want to scare her. Her eyes, staring down at him, were wide with fear, but also excitement.

He kissed her like he had before, intimately, sliding his tongue into the heat of her desire. His own body ached and throbbed, demanding release. But he waited until she came, her hands clutching in his hair as she screamed his name. Then he pulled her to the edge of the high mattress. And he thrust inside her—again and again. She met him, rising off the bed, her legs wrapped around his waist, her hands in his hair then gripping his shoulders. She nipped the straining muscles in his neck as she came again, shuddering as her orgasm bubbled hot and sticky over him. Her inner muscles clutched his erection, squeezing and squeezing until he could control his need no longer.

Passion exploded with one last nearly violent thrust, and he came. "Sienna!"

They collapsed onto the bed, his face buried in the sweet temptation of her neck. He slid his mouth along her throat then parted his lips so his fangs scraped across her skin. "Sienna, let me turn you."

"What?" She tensed beneath him.

"Become a Vossimer," he urged her. "Become my wife."

CHAPTER FIVE

SIENNA'S HEART CLENCHED with excitement then dread as she remembered, "All Vossimers are vampires." She'd finally said the word, but she could never become one. "Why, Julian? Why do you want me to marry you?"

"It's the only way I can protect you."

She should have been relieved he hadn't professed love, because it was too soon and would have proved him a liar, yet disappointment squeezed her heart. She sucked in a shaky breath and asked, "Who are you protecting me from?"

His arms tightened around her, holding her closer as if he was using his body to shield her. "People who will hurt you."

"They'll do more than hurt me," she realized. "They intend to kill me. Why?"

"Because of what you know."

"About you?" She'd said it once, but she could not manage to utter the word again around the lump of emotion choking her. "About what you are?"

He nodded. "I'm not the only one."

"You told me that all Vossimers are," she recalled. "So you have family?"

A muscle twitched in his cheek. "Yes. Relatively speaking."

"You're not close, then?"

"Not at all," he admitted. "But there are more than Vossimers. There's a whole Underground Society."

"I had no idea…" she murmured, stunned. "I would have never imagined…" Not only his existence, but his passion.

"You're not supposed to know. No mortal is."

She shivered as understanding dawned. "And that's why I'm in danger."

He sighed. "Any time a human has learned about our existence, bad things happen. The undead are destroyed."

The thought of him dead knocked the air from her lungs, filling her with a sense of loss even greater than she'd already known. "But…how…?"

"There are ways."

He might have wanted to spare her the image, but she closed her eyes and it was there—in her mind: Julian lying on the ground, a stake through his heart. She shuddered. "No…"

"When humans learn of our existence, they react with fear. They think we pose a danger. So they try to eliminate that threat."

"You keep telling me that I'm in danger," she

said, "that's why you brought me here." Why he'd proposed.

"Because you know. Because of what happened when other people found out, the Underground Society made a rule—for our protection."

"How many people have found out?" she asked, having to know how many mortals were killed—and how many Julian had personally killed.

Had she made love, not just with a vampire, but a cold-blooded killer? Goose bumps lifted her skin as dread chilled her to the bone.

"It was believed that your grandmother knew our secret," he said.

"But she died from a horrible disease," she said, flashing back to Nana's suffering. "No one killed her."

"No. There was actually no proof she knew...until the end."

"Until she told me."

He nodded then grimaced and admitted, "There was someone else who knew, who planned to write an exposé on the Secret Vampire Society. He was going to reveal our whereabouts and order our deaths."

Sienna's breath caught. "And this man? He was killed?"

Julian nodded. "Him and his wife."

"Was I alive when the murders took place?" she asked, wondering if she'd read about them. If the man had been a famous reporter or writer, his death could have been sensationalized, like her father's had been.

"You were seven," Julian answered, his deep voice raspy with emotion, "and in the backseat."

Her breath hissed out. "My father? How had he found out?"

"I don't believe your grandmother ever told him, but he inherited her gift. He knew things...he would have been better off never knowing. Then he investigated until he discovered other things—things you would have been better off that he never learned."

Grief pressed heavy on her heart. "I guess it's good that I didn't inherit that family gift—that I took after my grandfather instead."

"He was a simple man," Julian said.

"A good man," Sienna defended him as she twisted on her finger the engagement ring that her grandfather had put on her grandmother's.

"You're wearing that ring," Julian observed.

She nodded. "Nana gave it to me, wanted the man I marry to put it on my left hand."

"Marry me," he urged her again.

She shook her head, tears burning her eyes. "I can't..."

"Because you can't forgive my part in the accident?"

"What was your part?" She had to know, her stomach churning with revulsion. Had she made love with—not once but twice—the man responsible for her parents' deaths?

"I didn't stop it." He dragged in a ragged breath. "I tried...but I was too late. Too late to save them. And too much of a coward to save you."

"But you did," she reminded him. "You saved my life." She wished he could have saved her parents, too, but she believed he'd tried.

"I got lucky—that you weren't more seriously hurt," he said, "because I couldn't get to you right away."

"I know—the crash was horrible. The car was so far down in the ravine that it was a wonder you found me at all."

"I saw the car go over," he admitted. "But the sun was coming up. I couldn't get to you...not without risking my own life."

Sienna tensed, shocked.

"So much for being your hero, huh?" he said, and he lifted his arm and let her slide away from him. "I'm sorry. But I can't be out in the sun...and live..."

"So much for being undead," she murmured.

"Is that why you won't marry me?" he asked. "Because of what I am?"

She wasn't certain if he was referring to his being a vampire or his not being the hero she'd believed him to be for the past twenty years. "No. I made my grandmother a promise on her deathbed."

"To wear this ring?" He ran a fingertip over the diamond then over the scar on his chin.

"She did that? My grandmother?"

His lips curved into that wickedly sexy grin. "She didn't like what I said about your grandfather."

"She was feisty." Sienna wished she possessed her grandmother's spirit, as well as her face.

"She was stubborn," Julian said. "You can't be stubborn. The rest of the Underground will find us. I won't be able to save you this time."

"Unless I become your bride…" She glanced down at the diamond. Could she let this man—this one whose interest in her grandmother had caused her family so much pain—switch the ring to her left hand? She shook her head. "I can't…"

"You're exhausted," Julian said, brushing his fingertip under her eyes, over the dark circles she hadn't been able to hide with makeup. "Sleep on it."

She nodded and lowered her lids. But no matter how much rest she got, she wouldn't change her mind. She had made her grandmother a promise. Like Carolina Briggs, Sienna would only marry for love. She couldn't marry a man who offered just protection or even immortality. She could only marry the man who offered her his heart.

She couldn't marry Julian Vossimer…even if that decision killed her.

SHE WAS GONE. Julian didn't need to open his eyes to confirm Sienna's absence. After what he'd revealed, he wasn't surprised that she would have slipped away while he slept. He should have locked the door behind himself, but he'd been juggling the tray of food that sat beside the bed, mostly untouched. The champagne still filled the glasses, but no bubbles rushed to the rim. It had gone flat.

"Sienna?" he called out. Maybe she could hear him the way that Orson could. Maybe she had her grandmother's gift, but had been unaware until now, as she'd been unaware of the kind of man he really was.

She must hate him—so much that even if she had the gift, she'd block him from her mind. And from her heart.

"Sienna!" His voice cracked with urgency. He had to find her. Yet even though the bedroom was dark, all the candles burned out, he knew it was day. Because he had to fight for the energy to leave the bed.

Even if she wouldn't accept his proposal, he had to find a way to save her. He couldn't let the others kill her…because that would kill him as surely as his leaving the darkness.

Moments later, he climbed the stairs to street level. Light penetrated low-hanging gray clouds and the shower of falling snow. He lifted the collar of his trench coat and slid dark glasses onto his nose. But those precautions were ineffectual as the daylight seeped through his clothes, through his skin and weakened his spirit—draining his soul.

"Sienna…"

His eyes already squinted against the light. He closed them fully and blanked his mind…until she appeared. First as she'd been in his bed—naked and passionate. And then he found her—in the present. In her house, sobbing softly….

She didn't cry for him; he was sure of it, convinced that she hated him now that she knew everything about him. As Orson had said, he was too much trouble. He'd brought Sienna nothing but pain.

And now pain filled him, burning him alive—zapping his strength. But he couldn't turn back. Because he could see more than Sienna; he could see what she had yet to realize—that she was not alone.

CHAPTER SIX

TEARS STREAKED DOWN Sienna's face while sobs burned her throat. She'd already broken her promise to her grandmother. She wasn't supposed to cry But these tears weren't just over missing Nana; she missed *him*.

"That's another promise I broke," she admitted miserably as she twisted the ring on the finger of her right hand. "I love a man who doesn't love me."

While she hadn't been able to keep all the promises she'd made Nana, she would keep at least one of them. She glanced toward the tree, which stood before the bay window in the front parlor. Its finely needled branches were bare of lights and ornaments. Sienna had barely found the time to buy the tree; she hadn't been able to decorate it before Nana had passed.

But she'd promised that she would, that she'd deck the halls and celebrate the holiday. She wouldn't let another loss, however devastating, destroy her. She was stronger than that—stronger even than the threat of which Julian had warned. Dashing her tears away with the backs of her hands, Sienna dragged her weary body from the chair. The last thing she felt like doing, after taking the train from Zantrax, was decorating. But this, at least, was one promise she could keep.

Clad in the red velvet dress she'd found in the bathroom of Julian's apartment, Sienna hesitated at the door to the cellar stairs. Jeans and a sweatshirt would be more appropriate attire for digging through cobwebs and dusty boxes. But Nana had loved the velvet dress. And from the desire in his eyes as he'd stripped it from her, so had Julian.

Every thought returned to Julian, like Sienna ached to return to him. Maybe she could get back before dark, before he awakened and noticed that she'd gone. But could she, who feared the dark, turn into a creature who dwelt only in darkness? Even now, panic pressed on her chest as she opened the door to basement. Shadows fell across the steep steps that led to the rough concrete floor.

She'd always hated the cellar, but something more than panic assailed her. A sense of foreboding joined her usual fear, and her legs shook as she descended the rickety stairwell. "Hello?" she called out, as goose bumps lifted on the skin on her arms and the nape of her neck. Instinctively, she knew she was not alone. "Hello?"

Had Julian braved the daylight to come to her? No, she would have known the minute he was near; her body would have reacted, with heat and anticipation, to the closeness of his. But she was not alone. "Who's there?"

"Maybe you do have your grandmother's gift," someone mused from the shadows. The voice was feminine and familiar.

"Ingrid?" The hospice nurse had helped out with Nana at night, so that Sienna had been able to get some rest. She had helped only at night, coming by just after the sun had gone down. Was she one of them? Of the Secret Vampire Society? "What are you doing here?"

"I think you know," the beautiful woman said, her dark eyes glowing eerily in the shadows.

Fear pounded in Sienna's veins. Julian had told her the truth; she was in danger. Maybe she could convince the vampiress that she had no knowledge of their society. "No. I expected to see you at the funeral home—not here."

"I was there," Ingrid said. "At the funeral home *and* when your grandmother told you about us."

Sienna shook her head and infused confusion into her voice as she asked, "About us? I don't understand."

Ingrid's lips, either naturally or painted a deep red, curved into a slight smile. "About Julian Vossimer. She told you about Julian."

"She never said his name," Sienna maintained. "Not that I paid much attention to anything she was saying at the end. She wasn't making any sense." A twinge of pain struck her heart as she remembered, "She was out of her mind with pain."

"She was completely lucid, right until the end," Ingrid said, with a trace of respect for Carolina Briggs. "She got you to make some big promises."

"To celebrate Christmas."

"That's how I knew you'd come down here," the nurse explained.

"To get the decorations." She suspected Ingrid had actually come down to the cellar in order to get away from the sunshine streaming in through the upstairs windows. "The tree looks so naked…"

The image flitting through her mind wasn't of tree branches, though. She imagined Julian instead, how he'd looked—sculpted muscles rippling beneath taut skin, as he had moved over her—then inside her. Despite the dampness of the basement, heat suffused Sienna, spreading throughout her body. She had never been satisfied—*pleasured*—as thoroughly by any other man, and she wanted him again.

Would she even get to see him one last time—now that she'd been found?

"You look like her, you know," Ingrid remarked from where she lurked yet in the shadows.

"My grandmother?"

"This angel." The vampiress held up an ethereal blond doll. "I can understand why he fell for you."

Sienna's heart kicked against her ribs. "Who?"

The slight smile flashed again, but still those dark

eyes glowed eerily—with madness and an anguish that struck a chord within Sienna. "You're beautiful," Ingrid said, "not stupid. You know Julian has fallen for you."

"If I believed that, I wouldn't be here," Sienna pointed out. "I'd still be with him." In his bed, in his arms—her head against his chest, his heart beating steadily beneath her cheek. Why had she left him? Then she remembered. "He doesn't love me."

"I can understand your doubts," Ingrid admitted and continued as if they were friends commiserating about men. "Julian wouldn't have professed his love. He probably doesn't even realize he loves you yet. Men can be so dense." Now the anguish thickened her voice. "They sometimes deny their feelings until it's too late…."

"Was it too late for you?" Sienna asked.

Ingrid released a shuddery breath. "I heard the words. Despite the stake buried in his heart, he managed to tell me he loved me. It was the last thing he ever said."

"I'm sorry…."

"You should be," Ingrid said, rage chasing the sadness from her voice and eyes. "Your father is the one who drove in the stake."

Sienna gasped as another one of her idols fell. "My dad? You're talking about his exposé? I thought he died *before* it was published."

"Julian told you about the exposé?"

She nodded.

"But he didn't tell you what your father did," Ingrid said. "He wanted to spare you the truth."

"What is the truth?" Sienna had to know.

"My...Michael...was your father's source for the article. Michael was so trusting. He didn't understand that he was putting us all in danger—until it was too late, until your father murdered him. He didn't just write the article. He killed Michael. My lover's blood was on your father's hands."

"You got your revenge," Sienna said, suspecting her father's blood was on Ingrid's hands. That the vampiress was the one who was responsible for Sienna's parents' deaths. "You don't need to hurt me."

"You're human. You can't be trusted," Ingrid insisted.

"You were around me for months," Sienna reminded her. "You know me...you know I would never hurt anyone."

"You've already hurt Julian," Ingrid said.

Sienna shook her head. "No..." He was the last person she wanted to hurt.

"You rejected him."

"H-how do you know?"

"Because you're here, and he isn't," Ingrid pointed out.

"That's because he doesn't love me..." That was why she'd turned him down, she realized. Not because she wasn't certain she could become what he was… but because she couldn't even consider changing without his love.

Ingrid shook her head, as if disgusted. "The guy gave up his life for you. What more does he have to give up to prove his love?"

Shock and pain staggered Sienna so that she had to grip the stair railing or tumble down the last few steps to the concrete floor. "No! He's not dead."

"Not yet. But Orson Vossimer warned him. If he didn't kill you, he would be killed."

"Orson Vossimer? He's related to Julian. How could he kill him?"

"Orson Vossimer is Julian's grandfather. And he gave Julian another option besides death. He could turn you."

And Sienna had refused. "I didn't know…"

"It's too late now," Ingrid said. "You're both going to die."

And Sienna would never have the chance to tell Julian that she loved him.

LIGHT BLIND, Julian staggered through the house. Every muscle ached in protest of his movements, but he forced himself to continue, feeling his way along the walls. "Sienna!"

"Julian?"

Her voice, quavering with fear and shock, drew him toward an open door. He stumbled, nearly falling down the stairs.

"Julian!" An arm slid around his waist, a warm body wedging against his side to support his weight. "Oh, my God...what happened to you?"

"You," Ingrid said with blatant disgust. "You happened to him." Then the vampiress turned toward him. "Saving Orson the trouble of killing you?"

The only one he wanted to save was Sienna, but he could barely stand or talk. He didn't have to be a nurse, like Ingrid, to know that he was dying. But with his last ounce of strength, he would fight to protect the woman he loved. "Leave...her...be..." he murmured.

"You're in no condition to be issuing orders," Ingrid said with a vicious laugh.

"Julian, you have to leave," Sienna whispered urgently. "Just leave..." Her small hands pushed at his chest, trying to shove him up the stairs.

He swayed and stumbled back a step. But other hands were there, not to catch him, but to hold him. He didn't need to turn around to know that Ingrid had summoned her reinforcements. He lowered his head, focusing on Sienna. She stared up at him, her blue eyes wide with fear and glistening with unshed tears. "I'm sorry," he said.

She shook her head. "You have no reason to be sorry. It's my fault. I should have listened to you."

"I didn't tell you what you needed to hear," he said. But he couldn't say it now—he couldn't say in front of all these people the words he should have given her when they were alone and in each other's arms. He knew now what it would have taken for her to accept his proposal. His love.

"I'm sorry I'm not your hero…."

CHAPTER SEVEN

SIENNA'S HEART POUNDED a frantic rhythm. And she couldn't stop trembling—not just with fear, but from the cold. After night had fallen, they'd left the cellar, and they'd flown...to wherever they were now. But they hadn't used a plane, or a helicopter or any other type of machine. They'd just...flown. They hadn't flapped their arms or kicked their legs, but somehow they'd moved through the frigid night air.

Sienna was surprised they hadn't killed her then. The man who'd carried her would have had only to drop her. The fall would have killed her, leaving her body broken beyond recognition.

But Ingrid had ordered them delivered here—to another underground dwelling even more opulent than the apartment to which Julian had brought her. He lay now, unconscious, on a hard marble floor. Sienna knelt at his side, stroking her fingers over the chiseled angle of his cheekbone and jaw. "Wake up. Please wake up..."

He wasn't just sleeping. She wasn't even sure he was breathing anymore. So she moved her hand to his throat and felt for a pulse. But her fingers were numb and his skin so cold, she could find no reassuring beat.

"Julian," she whispered.

The men who'd flown them here stood around, glaring at her as she'd already been warned to keep quiet. They were beyond big, beyond her ability to fight. If only Julian were awake...

"He's dying," Ingrid said, her heels clicking against the marble as she walked back into the room from wherever she'd been.

And it's all my fault. Guilt clutched at Sienna. If she'd listened to him, if she'd believed him—they'd both be safe now.

"It is all your fault, girl," a man's deep voice spoke to her thoughts.

Tearing her gaze from Julian's pale face, she glanced up and then gasped. "You..." He looked so much like his "grandson"—even approximately the same age.

"We don't age, girl," he explained. "But we can die." He knelt near Julian and brushed a trembling hand through his grandson's hair. "That's why it's too risky for humans to learn of our existence. It makes us vulnerable."

"I won't hurt anyone," Sienna promised.

"Too late," the man snapped, as he rose to his feet and stared down at her. "You've already hurt my family."

"Your honor."

"Twice now," he said. "Vossimers are Underground royalty. Royalty does not offer marriage to commoners only to have those commoners reject them."

If Vossimers were Underground royalty, Julian was their prince and this man considered himself king. Regrettably, so did the burly men who hung on his every word as if he were issuing royal decrees.

"I'm sorry," she murmured demurely. "I was wrong to turn Julian down. Help him, please…"

"It's too late for my grandson," Orson said. Whatever affection he'd betrayed when he'd petted Julian's hair was gone now. "He has brought dishonor to our family too many times. And he's brought danger to the rest of the Underground."

"It wasn't his fault," Sienna defended him. "He never said anything to my grandmother. She had a gift. She knew things. Ask Ingrid."

The older Vossimer turned toward the beautiful vampiress. "Is this true?"

After a slight hesitation, she nodded. "But it doesn't change what happened. *She* knows our secret. *She* cannot live."

Pride lifted Sienna to her feet. "I don't care what you do to me. Just save him. Save Julian."

Orson Vossimer narrowed his eyes and studied her. "You act as though you care about my grandson."

"I love him," she admitted.

The older man laughed. "You think me a fool. That I will believe your lies?"

"I love him," Sienna insisted. "I'm not lying."

"Then you're the fool, girl," Vossimer said.

"He's a good man," she defended her lover again. "He's my hero." No matter what he believed; she knew the truth now.

"Then why would you turn him down when he offered you marriage, when he offered you a way to keep your life   for eternity?"

She sucked in a shaky breath. "Fear." Not just of the dark, but of the risk of giving her heart to a man who wouldn't give his in return.

"You are a fool, girl."

"Yes," she agreed. "I should have said yes. If I could go back…" She glanced down at Julian's lifeless body and remembered the passion with which he'd made love to her. "Please, help him…"

"It's too late, girl," Orson said, emotion turning his voice into a rough rasp. "It's too late…"

"Ingrid," she turned to the other woman. "You're a nurse. You must know what to do…how to save him…"

"His life is ebbing away," Ingrid said with a weary sigh of her own.

"But he's not dead yet." She refused to believe that, refused to let him go. "Please, help him," she beseeched the other woman. "*You* can help him."

Ingrid shook her head. "No, I can't. But you might be able to…"

"How?"

"Let him take your life."

"He can have it," Sienna offered. If not for him, she wouldn't have lived as long as she had. No one would have ever found the wreckage of her family's car. She wouldn't have survived without him. "I owe him…my life."

"Is this a trick, girl?" Orson asked.

"This is love." Love was selfless, like Julian endangering himself to find her and try to rescue her. It was her turn to rescue him—even if it killed her.

THEY'RE GOING TO KILL HER. The horrific thought chased the blackness of unconsciousness from Julian's mind. He fought the heaviness of his lids to blink open his eyes, gritty with fatigue.

"Sienna!" He tried to shout her name, but it escaped as a weak rasp. "Sienna!"

A soft hand brushed hair back from his face. "I'm here," she assured him, with a sigh of relief. "And so are you…"

She blurred before his weary eyes, and he blinked again until he could clearly see her. Even tense and pale with concern and fear, her face was beautiful. Then his gaze moved beyond her to register their surroundings—the marble floors and walls. "We're at my grandfather's."

She nodded. "He had us brought here...to this bedroom..."

"My bedroom," Julian said, with a surge of hope. "Are we alone?"

A laugh, high-pitched with a hint of hysteria, slipped from her lips. "You can't want to..."

"I will always want you," he said.

"But you're so sick."

If that was all he was, he could rally the strength to help her. But his situation was worse than that. Her situation didn't have to be the same. "I can tell you how to get out of here," he said.

She shook her head. "I'm not leaving you!"

"There's a bathroom behind that door..." He tried to lift his arm to gesture, but his limb was too heavy, his muscles too weak to move. His lungs ached as he struggled for breath with ragged pants. "There's a vent in the ceiling. If you climb on the vanity, you'll be able to reach it."

She pressed her fingers across his lips. "Shh... save your strength."

What strength? If he had any left, he could carry her into the bathroom, lift her to the vent and help her get away from the Underground. But once again, he was too weak to be her true hero.

"I'm *not* leaving you," she said, her voice firm and her statement implacable.

He managed to curl his fingers into the curve of

her hip. "You *have* to..." He pushed her. "You have to go. Now."

"There's no time," she said.

"There's time," he argued, "for you to get away." But how long could she stay hidden from Ingrid and Orson?

"I'm not leaving without you."

"I can't move," he admitted with frustration and stinging pride.

"You don't have to do anything," she said as she wrapped her arms around his neck. "But bite me..."

He tensed; maybe he was so weak that he'd imagined what she'd said. "What?"

"*Turn* me, Julian."

He moved his head, to shake it, but she'd put her neck there so that his lips brushed across the silky skin of her throat. "No...it's too great a risk."

"They're going to kill us both if you don't," she reminded him.

"But I might kill you," he said, dread twisting his stomach in knots. "I've never turned anyone before." And fatigue had stolen his usual cocky assurance, so that he wasn't convinced, even if he wasn't so weak, that he'd know how to turn her without killing her.

"You're going to die if you don't," she said. "Ingrid told me that this is your only chance—to use my life to save yours."

He shook his head. "I can't..."

"Julian, you're dying now. This is your one chance. I'm your one chance."

"No…"

"I love you, Julian."

Her words suffused him with heat and passion. "You love me?"

She nodded. "Yes."

"But you left me." Pain, more emotional than physical, staggered him as he remembered waking alone and finding her gone. "I thought you couldn't accept my part in your parents' tragic deaths. I thought you hated me…."

"I had to get away to think," she explained, "to consider the life you offered me."

"The life you rejected when you rejected me."

"I rejected the life—not you," she insisted. "We made love…twice…" She entwined her fingers in his hair. "I love you."

He wanted to believe her, but nobody had ever said those words to him, let alone meant them. Did she? Or was she only trying to help him because she was used to taking care of people?

"I only take care of people I care about," she said.

"What?" Shocked, he met her gaze, her blue eyes wide with awe.

"I can hear your thoughts," she told him, as shocked as he was.

"You have your grandmother's gift."

She nodded. "I just realized that now. I wish I would have realized it sooner. If I could have heard your thoughts earlier, maybe I wouldn't have left you and then you wouldn't have had to risk your life in the daylight. It's my fault, Julian, that you're dying. You have to use me to save you."

"Sienna…"

"If you don't, we're both going to die anyway," she said, "because I'm not leaving you."

"C'mon, Sienna, you can go out the vent," he urged her. "You can save yourself."

"For the moment. You think they won't track me down again? Where am I supposed to go? I have no place else to go—no one I want to be with but you." She kissed him, her lips pressing against his until he opened his mouth. Then she dipped her tongue between his lips, sliding it across the sharp tips of his fangs.

Hunger stirred within Julian, but it was nothing in comparison to the power of his love for her. "Sienna, if this doesn't work—"

"If it does, we can be together forever," she pointed out. "Unless that isn't what you want…?"

His heart contracted at the image she painted—the image of the two of them, in each other's arms, for eternity. Making love, making each other laugh— making each other happy. "It's what I want—more than anything else in this world, more than my own life. I can't…"

"You have to," she begged him. "Before it's too late for us. You have to—" And she kissed him again, first his lips. Then she slid her mouth over his chin and along the line of his clenched jaw.

He wanted her so badly. Not just now, but forever. "Are you sure, Sienna?" he asked.

"Absolutely," she assured him. Her fingers in his hair, she tugged up his head until his lips brushed across her throat. A moan slipped from between her lips. "Please…turn me…"

His heart, which had been beating weakly, kicked against his ribs—with anticipation and fear. "This might hurt."

"Just do it," she urged. "Just…bite me…"

He rubbed his lips back and forth across her throat, lifting goose bumps on her skin. She shivered. "Julian…"

He curled back his lips and pressed his fangs against her skin. And pressed harder until her skin broke.

She gasped, her breath hissing out between her teeth. But when he moved to pull back, she tightened her fingers in his hair and clutched him to her. "Turn me…"

He couldn't argue, not with her sweet taste sliding over his tongue. Heat and passion and love filled him as he drank. Too much or too little? The line was fine. One way would kill her; the other would leave her human and in danger of the Underground Society killing her.

Reenergized with her spirit, he pulled away from her. Her body had gone limp against him. He rolled her onto her back on the mattress and leaned over her. Her eyes had closed, her thick lashes lying against her pale skin. His hand shaking, he stroked his fingers over her cheek. "Sienna!"

Her skin had paled to a porcelain so clear her veins shone beneath the thin surface. Her pulse barely moved in her throat. Had he killed her?

"Sienna!"

The bedroom door squeaked open on rusty hinges. "Julian," his grandfather called his name. "You're all right?"

He shook his head, his eyes burning as he studied Sienna's beautiful face. "No, I'm not all right."

Strong fingers squeezed his shoulder. "You're alive. She's not—that's what needed to happen."

"She's not dead!" Not yet. Although faintly, her heart beat beneath the palm he pressed to her chest. "She can't die! She can't…"

She'd promised him eternity.

"If it's meant to be—if you're meant to be—she'll come back to you," Orson assured him.

"We're meant to be," Julian insisted as he stroked her hair back from her face. "We're meant to be."

"You have to prepare yourself," his grandfather warned him. "In case she doesn't make it."

Finally Julian tore his gaze from her and focused on the man who'd raised him in the ways of the Underground. "If she doesn't make it, neither will I."

"You say that now, but you'll get over her…like you got over her grandmother."

"I won't. I love Sienna." And yet he'd never given her the words. He'd never proved his love—like she had proved hers. For him she'd given up her life.

CHAPTER EIGHT

LIGHT FLICKERED, glowing through Sienna's closed lids—calling her back from the darkness. Her body ached in protest as she shifted under the blankets pulled to her chin, her muscles weak and cramped. But the pain was good; the pain convinced her she wasn't dead.

Unless this was hell.

She dragged her eyes open to a room bathed in candlelight, as it had been the first time he'd brought her here. Plaster walls rose to that ornate coffered ceiling with the chandelier hanging low and dark above the bed. This wasn't hell; this was where she'd found heaven in Julian's arms.

Julian! Had it worked—had he drunk enough of her spirit to revive his dying body? "Julian!"

"Shh…" a deep voice murmured, then strong arms closed around her, pulling her tight against a muscular chest. "I'm here."

"You're alive!"

"And so are you…" His breath escaped in a shuddery sigh of relief. Lips skimmed across her cheek then brushed over her mouth. "You're alive!"

She blinked again, unable to believe that they were together. Free. "He let us go?" she asked, confusion muddling her weary mind.

"Yes."

Because Julian had done what his grandfather had wanted. He'd taken the only option the old man had given him besides her death. She glanced down at herself, her arms bare as she pulled them from beneath the blankets. Her throat dry, she swallowed hard and managed only, "Am I...?"

"You're back to not being able to say it?" he teased, his lips curving into that wicked grin.

"I could accept your being one," she said. "But me..." How could she have become what she didn't understand?

"You didn't think it through," he said, worry furrowing his brow.

"I thought only of you, of saving you," she admitted. "I didn't care about myself."

"That's why I love you," he said, "so much."

"I know you love me," she assured him. "Going out in the sunlight, you risked your life for me. You proved it."

"That last time I had," he agreed, but guilt haunted his dark eyes, "but I could have saved you from the wreck earlier and I waited..."

She reached up, pressing her fingers across his lips. "Shh...if you'd come out in daylight then, you would have died. And I would have died, too. To get me out, you had to pull apart that twisted metal—no human could have managed that. You wouldn't have had the strength to do that if you'd come out during the day." She narrowed her eyes, as she noticed her fingers—her ringless fingers on her right hand.

Julian lifted her left hand from the comforter. "The ring is here. I moved it."

"To my left hand?" She stared at the ring, which glinted in the faint candlelight. "But I turned you down."

"Because you didn't think I loved you," he guessed. Correctly.

"How do you know me so well?" she asked.

"We have a connection."

"Because you have my blood?"

"We had a connection even before that," he insisted. "We've had a connection for years. That was why I asked you to marry me—because I couldn't lose that connection. I couldn't lose you."

He had loved her—even before he'd realized it, as Ingrid had suggested.

"So why didn't you ask me again? At your grandfather's house?"

"I didn't know if I'd make it. I didn't know if either of us would make it. And I didn't know what I had to offer you," he explained. "And every minute you've been unconscious, I regretted not asking, not moving this ring to your left hand when you were awake and could answer me."

"So ask me again," she suggested although, from how she ached with exhaustion, she still wasn't convinced that she could survive the turning. Or hadn't she been turned at all? But before she could open her mouth to take back her advice, Julian slid off the bed and dropped to his knees beside it.

His hand grasping her left one, where the diamond twinkled, he asked, "Will you become my bride, Sienna Briggs?"

She focused first on the ring, then on his face, where the diamond-shaped scar marred the masculine perfection of his cleft chin. "Are you sure?"

"Sienna!" he exclaimed, his face paling with shock. "I'm so sure. I love you so much."

The words warmed her heart and curved her lips into a smile. But…

"That wasn't what I was referring to—I mean, the ring? Are you sure this is the ring you want me to wear…as *your* fiancée, as *your* bride?"

He stared down at the ring, too, now. "Oh, my God, I didn't think… Did you want me to buy you a new ring? One that I picked out?"

She shook her head, tears stinging her eyes, as she remembered her grandmother, using the last bit of her fading strength, to slide the ring onto her finger. "No." If she had believed she would be strong enough to risk her heart again, she would have wanted to wear this ring. "This is the one I want. It symbolizes the greatest love I'd ever known…"

"Until now," he said, "until ours."

Her heart warmed more as it filled with the love of which he spoke. Their love. The greatest love she would ever know.

"But this ring doesn't mean the same thing to you that it does to me," she said. She managed to raise her hand to touch her fingertip to the scar on his chin. "To you it means rejection. To your grandfather it means dishonor."

"Your grandmother and I—we weren't meant to be," he said. "I think I even knew that then. I was just being an arrogant jerk. She had every right to hit me."

"Yes, she did. You insulted my grandfather—the man she loved more than life itself."

"More than the eternal life I offered her."

"It wasn't enough. You didn't love her."

"I didn't know that I could love," he said. "I didn't think I was capable until I met you. This ring—" he slid his thumb over the sharp points of it "—means something to me, too. It reminds me how much I changed—how much *you* changed me. It represents our love, too."

Tears blurred the ring, and his handsome face, from Sienna's gaze. "Yes, it does." And her grandmother's gift had been accurate again—that the right man would come along someday and slide it onto Sienna's real ring finger.

"That's the right answer," Julian said, "but to the wrong question."

She blinked back the tears. "What?"

"You haven't answered my first question," he reminded her. "Please, woman, put me out of my misery and respond to my proposal. Will you marry me?"

"Yes!" She tried to lift up from the pillow, but her body was limp, her muscles weak. "If only I were stronger, I would marry you now. Right this minute."

Because she wanted to be part of him…for the eternity he'd promised her. Fear tempered her happiness; she doubted that the "turning" had worked. Instead of eternal life, she would have to leave him… like her grandparents and parents had left her—to death.

"I'm sorry," she murmured. She'd taught him how to love, only to leave him—only to leave him to the anguish she'd had to endure when she'd lost the ones she'd loved. "I'm sorry…"

PANIC PRESSED ON Julian's lungs, so that he struggled for breath. Like Sienna struggled for breath. He could not lose her now. "You have no reason to be sorry," he assured her. He was the one who'd messed up—as usual.

"I'd hoped it would work…that we could be together…forever," she said. "But I'm so tired…" Her thick lashes brushed against the dark circles beneath her eyes as her lids closed.

He couldn't let her slip into unconsciousness again. He couldn't lose her again. He cupped her cheek in his palm. "Come on, Sienna, stay with me."

She blinked her eyes open, giving him hope. She hadn't slipped away yet.

And he wouldn't let her. He would do anything to keep her with him. "I know how you can get stronger," he said. "Use me." Like she had insisted he use her.

"What do you mean?" she asked, her blue eyes still dim with fatigue.

She wasn't dead yet. But he'd hurt her. His stomach clenched with dread and regret.

"I want you to do the same thing to me," he explained, with sensitivity to her unease about the vampire lifestyle, "that you had me do to you."

She shook her head. "I don't think I can. I'm going to have to find another way…to live…"

"There are other ways," he assured her. "We don't *feast* off people for sustenance. But I'm not talking about sustenance. I'm talking about survival—and about the connection between your soul and mine. It can only be complete when the same blood flows through us."

"It does."

"No, I have yours," he clarified, "but you don't have mine. Take *mine*."

"Julian…" She sighed. "I don't even know how. I don't have—"

He kissed her, deeply, sliding his tongue through her parted lips, stroking it over hers before tracing the line of her teeth. Her tongue followed the path of his then she tensed. So he pulled back.

"I have them," she murmured, in shock. "I have fangs…"

"It worked." He hadn't been entirely convinced himself until now. He had actually turned her. But she was still so pale—so weak. He could still lose her…if she didn't do as he asked.

"You're as surprised as I am."

He tensed, startled that she'd read him so easily. "What?"

Her lips curved into that faint smile. "I can hear you—your thoughts. Remember?"

Their connection was complete already. But it had to last. "Then you should remember what happened the last time you didn't do as I asked."

A grimace momentarily twisted her delicate features. "I almost got us both killed."

"So obey me, woman."

"Obey?" she asked as she lifted a blond brow. "That won't be part of our vows."

"We won't be able to exchange those vows if you don't get stronger," he reminded her. "Use me to regain your strength."

"Julian…"

He did as she had, just the day before, he leaned forward and pressed his neck against her lips. "Bite me…"

Her lips parted, the heat of her faint breath warm against his skin. His body tensed again, with desire, with desperate need of hers. He wanted her completely—body and soul and her indomitable spirit. "Come on, Sienna."

"I can't…"

"You have to…for us," he urged her then groaned as her teeth nipped his skin.

She stopped and moved her mouth away. "I hurt you."

"No," he assured as he joined her on the bed, pressing his lower body into her hips so that she could feel his arousal. "You only hurt me by stopping. Don't stop this time."

She lifted her arms, wrapping them around his shoulders, and pulled him fully down on her. Then she sank her new fangs through his skin, into his throat, and she drank him in the way he'd drunk her.

Instead of feeling drained by her possession, Julian felt energized—completely invigorated. He vibrated with passion for her. "Sienna…"

She pulled her teeth from his skin and licked the small wound she'd created. "I feel…"

"What?" he asked, rolling them both to their sides

so he could see her face. Her skin, once so pale, was now flushed, and her blue eyes sparkled.

"I feel alive."

And for the first time since he'd tried to turn her, she looked alive. Vibrantly alive.

"You're beautiful," he said, his hand shaking as he palmed her cheek. "So beautiful…"

"You're beautiful," she said, her steady fingers clawing at the buttons of his shirt to open it. "You're perfect. And you're mine."

"All yours," he assured her with a chuckle as she shoved his shirt from her shoulders. He reached between them and dragged the blankets off her, baring her to his sight…and touch. He'd taken off her dress, so that she wore only those tantalizing scraps of lace. For the moment.

He intended to take them off her soon. But first he rose from the bed. Or tried to. Sienna clutched his shoulders, then his waist and murmured in protest.

"You're not going anywhere," she told him.

He shook his head as he unclasped his belt and dropped his jeans and boxers. "I'm not going anywhere—not without you. We're spending eternity together, my love."

"I wonder if that'll be long enough," she teased with a mischievous twinkle in her eye.

"Long enough?"

"To do everything I want to do to you." She reached for him, her hands sliding over the muscles of his chest then his hips to his straining erection. First she stroked her fingers down his length, then she closed her lips around him and sucked him deep in her mouth. Her fangs scraped over the sensitive flesh.

He groaned, as passion like he'd never known surged through him. "Sienna!" He tried to pull away so he could reach for her.

But she was strong now, stronger than she'd been. And she grasped his butt, holding him to her—as she tortured him with her lips and tongue and the tips of her new fangs. He tangled his fingers in her hair and pulled, but it was too late. As her lips slipped down the length of him, he came, his legs shaking, his body shuddering as his orgasm spilled into the warmth of her mouth.

She licked her lips and lay back on the bed, as if she were satisfied. But he shook his head. She'd no idea the satisfaction he intended to give her.

"Promises, promises," she teased, speaking to his thoughts.

He joined her on the bed, pushing her into the mattress with his body—tense again already with desire for his fiancée. And he kissed her, tasting his own desire on her lips and tongue. Their teeth clinked, scraping across each other's—raising the hair on the nape of his neck. "Just when I thought I couldn't love you more…"

"You love me more," she said, scraping her nails down the rippling muscles of his back.

He dipped his head, nuzzled her neck.

"Bite me," she invited him.

He shook his head. "I want to taste you another way." He skimmed his lips down her throat to the slopes of her breasts. With just the tip of his tongue, he teased each pebbled point. Then he suckled the nipple deep into his mouth, his fangs nipping lightly into the soft flesh of her breast.

She moaned and shifted beneath him, pressing her hips into his—rubbing her damp curls against the erection that strained again to possess her.

But he denied himself the pleasure of burying himself inside her. Instead he moved again, sliding down her body until he could taste her desire for him. He pushed his tongue through her folds, dipping inside the moist heat. She arched again and clutched her fingers at his head, clasping his mouth to her so tightly that his fangs pressed against her mound.

She moaned and shifted and came, pouring honey into his mouth. Burning with desire for her, he rose up and thrust himself inside her.

She arched so abruptly she nearly bucked him off, then she turned them—so that he lay flat on his back and she straddled him. He sank deeper than he'd gone before. And his hands, shaking slightly, grabbed her hips.

She rocked back and forth then lifted her hips, sliding his erection in and out of her wet folds. "Julian!" she said, desperation in her raspy voice and dilated eyes.

He moved his fingers to her butt, clasping her soft skin with one hand while he raised his other hand to her breast and massaged the swollen flesh. She lifted her hands to his shoulders, digging her nails in as she rode him.

Her mouth had taken the edge off his urgency, so that he could take his time now, teasing her to the brink of release only to pull out again. Her muscles clutched at him, pulling him deeper. And she knocked his hands aside to cup her breasts and roll her nipples between her thumbs and forefingers. Julian sat up and flicked his tongue across the tips she teased herself. Then he reached between them, sliding his thumb across the most sensitive part of her.

And she came, screaming his name—pouring her passion over him. He dug his fingers into her butt, lifting her up and down, until another orgasm slammed through him—this more violently than the last. "It's a good thing we can't die," he murmured between desperate pants for breath, "or you'd kill me for sure."

She collapsed against his chest, pressing her lips to where his heart pounded hard in rhythm with hers. "I will never hurt you," she promised him.

He smoothed his hands over the perspiration-slick

skin of her bare back and asked, "So are you ready to make an honest man of me now?"

Her lips curved against his skin, into a smile. "Honest man?"

"When are you going to marry me?" he asked, urgency rushing through him despite being completely sexually satiated. He couldn't wait for her to become his bride.

"Now too soon?"

"Now is perfect—as perfect as you are." As perfect as their life together promised to be.

CHAPTER NINE

STARS GLITTERED IN the night sky as brightly as the lights wound round the boughs of the pine trees lining the park path. Big snowflakes drifted softly out of the darkness, sparkling as they hit the lights and the path. The flakes dropped onto Sienna's face and slid down her cheeks like the tears she fought from falling.

She would not cry. Not when everything was so perfect…and Julian awaited her, standing next to an Underground minister beneath the tallest pine in the park. Clutching tight to Orson Vossimer's arm, Sienna started down the aisle toward her groom. But the elder Vossimer's steps slowed, and he turned to her.

Had he changed his mind? Was she not good enough to be a Vossimer bride?

"No," he answered aloud her unspoken thoughts. "You're perfect. The perfect bride for my grandson—the perfect princess for the Vossimer prince."

"Because he turned me?" She had to know.

The older man shook his head. "Because you love

him as he's always deserved to be loved—completely and unselfishly."

"The same way he loves me."

"I see that now," Orson admitted. "I'm sorry…"

"For trying to kill me?"

The older man's handsome face, so eerily similar to Julian's, lifted in the wicked grin his grandson had evidently inherited from him. "Honey, if I'd actually tried, you would be dead. Not *undead*." He covered her hand with his and squeezed. "I may not be the nicest man, but I'm not a killer."

"But you threatened Julian," she reminded him, unwilling to let the man rewrite history. "You told him—"

"I warned him. I suspected how he felt about you. Ever since he'd pulled you from that crash, he'd had an attachment to you. I wanted to test that attachment."

"So it's not a rule that no human can learn of the Underground?"

He sighed. "It's a rule that fortunately hasn't had to be enforced too often."

Just with her parents. She winced, reliving the accident—reliving her loss. But she wasn't afraid of the dark anymore. Or of loving with her whole heart—the way she loved Julian.

"You wanted him to turn me," she realized. "You wanted us to be together?"

"I wanted my grandson to be happy," he said as

he turned toward where Julian waited beneath the lit pine tree. "You make him happy."

"And he makes me happy."

The old man nodded, then added with satisfaction, "And your gift would have been wasted on a human."

"Gift?"

"Telepathy, like your grandmother had," he said and admitted, "and I have."

"I don't have telepathy."

"But you know what Julian's thinking."

Right now she knew he was getting impatient, waiting for his grandfather to bring him his bride. Her lips curved into a reassuring smile she hoped he could see. Or at least feel. "Only Julian," she said. "We have a connection."

"Because of your gift," Orson said.

She shook her head. "Because of our love."

"Love…" Orson sighed. "I guess I might actually have to try it for myself."

They started forward on the path, which wound through chairs that had been set up in the park. Members of the Underground, friends of Julian's who had already accepted Sienna, occupied the chairs. One of those was Ingrid.

"Just be careful," she advised the Vossimer king. "Not all love stories end like Julian's and mine."

Happily ever after. She hadn't thought it existed—despite seeing her grandparents' love for each other.

And she never would have believed a man such as Julian existed.

"I'm real," he assured her as he took her hand from his grandfather's arm. "And our love is real."

"And eternal."

"You two are skipping ahead on the vows," the Underground minister teased.

"I guess we didn't need you after all," Julian shot back with a wink.

We didn't, Sienna silently agreed. They'd already forever joined their souls.

Julian winked at her, as if he'd read her mind, which he no doubt had. The two of them were one; they didn't need to repeat the minister's vows to seal their union. But they exchanged their promises and rings, a plain gold band for Julian and Nana's diamond for Sienna, so that they could celebrate their love with their friends and family, those dead and those undead.

Breaking away from the passionate kiss that punctuated their wedding ceremony, Sienna smiled and laughed.

"Happy?" Julian asked, his handsome face beaming with his own joy.

"Yes." And so was Nana. Despite her grandmother being dead, Sienna felt her approval shining down upon her as clearly as the stars and the twinkling Christmas lights.

Reading her thoughts again, Julian nodded. "Even Orson's happy for us."

"He loves you," she said and repeated when she felt her new husband's doubts. "He loves you. He just doesn't know how to express it."

"He doesn't know how to *feel* it," Julian scoffed.

"He wants to try," she defended her new relative.

Julian gestured toward where his grandfather stood near the dark-haired vampiress. "I hope he's not going to try with her."

"I don't think so." Orson was too clever to waste his time with someone who couldn't return his feelings. She sighed and admitted, "I feel sorry for Ingrid."

"Why? If she'd had her way, you'd be dead now," Julian reminded her.

Sienna shook her head. "No, if she had her way, she'd be with the man she loves." A twinge of guilt tempered her happiness. "I'm so lucky that I am…"

"We're so lucky," he said, "to have each other."

Music began to play, softly, from a string quartet set up near the Christmas tree. Julian took her hand in his as he wrapped his other arm around her waist and drew her against his body. Then he began to move in time to each sweet chord.

"We are lucky," she agreed.

"And brave," he said.

They had been brave to open up their damaged hearts to love. "Yes," she agreed.

"You were brave to trust me to turn you," he clarified his compliment, "and not kill you."

"Trust had nothing to do with it," she said. "It was love...."

With them, it would always be love.

For all eternity.

* * * * *

UNWRAPPED
Bonnie Vanak

ABOUT THE AUTHOR

Bonnie Vanak fell in love with romance novels during her childhood. After years of newspaper reporting, Bonnie joined an international charity, and she now tours destitute countries to write about issues affecting the poor. She turned to writing romance novels as a diversion from her job's emotional strain. Bonnie lives in Florida with her husband and two dogs. Visit her website at www.bonnievanak.com or email her at bonnievanak@aol.com.

For my mother, who taught me to believe
in Christmas magic and miracles.
Miss you, Mom. Love you always.

CHAPTER ONE

FOR THE SAKE of a werewolf, he was risking his life.

Adrian was a vampire. Powerful and fearless, he could move swifter than the eye could blink. But not now. Peeking over the gray ocean's horizon, the rising sun began to sap his enormous energy.

He was doing all this for Sarah. She was a Draicon, werewolves who once used their magick to learn of the earth, who were now hunted by the more powerful Morphs—former Draicon who embraced evil by killing one of their own.

The Morphs shuffled forward on the beach, saliva dripping from their yellowed fangs. Adrian tensed, waiting to see if they would shift to attack. Sarah's enemies could turn into any animal or insect.

A cluster of hooded vampires suddenly glided onto the nearby dunes. Clad in thick robes to protect them against the encroaching dawn, elders from his clan had come to rescue him. But they would not help until Adrian begged. Those were the rules. This was not their war, and he had broken with his clan to fight in it.

Vampires and werewolves can never be allies, his father always warned.

Sarah rushed past him, kicking up eddies of sand. She stabbed the Morphs in the heart with a steel dagger, killing them instantly. The Draicon was a tough little fighter, but he knew she couldn't face her enemies alone. She'd asked Adrian to join her. No one else stood with her—not her pack, her sister or even her own father.

Only two Morphs remained, but where the hell had they gone? Adrian turned around. His heart jumped into his throat as he spied the pair shifting from seagulls, assuming their true shapes behind Sarah. Their dark, soulless eyes glowed red. With the last bit of his strength, Adrian sped to Sarah. He pushed her to safety and turned to take her enemy's blows upon his weakening body.

Sensing his weakness, a Morph slashed his cheek with its razor-sharp talons. The creature howled in triumph as Adrian collapsed.

A collective hiss of disapproving anger echoed over the dunes. The Morphs turned and saw the vampires. Their shrieks of outraged fear turned into the cries of seagulls as they shifted and flew off.

He'd failed to defeat the enemy. The price would be banishment, if he lived long enough. Through a dazed fog of pain, he struggled to stand. Adrian held out a hand to Sarah. "Help me," he told her.

Her terrified gaze whirled to the vampires. Iridescent sparks filled the air as she shifted. In wolf form, she raced off. Blood trickling down his face blurred his vision as he stared in grief-stricken disbelief. Sarah, the Draicon he secretly adored. Sarah, now leaving him to die.

The ocean's tumultuous waves crashed over his trembling body, saltwater sealing the deep gouges on his face. The sun's cruel rays touched his skin. A scream tore from his throat as he smelled his flesh scorching. Adrian finally pleaded with the vampires for aid. But instead of rescuing him, his family began mocking him in a chorus of singing laughter…

Singing?

Adrian Thorne struggled out of the throes of the dream that had haunted him for the past decade. In the darkness, he opened his eyes and then snatched up a thick burgundy robe and belted it on, marching toward the window. After depressing the button that opened the heavy metal shutters, he swung open the glass panes. Twilight glimmered on the waves crashing against the sweeping, pink granite bluffs below, reflecting the deep rose and crimson hues of a spectacular Maine sunset. Cold wind whistled inside, whipping back his shaggy black hair.

Adrian stared down at the scene on the deck of his two-story mansion. A chorus of green, grinning faces greeted him. Six gremlins dressed in Santa Claus outfits warbled an off-key rendition of "Jingle Bells." Adrian winced and shouted down.

"Are you trying to raise the undead? Do them a favor, let them rest."

"Adrian!" one squealed at him. "Come down and get your Christmas gift."

"Dare I hope it's peace on earth, or at least peace in my house?" he suggested.

As he shut the window, the gremlins belted out a rap song about "peas on earth." Adrian shook his head and scrubbed the day stubble on his jaw. In a few days, elders from his clan would arrive for the winter solstice convocation. Ten years ago, his father, the clan's leader, had banished him until Adrian restored his honor by killing the Morphs that nearly killed him. But Morphs feared a vampire's power and though Adrian had funded numerous efforts to find them, he had failed to do so.

Only Sarah could lead him to her enemy. And she had vanished without a trace.

Downstairs, he went outside onto the wood deck, relishing the harsh winter wind stinging his cheeks. Squealing, the gremlins rushed over, the pom-pom balls on their Santa hats bouncing. The tallest, only four feet, had tinsel dangling from his pointed ears. Six faces beamed at him, showing rows of serrated teeth.

Snark, oldest of the six brothers, thrust a wrapped package at him. "Merry Christmas!"

Adrian felt a small tug of pleasure as he examined the shoebox-size package, his first gift in years. It was wrapped in gold-and-red striped paper that bore faint stains, and the red ribbon smelled like oranges and sour chicken. He raised a dark brow.

"Have you been rooting through the garbage again?"

A chorus of innocent nos with equally innocent looks confirmed his suspicions.

"Open it, open it," they began to chant.

"We got you exactly what you wanted. Just add water and read the note," Snark added.

Curiosity consumed him. He headed for the nearby pool house, the gremlins skipping in his wake. Inside, he switched on the soft overhead lights and sat at the wrought-iron table. Slowly he began to unwrap the present, wanting to make it last. The gremlins squealed with impatience.

Oh, very well. Adrian ripped the paper and tore off the box lid. He lifted a thin layer of tissue paper.

Beneath it lay the ugliest doll he'd ever seen. The smile died on his face. A black, Frankenstein-like scar snaked down the doll's right cheek. Tufts of hair grew from a balding scalp. She was dressed in a lime-green polyester pantsuit. A silver bracelet was included in the box, along with a small white card. He read the card. *Congratulations, you are now the proud owner of a Sally Ugly Bunch doll.* There was an 800 number and a website address at the bottom.

"Have fun playing with your gift!" Snark chortled, and they scampered off.

A hollow ache filled his chest as he lifted the doll. His fingers stroked the deep gouges on his left cheek. The doll stared sightlessly back at him, its own scar mocking him. Adrian glanced in the direction the gremlins took.

"I thought you were my friends," he whispered.

Grief twisted and writhed like hissing snakes in his belly. Primitive rage exploded, making his fangs descend. Adrian shook the doll, his voice a strong roar that echoed through the pool house's open glass doors and over the five acres of his cliffside estate.

"Damn you!" He threw the doll against the wall.

"Ouch."

He froze. Were the gremlins playing another trick? Snark said to add water. Adrian picked up his Christmas gift and marched outside. The pool was heated, and remained uncovered for the gremlins' nightly swim. Wind billowed his robe, fluttering it open and exposing his strong, muscled legs. He flung the toy into the water.

Shock filled him as the doll began to thrash. Stiff limbs became arms and legs beating the water. The doll grew to life-size, dark hair sprouting from its balding head. No longer a doll, but a woman.

She sank, only to surface again. "Help me," she choked out, before she went under.

This time she did not surface.

He was no hero. The last time he'd played the part, he'd been left to die. But he was no ogre, either. Shrugging out of his robe, Adrian dove into the pool. He swam underwater, grabbed the woman and dragged her upward. Swiftly towing his gift to the pool's edge, he then climbed out and hoisted the woman up into his arms.

Inside the warm pool house, he gently laid her down on the tiled floor. He inhaled, taking her scent into his lungs. Fangs exploded in his mouth as a familiar hunger seized him.

Only one woman could cause this kind of volatile reaction. Stunned, Adrian took a closer look. The repulsive scar was gone, replaced by smooth flesh. Instead of a chubby moon face, bulbous nose and thin mouth, she had full lips, a pert nose, high cheeks and long lashes.

Shocked, he sat back on his haunches. Adrian bent closer. "My beautiful Sarah," he whispered. "Just as lovely as when you left me. Traitor."

She lay still as cold marble. Very gently, he turned her head to one side. Adrian straddled her hips. Decades ago, he'd given CPR to a little boy who'd nearly drowned. Now he avoided everyone and was dead inside. But maybe he could give life again.

He compressed her chest. She coughed, and a stream of water spilled out of her lips. Satisfaction filled him as color returned to her cheeks. He did another compression and she coughed again.

The delicate blue vein in her throat throbbed with life. Just as he'd always done in the past, he fought the ferocious urge to take her blood. Instead, he stroked her throat, marveling at the feel of satin skin beneath his caressing fingertips.

Blood pulsed just beneath smooth flesh, calling to him in a siren song. He hadn't been near a woman in years, not even to feed. Adrian didn't trust the darkness inside him. His private blood bank took care of his needs.

Clenching his fists, he stared at her lying beneath him. He envisioned Sarah naked, her long legs open, her body sultry and inviting. Flat on her back, the perfect position to sink his fangs, and his body, into her. The strong sexual pull he'd always experienced around her, and never fulfilled, roared to unwelcome life.

Sarah was forbidden. He'd hungered for her, would have given her the world, but destiny promised her to another of her kind. Adrian had honored her chastity, guarding it from all, even himself. He had never even kissed her.

He could not help himself now. His fangs lengthened, echoing the raw desire pooling much lower. Adrian leaned down, and brushed his mouth against hers. Warm, wet lips moved beneath his. She tasted as delicious as he'd imagined.

Enchanted, he deepened the kiss, moaning at the honey of her mouth. Adrian reluctantly drew away. How the hell had she gotten here? He fetched the note from the doll's box.

"Dear Adreean," (the gremlins had never learned to spell, despite his best efforts to teach them). "Puleze accept with thankz thiz fer letting uz stay on yur guezt houze without pay. We finds her after we smells wolfie when letting air out of car tyers in town. Put thee bracelet on her and she cant do magickz. Meerry Chrismes."

He crushed the note beneath his fingers. Adrian smiled darkly as he retrieved the silver bracelet. He had a pretty Christmas present. And he wasn't about to let her go.

Not until she lured her enemies to his house so he could destroy them and gain admittance back to his clan. Take his rightful role as his father's heir and future ruler of the powerful clan of vampires.

As he snapped the bracelet on her wrist, feeling the chilled but soft skin beneath his fingertips, he only hoped the old feelings he harbored for her would not destroy him first.

CHAPTER TWO

A NAKED MAN had kissed her. The warmth of his wet mouth had spread through her icy body like lava. Making her blood sing, filling her with life.

I'm hallucinating.

Shivering and coughing, Sarah Roberts tried to clear the thick haze in her mind. Her eyes fluttered open. She tried to get a bearing on her surroundings. Her powerful senses picked up distant waves crashing against rocks, the mournful howl of a bitter wind skirting over the cliffs, smelled chlorinated water.

She was wet.

Remembering her pursuers, Sarah bolted upright. She raised her hands to ward off the enemy. A curious draining sensation made her limbs lethargic. Her gaze fell to the circle of silver encasing her right wrist.

Trapped by silver, she couldn't shift or perform magick. Terror and confusion collided together. Sarah fisted her badly shaking hands. They wanted her afraid. The Morphs would feed on her fear as she lay dying. Let them try. She'd go down fighting. A growl rumbled deep in her throat.

"Feisty little thing, aren't you?"

The deep timbre of the sensual voice sounded both familiar and dangerous. She inhaled and a delicious, spicy scent filled her senses, tugging at her memories. This was no Morph. She smelled vampire.

"Who are you?" she demanded.

"Ho, ho, ho."

She knew that voice. From where? Sarah turned. A man sat on a chair, a damp robe clinging to his powerful body. His face was hidden, his body silhouetted by the outdoor lights ringing the pool. The scent of chlorine covered him, as well.

He'd briefly, sweetly, kissed her. No, not a man, but something much more powerful and deadly, someone she knew. Her fingers grasped her wet clothing with growing dismay.

Yuck. Polyester. How did she wind up wearing this?

Then she remembered.

She'd been driving home after visiting distant relatives in Maine in hopes of finding a mate and had been in such a rush that she'd failed to wear the perfume that usually masked her scent. The Morphs picked up her trail. And sensing a vampire nearby, and knowing how Morphs feared them, Sarah detoured through the tiny seaside town of Anderson. But in town, the aging Ford's transmission finally bought it. A band of gangly Santas cheerfully bearing tools offered help. But instead of Mr. Goodwrench, she got...

Gremlins.

They had been in human form, then shifted into little green headaches. They took the watch from her wrist, chanted something, and she found herself trapped inside a plastic body.

She gingerly touched her temple, recalling the man's warm mouth moving over hers.

"Why did you kiss me?" she accused the silent figure.

"I saved you from drowning." The man stood and hovered over her, his face in shadow. "It's called CPR," he drawled.

He bent over, grasped her hand and pulled her to her feet. Surprised by his strength, she studied her rescuer. The gap in his robe revealed an intriguing triangle of muscled chest. Fascinated, Sarah reached out to run her hand over it.

He stepped back. "Get out of those clothes. I have towels and a warm robe."

Panic raced through her. "I'll just dry off like this." Sarah shook her body, flinging water droplets.

"I would expect as much. You always were very much the wolf." Stray moonbeams glinted off two gleaming fangs as he flashed a humorless smile.

She shivered. But an odd, poignant yearning collided with instinctive caution. The vampire turned his face to the light. Sarah recoiled in startled recognition. Once she'd thought he was the world, then her world changed and everything spun around like a crazy carnival ride.

"Oh, Adrian." Joy filled her as she stepped forward to hug her old friend. "I thought I'd never see you again."

He swept her a courtly bow, his gaze mocking as he straightened. "A valid assumption, Sarah, since the last sight I had of you was of your lovely ass racing away as I was dying. I believe we have a score to settle."

He hadn't forgotten or forgiven. Sarah dropped her arms. "How did you find me?"

"My little green friends are quite adept at flushing out scents, especially wolf, since few Draicon invade my territory." His white teeth gleamed in the moonlight.

"Adrian, you've got to take the bracelet off. The two Morphs that escaped are after me and if they come here, you'll be caught in a very personal, ugly war." Her voice dropped to a pained whisper. "I don't want to do that to you again."

Adrian raised a dark brow. "You're not leaving. Not until you help me settle old business."

He flicked a switch and light flooded the room. Two deep gouges demarcated his cheek.

Sarah smothered a gasp with the back of her hand. "You can't get hurt, you're a vampire." Contrary to human myth, vampires were living, breathing creatures born to their extraordinary powers. Their beauty, swiftness and grace made them deadly enemies.

The sneer on Adrian's mouth became more pronounced. "Do you like the artwork? The sunlight weakened my ability to heal."

Her hand automatically went to her bad leg. "Adrian, I didn't want to leave you, but your family had arrived. I knew they would rescue you."

A shadow chased across his face. Was it regret? "Did you assume as much? They would not. My clan's code forbade rescuing me after I broke the rules unless I humbled myself by begging for help. So I begged, they saved me and then banished me for a decade. I've been alone, except for the gremlins, my daylight guardians."

"I don't understand your people. Why should you have to beg for help?"

"Because I'm the next in line to lead our clan, and when I break a rule, it holds more consequences than if the others do it. My punishment is greater. The rules were meant for a reason, to keep me safe and separate me from all except our people." Adrian looked as if the confession pained him.

Shock slapped her like a wet towel. "You're Marcus's heir? You never said anything."

"Because I didn't want you to feel intimidated or treat me differently. When you asked for my help, I gave it to you, despite my father's angry objections." Ice coated his voice as he stepped closer. "I never imagined you'd run away when I needed you most."

His warm breath feathered over her chilled skin. "Do you know what it's like for a future leader of the most powerful vampire clan to be defeated by the enemies of another species? To admit a weakness to his family? To cast aside all he is and condemn himself to years of solitude? It's not half as agonizing as feeling your flesh burn until you'll say anything, do anything, to escape the sun."

She could feel the heat of his barely banked rage as if emanating from that very sun, but this heat held an icy blast. Sarah wrapped her arms about herself.

"I didn't realize…"

"I abandoned my family and took the side of a werewolf. I did it all for you, because you asked me."

His voice dropped to a bare whisper. "Once I would have done anything for you."

Her heart stilled. "I called you a couple of days after the battle to see how you were recovering, but the phone was disconnected. And I couldn't risk more than that phone call, much as I wanted to go back to you. It was too dangerous for us."

"I was already gone, banished to Maine, and shunned by all other vampires."

"I'm sorry, Adrian. I never thought it would come to this."

"It has." Icy-blue eyes met hers. "And now you're mine."

A slight shiver skated up her spine at the possessive note in his voice. She had to put distance between them. The Morphs were dangerous, but the feelings she still harbored for this vampire were also lethal.

"Revenge is an asinine motivation," she told him.

"Not revenge, Sarah. Something much more important." His expression hardened. "You're very necessary to me right now. If I can't find and defeat the Morphs who escaped me, I'll be banished for good and never rule the clan after my father steps down."

She closed her eyes against the coolness in his gaze. Once she had basked in the warmth of his presence, cherished their time together as they met in secret. Ignoring stern warnings from their families, they'd formed a close friendship eleven years ago, linked by a common love of old movies, books and engaging discussions about world affairs. Sarah's pack was wary of vampires, and his clan disdained all Draicon.

And then she asked Adrian to fight with her against her enemies because she could not face them alone. Never had she imagined he would pay such a terrible price.

Little could be done about the past. She must focus on the present. Her father was safe for now, entrenched among the human world after she'd phoned him last night. But he'd worry, and track her down if she didn't get home to Connecticut by Christmas. James was blind. Without her, he couldn't go anywhere without resorting to magick. And magick would leave a bright spectral trail for the Morphs to follow, as shiny as gold coins winking in the sunshine.

"If I could have changed things, I'd never ask you to stand with me. But you can't keep me here now."

"You're my Christmas gift. I never return gifts." He circled around her with a vampire's deadly grace and lethal quiet.

Her chest felt hollow as she realized her friend was gone for good. In his place was a dangerous vampire who wanted to use her as he wished. With the bracelet on her wrist stripping her powers, she was helpless against him.

I'll find a way out. She must. Her father depended solely on her.

In the moonlight Adrian's blue eyes gleamed like lasers. He caught her in one hand beneath her chin. Breath caught in her throat as he studied her face as an artist would study a sculpture in progress. His gaze dropped to the slender curve of her neck.

"Like what you see?" she snapped.

"You'll do nicely." He dropped his hand.

"For what? I warn you, I bite."

A deep chuckle rumbled from his chest. "So do I." He leaned closer. "My bite is better than yours.

You wouldn't feel anything, except a slight sting, and then...ecstasy. I make women cry out, even scream before they faint from the pleasure."

Sarah's insides tightened at the thought of his warm mouth pressed against her chilled skin. Kissing his way up her throat, those white fangs sinking into her neck as she clutched him, moaning as he suckled her.

Hunger flared on his face. She waited in breathless anticipation to see if he would finally capitulate to the need driving him each time they were near. But he only snagged a thick terry-cloth robe from a clothes-peg and draped it over her shoulders. "You'll find out soon enough what I want. In the meantime, let's get you into the house and warm."

CHAPTER THREE

SITTING AT THE kitchen table, Sarah kept her face expressionless. Once his friend, now Adrian's captive. Though she had to admit, it was a beautiful prison.

The mansion was tasteful and welcoming. Brown leather sofas and overstuffed fabric chairs sat before a river rock fireplace in the living room. French doors that opened to the pool deck held a stunning view of the jagged cliffs and moonlit ocean beyond. A recessed bar featured gleaming crystal stemware and a wine rack. Inside a locked glass cabinet was Adrian's rare collection of Revolutionary War muskets and cannonballs. Books were strewn about the coffee table. Seeing the wine and books had given her a pang of nostalgia, remembering the times they'd spent talking about books while sipping the fine vintages Adrian liked to collect.

He'd shown her to a lavish bedroom. Adrian allowed her to shower. Sarah had sighed with pleasure at the luxury of all the hot water she needed. By the time she'd emerged from a bathroom the size of her apartment, she'd seen that her battered suitcase now sat on the plush blue rug. She'd dressed in a cranberry sweater, her one pair of good black corduroy trousers and boots, and went downstairs. The designer jeans, the ones she'd sweated and saved for, were in shreds. Adrian actually looked slightly abashed when she told him.

"I apologize. The gremlins' taste usually runs to Dolce & Gabbana, not Guess."

He offered to purchase another pair. Sarah demurred. Adrian could afford to buy a yacht filled with Guess jeans, but she didn't take handouts.

Sarah now studied her captor. Adrian stood well over six feet, with wide shoulders and a hint of muscle beneath his clothing. In black wool trousers, a black silk shirt and designer loafers, he had an air of elegance and sophistication.

He was breathtakingly handsome. Heavy, dark brows sat over sharp blue eyes. His chin was strong and square, his lips sensual and full. Dark brown hair fell almost to his collar, clipped shorter than when she'd last seen him. The two deep gouges on his left cheek stood out in stark relief. Even the scars did not mar his beauty, but gave him a dangerous look.

Arms folded, Adrian leaned against the Sub-Zero stainless refrigerator.

"Release me, Adrian. I have to get back home, where it's safe."

"Back to your mate? He can't protect you as much as I can."

Arrogant, confident vampire. "I have no pack anymore, and no mate."

His expression remained hooded. "He's out there. You'll find him eventually, as all Draicon do with their destined mates."

"If they're still alive. Mine isn't. My destined mate died long ago."

Was that surprise flaring in his keen gaze? "You were waiting to find him when we were friends. I honored your commitment to mate with him. I never even…"

His voice trailed off, but she knew what he meant. *Never even kissed you.*

She bit her trembling lip, remembering his soft kiss after he'd rescued her from the pool. "He was killed when I was just a child, years before you and I ever met."

Adrian's mouth thinned. "Your father told me he was alive."

"James was afraid of you becoming too friendly with me. Draicon males can scent when another male has been…intimate with a female. And a vampire, well, a vampire is to the Draicon, you know."

"No, I don't know. Why don't you tell me? Lay it out, Sarah. What are we? Enemies?"

Bitterness lashed his voice. He looked as remote as the Arctic.

"You know your clan and my father would never approve of us," she whispered. "Your own clan punished you for taking my side. My father warned that vampires and werewolves can't be friends. Our passions run too high. Family loyalty must come first or we lose everyone close to us. You and I..."

Words hung unspoken in the air. *We were never meant to be.*

"I already lost my clan for ten years and high passions can also make for very pleasant pastimes, Sarah," he said in a dangerously soft voice.

"Why did you bring me here, Adrian?"

"I've never taken a werewolf before. I hear they are quite wild in bed."

Tendrils of heat curled through her at the image of his muscular body naked as he turned to take her into his arms. Adrian's gaze burned into hers.

"What do you really want?" she asked again, her heart racing.

"You."

He glided toward her with inborn grace and bracketed his arms on the chair, caging her. She breathed in his masculine scent. Even among all the males of her kind, none had ever compared to Adrian.

Ice filled his gaze once more. "My clan won't take me back until I restore my lost honor by defeating the Morphs I failed to kill. Any efforts I've made to find them have failed. My clan arrives in a few days for the convocation at midnight on Christmas Eve when I must prove I've killed the enemy. I need you to lure the Morphs here for me."

Real fear replaced rising desire. "I've hidden from these Morphs for ten years and now you want me to be bait? You must hate me, Adrian."

His gaze softened. "I would never allow them to touch one hair on your pretty head. I'll protect you, Sarah."

"And during the day?" She tried to push away, but he kept a firm grip on her chair.

"The gremlins will watch over you. Their magick is very powerful."

"Oh, sure. They managed to convince me that they could fix my car. That's magick."

His mouth crooked up in a charming grin. "They did fix your car instead of eating the engine. I'd say that was very good magick."

The grin stilled her. She saw the old Adrian, full of mischief and fun. For a moment, time slid back. How she wished she could have told him the full truth when she pleaded for his help that night on the shore.

Regrets were a waste of time. "You don't seem to understand. These Morphs will stop at nothing until I'm dead."

"Why do they want you so much, Sarah? There's a host of other Draicon out there to feed off. What is it about you they crave?"

Raising her chin, she met his hard look with a brave one. "James and I are on our own. We're packless, and more vulnerable because we have no one to stand with us against an attack."

"What happened to your mother and sister?"

Tears burned in her throat. "Dead, that day you and I fought on the beach. My father and I ended up running for our lives."

He looked stunned. "I'm sorry, Sarah. How did it happen?"

"An unexpected enemy killed them."

Adrian pulled out a chair, sat beside her. His gaze sharpened even as he held her hand in a comforting gesture. "That day we fought on the beach, you said you needed my help because your pack was protecting your mother. She was pregnant with the heir, and your sister and father stayed behind to guard her, as well. So what happened? Where's your pack?"

She said nothing.

"Tell me."

His voice carried a hint of command, layered with a vampire's natural enthrallment. Sarah fought against it.

"They scattered. It's a moot point, okay? What's important is the Morphs after me will destroy anything and everything that stands in their way."

He leaned closer, so close she could count the bristles shadowing his hard jaw. "Bring them on. I'll defeat them for you, win back my clan's approval. No Morph can best me."

Power shimmered in the air. She didn't doubt

he could take on a legion of them without breaking a sweat. The ones he'd battled would never have scratched him, if not for the rising sun.

The Morphs could take her life. But Adrian could take her heart, and then shatter it like glass. She'd spent the past decade picking up the shards of her former life. Hadn't she already endured enough?

Sarah pushed away from the table. He blocked her way. Adrian's long fingers gently caught her wrist. "You will stay here." His thumb stroked over her skin, creating a flare of pulsing desire. "I'll keep you safe, Sarah."

His touch soothed her. For a moment she wanted to stop running, and fall into his arms. Sarah pulled away from the temptation. Never would she allow anyone to draw close. There was no one she could trust, especially not Adrian.

His eyes grew brilliant as he watched her. White ringed the blue irises, as if they shimmered with light.

"The Morphs who are after me have learned a few tricks. I can't stay here."

Adrian released her wrist. "I've learned a few tricks, as well. And so have you, to evade them, and me, all these years. Why did you run away from me, Sarah? Such a mystery. I will find out why."

She hid a wince as cramps tightened her left leg. Sarah drew in a deep breath, working past the pain. Shoulders squared, she studied her captor.

"If you're done with the inquisition, I'd like to go to bed."

A slow smile touched his mouth. "Do you?"

Her heart gave a funny little jerk. "Maybe I'll settle for a walk on the beach," she muttered.

Adrian raised a dark brow. "It's cold on the shore."

Not as cold as it is in here. "I'll survive." She gestured to carving knives on the counter. "Those steel?"

Adrian nodded.

Gritting her teeth against the pain of her bad leg, she tried to walk normally to examine the blades. But it proved impossible. Her left leg pulled like a lead weight.

A frown touched his face. "Did I hurt you when I threw you into the pool?"

"You can't hurt me," she shot back. "I'm tougher than that silly doll."

"I don't doubt it."

She selected two knives, slid both through her belt. Adrian watched.

"Since when do you arm yourself to walk on the beach?"

Her chest felt compressed. "Since my old life went to hell. But you wouldn't know anything about what that's like."

"Hell isn't reserved exclusively for Draicon," he said quietly.

Arms folded, he looked down at her, power surrounding him like a dark cloak. Sarah's heart gave a little lurch. She dared to place her hand on his arm, feeling the tensile muscles tighten.

His eyes darkened. Then Adrian jerked free of her touch and walked away. Just as she had walked away from him years ago. At the doorway, he paused and spoke over his shoulder.

"Take my coat from the hall closet."

Warmth surrounded her as she shrugged into Adrian's fur-lined black cashmere coat. She almost moaned in delight from the toasty feeling, the delicious scent that was uniquely his.

A cold ocean breeze whipped at her hair as she went outside. Pebbles crunched beneath her boots as she followed the pathway down the cliff to the sandy beach. Craggy cliffs, laced with outcroppings of pink granite, stood as a silent sentinel over the horseshoe-shaped bay.

Sarah watched the white froth of angry ocean waves. Salty spray stung her cheeks, but the briny air rejuvenated her. She and James had lived in urban centers, avoiding the pricier areas they couldn't afford.

After years of hiding, she and her father had finally settled, found jobs and had a little money. Their savings wouldn't even cover one month of Adrian's electric bill, but it was theirs. Now, thanks to her expedition to find a mate for herself and a pack for her father, they'd been discovered by the enemy. All for nothing. Her distant cousin Cameron hadn't wanted her any more than the other males she'd sought out.

Oh, the pack had been friendly and Terrence and Elaine, the alpha couple, couldn't have been nicer. Cameron even liked her. But then her cousin had "accidentally" caught sight of her as she emerged from the shower. The towel had covered all essential parts, except her legs. The shock on Cameron's face had quickly turned to revulsion. He'd left the house, leaving his parents puzzled and asking questions she didn't want to answer. Filled with shame, she'd given polite excuses and left.

Relishing the stinging spray on her face, Sarah began to hunt for sea glass. The simple pleasure washed away the hurt of Cameron's rejection, the uncertainty about being Adrian's captive. Something in the water caught her eye. Fish, jumping and leaping in the water, grayish moonlight glinting off their silvery scales. Suddenly the water began to churn.

Sarah backed off instinctively, drawing closer to the cliffs. The boiling mass in the ocean swam closer. Her blood ran cold as an explosion of white, sightless crabs spilled onto the shore.

Morphs.

Don't panic. She forced concentration, dragged in their scent. Morphs could mask their scent, but a skilled Draicon could detect a faint trace of their original packs. These were clones. Not as powerful, but still deadly. Oh, sweet mercy, they were coming after her.

Do something!

Sarah ran. She could hear them closing up behind her, their claws eager to snap at her flesh. Panic squeezed her throat. She forced it down, whirled. Both knives came out with practiced ease. *See them as they really are, they're evil, they're killers.*

Thoughts of Adrian loaned her strength as she remembered how he'd fearlessly engaged them. Shoulders thrown back, she screamed, "You can't do this to me anymore. Come on and fight me, bastards."

The mass of Morphs shape-shifted. Nausea boiled in her stomach.

"Oh, rats," she muttered.

A mass of dark rodents streamed toward her. Holding out the knives, she stood ready to pounce. They ground to a halt a few feet away. Dark power shimmered in the air as a rat shifted to a human form. A sob wrenched her throat.

It was a clone, an exact imitation of someone who'd loved her. The one person she'd sworn to never, ever forsake.

"Sarah," it whispered into the night wind.

It shifted again, the face contorting, body twisting. Sarah lowered her weapons.

"Why?" she asked brokenly.

Something rushed past her like a spinning tornado. She caught Adrian's tangy scent. In helpless anguish, she stood as if her feet were nailed to the pebbled sand. Movement blurred the air as the vampire killed the Morphs. One shifted into its true form, a hunched creature with yellow fangs, a red, wet twist of a mouth yawning wide-open.

In the blink of an eye, Adrian stabbed it in the heart. The Morph gave a dying shriek and dissolved into thick, gray ash.

Wind spun the dust of her dead enemies into a cloud. Something was clattering violently. Her teeth.

Adrian glided over, clasped her wrists, making her drop the knives. He gently rubbed her arms. "Are you all right? Did they hurt you?"

She shook her head.

"Sarah, why didn't you defend yourself?"

Wordlessly, she stared downward. Shame covered her like a wet blanket of fog. She could not voice her darkest fear. Not to him.

He pulled her against his muscular chest.

She collapsed against him, cherishing the feel of his arms drawing tightly around her. For the first time in years, she felt safe. He stroked her hair, each caress a soothing rhythm that settled her raging nerves.

Adrian rested his forehead against hers. "I told you I could handle them," he murmured. "You have nothing to fear."

Letting him this close was dangerous. He could break her heart and it would hurt worse than a thousand lacerations from a legion of Morphs. Sarah jerked away. "Yes, I do." *You*.

Wearily, she pushed back the hair from her face. "These were scouts, flushing out my scent. The original is hiding in the shadows, waiting to amass any weaknesses in your territory before it attacks."

Damn, she was tired. No sustenance since she'd left Terrence's pack. Combined with the silver bracelet draining her energy, she felt ready to drop.

As she turned to leave, her bad leg seized up. Stifling a cry, she pitched forward as her vision went gray.

CHAPTER FOUR

ADRIAN SWORE A low oath. Lifting her in his arms, he carried her into the living room. Her soft body felt good cradled against him. He laid her on one of the leather couches.

Her complexion was too pale, her cheeks looked slightly sunken. She needed food.

Covering her with a forest-green throw, he returned to the kitchen. Adrian opened the refrigerator. Nothing. There was a thick steak in the freezer. He placed it in the microwave.

While waiting for the beef to defrost, he perched on the sofa. Long, dark eyelashes brushed against the pale hollows of her cheeks. Her rosebud mouth was slightly open. Adrian stroked hair away from her face. When had she grown so thin and pale? The Sarah he knew was healthy, curvy and filled with laughter.

Pulled irresistibly by desire, he leaned close. He, the vampire who could have any female in his bed, had not taken a lover since the day Sarah walked into his life. She had waltzed in and stolen his heart as easily as she'd captured his friendship. Eleven years ago Sarah had boldly ignored the dividing lines between vampire and Draicon. She'd knocked on the door of his North Carolina beach home, asking for permission to hunt on his private lands during the full moon. Deeply curious about the lovely Draicon, Adrian had granted it, and had spent the night watching Sarah chase prey and then frolic in the churning, silver-splashed surf. When she'd shape-shifted back into her human form and thanked him, they'd started joking together about old, campy Hollywood vampire and werewolf films.

The microwave dinged, interrupting his thoughts. A few minutes later he carried a plate of rare roast beef to the living room. He waved it beneath her nose.

"Wake up, Sarah. You need food."

Slowly she opened her eyes and sat. Her nostrils flared as she saw the fresh meat.

Adrian sensed her deep pride fighting with the ravenous hunger. He set the plate down on the coffee table and walked to the window.

Soon as he did, he heard her quietly gulp down the meal. His heart ached. When had she last eaten? What the hell had become of her?

Why should he care? He hated to admit he still did.

He could not afford to care. After dispatching her enemy, he must send her on her way. Arms folded, he stared into the darkness. Any desire he had for Sarah must be controlled. Adrian was his father's heir, and no one would stand between him and his clan ever again.

Adrian studied the shadows. He spoke over his shoulder. "I'll place safeguards around the property to protect you."

"They'll find a way inside. Even your powers can't stop them."

His temper flared at the insinuation he was weak, but he held his anger. "I doubt it. You have no idea of the full extent of my powers," he murmured. "But it's obvious they've grown stronger. The new tricks they learned include cloning themselves and shifting faster."

"They prefer attacking as wolves, the original Draicon form. Takes less energy. They shift into their true Morph form to feed."

"I remember that. What else should I expect?"

The plate clanked down. "Everything. Everything beyond your darkest dreams, your worst nightmares." She added quietly, "Or mine."

Something inside him twisted at her pain. He wanted to pull her into his sheltering embrace, let her rest there. Eradicate everything she'd felt the past years, and restore the wide smile she'd once always worn. Fisting his hands, he steeled himself against the temptation. But he must know why she abandoned him.

Adrian sat beside her on the sofa. "Why did

you leave me, Sarah? Was it to save your own skin? Tell me."

Damn, he hated to use his enthrallment, the command in his voice no one, not even a stubborn Draicon, could resist. But he must find out, so they both could move on.

"Never. I would have died with you. I had to get home, save her."

"Save who, Sarah?" he demanded.

"I knew what was happening, I was stupid, ignored the danger signals, I didn't want to believe it…my mother, screaming…"

The sob wrenched from her throat stabbed his heart. He waved a hand before her face. "Hush," he soothed. "You will sleep tonight, sleep well and re-member only pleasant memories."

She blinked. Her hand slid over his, the warmth of her skin flooding him with the need to touch her further. Adrian stared down at her fingers encircling his. He lifted her work-scarred knuckles and kissed each one.

Contact sizzled between them. A fierce longing seized him. Couldn't help the wanting, the deep need to bury his body and his fangs deep inside her, so deep she could never get rid of him, would always carry his scent, the imprint of his passion. He wanted all of her, the Sarah who had laughed with him, bravely faced her enemies, the woman whose laughter sounded like the pealing of tiny silver Christmas bells.

He could not have her. Adrian dropped her hand.

"Go to bed," he said, retreating back to the window.

"I never like to be in debt to anyone," she told him. "If I'm to stay here, then I insist on paying my way."

Adrian turned and studied her clean but threadbare clothing, her slender shoulders stiff with dignity. Sarah could not pay him. But he knew well the importance of maintaining one's pride.

"Take charge of the delivery of fresh blood tomorrow from my private blood bank and stock the refrigerator. When I rise, have a bottle warmed and ready. That will suffice for payment."

As he heard her murmur good-night, he did not voice the other payment his heart longed for with all his might.

And kiss me, Sarah. Kiss me and let me hold you in my arms, and shut away the weary world.

CHAPTER FIVE

SARAH SNAPPED AWAKE in the darkness. The digital clock on the nightstand read 3:00 p.m. She switched on a lamp. Adrian had shuttered the windows against the glaring sunlight.

Last night, she'd called her father, trying to reassure him all was well and she'd experienced a slight delay. But he didn't buy it. If she weren't home two days before Christmas, he would fetch her himself.

A shower cleared her muzzy head. Afterward, she sorted through her battered suitcase for fresh clothing, selecting a powder-blue turtleneck and faded jeans.

Except she couldn't find her good bra.

A loud thud sounded. Outside, someone was having target practice.

She went downstairs.

Sunlight beamed through the mansion's lower floor. Adrian had thoughtfully left all the shutters open, either for her or his gremlin friends. She peered through the French doors.

Her heart went still, then anger raced through her. Sarah grabbed her worn sheepskin jacket and raced outside. Her breath fogged the crisp winter air. Ice crystals formed on overhanging tree limbs. New snow blanketed the grounds, the brightness of the day nearly hurting her eyes.

"Hey, stop it!"

With military precision, the six green gremlins had lined up Adrian's antique cannonballs. In the distance was a dummy. Two gremlins stretched out her white garment on either side, as a third placed two cannonballs inside. A fourth pulled it back like a slingshot.

"Incoming!" the gremlin bellowed, sending the balls flying toward the dummy.

They were using her bra as a launcher. Her one good bra she'd bought in a half-price sale at Macy's.

Sarah raced forward, snatched it from their startled grasp. "That's mine," she snapped.

"We's need it for target practice," the shortest protested. "It was the only thing that fit the ammo."

"Get your own," she grated out, staring in dismay at the stretched garment. Rust smeared the pretty white satin.

"In any war, there's sacrifices," the tallest stated. He peered up at her. "Adrian said there was a battle, and we's should prepare to remove the heads of the enemy."

Sarah wished she could take off their heads. "By fighting with my bra. Oh, that's rich. Adrian said your magick was powerful. I'd be better off guarded by the Three Stooges."

White sparks of power filled the air, nearly knocking her off her feet. Her gaze swiveled to the target. She stared at the smashed dummy, blown to bits by the burst of energy zinging from the gremlin's fingertips.

"Then again," she murmured.

The tallest gremlin blew at his index finger as if it were a smoking pistol. He extended a green palm toward her. "Introductions are necessary. Our mother always said we's shouldn't act as if we's was raised in a barn…"

"Even though we's were," another chimed in.

She shook the proffered hands. Snark was the tallest, followed by his brothers, Trip, Grimace, Wedgie, Short and the smallest was 404.

"Named after the computer error message," 404 told her.

Wedgie grinned, showing rows of pointed teeth. "Adrian said last night you had a bad case of crabs."

Laughter bubbled up in her chest. She tossed the bra back at them. "Here. I have another. Besides, it's ruined now. One question. Why did you dress me in polyester when you turned me into a doll?"

Grimace looked surprised. "We's thought it would drain your magick. We's used gloves, because it drains our magick. We's terrified of it."

"Makes sense," she murmured. "It scares me, too."

She glanced at the gray shingled home, sitting on the cliffs in aloof splendor as it overlooked a gray sea. Soon it would be turned into a battle zone. Her chest felt hollow with regret as she thought of Adrian dying on the beach, his clan silently waiting for him to call for help.

If I had only known...

Sarah turned her face to the sun. Light was her friend, for Morphs couldn't use the shadows to hide. It was Adrian's enemy, and had burned his flesh. If only she could take back that day.

When she went inside, the gremlins followed. She looked at them. "What are you doing?"

Trip looked surprised. "We keep Adrian's home safe during the day and Adrian told us to make sure to guard you, as well."

His edict touched her. No one had seen to her needs in a long time.

No one would again, after Adrian released her. As Sarah shrugged out of her jacket, a soft chime at the front door reminded her of the promise she'd made. After signing for the collection of blood, she unpacked the cold case and stocked the bottles in Adrian's glass wine refrigerator.

The gremlins watched in silence. She turned to them. "How did you know it was me when you were in town?"

Snark looked impish. "Come with us."

They led her to a dark study upstairs, switched on an overhead light. A massive mahogany desk and matching credenza dominated the room. On the desk sat an LCD computer screen.

"Adrian's computer. He keeps tabs on all his businesses from here," Short told her.

Grimace slid into the black leather chair, pushed a button on a slim tower sitting beneath the desk. The gremlin shot his brother an accusing look, "404, have you been playing games on the computer again?" He pointed to the blue screen.

"Oops," came the reply.

Snark sniffed. "Short, nothing more."

Short went beneath the desk, fiddled with cables. "This may take a few minutes."

The clock indicated it was nearly sunset. Adrian would soon rise and be hungry. While the gremlins worked on the computer, Sarah fetched a bottle of blood. She warmed it in the kitchen and placed it on the counter for Adrian.

When she returned to the study, the computer was finally powering up. Grimace tapped a few keys. "This is how we knew who you were," he told her as the computer kicked into screen-saver mode.

Breath fled her lungs.

A face stared at her from the screen. A face she barely recognized, molded into a laugh, eyes sparkling with life, the dark hair shining in the sun's setting rays. Beneath the photo was a caption: *Sarah Roberts, sunset on the beach.*

Adrian put her photo on the computer.

Sarah's finger traced the digitized cheek. Had she been that happy? She'd forgotten.

Adrian had not.

404 peered at the screen. "Where is this?"

"North Carolina. We were walking on the shore. Adrian insisted on testing his new camera. He said I was more photogenic than…"

"The prettiest sunset."

The deep velvet voice came from the doorway. She turned. Fascination stole over her as she realized Adrian wore only black silk pajama bottoms. Never before had he exposed to her so much luscious, tanned skin. Broad, sculpted shoulders rippled with muscles. Muscles ridged his flat abdomen. She stared in fascination at his smooth chest, wondering what it would feel like beneath her exploring fingertips.

Her gaze flicked up, saw him studying her with dark intensity. She turned away, feeling heat flare on her cheeks.

"Your dinner, or breakfast, is in the kitchen," she mumbled.

But he went to her, gently snagged her wrist. "Come with me. I hate to eat alone."

She followed him to the kitchen. Adrian grabbed the bottle of blood, poured a glass and drank.

Sarah watched in fascination as his throat muscles worked.

Suddenly he spewed out the contents. "Warm, unsweetened cherry Kool-Aid!" He gagged.

"I filled the bottle with blood just as you asked!" Sarah tensed, expecting him to yell.

Stunned, she watched him wipe his mouth with the back of his hand, throw back his head and laugh. Her appreciative gaze hungrily drank in his powerfully muscled body, the smooth firmness of his chest, the black satin pajama bottoms clinging to his long, athletic limbs.

Filled with amusement, those sunny blue eyes glanced at her. "The gremlins. I should have known. They've done this before, and I told them they would never pull this one on me again. They can't resist a challenge."

"Put a lock on the refrigerator," she suggested.

"Tried that. They ate the lock. Said it was delicious."

Together they burst into laughter. When they finally ceased, Sarah felt wistful for the emotional connection they'd shared—the vampire and the werewolf who liked to watch old movies and discuss books and theater.

When she asked if he worried about the gremlins, he grew serious.

"I took their blood, so I could track them. If one of them were dying, I'd instantly know it. I do it for everyone I care for, including my father, except I was required to take his blood. If my father dies, I instantly sense it and know I must assume leadership to keep the order."

"Why didn't you ever take my blood?" she asked.

He gave her an intent look. "I honored you too much, Sarah. If I took your blood, it would lead...to other things."

He'd never touched her. Adrian's sense of honor had guarded her chasteness.

To hell with honor, she thought suddenly. *Does he want me?*

The same funny flip of her heart happened again, this time combined with a powerful erotic tingling. Her gaze roved over the firm muscle and sinew of his body, the carved planes of his face, the sensuality of his full mouth. His dark brown hair was rumpled. Sarah started to lift her hands to run them through the soft strands.

Clenching her fists, she gritted her teeth. Survival and desire were not good companions.

But she wanted to push him downward, climb over him, run her tongue over that firm, smooth skin, taste him...

An intent look replaced his amused one. Adrian closed the distance between them. His long, tapered fingers slid around her neck, caressing the bare skin beneath the fall of her hair. Sarah's body tightened with each slow stroke.

He pulled her toward him, his mouth lowering on hers. Sarah slid her arms around his neck, closing her eyes. Feelings surged through her at the languid way he kissed her. He deepened the kiss, coaxing her mouth to open beneath the insistent pressure of his.

His hand went to her breast, cupping the heavy weight, his thumb stroking over her hardening nipple. Sarah whispered encouragement as he touched her, each flick of his thumb making her blood run hotter, her body ache with ceaseless yearning.

When she reached behind him and cupped his taut buttocks, he shuddered with pleasure and broke the kiss.

Adrian nuzzled her neck, his hot breath feathering over her skin. He cupped her bottom, lifted her up against the cold steel of the refrigerator. He nudged her legs open, and stepped between them as she wrapped her thighs around his hips. Sarah arched against him, feeling the steely length in his groin. He lifted her so the opened juncture between her legs was centered against his hardness. Sarah dug her nails into his shoulders, tasted the tangy saltiness of his collarbone as she licked his flesh. She rubbed herself against him, gasping with pleasure, hearing him softly encouraging her to let go, surrender to it….

The feelings built to a crescendo, and with a tiny

cry she let go. Her head hung back limply, sweat dampening her temples as she gasped for air.

Slowly he lowered her trembling body to the floor, his gaze burning into hers. Sarah ran a hand down his front, gliding over his flat abdomen, down to the silkiness of his pajama bottoms and his thick erection. She stroked through the thin covering, watching his heavy-lidded gaze darken.

Adrian growled deep in his throat, lowering his head to the vulnerable curve of her neck. She felt the erotic brush of his lips nuzzling her tender flesh, then the intriguing, sharp rasp of his fangs gently scraping her skin.

Ready to pierce, take her blood, marking her as his exclusively.

Reason returned like a hard slap to her cheek. Sarah jerked away, startling him. The dark intent in his eyes flared again as he regarded her.

"This is crazy," she muttered, holding her hands out as if to stop him. As if she could stop him, this powerful vampire accustomed to getting anything he wanted. In her weakened state, he could topple her with the flick of a finger. He could take her blood, those long fangs sliding into her flesh, and she couldn't stop him, wouldn't have the strength.

Or the will.

"I can't do this. I'm still untouched, understand, Adrian? I'm a virgin because I need a mate of my own kind willing to take me in and that's all I have to offer. I can't go to another male marked by the scent of a vampire who took me and my blood."

"Sarah, look at me," he said quietly.

She didn't want the enthrallment in his eyes to spellbind her. But the command in his tone made her lift her helpless gaze.

Hands clenched into trembling fists at his sides, he studied her. The haunted look on his face twisted her heart. She wanted to wrap her arms about him and never let go and give in to the passion they both shared.

It wasn't possible.

"I will never, ever, do anything to hurt you. Do you understand? Even to the extent that it might hurt me. I will never do anything you don't want me to."

Slowly she relaxed, but his body tensed even more. He jammed a hand through his mussed hair. Something she couldn't read flickered in his eyes.

"Have dinner with me. Tomorrow night." His mouth twisted up in a mocking smile. "I promise I won't bite. Please."

Sarah nodded, leaving the room. *Won't bite*. She could trust he wouldn't.

But never trust herself not to want it.

CHAPTER SIX

THE GREMLINS WERE having trouble with the Christmas tree.

All six struggled to straighten the seven-foot balsam pine delivered that afternoon. Fresh pine tickled her senses. Sarah smiled as she unpacked the boxes of decorations. She'd seen little of Adrian last night, as he had a meeting in town. Now she enjoyed watching the little green monsters try to best the tree. The tree was winning.

"It's crooked," she teased them.

"We's know that," Wedgie said. "We's just trying to decide what to use to anchor it to the wall so it's straight."

"Sometimes whatever you have on hand works best," she replied, and went upstairs to change for dinner.

An elegant, floor-length red dress was laid out on the bed. Sarah picked up the garment, stroking the red velvet designer dress. Two diamond clasps were at the shoulders, the bodice was a deep V. She spotted a note in Adrian's firm, bold handwriting.

"Please indulge me and wear this tonight. The shoes are in the closet."

Clutching the treasure, Sarah padded over to the room-size closet.

On the floor were red Jimmy Choo shoes. They fit perfectly. A smile touched her mouth as she headed into the shower.

Her cell chirped softly. Sarah's heart sank when she saw the number. Terrence. Probably questioning her hasty departure. She answered it.

The startling conversation that followed filled her with joy and hope. When she closed the phone, she studied the bracelet holding her captive.

"Distant cousins or not, you and your father are family," the alpha male had told her. "Cameron admitted what happened. He's ashamed and wants to apologize. My mate and I would be honored if you and your father would join our pack. We'll help you defeat your enemies, honey. Draicon must stick together."

Draicon needed to stick together. Not Draicon and vampires. She could finally bring her father to a pack that wanted them.

Sarah fiddled with the silver binding on her left wrist. It was looser. The gremlins had made one mistake in fashioning the magick handcuff. They'd failed to take into account that the metal shrank in the cold outdoors, but would expand inside the warm house.

She tugged harder, succeeding in inching it a

quarter of the way down her hand. Sarah stared at the bracelet. She was strong enough to yank it off now, if she risked the pain. Escape was in her grasp.

With trembling hands, she stroked the soft red velvet. One dinner with Adrian surely could not hurt. She had tonight. Tonight must be enough.

Even though in her heart she knew it could never be enough.

Sarah dressed carefully, pulling white silk stockings over her long legs, enjoying the swish of heavy velvet as it cascaded to her ankles.

The image staring at her in the mirror was stunning. Sarah touched the glass, hardly able to believe it was her. "I look pretty," she murmured.

Jazz played softly in the background as she went downstairs. In the dining room a polished walnut table was set with china, sparkling crystal and heavy silver. A setting of red poinsettias and fresh holly adorned the center. But it was Adrian, clad in a black designer dinner suit with a white starched tie and pearl-buttoned shirt, who made her breath catch.

She murmured a compliment, gratified at the admiration in his own eyes. "You're so beautiful," he said in a husky voice.

Her hand lovingly caressed the red velvet. "Your favorite color."

A roguish grin touched his full mouth. "The color of passion."

The same color tinted her cheeks. Adrian's smile

deepened. He held out her chair, but instead of pushing it in, easily lifted the chair with her in it to the table. Sarah turned with a teasing look.

"Show-off."

"Always," he murmured, and they laughed.

He expertly uncorked a bottle of wine and sampled it. He poured her a glass. They sipped the vintage. Sarah sighed with pleasure.

"You always did appreciate the finer things in life," he noted.

More so now than before, since I have no money, she thought. But she wouldn't let even that gloomy thought ruin the splendid evening. She raised her glass.

"To Rick," she offered.

His dark, heavy brows knitted together until comprehension dawned on his handsome face. "Ah yes, *Casablanca*." He looked boyish suddenly as they clinked glasses. "We'll always have Paris."

Sarah drank and set her glass down. "I always wonder whatever became of him. Did he ever find happiness after the war, after letting go of his one true love?"

A mask dropped over Adrian's face. He toyed with the stem of his glass. "Maybe he couldn't let go emotionally, but kept her guarded in his heart, like a secret never shared with the world."

She didn't know how to respond to that.

Dinner was rare prime rib. Sarah ate heartily as

Adrian drank from a crystal goblet filled with dark crimson liquid. She gestured to it.

"Did you put a new lock on the fridge?"

"No, I simply warned them if they tampered with my food supply anymore, no more Friday night DVDs."

"The gremlins like to watch DVDs?"

"Not watch. Eat," he replied.

They laughed again.

He leaned forward, reaching out for her hand. "I've missed your smile, Sarah."

Her hand trembled in his. Adrian stroked a thumb slowly over her wrist, the burning intensity of his gaze filled with sexual promise. Her nostrils flared as she caught his delicious, woodsy scent. She studied the hardness of his body, wondering what his muscled weight would feel like lying atop her as he pushed inside her. Moisture trickled between her legs, preparing her flesh for him. She wanted him with a hot, insane need.

Sarah withdrew her hand.

"I need to tell you. The pack I visited, the alpha called and they want to take in my father and me. When I leave here, I'll have a family again."

His expression quickly shuttered. "I'm pleased for you."

But he sounded distant, as if her news was an unwelcome reminder of the barriers sharply dividing their worlds.

They finished eating. Adrian led her into the living room. A window was cracked open, allowing in the cold ocean breeze. Glittering with gold garland, colored lights and brightly colored balls, the Christmas tree stood in a corner. Sarah walked over to it, murmuring with pleasure.

"I wonder how they got it to stay upright."

A small, teasing smile touched the corners of Adrian's mouth. "Look in the back."

She did. Sarah stared at the white, rust stained garment tied to the tree and nailed to the wall. Her bra.

"They needed something rather large and supportive." This time he chuckled openly and she went to mock-punch him.

He caught her wrists as the music system began playing a sultry jazz tune. His playful expression turned serious. "Dance with me, Sarah."

So few indulgences she'd enjoyed. For once, she threw caution to the wind. One dance. All she had was tonight, and Adrian's own special brand of magick.

She went into his arms. He held her tight as she rested her head against his broad shoulder. Adrian guided her around the room, humming into her ear. Each shift of his body pressed his hard muscles against her softness. It felt good, so right, as if she belonged here. He rocked against her, eradicating everything but the thought of him. If only the night were endless, and the hours would never cease.

All too soon, they would. And soon she would leave him once more.

"The night I fled the beach, I whispered a promise to you." Sarah's throat tightened with the admission. "You were my only friend, Adrian, and it broke my heart to never see you again. So as I ran away, I promised I'd come back to you someday."

He stilled, his expression filled with tenderness. "I never stopped looking for you. Needing to lure in your enemies was an excuse. It was you I searched for all these years, Sarah."

When his lips captured hers, she sighed into his mouth. It was here and right, this moment, living only for the passion of his kiss. Adrian cupped the back of her head, tunneling his fingers through her silky hair. He kissed her with an urgent desperation, as if he never wanted to let her go.

As she kissed him back, she remembered he would have to release her. Their people despised each other. Adrian was needed as his clan's future leader. A Draicon like her, especially a crippled one that no man wanted, could never fit into his world.

All too soon he broke the kiss. Torment filled his gaze as Adrian solemnly regarded her. She put a finger to his warm, wet mouth. "Don't say a word. Just dance with me, for every moment we have left."

They resumed dancing, Sarah resting her head against him. She breathed deeply, taking in his delicious masculine scent of pine and forest, mixing with a faint, odd fragrance of…fruity cologne.

A familiar tingling ran down her spine. She only experienced it when a certain Morph was present. Sarah wrenched away and ran to the French doors.

He was right behind her. "What is it?"

"They're out there."

Adrian frowned. "I can't scent them."

"They've learned to disguise their scent. I've discovered how to detect it. The Morphs last night were sent in to assess weaknesses and find their prey. Now that they know I'm here…"

Her voice trailed off. "But how could they track me so fast, especially since you killed all the ones last night?"

Adrian studied her with a calm look. Suddenly she knew.

"You let a couple escape to bring the others straight to me. Adrian, how could you?"

"I did what I must. The safeguards around the property will protect you."

"And I warned you they can find a way past your damn safeguards. Killing them is everything, isn't it? And here I thought I mattered." She clenched her fists. "You'll do anything to get your justice, and you don't care who stands between you and them. Even me."

"Not true, Sarah." He folded his arms across his chest. "But why have you spent the past ten years running away instead of confronting them? You're a fighter."

"I'm not running now. I'm going out there to face them, even if they kill me."

"Dammit, why won't you tell me what's really going on?" He pushed forward, crowding her until she was pressed against the glass doors. "Don't you trust in my ability to defeat them? I told you I'd never let them hurt you."

"It's not that. I have to do this alone."

His gaze sharpened. "Why, when before, we faced them together?"

"Because there's one Morph I must find the courage to face by myself." She slipped beneath his grasp.

"Where are you going?" he demanded.

"Upstairs to change. Then outside, to do what I couldn't do ten years ago."

WHEN WOULD SARAH trust him? Adrian wondered.

He sped outside into the cold, bitter air. Adrian loosened his tie, dragged in a lungful of air, smelled nothing. Even his adroit senses could not pick them out.

But Sarah could. She had spent years learning about them, fleeing from them. It was quite possible they could break past his defenses.

He couldn't let her rush headlong into danger. *Even though you placed her in it,* his conscience nagged.

Minutes later, dressed in old jeans, a faded Steelers T-shirt and her sheepskin jacket, she burst out onto the deck. Adrian snagged her about the waist.

"I have to show I'm not afraid," she shouted, struggling to release herself. "Let me go."

"Why now, Sarah?" His arms anchored her to him. She possessed the strength of her kind, but he was far stronger.

"Because I can't run anymore, I have to make a stand."

"Just like you did on the beach? When you trusted me to stand with you?"

Her struggles ceased. Dark eyes wide in her face, Sarah stared at him with a woebegone expression. Adrian's heart lurched. "Sarah, together we can defeat them. You can't fight them alone."

"I have no choice," she whispered brokenly. "This is my problem. My war."

"No, you made it my problem and my war the day you asked for my help."

Her gaze grew flat. She inhaled deeply. "The scent's gone. They're gone."

They went back inside. Adrian crossed the living room to stand near the Christmas tree and touched a seashell ornament. A hollow feeling settled in his chest as he stroked his fingers over it. Sarah had made the ornament for him as a gift.

A sickeningly sweet odor filled his nostrils. He studied Sarah shrugging out of her coat. "Are you wearing perfume?"

"I only wear it to cloak my scent and haven't since I've been here."

"Odd," he mused. "I smell citrus. But I never eat fruit and the gremlins detest anything healthy."

Sarah went preternaturally still. "Oh, crap, why didn't I see it before? Those defenses you set, the safeguards, they were against anything coming onto your property unless it was invited in, right?"

"Of course. Why?"

She lifted a trembling hand to the tree. "Because you invited them in, Adrian. They've been hiding in the Christmas tree the gremlins brought into the house. That's how they got inside past your safeguards."

He swore softly, and went to her when a swarm of insects flew out of the pine branches, flooding the room in a dark cloud. Adrian's protective instincts flared. He threw Sarah to the ground, covering her as the mosquitoes flew at them.

They were trapped.

CHAPTER SEVEN

THE WHINE OF thousands of mosquitoes rang in Sarah's ears. She lay still beneath Adrian's sheltering weight.

"Adrian, don't let them suck your blood or they'll absorb your DNA and can clone themselves into you," she told him.

As he pulled her upright, a wave of enormous power filled the air. The black cloud of mosquitoes buzzed and then hit the protective magick shield he'd erected around each of their bodies.

The cloud divided into two. Half shifted into a pack of snarling wolves. They balefully eyed Adrian, growling as they tested the shield again. The other half remained mosquitoes and flew out the opened window.

Adrian's power filled the room with crackling heat. "Stay here, don't move from this spot or you'll break the shield's protective boundaries. I'll kill the ones that escaped."

He sped outside. Yellowed fangs dripped saliva as the wolves growled. Sarah caught a familiar scent from the lead wolf. Her heart shattered as the tingling down her spine felt like an electrical shock.

She was here. The Morph that had pursued her for ten long years. Sarah fumbled with the silver bracelet on her wrist. Reddened eyes crazed with bloodlust stared her down. She willed herself to see the Morph as it really was. Evil, twisted, greedy for power. Not the Draicon who had loved her.

From the opened doors, she caught the scent of scorched earth, heard bellows of outrage followed by loud cheers. The Morph clones, shifted into a dozen fire-breathing dragons, were being hit with a spray of water from a garden hose by the gleeful gremlins. As the water extinguished their fire, Adrian destroyed each dragon. Breath caught in her throat as one dragon's jaws clamped around his arm before he could kill it. As the dragon died, she felt a faint connection die, as well. Sarah bit her lip. One of the Morphs that escaped ten years ago was now dead. Only one original remained: the deadliest Morph.

She had to help Adrian. Years ago she'd failed to eliminate her enemy and had abandoned Adrian on the beach. It was time to stand with him and finally do what she couldn't face all these years.

Sarah viciously tugged at the bracelet, wincing at the pain as it scraped her skin, leaving her hand bloodied. The bracelet slid off. Magick flowed into her, closing the flesh gouges in her hand. She stepped outside Adrian's protective shield.

She waved her hands, dispensing of her clothing, and transformed into wolf. Bones lengthened, her face became elongated, fur erupted on her body. Sarah snarled at the enemy, baring strong, white teeth.

The lead Morph raised its head. The wolf's howl sang out in her blood and bones.

Memories surfaced of home and a love she thought would never die. *Sarah, Sarah, remember me?*

She could not move, think or even speak, only stand there in mute remembrance. The Morph's form shimmered as if it shifted again.

Sarah raised her head and returned the wolf song in a long, mournful howl of her own.

Teeth bared, the wolves sprang forward. Once again she'd been a fool. Sarah cursed inwardly and mentally guarded her thoughts as she summoned the courage to defend herself.

Suddenly a microburst of air ruffled the fur on her back. Adrian.

He became a stunning blur of speed, attacking and ripping out Morph hearts. Sarah stared with dulled shame at the dead Morphs as their bodies dissolved into ash on the finely polished grained wood floor.

He'd destroyed them all, and she'd done nothing.

Holes made from the Morph's acid blood dotted Adrian's fine dinner suit. Adrian waved his hands, replacing the ruined suit with jeans and a black T-shirt. A single droplet of sweat trickled down his temple. He whipped around. "I see you removed the bracelet. If you were so damn intent on taking them on yourself, why didn't you attack?"

Adrian dropped to his knees, ran his hands over her luxurious gray fur. He buried his head against her neck. "Dammit, Sarah, they could have killed you."

She shifted·back, then waved her hands to clothe herself. Energy drained from her, leaving her cold and shivering. Adrian helped her to her feet.

She stared at the piles of ash. "I couldn't."

"Why? You're not a coward. What is it about these Morphs?"

Her throat closed up. Maybe it was finally time to confide in someone. Finally trust. How could Adrian hurt her any more than she already hurt?

Sarah fled into the kitchen, away from her dead enemies. She was finally safe.

And yet she felt only fresh grief, as if someone had sliced open a wound and let it bleed anew.

ADRIAN'S PULSE RACED as he followed her. Sarah seemed as frail as fine-spun glass.

A merry tune filled the air as a whistling, soot-covered Snark strolled into the kitchen. "What next, Adrian?"

"There are piles of ash in the living room. Put all of it into containers, Snark," Adrian ordered.

Sarah watched the gremlin leave. "Of course.

Morph remains are your trophy, to prove you defeated the enemy. Your ticket back to your clan."

Her breath hitched as if she struggled to contain her emotions. Adrian's heart shattered. He waited for her to let it out.

Sarah stared out the window as she braced her hands on the sink. "You lost your clan for a while, but you can return. Not like us. You don't know what it's like to run and keep running, and survive and just pray you can hang on long enough to bear the cold digging into your bones, the hunger digging into your empty stomach, afraid to shift, afraid of your own damn magick leading a trail for your enemy to track and finally kill you. Never fitting in, never belonging. Living as humans, never able to be one of them. Always outsiders."

She whirled, facing him. Moisture sprang to her beautiful brown eyes, shimmering like diamonds beneath the overhead halogen lights. Her body went rigid as marble. He knew her, her strength and pride, and refusal to succumb to weeping.

"I didn't want you to be hurt, Adrian. I never would have abandoned you if not for..."

Guided by the despair on her face, Adrian went to her. Gently, he cupped her cheeks as he tenderly regarded her.

"What, sweet? Why did you leave? Tell me."

Trust me, his expression urged. With all his heart, he hoped she would open up to him.

Her trembling hands clutched his wrists as if hanging on to a life preserver. "I had to save my mother."

"Why didn't the other males in your pack defend her?"

A sob caught in her throat. "Oh, Adrian," she half laughed, half cried. "Don't you get it? The Morphs we fought that day on the beach *were* my pack. I was too ashamed to tell you exactly who you fought. You had a family loyal to you. They loved you. And mine was filled with hate and greed."

Shocked, he could only stare. "How did this happen?"

Sarah released his wrists. "My parents had discovered that my mother was carrying a boy. Because my father hadn't any children other than my sister and me, he'd appointed my eldest cousin to rule the pack after him. When he found out my mother would give him a son, my father renounced Dave as his heir."

A sinking feeling settled in his chest.

"Dave was furious. After all those years, promised to be pack leader and then denied. My sister, Sandra, was angry, too. She was his oldest child, but wouldn't inherit because she was female. Dave needed more power to take over the pack. The only way for a Draicon to obtain more power is to embrace evil and turn Morph."

Adrian stared in growing horror.

"Dave killed his own father, and it set off a chain

reaction in the pack, some killing to turn Morph, others dying trying to defend themselves. My parents, my sister and I went into hiding. I made sure they were safe, and begged for your help to stand down my cousin and the other Morphs who were roaming the beach, looking for us.

"That night we faced them, I knew I'd made a big mistake. I could sense it, feel it because she was family and we were closely connected. I knew what she was thinking and planning. I hadn't hidden my parents to keep them safe. I had placed them with an enemy I didn't want to see, an enemy working with Dave to take over," she whispered.

"Your sister." He rested his hands on her shaking shoulders, gently rubbing them.

"When I left you on the beach, it was because I knew something terrible had happened. Sandra killed my mother, blinded my father and was about to kill him when I arrived… My father screamed at me to kill her. I couldn't. She was my only sister, and I loved her! She attacked me and then ran off. My father and I blended in the human world to hide because Sandra wanted us both dead. My only sister, my flesh and blood, who once loved me."

Her voice died on a shudder. Adrian went still, his heart stuttering in absolute fury and grief for her.

Sarah's mouth wobbled tremulously. She unfastened the metal button of her jeans, then jerked the zipper down, the rasp thundering in the kitchen.

"And this is the price I paid that night, when I couldn't fight her, couldn't see her for what she'd turned into. This is what she did to me."

Adrian didn't dare breathe. He struggled to contain his own emotions, knowing this was a moment he must not interrupt.

Color suffused her entire body now as she shoved the pants down to her ankles and stepped out of them. Sarah wrapped her arms about herself.

"Father and I gave our portion of rationed beef to my mom to keep her and the baby strong. My father and I lacked enough energy to heal properly. So now he's blind and I'm a cripple. No Draicon male wants me. Who would want a lame wolf as a mate?"

Her voice was like the hushed breeze pressing against the kitchen window. Adrian's gaze dropped to her left leg, the leg she instinctively tried to cover with her hand.

Deep, jagged scars zigged and zagged down from the top of her pretty lace panties, past her knee, down to her slender, muscled calf. Her flesh looked as if it had been shredded, the bones shattered and never fully repaired.

Silence draped the air between them. He studied her leg, then looked her in the face. Pride stiffened her stance as she yanked up her pants.

"Even when I shift, I can't run properly. I'm not an asset to a mate, but a liability."

Adrian cupped her chin in one strong hand, forcing

her to turn his way. "You are strong, sweet. You are strength, and survival and light in darkness. Any male worth his mettle should be proud to call you a mate."

Her mouth moved with uncertainty as she glanced at him. Lurking in her wide eyes were traces of suspicion and doubt, but a new emotion flickered there, as well.

Hope.

He dared to ignite the flame, make it burn brighter. Heaven knew what a cynical bastard he'd been, only green gremlins for company, but he could at least do this. For her.

Suddenly she meant more than anything else. Sarah in that moment became a beacon, focusing all his concentration. He must make her believe in her own worth, and see what he so plainly saw. Her courage, strength, and tremendous endurance, and the life that pulsed so fiercely within her. Like the brightest star in the heavens, guiding him home.

"I understand now, Sarah. If I had known what was happening to you, trust me, sweet, I would have fought my way through a thousand burning suns, a legion of Morphs, hell, a pit of lava, to reach you and keep you from harm. How I wish I could have spared you..."

His voice trailed off.

"I've been so lonely," she said in a small voice.

"But no man will ever look at me the same, no man will want me…"

Adrian pulled her roughly into his arms. "This one does," he said thickly.

He kissed her, pouring all he had into the kiss, fusing their lips together in desperate urgency, as if his mouth could soothe away all past hurts. Heal all she'd hidden inside for so long.

After a long moment, he pulled away. Adrian traced the outline of her kiss-swollen lips. No longer could he hold inside what he'd felt.

"Do you know what it was like to be near you, and yet so far away?" he murmured. "Never to touch you, knowing I can never have you, each agonizing moment thinking you had a mate somewhere who would have everything I wanted so badly, to wake up beside you, spend the years with you…"

"I only wanted you. But it wasn't possible," she whispered.

He ran a thumb along her jaw, marveling at the delicate bones and frailness, knowing the steely strength inside the woman. Sarah's eyes closed as she leaned into his touch.

"I don't have a mate, and every male I've sought as one rejected me. I never really wanted them because I could never forget you, Adrian. I'd gladly damn any opportunity to be with another male, if you wanted me, too, even if it were only for tonight."

Adrian brought her face closer to his.

"I'd rather risk a lifetime of loneliness than never touch you at all. One night would never be enough—hell, an eternity of nights with you would never be enough to satisfy what I feel for you, but I would take it and cherish each second. If I had you just for one night, I could walk into the sun and not regret my life leaving me, because I'd be carrying the memory of your smile in my heart."

She tenderly caressed his cheek. "Then let's have tonight."

CHAPTER EIGHT

THEY WERE NAKED together, just like in her dreams. Except this dream was real, and she was standing before the full-length mirror in his bedroom. Sarah stared at Adrian's reflection, his muscles rippling with strength.

Behind her, Adrian gently wrapped her in his arms, as if he could shelter her from all past pain. He brushed aside her hair, blew a breath on her neck. He kissed her there, sending a quiver racing down her spine as he ran his tongue down her throat.

His hands slid down her trembling thighs, reached in front and cupped her. Spreading her wet folds open, he drew a finger across her slickness. Sarah threw her head back against his shoulder, moaning.

"Look in the mirror, Sarah. Look at yourself, and see how beautiful you are," he softly told her.

She saw herself, flushed, her body trembling with desire, being loved by a man who could have any woman. He'd chosen her.

As she lay down on the massive bed, Adrian knelt before her. He gently pulled her thighs open and stared at her glistening center. Embarrassment at this vulnerable position faded beneath his worshipping gaze. "You are so beautiful," he murmured.

Then he lowered his mouth between her legs.

She felt the slight scrape of his fangs as his wicked tongue stroked over her center. Each delicious flick made the waves of pleasure grow higher and higher. Her hips pumped upward in nameless instinct, but he held her down. Sarah cried out as she shattered like a million pieces of light.

Adrian's gaze was fierce as he straddled her. He palmed her breasts, his thumbs flicking over her cresting nipples. Each sensation spiraled her higher as he gazed down at her with possessiveness. No man had ever wanted her this much.

Nor had she ever wanted anyone else.

As she slid her arms about his neck, Sarah bent her head to the curve of his shoulder, tasting the saltiness of his skin. She nuzzled her cheek against his shoulder, marking him with her scent. "Make love to me, Adrian, be with me, even if only for tonight."

"I'd be with you forever, Sarah," he whispered.

Her hand slid down his muscled abdomen, feeling him quiver beneath her touch. She slid her fingers through the dark, crisp hairs at his groin to his rigid, long arousal. Slight trepidation filled her. He was huge, and she didn't know if she could take him.

He studied her with such a tender look, she felt nothing but absolute trust.

Nudging her thighs open, he settled his hips

between them. The tip of his erection touched her wet core. He pushed forward slowly.

"Look at me, Sarah, when we become one," he commanded.

As she did, he gave a powerful thrust, sinking deep inside her. The pain was sharp and immediate. She gasped and writhed, instinctively recoiling from it. He brushed his mouth against hers.

"Shh," he murmured. "Hold on to me. It will get better."

Sarah clutched his broad shoulders. Adrian's powerful muscles quivered as he held still. He was thick and hard inside her. She savored the feeling of being joined so intimately with him at last.

When she relaxed, he began to move slowly. Pain faded into pleasure, then a deep, intensified need with each stroke. She raised her hips to meet him, demanding more.

"You're mine now, Sarah. Mine," he breathed.

With each commanding thrust, it felt as if he sank into her very soul. He took her, marking her as exclusively his, his cock buried deep inside her, his body melded to hers. As if nothing could ever part them.

Adrian loved it, her tiny, excited cries, the delicious scent of her sex, how her tight, slippery heat surrounded him. Masculine pride filled him as she moaned with pleasure. The tips of her hardened nipples brushed against his damp chest as he slid over her. Pushing himself up on his hands, he watched her face. Wonder filled her darkened gaze as he tutored her in passion. He wanted to claim each succulent inch of her, bond them together in the flesh so she could never forget him after this night.

Wrapping her legs around his pumping buttocks, Sarah raised her hips to meet the rhythm he taught her. The sweet, intense pressure built higher. She arched against him, crying out his name as it burst inside her. Adrian groaned, shuddering, as his own release came. He collapsed atop her, his breathing ragged against her ear as she tenderly caressed him.

When they'd lain awhile, trembling and spent, he touched her face. "Are you all right?"

Sarah nodded in a languid daze.

They had tonight, and with dawn, it would end. She must not think of tomorrow. Adrian pushed up on his elbows to regard her in the gathering moonlight.

The stark hunger on his face made her shiver with anticipation as he ran a thumb over the vein in her throat. "I want you, Sarah. I have to taste you," he murmured.

"If you take my blood, won't your clan banish you for good?" she asked.

"Only if you take mine. My blood is powerful and healing, and it's forbidden for me to share with anyone except another vampire. But if I take your blood, I'll create a bond you can never break."

She tilted her neck to the side. "Do it."

The look in his eyes made her heart turn over. "I will not hurt you, sweet. Just lay back, and try to relax."

A low growl, startling in its possessiveness, rumbled from his deep chest. He brushed aside her hair, held her trembling body against his, murmuring reassurances. She felt the sensual sweep of his warm tongue. A slight, stinging pain followed, a sensation of pressure, then a warm tide of intense pleasure. Each erotic suck sent all her nerves tingling, as if his mouth were pressed between her legs. It was too much.

As the pressure built, her muscles clenched, and she shattered, screaming as another intense orgasm swept through her.

He ran his tongue over the puncture wounds, kissed her as she lay in his arms, her body still spasming.

"Wow," she managed, staring up at his tender, amused expression. "No wonder you use a blood bank. You'd have legions of groupies banging at your door if you did this all the time. Even dignified blue bloods."

Adrian stroked a thumb over her trembling lips. "I like hot, red blood. Yours."

She cupped his face, searching his deep blue eyes. "You took me as your kind does, so I belong to you. Now take me as my kind does. Mate with me."

Passion glowed in his hooded, dark gaze. Sarah

rolled over and knelt before him. From behind her, he ran his hands down the backs of her thighs. Then he caressed the inside of her thighs, and put his hand between her legs, rubbing gently. She felt soaked from wanting him, every cell crying out for him to take her.

With one hard, rapid thrust, he entered her. Sarah cried out from pleasured shock. He was bigger, harder than ever. He cupped her hips as he rocked against her, his flesh slapping heavily against hers. His breath rasped out in rapid pants, thundering with hers in the night air.

In this position, her wolf flared to life. It howled and demanded. Adrian thrust harder and faster. She screamed, nearly blacking out as she climaxed, hearing him cry out her name as he followed.

Minutes later, they lay tangled together, sweat cooling on their bodies. Blissful and languid, Sarah snuggled against him. She felt cherished. In the safe cocoon of his bedroom, it didn't matter they were werewolf and vampire.

But her practical side warned that time marched forward. They had the moment. The moment could never be enough for her.

Mirrored in his eyes was a reflection of her own torment. "I can't let you go." Adrian brushed back a strand of hair from her face. "I care about you too much."

It felt like hot knives lacerated her heart. She

pressed a kiss into his palm. "I feel the same way and I don't want to go, either, Adrian. What can we do?"

"Let's not think about it now," he murmured.

He quieted her with a kiss, his mouth moving over hers. She ran a finger down his smooth, muscled chest, toyed with a small brown nipple, delighting in his sharp intake of breath.

What would it feel like to remain forever in his arms? But how could his family accept her, the despised Draicon?

Adrian glanced at the clock and muttered a low curse. "My father's arriving tonight, Sarah, in preparation for the ritual. I must get ready."

He gave her a tender kiss. She watched him walk naked to the bathroom, admiring the taut curves of his ass. Sounds of the shower began.

Sarah went to the French doors overlooking the dark, rolling sea. Beneath the silvery moonlight, foaming whitecaps crashed against jagged, unyielding rock. She and Adrian were like that, ocean and rock, smashing against each other in the stern restrictions of their separate worlds. How could they merge and have a life together without one having to give up altogether?

She went to her own room, showered, as well. When she returned to his, Adrian was toweling his long, dark hair. Her gaze met his in the mirror.

"I'd like to formally meet your father," she told

him. "And apologize for what I did to you that night on the beach."

Vampires did cast a reflection, contrary to myth. But the tormented look in his eyes made her suddenly wish they did not.

He dropped the towel, braced his palms on the dresser. "It's best you don't, Sarah. Not now. He refuses to associate with Draicon."

Emotion tightened her throat. "Why does your father hate werewolves?" she asked him.

"He doesn't hate your people. He merely wants to preserve the purity of our bloodlines. Marcus has always held to the belief that our clan should never mingle with outsiders. He made that rule long ago for that express purpose. My family is one of the oldest and most noble clans." He sat up, jamming a hair through his thick hair. "The rules must not be broken."

"Then you can't break them by having me in your life," she pointed out in a small voice.

His hard jaw ticced violently. "I'll figure something out, Sarah. In the meantime, you must remain hidden from my family."

Hidden? In the shadows, lurking as before, never accepted? "So you want me to hide again, like I used to when your family came around at your beach house in North Carolina? Where this time, Adrian? Should I run into the closet and douse myself with cologne to mask my scent? Or do you have another hiding place in mind?"

Cold dread gathered in her chest as Adrian's mouth thinned. "This convocation is critical to me, Sarah. I must show my father and my clan I'm worthy of returning as his heir."

Yet in his family's eyes, she would never be worthy. Suddenly she realized she no longer wanted to remain hidden. "I've been in shadow all my life, Adrian, even before I got injured. I was always hovering in the background. That's not a life. If we're to be together, I won't be a secret. All that time we spent together, hiding our friendship from our families, as if you and I were something to be ashamed of. I can't live like that."

His knuckles clenched, he stared at her in the mirror. "I can never be ashamed of you, Sarah. But my family won't understand or accept you and I together. Would your family?"

The truth hurt deeply. "No, they wouldn't," she whispered.

Adrian hung his head. Sarah realized what she must do. Once she had hurt him, deeply, out of necessity. Now she must do so again.

"I have to leave, Adrian. I need to get my father settled into Terrence's pack, so I might as well do it now." She struggled to keep her voice even. "It's time for me to go."

He lifted his head. For a moment something fierce

glittered in his eyes. She rushed on. "It's best if I leave. You know that vampires and Draicon, well, we're like oil and water."

His expression shuttered. "You and I aren't. Sarah, I thought…"

"You thought wrong. I could never be happy with a vampire, anyway." She offered a bored shrug.

The pain in his deep blue eyes felt like a hot razor across her skin.

"Sarah, I meant what I said earlier when I told you how much I care," he said in a low voice.

Tears she seldom shed now clogged her throat. Sarah forced herself to speak past them. "I didn't. I feel nothing for you other than friendship," she lied.

Adrian's expression shifted to ice. She turned away, each step like a lead weight.

Sarah went to her room to pack. It was time to return to her own world, and leave his behind.

CHAPTER NINE

ADRIAN WAS ABOUT to get everything back. Why did he feel as if his heart was shattering? He dressed for the convocation, his chest aching. He knew why. Sarah.

His father and elders from the clan waited downstairs to begin the ceremony of trust to return him to the fold. In the two days since Sarah's departure, Adrian could not forget the Draicon sealed into his heart.

He wanted Sarah at his side each night, in his bed each morning, wanted to make her happy. Adrian longed to watch her eyes darken with arousal as he pleasured her, listen in loving tenderness as she clung to him and called out his name in passion.

But her needs came before his wants. And that was why he let her go. Back to her people, to forget this stabbing insanity crying out they could make it work. Too much was against them. She belonged with the Draicon.

He must release her forever, turn around and never look back.

Feeling as if someone crushed his heart beneath an uncaring fist, Adrian went downstairs to return to his old life.

A SHAFT OF dying sunlight dappled balsam pine branches lining the pebbled drive.

The scent of pine mingled with tangy brine of the sharp, cold sea. Standing on the walkway, Sarah stared at the blue-gray shingles of Adrian's house. She inhaled the crisp air.

James had arrived and settled into Terrence's pack. They had both been welcomed. Sarah boldly faced them and told them she'd loved a vampire, but to her surprise, they accepted her anyway. Even her father seemed to understand. Cameron apologized profusely, confessing Sarah's scars embarrassed him because she had been tested in battle, unlike him. Yet, for all the welcoming hugs and assurances of affection, Sarah found herself throwing up a mental shield.

The only one who could invade her mind and use her emotions against her was dead. Still, she felt the need for caution.

Returning to Adrian's seemed foolhardy, but she couldn't dismiss the urgent instinct to check on Adrian. Sarah glanced down at the notarized statement in her hand in which she testified that she'd witnessed Adrian defeating the enemy. The lightweight parchment was equally thin as an excuse to visit.

Her finger shook as it depressed the doorbell.

Adrian answered. No, not Adrian. This man had his prodigious height, the same chiseled features and burning blue eyes and air of quiet pride, but no scars were on his left cheek and his hair was silvered at the temples. Like Adrian, his fingers were long, lean, elegant, but one fact separated them. On his right pinkie he wore a gold signet ring with an elaborate crest.

The ring was a symbol of his power. Adrian once told her his father never removed it. Ever.

Behind him, she heard people talking, laughing and glasses clinking. The entire convocation must have arrived for the ceremony. But something felt off-kilter. Every Draicon sense alerted her to danger. Hairs on the nape of her neck saluted the air.

"You're Adrian's father," she said, studying him. "I need to give him this. It's my signed statement that I saw him kill the Morphs that escaped him on the beach."

The vampire's piercing gaze focused on her like a laser. "You're the one who asked him to fight on the beach. Sarah, the Draicon. The paper isn't necessary. The Morph ashes are proof enough for tonight's ceremony."

She swallowed hard. "Had I known what would have happened, I'd never have asked him to fight with me, sir."

Sarah looked him in the eye. As an equal, even though this powerful vampire could probably snap her neck like a matchstick.

Something flickered in his gaze.

"Please, I must see Adrian."

Please, let me see him. Please, just one last time.

His fierce look thawed slightly. "He doesn't wish to see you."

"You're assuming…"

"No," the vampire said almost gently. "He looked out the window to see who was at the door. He asked me to answer it."

Her heart lurched at the dismissal. Sarah clenched her fists. "I just want to see him, make sure he's okay."

"He's fine…" Marcus frowned as he glanced around. An insect's incessant whine buzzed in her ears. Scenting danger, Sarah went absolutely still.

"Damn mosquitoes! They've been buzzing around since this morning."

Breath caught in her throat. Her senses cried out a warning.

One Morph wasn't dead, after all.

Marcus flinched and then slapped his arm. "Dammit, missed again," he muttered.

"There are no mosquitoes in Maine in winter," she said, her heart pounding frantically. "Please, I must see Adrian. You're all in danger."

Pity shimmered in his gaze as he stepped back. "You need to leave. Now."

Her fists pummeled the sturdy oak as the door shut in her face. "Adrian, open it. It's me, Sarah. You've got to listen to me! Please." Tears trickled down her face.

The door remained locked against her, while inside she knew what would soon happen.

A low, malicious chuckle echoed in her mind.

Sarah whirled and ran off. She could no longer handle this alone.

It was time to call in reinforcements.

CHAPTER TEN

DARKNESS COVERED THEM as the twenty male Draicon hovered just outside Adrian's mansion. The midnight hour rapidly approached. Alpha leader Terrence turned to her, his expression troubled. "Sarah, are you certain there's something wrong?"

Beside her, her father tilted his head to the air. "Trust my daughter," he murmured. "I sense it. Something smells off."

The other Draicon looked at James with respect. Of all of them, he had the sharpest sense of smell, another reason why Terrence wanted him in their pack.

Sarah took a deep breath. "The Morph that wanted me dead wants me to suffer first. It's after Adrian. It knows how I'll feel if something happens to him."

The Alpha male nodded, his gaze narrowing. "Call us if you need us."

Emotion overwhelmed her. She was alone no longer, and it felt good.

Hugging the fur collar of her sheepskin jacket, Sarah slipped through the shadows. Silent as her wolf, she crept around to the back French doors opening to the living room, and crouched down to watch.

The vampires entered the living room. Removed of furniture, with large red candles in ornate stands placed about the room and only the Christmas tree brightening the corner, the room looked slightly forbidding.

The twenty red-robed figures, cowls concealing their faces, could have been wraiths. She didn't fear vampires, not even these, but something wasn't right.

Marcus stepped in front of the vampires as they assembled in a line. Sarah's nostrils flared. Head bowed in supplication and wearing his crimson robe, Adrian knelt before his father. A heavy sword in his hand, Marcus gazed down at his only son. The air thickened with malice.

If she interrupted this sacred ceremony now, Adrian would never forgive her. The other vampires might kill her.

Marcus raised the sword in the act of laying it just against Adrian's neck in his gesture of absolute trust for his clan. Sarah's gaze whipped to Marcus's right pinkie.

It was bare.

Dread pooled in her stomach. She drew in a lungful of air, catching the fruity scent and feeling the tingle race down her spine.

The glass shattered with a direct pulse of her

powers. Through the broken, wide opening of the doors Sarah burst through. "No!"

The shout was just enough to startle Marcus into pausing. Sarah didn't stop, but barreled forward, pushing Adrian aside to safety.

Sarah's frantic gaze met Adrian's venomous one. He stood, tossed back his cowl, blue eyes icy as glaciers as he towered over her. "Sarah, what the hell?"

She heard the outraged murmurs. The others did not matter. Only Adrian.

"It isn't your father, Adrian, but an imposter out to kill you."

Adrian's brow furrowed as Marcus lowered the sword, glaring at Sarah. "Enough, Adrian. Get rid of this intruder before I dispatch her myself."

Ignoring all else but the vampire before her, Sarah raised her pleading gaze to Adrian. "Adrian, please trust me. I'm telling the truth. I can scent it, it's a Morph."

"Ridiculous," one vampire scoffed. "Do you think we would not know our own leader, wolf?"

"Why would a Morph want me dead, Sarah?" Adrian remained motionless, pinning her with his intent gaze.

Sarah's throat closed. "Because it knows if it kills you, I will die inside. And then when it kills me, my grief will fill it with power it hasn't experienced since the day it killed my mother. It's my sister,

Sandra. She knows how much I care about you. I was lying when I said I felt nothing for you other than friendship."

Sarah prayed he would believe her, and take her side once more.

"My son, believe her and you will be banished forever," Marcus warned.

Adrian hesitated and she saw his tormented indecision. Whom to trust? Side with his clan, or once more break with them?

Something flashed deep in his gaze. Adrian calmly regarded the others. "I trust Sarah and I'm taking her side."

Through the ripples of shocked outrage, danger crackled in the air. Marcus snarled. The vampires cried out in alarm as vampire shifted.

The hunched figure with its wispy hair, black, soulless eyes and wet, red mouth hissed at them. The creature shifted, and burst into an explosion of bees, swarming straight at the vampires, then flying upstairs.

Looking severely shaken, the vampires stared at her. Sarah realized they finally understood she was on their side.

"I could use your help," she told them. "You're swifter and more powerful than we are."

Respect filled his gaze as Adrian regarded Sarah. "None of us can scent the Morphs, but Sarah's pack can."

When the shaken vampires nodded, she stepped back and waved her hands, shifting into wolf. Sarah released a blood-curdling howl, calling forth her new pack. Minutes later, they streamed into the house, shifting as they ran.

Adrian took charge. "Each vampire team with a Draicon, find the Morphs and kill them."

He bent down, caressed her fur. "You're with me, sweet. We make the best team of all."

They raced through the house. Sarah immediately scented Morphs hiding in Adrian's closet. When she flushed them out, they shifted into wolves to attack and Adrian killed them. One by one, the vampires and Draicon hunted the enemy.

When the last Morph had been destroyed, and the other teams combed through each corner to ensure this, she and Adrian went downstairs. Sarah shifted back, clothed herself. "I think we got them all, but I need my father to sweep the downstairs," she mused. "His sense of smell is the strongest."

"I'll get him."

As Adrian raced upstairs, Sarah sank into a chair. Weariness overcame her. Still, she couldn't erase the prickly feeling warning her it wasn't over yet.

Sarah saw a small brown cockroach crawling toward her. A familiar, unwelcome tingling raced down her spine.

Pulse racing, Sarah waved her hands, summoning a steel dagger into her hands.

The roach wriggled, and began to shift. It became someone she once knew so well. Until the day she killed her mother.

"Sarah, I've missed you." Large brown eyes, exactly like hers, gave her a pleading look. "Let's forget all this. I'll leave and you can go on your way. Truce, okay?"

The knife wobbled in Sarah's hand as she stared at her sister, Sandra. Her mirror image.

"Remember all we shared, remember how we loved each other!" Sandra sobbed.

The dagger fell from Sarah's outstretched fingers, clattering onto the floor.

"Sarah!"

The roar of that beloved voice broke through her anguish. Adrian regarded them with a shocked look.

"Hellfire. You're identical twins. No wonder you couldn't face her. It's like facing yourself." Adrian's head whipped back and forth between them. "Sarah, which one are you?"

Sandra's expression shifted into terror. "Adrian, end this before she kills me!"

But the vampire studied her twin. "Do you want me to prove my love by killing her?"

"Yes," Sandra replied eagerly.

"Liar," he said softly. "Sarah would never ask that of me."

Sarah cried out as Adrian lifted his hands to blast

her twin. He looked at Sarah, hesitated. Sandra sprang forward, retrieved the dropped dagger and tossed it at him.

"No," Sarah screamed, flinging herself in front of Adrian.

White-hot needles suddenly pierced her chest. Gasping, she looked down at the dagger protruding from her body.

A cruel smile touched her twin's face. Sandra shifted into her true Morph shape and opened her mouth. Finally, Sarah saw her twin for what she truly was. Sandra began to inhale, absorbing her dying energy.

With all her strength, Sarah wrenched the dagger out and raised it in her right hand. Gasping for breath, she stared one last time at her twin, the sister she once loved.

"You're not Sandra. She died on that day."

The dagger went straight into Sandra's heart. Air blurred as an outraged snarl filled the air. Adrian. Her world going gray, she watched him finish off her twin.

As her sister screamed and died, Sarah collapsed.

CHAPTER ELEVEN

ADRIAN'S BLOOD RAN cold as he ran to his lover. Blood gushed from the terrible wound in her chest. She must not slip away. He could make her live.

Around him, both vampire and Draicon gathered. Ignoring them, he dropped to his knees. Gently he cradled Sarah in his arms. Feeling her anguish, the agony from the deep wound piercing her heart.

He pressed his lips against her chilled forehead. "Take my blood. It will heal you."

"D-don't," she pleaded. "If...if you do this, your father will forever banish you."

Adrian removed his robe, unbuttoned his shirt. He forced his fingernail to lengthen and made an incision over his heart. His life's blood.

Pressing her mouth against the wound, he urged her to drink. His eyes closed as she finally did. Pleasure at this intimate connection between them warred with frantic desperation. Gently he rocked her as color gradually returned to her pale cheeks. He felt the reassuringly strong pulse beneath his thumb as he stroked her throat.

Trembling, he allowed her to pull away, watching

in relief as the wound closed over. The laceration in his own chest healed as he gazed tenderly at her. Nothing mattered at the moment but his beautiful Sarah.

He would pay for this later, but didn't give a damn.

They found Marcus unconscious, gagged and tied with heavy silver chains to the cliffs. The gremlins were nearby, buried to their necks in the sand, gagged and tied with polyester.

After freeing them, Sarah wondered aloud why her sister hadn't merely killed them. Adrian's jaw tightened. "Your sister must have ascertained what you knew, that if they died, I'd instantly sense it. So she left my father to burn in the sun and the gremlins to drown at high tide, while she set about killing me."

Minutes later, as her pack gathered on the patio, Sarah watched in stunned awe as Marcus walked outside, looking fully healed. The vampire clan chief thanked each Draicon. Respect filled his face as he shook her father's hand.

"Once I thought vampires and Draicon could never be friends. I was wrong," Marcus said.

James nodded. "It seems we were both wrong."

At Marcus's request, her pack went into the mansion for refreshments the vampires had prepared for them.

"I don't understand how your twin knew what

weakened the gremlins or what I meant to you," Adrian remarked.

Sarah sighed. "We were so close we were psychically bound together. That's how she knew I loved you, Adrian. She felt my emotions and knew my thoughts."

"But how did you know Sandra was masquerading as my father?"

"Your father's ring. You told me he never removed it because it was a symbol of his power. Sandra never knew it because when I remembered it, I had put up a mental block to keep her out."

Marcus gave Adrian a long, thoughtful look. "You broke the rules, again. You gave a werewolf your blood. The consequences of this cannot be ignored."

Adrian hugged her to his side. "I love Sarah," he said quietly. "I don't care that she's a werewolf and I'm a vampire. All I know is I'd rather face the dawn tomorrow than spend another day without her. Even at the expense of losing my clan."

She wrenched out of his grasp. "Adrian, you're his heir."

"That's not as important to me as you are. I will always love my family, but I can't bear the pain of being separated from you again." His fingers trailed over her cheek. "But I'll understand, and let go, if you wish to return to your new pack. I only want you to be happy, Sarah."

Love for him filled her, so much she could see nothing but Adrian. She cupped his solemn face in her hands.

"My father has a pack now, but I never wanted that for myself. All I ever really wanted was you." She struggled to speak through her tears. "I'd be honored, and happy, to be with you. Even if it means abandonment by everyone else."

"Then I have no choice," Marcus said gravely.

Adrian tensed. But the elder vampire's next words filled her with shocked awe.

"In my foolish pride, I never wanted vampires and werewolves to be allies, for I saw our race as superior. Centuries ago I made rules to protect our people against involvement with the Draicon, desiring to keep us apart and separate from those I considered beneath us."

"You always did live in the eighteenth century, instead of getting with the times, Dad," Adrian said drily.

Marcus looked thoughtful as he threw back his cowl. "Indeed." He glanced at Sarah. "It was a mistake. You saved my son, Sarah, and I am forever grateful. You taught us the value of trusting a Draicon and learning to work with others."

The elder vampire studied Adrian. "I cannot break my own rules, son. But those rules could be changed by a new leader. It's time for our clan to embrace this new century. If you will accept that leadership, Adrian."

Hope filled her heart.

"If I do, you must know I will change the rules, even to the point of taking a Draicon as my mate. If she will have me." Adrian's gaze at her was tender. "If you will have me, Sarah."

Her answer was to slide her arms around his neck and kiss him. When they finally parted, Marcus gave a deep, rich laugh startlingly like his son's.

"I think a Draicon could teach our people much. We would welcome you, Sarah. And I look forward to getting together with your pack, to learn how we can benefit from working together." Marcus clapped Adrian on the shoulder. "Now, if you will, I could use a glass of wine. You have a fine collection of vintages I'd like to sample."

"Open a few bottles, Father. But what about the ceremony of trust?" Adrian asked.

Marcus looked emotional. "You have already proven your trust, my son. To the most important person of all. Her."

Adrian's father went into the house as they stared out at the ocean. Now she understood. The sea crashed against rocky cliffs, but their individual strengths gave the meeting a raw, powerful beauty. Between both existed an unbreakable bond. She and Adrian were the same. Their individual powers made their love even stronger. Theirs would never be a serene, unruffled relationship. Yet she wished for nothing less. Stormy sea meets strong rock in raw power and passion.

Sounds of merriment drifted through the smashed French doors. The gremlins were verbally butchering "Frosty the Snowman" into "Frosty the No Man."

Adrian's hands tightened on her waist. "I know why the gremlins turned you into a doll. We were watching a movie about a man who fell in love with a beautiful mannequin that came to life. They asked if I could ever love an ugly doll." He brushed away a strand of hair from her face. "I told them yes, if the doll were you. Because you would always be beautiful in my eyes, Sarah."

Joy filled her heart. She splayed her hands against his firm chest, feeling the reassuring, strong beat of his heart. "I always thought Christmas was a time of miracles. Now I know it's true. Because I have you, Adrian. I know vampires and Draicon can be friends, and much more."

"Much more," he said softly, and then kissed her.

* * * * *

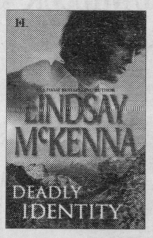

Try these Healthy and Delicious Spring Rolls!

INGREDIENTS

2 packages rice-paper spring roll wrappers (20 wrappers)

1 cup grated carrot

¼ cup bean sprouts

1 cucumber, julienned

1 red bell pepper, without stem and seeds, julienned

4 green onions finely chopped—use only the green part

DIRECTIONS

1. Soak one rice-paper wrapper in a large bowl of hot water until softened.

2. Place a pinch each of carrots, sprouts, cucumber, bell pepper and green onion on the wrapper toward the bottom third of the rice paper.

3. Fold ends in and roll tightly to enclose filling.

4. Repeat with remaining wrappers. Chill before serving.

Find this and many more delectable recipes including the perfect dipping sauce in

REQUEST YOUR
FREE BOOKS!

2 FREE NOVELS
FROM THE SUSPENSE COLLECTION
PLUS 2 FREE GIFTS!

YES! Please send me 2 FREE novels from the Suspense Collection and my 2 FREE gifts (gifts are worth about $10). After receiving them, if I don't wish to receive any more books, I can return the shipping statement marked "cancel." If I don't cancel, I will receive 3 brand-new novels every month and be billed just $5.74 per book in the U.S. or $6.24 per book in Canada. That's a saving of at least 28% off the cover price. It's quite a bargain! Shipping and handling is just 50¢ per book.* I understand that accepting the 2 free books and gifts places me under no obligation to buy anything. I can always return a shipment and cancel at any time. Even if I never buy another book, the two free books and gifts are mine to keep forever.

192/392 MDN E7PD

Name	(PLEASE PRINT)
Address	Apt. #
City	State/Prov.	Zip/Postal Code

Signature (if under 18, a parent or guardian must sign)

Mail to The Reader Service:
IN U.S.A.: P.O. Box 1867, Buffalo, NY 14240-1867
IN CANADA: P.O. Box 609, Fort Erie, Ontario L2A 5X3

Not valid for current subscribers to the Suspense Collection
or the Romance/Suspense Collection.

Want to try two free books from another line?
Call 1-800-873-8635 or visit www.morefreebooks.com.

* Terms and prices subject to change without notice. Prices do not include applicable taxes. N.Y. residents add applicable sales tax. Canadian residents will be charged applicable provincial taxes and GST. Offer not valid in Quebec. This offer is limited to one order per household. All orders subject to approval. Credit or debit balances in a customer's account(s) may be offset by any other outstanding balance owed by or to the customer. Please allow 4 to 6 weeks for delivery. Offer available while quantities last.

Your Privacy: Harlequin Books is committed to protecting your privacy. Our Privacy Policy is available online at www.eHarlequin.com or upon request from the Reader Service. From time to time we make our lists of customers available to reputable third parties who may have a product or service of interest to you. If you would prefer we not share your name and address, please check here. ☐

Help us get it right—We strive for accurate, respectful and relevant communications. To clarify or modify your communication preferences, visit us at www.ReaderService.com/consumerschoice.

MSUS10R